The Hidden One

Norm Mitchell

**CALUMET
EDITIONS**

Minneapolis • London • Nuremberg

CALUMET EDITIONS

Minneapolis • London • Nuremberg

SECOND EDITION DECEMBER 2022
The Hidden One. Copyright © 2018 by Norm Mitchell.
All rights reserved.

This is a work of fiction. Names, characters, places and incidents either are the product of the author's imagination or are used fictitiously.

10 9 8 7 6 5 4 3 2

Cover and interior design: Gary Lindberg

ISBN: 978-1-959770-90-9

The Hidden One

Norm Mitchell

ONE

15 to 28 May 1962
Cambridge & Boston, Massachusetts

1.

After the lacrosse game, Ashley Cooper stood under the hot shower and let it blast away the blood and dirt. The water massaged his bruised shoulders and stung the small cut on his forehead. He thought about how it was always a brutal match-up when he played against that swine Alex Dragovitch. His first encounter with "Drago" was a soccer match during the fall of '57, and the bastard had nearly sidelined Ashley for the whole season. Despite a concussion, Ashey had hung in for the whole game—a victory of sorts—and since then he had gone against Dragovitch three more times, once in soccer and twice in lacrosse, improving his performance each time.

Today, having done his research, he anticipated the giant defender's moves and scored the game winner. Even better, Dragovitch looked completely stunned. Ashley loved that look and wished Olga could have seen it. She always cheered the loudest, and afterwards she would give him a glorious back rub. She certainly deserved a lot of the credit for his goal, because she had observed Dragovitch over the years and knew his weaknesses. But she was absent from the game today, and no one on campus knew where she was or when she would return.

Team Captain Adams took the showerhead to his left. "Congratulations, Cooper, on slaying the infamous Blue Dragon. I hear he's going to AC Milan Football after he graduates in June."

"Thanks. Glad to be rid of the cheating bastard."

"Not more than me. Tried to get past him for four years now. No cigar."

Cooper felt surprised by this admission. Adams had five more goals than he did to lead the team. "Well, you did score once today."

"Not the same. That was against Samuels."

"Hey, a goal's a goal."

"Anyone ever tell you how profound you are?" They both laughed and looked around the sunlit room as their teammates continued celebrating.

"Well, if it isn't our freshman sensation, Ashley Cooper. Finally scored on Alex."

Ashley recognized Nick Stevens' annoying Indiana drawl before seeing the big defender at the showerhead on his right.

"Wonder what genius scheduled us for the very tough Yale squad after playing Princeton just four days ago."

Ashley would follow the Colonel's advice… the best way to handle a fool is to ignore him.

"What, you little weenie, you think you're too good to talk to me now?"

This guy really never learns. "I enjoyed both games. I guess you're just out of shape. Of course, must be pretty hard on you and your buddy just standing around for most of the game because of our stellar offense."

"You know what? Nobody likes you. You're a weirdo, a freak, but an athlete, so we put up with you. Besides, Drago really put the hurt on you. In my book, he won. You know why? Me and him are not just defenders, but warriors. Our job's to put the hurt on weenie attackers like you. We don't run around the field like a bunch of chickens with their heads chopped off."

"Stevens, are you really so stupid you want to cheese off all your attackers and midfielders too? Even in this clamor, they can hear your obnoxiously loud and distinctive voice. So, before you pontificate again, like Dr. Johnson said, 'it is better for men to think you are a fool by remaining silent than to open your mouth and prove them right.'"

"Yuk. Yuk. You think you're so damn smart, Cooper. Then how come I'm screwing Pen, and she can't get enough of me? We laugh at how she cock-teased you the whole time you two were going steady."

"Haven't you discovered yet she's a spoiled psychotic bitch? No, I guess not. Probably can't get enough of you because she never has orgasms."

"Girls can't orgasm. Everybody knows that. I know you're screwing that old maid, our weird Russian Lit prof, Olga what's-her-ass. You must really be desperate."

"You moron, a woman at thirty-one is in her prime. You can't imagine how fantastic it is to have an experienced lover. Pen never had a clue about sex. She's just dumb enough to get the clap from you."

"Bullshit. If anyone's got the clap, it's you from your Frenchie. She's probably spread her legs across two continents. French girls are well-known easies."

"Like you'd know anything about European women. I can see the hayseed in your hair, Hoosier boy. But then everyone knows the only reason you're at Harvard is because you're a legacy, thanks to your old man, the bogus diplomat."

"Cooper, be careful who you're calling a boy, weenie."

"Look, you moron, you've been on my case ever since I got here. I never did anything to you. Besides, didn't I beat you badly enough after Princeton to knock some sense into your thick head?"

"You only won because you fought dirty. Here at Harvard, we have rules."

Captain Adams came over. "Enough, Cooper. No need to slam him again. I need Stevens well for Tufts on Saturday.

And you, Stevens, why do you insist on provoking him? You're supposed to be teammates. So, start acting like it. Whatever your problem with Cooper, forget it. If you can't control your emotions, you've no place on the team. Clear?"

"But what about Cooper?"

"What about him? You've been riding him all year. I think he showed commendable restraint to have waited through most of the season before wailing on you. Now, I want the two of you to shake hands."

"No way, Jose."

"No, thanks. I'm not putting my hand in his big paw so he can damage or break it." Ashley returned to his shower while Adams took Stevens to the other side of the room.

2.

After dressing, Ashley was not eager to run "the Gauntlet." Outside the dressing room, very aggressive young women, and even high school girls, waited. They all wanted to go to the team's fabled party. And they would promise the players anything to get there. Once outside, he saw tall, blonde Penelope Farwell standing impatiently in the front with her arms tightly folded under her prominent breasts. He assumed she was there for Stevens. Instead, she came over to him.

"Ash Cooper, Nick's going to play professional football next fall for the Boston Patriots. That's so exciting."

"I know. Should I be impressed or something? AFL?"

"No. It just means he won't be around, and I thought we could get back together. And it's time we put our differences behind us. And going to the party today would be a good start."

"Stevens gave you the brush-off then?"

"Ash Cooper, that's one of the meanest things you ever said to me. Just thought we could get back together. You must know, by now, your weird Russian witch has left you and Harvard… probably forever."

"Pen, I give you points for sheer gall. But Olga and I are doing just fine. She'll be back soon. You've made your bed. I'm sure you know the rest."

"When that old witch's dead, you'll come back to me."

"Dream on, princess."

"I've seen the future, and you're mine."

"Sure. And if we all believe in fairy dust Peter Pan can fly."

"Ashley." He recognized Corinne's accent. She came up and kissed him on both cheeks in her lovely French way. She then looked over at Penelope. "Good afternoon, Miss Farwell."

"And to you too, Madame Duval. Well, I should be going. I can't wait."

Ashley nodded. "Yes. Good idea."

As Penelope disappeared into the crowd, Corinne asked, "And what vile scheme was she proposing, and what can't she wait for?"

"Oh, probably getting her check from Daddy. She's heard Olga's out of town and wants to get back together. Suggested I should take her to the party. Now, what brings you to the Gauntlet. I doubt you want to come to the party."

She smiled. "While it might be fun, I must get back to the office. Anyway, I'm very glad I found you. Olga's returned from Montreal, and she's most eager to see you. I thought she'd be at your game, but she had some errands first. She must be at her pad."

"Great news. Let me escort you out of this chaos." They began walking arm-in-arm. "Have you heard anything from Rand?"

"Oh, he thought he might be able to come up for the weekend. But he's busy studying instead. *Alors*, I saw the game. I thought you were *magnifique*, especially against that big, horrible Dragovitch. Olga's told me about him. You must be thrilled to finally defeat him." Stopping, she again kissed him on both cheeks and hurried to her car.

Ashley made his obligatory appearance at the party to receive a new star on his helmet and then began running across the campus. *Damn, never letting Olga out of my sight again. What was she doing in Montreal? Ah well, I'll make everything right again. Just like we were.* Ashley ran up the stairs in the two-story building on Dow Street.

Unlocking the door to Olga's anteroom, he smelled the familiar residual incense, neglected cat box and Olga's earthy scent. He smiled at her large poster, *The Spirit of Anarchy*, where a bare-breasted young woman, a black bandana covering her hair, heroically clutched the staff of the flowing black flag, confidently leading the world's multi-hued masses into the future. Olga wanted everyone to know her political passion as they entered.

Ashley noticed on the shelf below the poster that her Russian Orthodox icon of Sainte Elizabeta was missing. Curiously, the three candles, which always surrounded it, were also gone. Olga had sworn several times that if she ever lost the icon, serious trouble would follow. He hoped she was all right.

In the main room, which was cluttered and chaotic as usual, he felt relieved that her most precious possession, "Tiffany," an authentic stained glass floral lamp, remained on the bedside table under her woolen anarchist flag on the wall. However, on her unmade brass bed, he saw a cream linen suit, next to a matching pillbox hat. Olga seldom wore anything besides black turtlenecks, short skirts and dance tights. So, the white brassiere and briefs with the tags attached puzzled him. Next to the clothes lay a one-way Air France ticket to Paris for tomorrow and beside it was his name written on a light-blue envelope. He stuffed it in his jacket pocket, and when he saw the closed bathroom door, he knew Olga was in trouble. She never closed that door because that would be too bourgeois.

He went in. Olga lay naked on the white tile floor, her pregnancy showing, eyes shut, with blood flowing freely and more blood in and around the toilet. He ran to the kitchen telephone to call an ambulance, then rushed back, wedging her anarchist flag between her legs. She briefly opened her eyes, which appeared lighter than usual as she shivered and became paler. He covered her with his blazer. *It'll probably be ruined, but I don't care. It may just save her.* Now, feeling scared, he held her hand and felt her trying to squeeze it until the ambulance finally arrived.

3.

Later, in Massachusetts General Hospital's waiting room, Ashley knew Olga would now be in better shape had he not gone to the party. And, as he cursed himself, he noticed dried blood on his hands. He also saw a large bloodstain on the right knee of his khakis where he had knelt over Olga. After going to the men's room to wash, he abruptly stopped scrubbing. She had often spoken about the blood. Initially, he had thought that this was some crazy Russian peasant superstition. However, as she revealed herself, he began to appreciate its importance. He left caked blood in his cuticles. In the mirror, he saw his flushed face and felt feverish. Oh no, not an *Andronyi*. Not now. As a precaution against this unpredictable force, he sat in a locked stall and waited, as calmly as he could, until unfamiliar color images rapidly appeared in his brain.

An elegant, black-haired lady and a distinguished older man chase a black-haired and laughing little girl through a lush estate garden. Later, the lady, the man and the girl run down a road amidst ruined buildings, corpses and cars as bombs fall. Ashley hears dive-bombers screaming down and more explosions until nothing for a while. Then, images of the war continue; Nazi flags, German soldiers all over Paris until liberation. After the war, the pretty girl with dark-blue eyes graduates from gymnasium before going to the Sorbonne... and then disappears for a long time. The distinguished man is gone, replaced by two young boys. Ashley sees among all the strangers another older man, a professor, who becomes Olga's lover. Later, he sees Corinne and himself.

He knew sending these intimate memories could not be a good sign for Olga's survival. He rushed to the duty nurse and asked about Professor Olga Andreyeva.

"The professor remains in surgery as of 11:40 p.m., a few minutes ago."

Well then, she's alive, still fighting for life. *Wow, am I stupid. I must call Corinne. She'll know what to do.*

Ashley ran out to the hall phone booth and called Corinne. She picked up immediately. "Ashley, what's wrong?"

"It's Olga. I found her passed out, bleeding, uh, intimately. She's in surgery now at Mass General."

"*Mon Dieu*, I'm on my way. Don't sign or do anything until I get there."

Returning to the waiting area, he found it now deserted except for a man smoking. Ashley wandered to the window and stared at Boston's lights, trying to make sense of this, when his head began to ache from the *Andronyi*. When he finally sat, a little after midnight, he remembered Olga's letter.

14 May 1962 p.m.
My Dearest Brother:

He smiled. She meant "brother" in the sense of a comrade in their heroic struggle to create a perfect world.

Shortly after you left for the Columbia game
on Saturday, Dean MacNamara summoned me
to his office. Nicholas Stevens and Penelope
Farwell saw us walking arm-in-arm down
Oxford Street that night after Corinne's party
and reported us. Moreover, I tried to disguise my
condition from him. It didn't work. I agreed to
quietly resign in exchange for your safe return to
the college next year because Harvard is where
you belong. My love, my charge is done.

He shook his head, wondering what she meant by "my charge is done."

After that, I went to Montreal on personal
business for several days and that's why I
wasn't here when you returned to campus. I
came back today for the Yale game, and I leave
tomorrow for Paris. Mamman has agreed to
accept her prodigal daughter, as I'm no longer
safe in Boston. I've been followed the last few
days. (Such is the lot of a Russian émigré.)
That's why, in a moment of extreme fear and
weakness, I wanted you to stay with me last
Saturday. But, of course, you couldn't do that,
and I couldn't tell you why you should because
I've never lied to you. However, I'm guilty of
the sin of omission. I did that to protect you
from forces you can't begin to comprehend.
Not because you're dull, but because they're so
alien to anything you know.

YOUR IGNORANCE OF THESE EVIL MEN
AND WOMEN AND THEIR WAYS AND
DEEDS, WILL KEEP YOU SAFE. PUMPKIN,
DO NOT TRY TO CONTACT ME! PLEASE.

He recognized their Pumpkin code reversing the following
words' meaning.

My most precious, I'll always treasure our time
together as I now most joyfully carry our love to
fruition.

I must assume our baby's dead. I vow we will try again.

I'll always love and treasure your easy, romantic
nature. You're already a man of extraordinary
talents and abilities. But not even you have no
inkling of what you'll achieve.

He smiled at her characteristically Russian double negative and romantic praise.

> Never doubt for a moment I love you with all
> my soul and heart. Your path will not be an
> easy one. You must never let the crowd seduce
> you. Always stand up for the truth and you will
> always stand out. You must be strong, as I know
> you are. I've every faith when you are at last
> called, you'll prevail in your quest. Remember
> all I have taught you and my spirit will always be
> with you. Finally,
>
> Yet, I secretly cast spells over the future,
> whenever the evenings are quite blue,
> and I have a foreboding of a second meeting,
> an inevitable meeting, with you.

Yes! We'll meet again. Ashley closed his eyes, remembering the first day of class last fall. Olga recited Anna Akhmatova's *I Rarely Think of You Now*. And hearing those four lines, he felt as though she were speaking only to him. And now he knew she was. She had smiled serenely and slowly closed her eyes, reciting the whole poem in Russian. At that moment, he fell in love with this strange, exotic woman, so authentic, like no one he had ever met.

Ashley sensed someone staring and felt afraid when he saw flat, dull eyes looking at him.

The man who had been smoking laughed and handed him an icon. "Kid, I think, perhaps, you may have been seeking for her."

As they both rose, Ashley asked, "Where did—?"

"Not so important."

"To me it is. Did you open the icon?"

"Of course. To establish I possessed correct one."

"See anything unusual about the icon?"

He shook his head. "No, what is important right now is your paramour is not going to survive. You remain safe for the present.

But, things change." He laughed, tapped an English Oval on his gold cigarette case and lit it with his matching lighter. He blew the smoke out in a shimmering ring.

Ashley knew the smoker had lied about the icon. Sainte Elizabeta possessed many secrets.

As he walked over, a fatigued surgeon in a gown and cap yelled, "Extinguish that filthy thing!"

The smoker took a final drag, dropped his cigarette on the floor and ground it underfoot. He blew smoke in the surgeon's face before laughing and shaking his head as he left. The surgeon fanned the smoke away with his clipboard.

"You must be Ashley Cooper for Professor Olga Sergeyvna Andreyeva." He had stumbled over her name before studying him. "What's your relationship?"

"Her half-brother. Our mother's divorced, lives in Paris."

"Where's the professor's husband?"

"Not married."

"I see." The surgeon spoke sternly. "You know your older sister's pregnant?"

"Yes. Is this a miscarriage?"

The surgeon grimaced. "Yes, this is some of the worst hemorrhaging we've seen. Now, where's the father?"

"No idea. A real free spirit." He leaned forward. "But she's going to be all right?"

The surgeon scribbled on his clipboard. "She regained consciousness and said, 'My brother, Ashley Cooper,' then relapsed back into a coma. We were unable to stanch her bleeding. I declared her deceased at 12:34 a.m., about five minutes ago. I'm truly sorry."

No. That can't be. She never gives up. A fighter. Too young to die. Don't believe she'd let me down like this. We've unfinished business. Ashley could hear Patricia, his late mother, and her crisp English accent telling him to show no emotion in public. Olga wanted him to scream and yell. These two women fought for his soul. Mother prevailed.

A few minutes later, Corinne arrived, softly repeating "*Ma belle*," as though a mantra, before dabbing her eyes with a light-blue handkerchief and regaining her composure. "Very well, Doctor. I'm Madame Duval, Professor Andreyeva's attorney and personal representative. I'll be making the arrangements for her return to Paris later today. Now, we'll see her body."

The surgeon led them into a white room where Olga lay on a silver gurney under a sheet, with only her head exposed. After she identified the body, Corinne and the surgeon went to the far side of the room to sign papers. Ashley intently studied Olga's face, taking mental pictures. He saw tangled, matted black hair, open washed-out blue eyes and her slack jaw. Yet, he sensed life still within her.

Lifting the sheet, he saw her small Orthodox cross with the squiggle nestled between her breasts. Thankfully, the smoker had not stolen it because she believed she could not enter paradise without it. Olga had refused to tell him what the cross's squiggle meant. For some reason, his intuition had never worked with her, even though she had taught him how to better focus it. Olga died with many secrets, and Ashley felt cheated because she had not revealed them.

When he touches the cross, electricity surges through his body. Olga's eyes shine brightly with intelligence and passion and, as her mouth closes, her erotic aura illuminates her face. He feels a strong tingling sensation in his chest, like his heart is racing.

Ashley shouts, "Doctor, I think there's some life left in her. Her eyes lit up and—"

"No, Ashley, this happens all the time. It's post-mortem involuntary muscle movements. You probably imagined something you wanted to see."

As he again looked down, the cross, which had left a burn mark on her corpse, was gone. He kissed her goodbye before pulling the sheet over her head. He smiled. She was on her way to the Russian paradise she had described to him... set in a dense forest clearing, where souls of the blessed could wander and commune together in their natural state, eternally young and free.

Ashley thought it sounded great, sort of like he imagined California. But he remained agnostic on life after death.

He went over to a shallow silver bowl nearby and studied the small human form of his son. Where was he now? If anywhere.

Fighting back tears, he heard Corinne. "We must leave. It's very late. You've classes tomorrow."

"No. I can't leave him."

"You must. There's nothing further to do. I know you fought to keep Olga alive. Come now, I'll drive you back to campus."

"No, if I hadn't gone to that damn party, she might be alive."

"No, Ashley, had you arrived an hour earlier it would've made no difference."

4.

Once outside, Corinne said, "Have no fears, Ash. Although the doctor was somewhat skeptical, I persuaded him Olga died of just the miscarriage. That means there will be no inquiry, no police, no delays in getting her body back to Paris."

"Good. I hadn't thought about that. When's the funeral?"

"I'm sorry, Ash. The funeral will be in Paris during your final examinations."

"But why won't there be one here?"

"First, Olga had few close friends here. Second, her will states her desire to be buried in the family crypt in Paris."

"But that's what I don't get. She hates her family."

"*Alors,* they've reconciled. She'd planned to return to them and, likely, a position at the Sorbonne. Besides, you must do well on your examinations. Dean MacNamara wanted you expelled before he made the deal with Olga."

"Why does MacNamara care one way or another about me? I mean, I can see he might be angry at Olga, but—"

"Very simple. You achieved what Olga denied him on several occasions. He has a long memory. Don't give him any excuse."

"Revolting old letch." He shook his head. "No, of course I won't. In the waiting room before you came, there was a guy who stole Sainte Elizabeta from Olga's pad."

"Were you able to get it back?"

Ashley heard the fear in her voice. "Absolutely. He gave it back when he told me Olga wasn't going to make it. But even he'd freaked when he opened it. That's why he gave it back. This big, powerful square was scared. He's not so tough."

"Don't get too confident. After all, he's not Nicholas Stevens. Now, please describe him."

"Well, about five-ten, light tan, very Slavic, well-dressed, silver hair, smokes English Ovals."

"Yes. Recently, he began following Olga, but I don't know his name." She smiled. "Doubtless, when he opened the icon, he filled with dread seeing the terrors of Hell which await him."

Ashley shrugged. "I've decided to call the square 'Ovals.'"

"Good name, Ashley, until we discover his true identity."

Ashley nodded. "You know how Ovals killed Olga?"

"At this point, I'd prefer not to speculate. I'm not even certain he's the assassin. However, whoever it was, I think it's of great significance they chose such a sadistic way to kill her. After all, it would've been much easier to shoot her dead. Now, don't worry. Olga's family, who are very well connected, will be conducting the investigation. Once I learn of anything definite, I'll let you know." She hugged him. "Ashley, I'm so terribly sorry for your loss. I know how much she meant to you. And, even more, how much you meant to her. Olga will always be with you. Come now, let's get you back to campus."

Once in her cramped Renault, they drove in silence all the way to Peabody Street. When she stopped at the Johnston Gate, Ashley said, "There's always been a part of Olga she kept hidden from me. I sense the same with you. I need to know what's really going on. Why was Olga killed? Who's Ovals? I have to know."

"No, Ashley, you don't. Such knowledge could get you killed. Moreover, don't fear Ovals or whomever. Your ignorance will protect you. That said, I vow to explain all to you at the appropriate time. Please be patient."

Showing his anger, he kissed Corinne on one cheek but not the other.

5.

Ashley again stands under the warm shower in the locker room, alone in the moonlight. The water feels good, but, as it abruptly becomes blood a voice in his head says, "This is the blood of your bond-mate, Olga. It is warm and healing. Do not fear it. Embrace the warmth."

Waking up, he wondered whose voice that had been, and what "bond-mate" meant. But he felt much better, his cuts, bruises and aches gone. *But my spirit's still unsettled. I need to commune with Sainte Elizabeta.* Sitting on the bed, he opened the five-inch icon's two hinged wings. On the middle panel, he studied Sainte Elizabeta's face and bright eyes. Each wing had an additional eye. As he focused, her four eyes glowed and grew larger. Light soothed him until he fell back.

6.

Next morning, Ashley heard a knock, asked who it was and unlocked the door. One of his suitemates told him that he had a call from Randell Speers, his best friend. He threw on a shirt and pants and ran down the hall to the pay phone.

"Hey, man, what's up?"

"Corinne told me your situation. Really sorry about the pain you're going through."

"Thanks. Even worse than Olga is our boy was killed."

"Wow! I'm truly sorry. But as your best friend, I feel I can ask you now. Why was Olga even pregnant? I'm certain she knew about birth control."

"Of course. I know this is tres bizarro. She said she was in her prime to have a child and wanted to have it with me. I could be as involved as much as I wanted. But this would be, primarily, her responsibility. As time went on, I wanted to become involved. As an only child, one thing I've always wanted is a bunch of kids with my wife, whoever that might be."

"I think you still have time to marry and have children. My money's on Pen."

"Never happen, Rand. You know about her and Stevens. They ratted Olga and me out to the dean. She had to resign. That's two sins I'll never forgive her."

"Perhaps you should, man. Your lack of forgiveness will burden and hurt you far more than it will her. Besides, if you want to get ahead at the Firm, you'll need her father's blessing."

"Right, except I'm not ever going to set foot in that damn place. Except to visit the Colonel. As far as I'm concerned, George and his daughter can go to Hell. They'll never be a part of my world. I'm going into poverty law when I finish law school. That's what Olga wanted for me, to fight for the little guy. I'm also breaking out of our golden ghetto to get a pad in the Village."

"Geez, never heard you this cheesed off before. But don't go burning any bridges just yet. Give yourself time to heal, to reflect. And then decide if that's really the life you want. Call me anytime to talk more."

"Thanks. You know, you're sounding more like a rector every day."

"Thanks, I've resolved the issues I had with Christianity last summer. So, I'm on track to be an Episcopal priest now."

"Great, I guess. But what did it for you?"

"Actually, quite simple. The French philosopher Blaise Pascal made a wager. 'If I live a good and holy life and there is no God, then I have lost nothing. But, if there is a God, I have gained everything.'"

"Cool. I like that. You've made me feel so much better. Thanks, man. You're going to be a hell of a priest."

"Great. I'll see you up on the Mount soon. I can't wait to beat your sorry ass in tennis."

"Dream on, Clyde. Later."

7.

Almost two weeks later, Ashley stood at the same pay phone, feeding it coins as he waited for Randell. "Hey man, we beat Tufts, and I had two goals. Also, I know I aced my finals. Your pep talk really worked. Thanks."

"'Sall right. I've my last exam in a few minutes, but we beat Brown in tennis last Saturday, and I won all my matches."

"Great. Tennis is definitely your game. Oh, got an airmail letter from Corinne. Said with Olga laid to rest in the family mausoleum, her American business was done. And so, she'll remain in Paris."

"I know. She invited me to come see her in Paris next week, and I've already accepted."

"Super. I'll drive you down to Idlewild."

"I can't let you do that with Ovals still on the loose. I'll get Dad to take me. Thanks anyway, man. Gotta run. See you."

That afternoon, crossing Harvard Yard, Ashley saw Ovals coming toward him. He braced himself confidently as Ovals came in close and said, "Things change, perhaps fast, perhaps not. You having now been warned."

I can't help it. My fists are clenching. There's a coldness and numbness in me and red around my vision. I'm really going to hurt this man. I see hands, not sure if they're mine, going out. Hitting his face.

Ashley laid face down on the grass, a knee in the center of his back and hands around his neck. "I see you have courage, kid. Courage alone can be suicide. You cannot defeat me because you are not warrior. You insult me with pitiful display. I do not like you. With little snap of neck now, your life gone. I have orders. When time comes, your death slow."

After Ovals left, Ashley rolled over, scared and confused, and looked at the sky and clouds, thinking. *Now, is Ovals serious*

*or just screwing with my head? I'll ask Olga. Get a grip, you're
on your own. My ignorance really isn't protecting me. Calm
down. Home tomorrow. The Colonel must know what's going on.
I'll ask when he picks me up.*

8.

The next day, Ashley's new stepmother, Veronique, known as
"Ronnie," arrived to drive him and his boxes home. He liked her
even though he had only seen her a few times over Christmas.
He had spent most of that time at debutante balls and lunches
with old friends. What he remembered was her English, seasoned
by her wonderful French accent with a hint of Slavic. And her
intense dark-blue eyes.

On the way home, he asked Ronnie to pull over near the
corner of Massachusetts Avenue and Dow Street, saying he had
to pick up something. He ran through the open door to Olga's
pad. Almost everything of value had been removed, and the
place was cleaned up. Her anarchist flag lay neatly folded on a
Formica table. He picked up the note on top. "Ash, bravo, quick
thinking. Thought you might like to have a remembrance. Love,
Corinne." He picked up the flag and crushed it against his face.
Even though it had been washed, blood crystals remained and bit
into his cheeks.

"Ashley, what are you doing?"

He dropped the flag, turned around, maintaining his
composure, and studied the tall, black-haired lady with dark
glasses up in her hair. Around her nose and those eyes, she
resembled Olga. But, even in khakis, a white blouse and heels,
Ronnie was elegant, just something Olga could never be. But she
had an aura almost as strong as Olga's. Interesting.

"This must be the flat of Olga Andreyeva."

He nodded. "Yes, but how do you—?"

Ronnie laughed. "Easter holiday, you said you were staying
in Boston, but you were really in New York. A friend of mine
spotted you two, obviously on very intimate terms, in that little

Cuban restaurant in the West Village. I never told the Colonel. He would never understand." She looked at the stained mattress against a wall and smiled. "Doubtless, she taught you a great deal about the art of love. She was always very adventurous. *N'est-ce pas?*"

"Yes, you seem to know a lot about her."

"We were colleagues. Professor Olga Sergeyvna Andreyeva was well-known as a crusader for equality of women. You were most fortunate to have had this great woman as both your mentor and lover. The whole world mourns her passing."

He heard the sadness in her voice.

She smiled and said, "Come, Ashley, the Colonel arrives from Russia this afternoon. He's very anxious to see you. And I have been working on my backhand all winter. He told me you play a *formidable* game of tennis."

Ashley could only nod, feeling his tears start from this room's wonderful memories.

"It is all right, Ashley." She came over and held him, filling his nostrils with her complex perfume. "Let it flow, all of it. We are family."

He cried and realized she was crying as well. She kissed his cheeks and dabbed his eyes with her light-blue handkerchief, repeating again, "We are family. Nothing to fear. You are safe."

After several minutes in her soft embrace, and getting very aroused, he opened his eyes when he felt that strange tingling in his chest. He still did not know what it meant, if anything. Ronnie soon left. A few minutes later, after looking around a final time and deciding Olga's flag would make a perfect summer blanket, he went down the stairs.

Quaker Mount, NY
June 21 to 29 1962

9.

June 18, 1962

Ash,

Corinne's dead, shot by several gunmen as we
left a party where Olga's family had honored
her. I was wounded and have been in the
Général Robert Nivelle Hospital in Paris. This
all happened a few days ago. Thirty-one's too
young to die. I won't soon fall out of love with
her. And, like you, I can't tell you how much she
taught me. But, it's so bizarre, we've both lost
our extraordinary women, who were so close to
each other, in a little over a month. However,
I've no regrets about accepting her invitation
to come over. And I now know she would have
been killed, whether I was here or not. But, that
this had been the best two weeks of my life made
Corinne's murder even more shattering. I still
can't believe something like this could possibly
happen. I'm feeling nothing. Wish you were
here.

Rand

After dealing with several international operators in both
English and French, Ashley finally connected with Randell.

"Allo." Randell sounded like he was in a tunnel, and Ashley
heard the line's static.

"Rand, it's me. I think the Colonel will probably understand
why I'm calling you. Had to talk. How're you doing?"

"How'd you ever find me?"

"Long story. Too long for long-distance rates."

"OK. Much better than when I wrote you. I can hear the sadness in your voice, so you must've just received it."

"Yes, I really liked Corinne. Could've been Leslie Caron's sister. You know, she starred in *Gigi*."

"Yeah, she hated that film and her too. People always telling her she looked just like Caron. She didn't see it."

"Well, she was always so happy and knew what to do in an emergency."

"Yes, we had such amazing times. Gangbusters."

"I'm glad you're feeling better. Guess you can't grieve forever."

"No, man, you can't. Just as you've recovered from Olga's death, I've begun to take the first steps to return to normalcy. Doesn't mean I don't miss her... I do, so much. But I'm powerless to do anything about her death. My life has changed, and I'm a changed person, just like you've become after Olga."

"I don't think I'll ever fully recover from Olga. But, each day I come to accept she's no longer here to love and guide me. Anyway, I'm going to book a flight to Paris. I want to help you. I've got some bread saved up and can't think of a better use."

"No, Ash. Doing much better and be home soon. Olga's mother's paying my hospital bill and has sprung for a first-class ticket to New York."

"That's great. But, look, after all you've done for me, I can't leave you in the lurch, even for a few days. Also, I must see Olga's tomb."

After a pause, Randell said, "Um, no. I don't know where the crypt is. And Olga's mother, who does, is too busy right now with the investigation to meet with you. She told me when the time's right, you'll see it. Besides, Paris is too dangerous right now."

Damn, someone's in his room coaching him. I can almost see her... tall, middle-aged with dark hair and stylishly dressed. Maybe Olga's mother? "Rand, is there someone there with you?"

"No. Just me. Look, I'll send you my flight info. The doctor just came in and wants to examine me yet again. Will you meet my flight?"

"Yes, of course. I can't be scared of Ovals anymore." *Bullshit*, he thought, *bullshit. I don't believe Paris is too dangerous. He's being coached. Very disturbing. Why don't they want me coming to Paris? Even worse, now that Corinne's dead, I'll never find out how Olga died and who killed her.*

10.

June 25, 1962

Ash,

I'll tell you more about my adventures when you meet my Air France flight 72 from Orly, arriving at Idlewild on the thirtieth. 10:05 a.m.

Anyway, I want to get down what happened the day Corinne was killed before I start to forget. And also, so you'll know as well. That morning, we received two packages. White tie for me, which fit perfectly, which was weird and a little scary. How did they know my exact measurements? Corinne was excited to try on a dark blue gown with a very low neckline and in the back, it went down to her lovely derrière.

She explained she was to be honored at a party on the Avenue Foch. When we arrived, the party, in a glittering ballroom, had already begun. The apartment was huge, occupying the entire top floor of a very elegant building. Even had this huge skylight over the ballroom. It felt like being in old Russia. Our hostess was the Grand Duchess Nadia Mytrovna Andreyeva. Olga's mother! (Dig it. Your beatnik professor was an aristocrat!) Nadia insisted I call her by her first name. Initially, I felt uncomfortable, wanting to show respect for her status and age. But she absolutely insisted.

(Honestly, these French ladies are so elegant, it's hard to tell their real age). Nadia then asked me a lot of questions about you and I replied that you were a gentleman and a scholar to all.

There was a wide variety of people there and I'm sure I saw McGeorge Bundy, Kennedy's national security advisor, in a long discussion with Nadia later. There were also several men, and some women, in military dress uniforms, including a few Americans. I wondered what I'd stumbled into. At nine, Nadia took Corinne by the arm and they promenaded around the great ballroom to thunderous applause. This was followed by a magnificent dinner. And oceans of excellent champagne, which was used to toast Corinne endlessly. I don't recall too much after the dinner, except Corinne looked absolutely radiant as we danced until dawn. People would come up to her to offer congratulations between dances. She said she would explain everything to me later.

Later never came. Nadia came to visit me at the hospital, where I have an armed guard outside my door. Nadia says it's standard procedure. She seemed truly concerned about my well-being, but deftly parried all my questions about Corinne. I'm now certain Corinne and Olga were part of a Russian émigré organization called 'Bleu'.

Later, Rand

Ashley sat in his desk chair upstairs in the Colonel's house, thinking. It felt right that Corinne belonged to this Bleu organization and had been promoted to some high rank. They would be hunting her killers and, probably, Ovals as well. Even though his intuition told him Randell was in no danger, he still felt uneasy about the phone coaching and the armed guard. Most of all, it deeply troubled him that Randell felt it necessary to write the letter when he would be home in a few days. He shook his head. What was this about Olga's mother being a grand duchess?

The Colonel was again in Russia, and Ronnie had been his companion, keeping his spirits high. But like Olga, there was a part she kept hidden from him, and his intuition did not work with her. She had told him Ovals had been arrested by the Boston Police the day after they left, and his trial for several murders had been going on for a week now, and Ashley had been following it. Ronnie came into his room.

"*Bonne nouvelle.* Just had a telephone call from the county sheriff. Ovals was caught at the Woodinville train station this morning, after being acquitted yesterday, and was shot dead trying to escape. You are free."

Ashley stood, and they hugged for several minutes.

"As I said in Boston, we are family. You are safe."

Ashley could not help himself from becoming aroused. And, in response, she did not pull back. "We celebrate your freedom with sets of tennis at the club, followed by lunch and swim at the lake."

Ashley, for the first time since leaving Cambridge, now felt happy. "Sounds like a great day. I'll be ready in just a few minutes."

"I shall stop by in five minutes. By the way, I intend to beat you in our match."

"Good luck."

11.

Even though she had beaten him, it had been a wonderful day. As he lay in bed, under Olga's flag, his thoughts were full of Ronnie. All day, he had focused on Olga's memories from the *Andronyi*, trying to find a way into Ronnie's hidden place and that was probably why he had lost. But it was worth it. He now knew she was the black-haired girl in the *Andronyi* and, thus, Olga's sister. This could not be coincidence. So, the elegant, dark-haired lady was Nadia. Ronnie had to belong to this Bleu organization, and that was why she was here, to protect him from Ovals. But would she stay now that Ovals was dead? His intuition remained silent, and as he turned out the light, he thought, *I'll pick up Rand tomorrow, and things will get back to normal. With Ovals' death, my freshman year is finally over.*

TWO

Wednesday, 19 May 1993
New York, NY

1.

At eleven a.m., Ashley Cooper and Randell Speers began their weekly match on the clay courts of the Riverside Racquet Club, and it quickly escalated with hard-fought, long volleys. They would briefly break between sets for sports drinks and try to psych-out each other by not speaking.

As one p.m. approached, Randell had the advantage. Both men were flushed; their whites and headbands were soaked, their sports drink bottles long since empty. The match point had lasted some seven or eight minutes, until Rand lobbed the ball over the net. Ashley hesitated, thinking what the—not now, as he ran toward the net and watched the ball bounce a second time. My God, that image was nightmarish. They shook hands at the net.

2.

In the Taproom, Ashley said to the venerable barkeep, "The usual, please, Francis. On my tab."

Francis nodded, congratulated Randell and offered condolences to Ashley. "You both look half-past dead. I shall include Uncle Francis's Magic Elixir in the fare for you both."

Going to their usual table, they passed the Wall of Fame's portraits with gold plaques underneath recording their championships. *Damn,* Ashley thought, *it's getting harder to pass my younger self each time.* Sitting in high-backed chairs, they quickly emptied their pitcher of ice water. Randell took out a small, dog-eared notebook. "OK, Rand, what's the overall score here at the Racquet?"

"First, today's the seventeenth anniversary of our first championship match."

"Amazing. But since we both gave up competition tennis back in '86, it's just not the same being in the stands and not on the court for the big one. Don't get me wrong, I love our Wednesday contests. But—"

Randell laughed. "We have our own championship series every Wednesday. If it's not competitive enough, I can still up my game. I was just being nice today."

Before Ashley could respond, Francis brought English ales and club sandwiches. "And here is Uncle Francis's Magic Elixir." He handed them each four brown tablets, which they took with their ales after he left.

"As a famous man once said, 'Dream on, Clyde.'"

Randell laughed. "Including each of our five championship victories, we've played six hundred and eighty-four games. You hold a four-match edge."

"OK. I now confess something to my priest about my championship victory over Joe Stevens. I cheated. Used my intuition to beat him just like his father."

Randell nodded. "I know."

"How?"

"It's not obvious, but using it, you play slightly differently. You can bet I wouldn't be playing against you if you were."

"Of course. But there's a downside to it as well."

"What? Your petit mal epilepsy."

"You're so wrong. I don't have that."

"I've seen you briefly check out many times over the years. There's no shame—"

"All right. I've something tied to my intuition. Olga called it *Andronyi*. I get all these images in my head."

"That why you hesitated on my final lob?"

"Yes. This time, just a color picture. A tall, skinny, naked girl. I'd guess ten to twelve. Her back's all ripped up and heavily bleeding. There's a handwritten sign in Russian around her neck... 'I am wicked girl. My punishment.' She's facing a woman in a Soviet officer's uniform. I couldn't see either of their faces."

"Mercy. Absolutely horrible. Who's she? Any more clues?"

"No idea. Short black hair. Not starving, exactly. Just painfully thin. I can see the back of her rib cage. Probably taken in the gulag. Had about thirty-six of these episodes since 1958, all different people's memories, but this was the first time for the girl. As to why and how, no clue."

"I'm sorry. I assumed you checked out because of the epilepsy. I never brought it up. Thought it would embarrass you. Waiting for you to say something."

"It's OK. Glad I brought it up then. Like my intuition, let's keep this to ourselves. I'm not embarrassed. Just something people don't need to know."

"Of course, I understand. I'm scoring our match a draw."

"No. This is part of the game. I used it to beat Stevens and to lose to you. That championship game with Joe was the fight of my tennis life. Simply couldn't lose to a Stevens. Although I won, I knew right then, my days of championship tennis were over."

"I was out then with a knee injury. Still bothers when it's going to rain."

"I remember. That was another factor in my decision. But if I had that match to do over, I wouldn't change a thing."

"Ash, you must get over your hatred of Nick. He's been out of your life for over thirty years."

"No. He was following me a few days ago. At odd hours."

"You sure it's him?"

"Fairly certain. Hasn't changed all that much. Still a big lug."

"OK. Why would he be following you now?"

"No idea." Ashley looked out the picture window. A tug was pushing Western Petroleum barges down the East River past the 59th Street Bridge. "God, can't get away from Western."

"Think George's having you followed for some reason?"

"You never know with him. The Colonel told me last week George's phasing out his duties as CEO of Western in favor of William."

"Interesting. I always thought he'd leave feet first. He's about eighty, after all."

"Me too. The old bastard's son's just too unstable to run the company. So, if George actually leaves, the company's stock will plummet."

"Probably. You know, you look tired. And that's another reason you lost. So, what's up? Beyond your visions? Noticed you missed services on Sunday."

Ashley turned back to Randell. "I still have trouble thinking of you as a rector. Especially after some of the unholy experiences we've had. Your ten-year anniversary as our neighborhood rector is soon. Any big plans?"

"No. Just another day at the office. Now stop trying to change the subject. I ask again… what's the matter?"

"Got in from Moscow at eight thirty last night. Damn flight's getting harder every time." He savored the aroma of the hops before sipping his ale. "OK. It's Pen. Been about eight months since she died. Keep on thinking it's going to hit me. She was the mother of my only child. I—"

"Perfectly understandable. You two had been drifting for a while. Especially after Annie was born. Until… nothing. As your priest, and friend, I'd urge you to start getting out more."

"I do. Seems like every hostess in New York has someone they want me to meet. All so pointless. Zero interest in getting married again."

"You should."

Ashley took a long drink from his ale. "Well, if I were, there's one person…"

"Tell me more."

"No. It's nothing."

"C'mon, let me decide."

"All right. This lady at the French diplomatic reception in Moscow a few nights ago. Tall, sleek, elegant, wearing a high-neck sleeveless couture gown. Fit immaculately. Not some twenty-something either. Probably mid-thirties. When she approached me, she smiled and spoke to me in a language I didn't know and had never even heard. Tried English, French and Russian. She smiled again and left. My intuition didn't work with her, like Ronnie and Olga, but I think she was faking on the language. Like this was some sort of test. I asked who she was, but no one would tell me. She's somebody important. Or somebody important's wife or mistress."

"A mystery lady." Randell smiled and took a large bite of his sandwich. After wiping his mouth, he said, "You know, under that cynical attorney's demeanor, you're a real hopeless romantic."

"Not so, Rand." Ashley shook his head. "You've been telling me that for years. Not so!"

Randell smiled.

Ashley again shook his head. "You'll never guess who she looked like."

Randell appeared to be thinking very hard. "Oh, let me make a really wild stab. She looked like—Olga." Randell looked at his watch. "Today's the nineteenth. She died on the sixteenth. Every year since, you get weird in mid-May."

Ashley laughed. "Just a reminder, Rand. You get a little flaky every year around the middle of June."

"Touché." He laughed. "See, that's it. We're now almost old enough to be their fathers and they peer at us through the years, eternally young, beautiful, wise and perfect." He took a long drink of his ale. "You know what still bugs me is that I still don't know any of the details of Corinne's death and—"

"Have you recently tried to contact, ah, Nadia?"

"No. First of all, I don't know any longer how to contact her. Second, Nadia must be in her nineties by now, assuming she's even still alive. Third, she told me all would be revealed at the appropriate time."

"That's what both Olga and Corinne said when I asked them about what was really going on. And come to think of it, Ronnie too. Well, be glad you escaped Paris alive."

"Of course I am. You at least know, substantially, how Olga died."

"Still don't know what actually killed her or even who or why. Believe me, over the years I've called in many favors from numerous people and agencies. No one knows or is willing to say. It's a complete dead end, so, today, I've finally accepted I'll never know. So, I'd like to propose a toast… all the Bleu Russian émigré business is now finished and done with. No more questions. No regrets."

After the toast, Randell said, "Excellent idea. It's long past time we did this. And I don't know about you, but it appears Uncle Francis has come through yet again to rejuvenate us."

Ashley nodded and laughed. "Looks like we'll live to fight another day."

3.

Her distinctive laugh caught Ashley's attention as Lana van Rouene led three other women in whites to their table.

Ashley said, "You know, Lana's something. I mean, she just waltzed in here one day, a foreign woman of independent means and ambiguous background. Then she began appearing at some of my other clubs. Married Ambassador van Rouene and after producing the long-sought male heir, I hear her laugh all over town. And I don't even know her original name. And I don't trust her."

Randell nodded and gave Ashley a very peculiar look. Lana raised her racquet in victory and smiled at them. When she came over, they both rose. She said, with her strong Slavic accent, "Good day, Doctor Speers. Ashley, wonder if I might have few moments when you finish lunch. Final details about tonight."

"Of course."

"Thank you so much for volunteering to be my escort. Ambassador has very bad grippe, and we greatly appreciate your cooperation at last moment."

"My pleasure. I hope he soon recovers."

"Thank you." She smiled and rejoined her party.

Randell leaned in. "Just had a horrible thought. She's about the same age as Olga and Corinne were—"

"You're right. A horrible thought. But Olga had more understanding in her fingernail than Ms. van Rouene has in her whole being." Ashley laughed. "Face it, they just don't make thirty-one-year-olds like they used to."

"Thus, hath spake all the generations." Randell laughed. "It's not every thirty-one-year-old profiled in *Vanity Fair* and *Vogue*, or named 'Hostess of the Year' by that fancy food magazine."

"Agreed. I didn't say she was stupid. She's not. Olga wanted a better world. Lana wants a better party."

Randell sadly took another bite of sandwich. "So, how was Russia, aside from the mystery lady?"

Ashley leaned in. "Followed in Moscow. I'm used to that. They follow all foreigners. However, these guys were very menacing. I think they were from this Minister Iskandarov guy I've been trying to negotiate with. He's a man of the shadows, so no idea what he looks like, but it's likely he was at the reception and saw me with the mystery lady. Could be his wife or, more likely, his mistress."

"If you pursue the lady, he might not be so understanding next time." Randell nodded again. "You know, sometimes the past doesn't like to remain the past."

"You know something you're not sharing?"

"Only this. Olga, you've told me several times, was preparing you for something, although she never said what."

Ashley nodded. "Think it's something to do with Iskandarov?"

"Is your famous intuition telling you something?"

"Uncertain. Don't know really anything about Iskandarov... only what others have said." Ashley shook his head and took another bite of sandwich.

"Think there's a link with Stevens following you?"

"No idea. George and Iskandarov might be allies. At this point, I don't care. I'm sick of going to Russia. A total mess. I'm going to do more phone work."

"Good idea. But what about the mystery lady?"

"A lady's always most alluring when she's a mystery. Looks like she'll have to stay that way."

"We'll see. Uh-oh, don't look now. Joe Stevens just walked in."

"No problem with him ever since I beat him. Doing a respectable job with Pen's Windimere stock as president of the company. If you remember, your endowment fund gets the growth on it every year."

Joe seemed determined and fit in his whites. "Mr. Cooper, Father Speers, good day."

They both stood. "Congratulations on your recent club championship, Joe."

"Thanks, Mr. Cooper. Wondering if you'd changed your mind about selling Pen's shares. Again, I'm prepared to give you a very handsome premium."

"Sorry, Joe. Sentimental value and all. Besides, they're Annie's when she turns twenty-one. You might talk to her in about four years."

"OK. If you or Annie change your mind, let me know."

"OK, Joe. You'll be the first."

As they sat, Randell said, "That was a very civilized interaction."

"I couldn't possibly care less about Pen's affair rumors. George wouldn't tolerate my divorcing his daughter. Pen knew just how far she could push. Even an affair. Got to keep old George happy, I do."

"Ash, I'm now speaking as your oldest friend, not your priest. You're one of the top international attorneys in the country. And it's been your talent, very hard work and, especially, your creative thinking, much more than George's largesse, that has made the difference."

Ashley raised his hand. "Perhaps, but I didn't exactly cover myself in glory on this last trip. Even though I got all the bilaterals signed off, I couldn't make any progress on the L'Enfant Bosnian Initiative with Iskandarov. I was dealing with three of his agents. They took my proposals to him along with my reasons why he should agree. The next day, they returned and gave me everything he'd signed off on. One of them told me Iskandarov would never agree to L'Enfant. And he had the power to keep it off the table forever."

"Don't see why that would be a problem for you. L'Enfant's really the Clinton Administration's responsibility, isn't it?"

"They need someone, like me, for delicate negotiations the government can't risk publicly losing. Net result, I screwed up."

"I'm sure it's not that serious."

"Elsewhere, perhaps not. But, at the Firm, there's no margin for error. Oh, it's all very clubby and collegial. But, as I've said before, the long knives are just beneath the pinstripes."

Randell smiled. "What's your intuition tell you?"

"Not good."

"Well, the Rastafarians say Jah, their god, never gives a man more weight than he can bear."

Ashley almost laughed before he realized Randell meant his comment seriously. "What do you say?"

"God moves in mysterious ways. Einstein said, 'God doesn't play craps with the universe.' And I'd add, nor with individuals. Should anything bad happen today, and I doubt it will, there's a reason."

"What might that be?"

"Perhaps God needs you to be elsewhere."

"Hmm, maybe He does. Thanks."

Randell looked again at his watch and sighed. "Got to run. Bishop wants to see me about something or other."

4.

Lana sat in Randell's chair, looking especially captivating in her whites, and spoke softly. "I missed you, *Kitzi*. And I need you. Can you get away early today?"

"Won't know until I get to the office. I slept in this morning."

"Playing hard to get?" She arched her back as she spoke, slightly shaking her blonde hair.

"No, not at all. Been in Russia since last Thursday and specifically came back for the Firm's weekly meeting, which begins at two thirty. No telling how long that'll go on." He looked around to see if anyone could be listening. "Now, why am I always so interesting the same time of the month?"

She shook her head. "I am most certainly not trying to get pregnant. No. That would be awkward. I use American birth control, especially now I have satisfied portion of contract with ambassador. No, I crave you constantly, but there are only few times in month when I am available. I am still hostess and companion for ambassador at many events. Despite his age and condition, he has busy schedule." She smiled. "You most sexy man. Much more handsome than portrait on wall over there. I have need of truly great fuck before benefit. And I am most used to getting what I want."

Ashley leaned forward, again looking around. "Is that all I am to you?"

"Is that not enough?" She laughed. "Seriously, best if we keep it there for now."

"OK. I'll call you when I know what's going on at the Firm."

She smiled. "Excellent. Call my studio." She studied him. "You seem troubled? Is it that Fischer person again?"

Ashley nodded slowly. He had forgotten he mentioned Larry Fischer to her. "Yes, while I've been out of the office, he's been spreading poison about me to the executive team."

"Most unfortunate. Fischer is Jew, yes?"

"Yes, but I don't see—"

"When I share myself with man, his problems become mine and his enemies mine. And I think have solution." She rose. "*Dasvidaniya*, Ash." She smiled and headed to the ladies' locker room, and he was reminded that she was relatively short. He also wondered what nefarious plan she had for Fischer. Nevertheless, an interlude with her, risky as it might be, would be just what he needed to get himself back on track.

5.

Ashley sat watching an ant trapped between two panes of sealed window glass. How the ant came to be in a supposedly hermetically sealed space amused him. Shoddy construction in George's building? Perish the thought. Beyond the ant, he enjoyed the unobstructed view of the harbor. After twenty years of service, he still took pride in being a partner of the most prestigious international law firm in the country. *I've recently felt unchallenged and L'Enfant was the challenge I needed. Boom!*

As he looked around the large, airy office, Managing Partner Charles Drew put down his phone and relit his briar pipe, protruding under his thick white moustache. Charles brushed the smoke away from his ruddy face. He stood and picked up his ancient briefcase from his mahogany desk. "Ash, you seem a bit out of sorts today. Something bothering you?"

"No, Charles. Just the usual jet lag."

He nodded. "Well, come on then, can't keep the Firm waiting." A few leather specks fell from Charles's pinstripes. Ashley smiled. Charles's father, Rupert, former managing partner of the Firm, had given him the briefcase when he made partner almost fifty years ago. Charles still proudly carried that well-worn case across the Brooklyn Bridge from his brownstone in Brooklyn Heights.

Ashley followed Charles through his door into the Firm's conference room. *Very peculiar. Charles calls me into his office on urgent business, and I just sit there.*

The long conference table shone. Pictures of the past seven managing partners, eight secretaries of state and three supreme court justices from the Firm hung on the dark, paneled walls. The partners and staff had gathered in many clusters, speaking quietly. Ashley felt surprised to see his father, Senior Partner Emeritus David Cooper, the Colonel. *He isn't due in town until tomorrow. What gives?*

The Colonel stood erect with his back to Ashley, carrying on a discreet but intense conversation with George, white-haired and lean, who faced Ashley. George reminded Ashley of a thirties hood ornament, a sense of motion even while still. *I've got to hand it to the old bastard... his trips to that Swiss rejuvenation clinic must've taken ten years off.*

George Simpson Farwell had been born into an old New York family. FDR, a family friend, had asked George to come to Washington in 1933. He had since used his State Department contacts to grow Western Petroleum into a major independent force. And he had become wealthy because Western had been able to go where "the Seven Sisters," for political reasons, feared to tread, and he had done business with some of the worst tyrants on the planet. Nevertheless, nothing had ever surfaced to tarnish his "statesman's image," and he continued to spread money around to ensure nothing ever did. It seemed a bad sign that George did not acknowledge Ashley, as he usually did.

Ashley shifted his focus to an exotic, well-dressed, raven-haired woman in her mid-twenties standing near George. Her blue eyes were heavily made-up, and dark red lipstick complemented her light amber skin. Initially, Ashley thought she might be a high-priced escort. Only George could get away with bringing a prostitute to the Firm's inner sanctum. But when he saw her busily scanning the room, he knew she was his new bodyguard. After all, George had told Ashley countless times that he had many enemies. Ashley realized he was staring at her when their eyes met. In that moment, he knew that, although relatively young, she could be a very formidable opponent, if it came to that. George called her *Anghelina* and asked her to join his conversation with the Colonel. Even though his intuition again remained mute, he felt something complex and problematic about her. *OK, I sort of get Olga and Ronnie, being sisters, could block my intuition, but how she does it is a complete mystery.*

Charles interrupted his thoughts when he strode to the head of the mahogany table, sat and gave the cue for all to sit by placing his pipe in its holder. The Colonel and George flanked him. The senior partners and the partners, all in high-backed, swivel leather chairs, sat around the table. The young, overworked associates and the silver-haired ladies sat in "the Ring" by the walls. These were the ones who made the place run, especially the ladies, and he always treated them all with respect. He noticed Anghelina standing near the main door.

Charles stood. Larry Fischer, across from Ashley, smirked contentedly. Ashley idly rolled his pen in his fingers, knowing his punishment for failure was about to begin.

"And now, I invite Ashley to stand." He rose, erect and expressionless. "Ashley's just this morning back from Russia, where he's successfully negotiated a series of very lucrative initiatives. At least, lucrative to the Firm." Charles paused at the muted laughter. Ashley looked at him incredulously. "As most of you also know, for the past six years, Ashley has been named by *Michaels Review* as one the Top Ten International Attorneys in the country. This year, he moved up to number one, mainly for his work on the Morrison Initiative. I should add that his work on the L'Enfant Bosnian Initiative has been exemplary as well." He again paused for polite applause. "Therefore, the Executive Committee of Goules, Argent, Orr and Drew, for his great contributions and loyalty, honors Ashley Cooper with senior partnership with all its privileges and honors, effective immediately. I should note, Ashley's the youngest man ever so honored."

As Ashley, smiling, walked toward Charles, he could hear the applause, mostly polite from his peers. Most of his colleagues hated his guts, and the feeling was mutual. Fischer looked as though the building had just fallen in on him, but he would soon be back causing trouble. Many of the gray-haired ladies stood, beaming and applauding loudly. The associates joined in competitive applauding to demonstrate their loyalty to both the Firm and Ashley.

While Ashley smiled, he also felt suspicious. *My intuition's never been this wrong before. And why all this puffery about L'Enfant?* Charles shook his hand and handed him the framed proclamation. *Something fishy going on here.*

The ceremony ended with Charles leading the ritual three cheers.

6.

After the meeting, Ashley, Charles, George and the Colonel gathered in Charles's office. Charles asked, "So, Ash, how does that jet lag feel now?"

"Fine, Charles—"

"No, Ash, call me 'Pinky.'" Charles smiled and patted him on the back.

"Well, Pinky, I'm somewhat confused then. I thought L'Enfant was the core of my trip. And I failed."

George shook his head. "Nonsense, son, you did better than anyone could've expected. Minister Iskandarov, who opposes L'Enfant, is, like Stalin, a ruthless, violent and unprincipled Georgian. I know all about those people from the Caucasus region. Blood of the Mongols flows in their veins. You may recall I was with FDR at Yalta." George paused, waiting for acknowledgement.

Right, as though I could ever forget something you bring up about once a day. Ashley nodded with interest.

"Besides, Iskandarov has links to the *Mafiya*. Very dangerous."

Charles added, "You're hereby relieved of any further efforts on L'Enfant. We can't have our newest senior partner getting himself killed or injured, now can we? So, no trips to

Russia without the permission of the executive committee. I'll be assigning this phase of it to Fischer. He has the, how shall I put it, unorthodox contacts to get the job done. Besides, if Aleksandr Iskandarov kills the little Jew bastard, well, no great loss, eh?" Charles and George laughed.

Ashley felt extremely uncomfortable but also relieved he would not be involved in bribes and *Mafiya* dealings. *Not that I couldn't handle it. Fischer as designated weasel seems very appropriate.* "So, what are my new duties, Pinky?"

"You'll have leave until Monday when your new offices will be ready. You'll be our liaison to Bob Dole's new kitchen cabinet. They need an advisor, a true expert, with real hands-on experience with Russia. They believe foreign policy is the Republican's ticket back to the White House in '96. This could be a fabulous opportunity for you, Ash. To begin, undersecretary." He paused. "Then, one day secretary of state." He again patted Ashley on the back. "You're a very lucky young man. All the details will be on your desk Monday morning, Mr. Senior Partner." Charles smiled. "Of course, you'll also keep in touch with Sarah Andrews, our liaison to the Democrats."

Ashley smiled. "Yes. Well, if there's nothing else, I won't take any more of your time. Again, thank you all for the honor you have bestowed on me today." *Damn it, I've been a Democrat most of my life. And now they want me to work with Bob Dole and his Fascists?* Leaving, he said, "Dad, would you join me in my office for a few moments? A few details about tomorrow night."

7.

Once in his office, Ashley wondered why his father had been uncharacteristically quiet. He also did not trust Charles and knew he had ulterior motives. His phone rang, and his assistant, Roberta, congratulated him before saying she had Sasha on the line. After pleasantries and congratulations about his promotion, spoken in Russian, Sasha told him Minister Iskandarov would like to meet him in the near future to discuss L'Enfant. Sasha would call him when the time was opportune. Ashley realized he still had an interest in L'Enfant and considered disobeying his orders.

Ashley asked if they could meet before next Monday. He had some important new information for the minister. Sasha told him the minister had pressing business in Sakartvelo, which took precedence. He asked Ashley what the information might be. Ashley dodged the question, thanked Sasha and said that if any openings did come up before Monday to call him on his home phone.

He called Roberta to see if she had told Sasha about his promotion. She had not. So how did Sasha know about it? If he did, then Iskandarov probably knew about it as well. What did he really know about Sasha? They had never met and only spoke over a secure line. From the beginning, Sasha had stressed that their relationship must be absolutely confidential. Now, since "Sasha" is the diminutive form of "Alexandr," could he be speaking directly with Iskandarov? Again, his intuition remained mute. While both names were common, he did notice Sasha's slight English accent, which sounded vaguely familiar.

He saw the Colonel standing in the doorway and motioned for him to come in and close the door.

"Ash, Ronnie and I are very proud of you. Senior partnership in the Firm is, truly, a great honor." His speech, after all these years in New York, still reflected his Georgia roots.

"Come on, Dad, this whole thing's a sham. I failed. We both know what that means. No more prime cases and a push out the back door." He paused. "How long have you known about this?"

The Colonel shrugged. "That's not important. Ash, just this once, take the brass ring and be happy." Ashley nodded. The Colonel's denial was confirmation that he had arranged it. He had many favors to call in. Surviving here longer than any of his colleagues, the Colonel still knew exactly where all the bodies lay buried and would not hesitate to use the information. The only question remaining was, why now?

"Ash, you've some free time coming up now. I want you to spend some of that with my only granddaughter. When was the last time Annie and you spent some... what they now call 'quality time,' together?"

"Dad, she's a teenager. I embarrass her simply by breathing. She's not my little girl anymore."

"Ash, I have been very successful in my ninety-four years on God's earth by knowing about people. I know Annie. She needs you and is sending out Maydays as surely as I'm sitting here."

"I know, Dad. I don't have a clue how to reach her."

"Ash Cooper, I don't buy that for one damn minute. You're one of the finest negotiators we have. Concentrate on your daughter rather than this L'Enfant business." He leaned forward across Ashley's desk. "I know you've probably already compartmentalized Annie and moved back to L'Enfant. What you want." He sat back and shook his head. "Your ability to ruthlessly compartmentalize is a great gift and a large part of your success. But look at the big picture, not exactly your strongest suit, I might add. Everything happens in its own good time. If you're meant to be the catalyst for L'Enfant, it'll happen. You can't force these things."

"You know, Dad, you're right. I do want L'Enfant."

The Colonel nodded, smiled, and spoke softly. "But speaking of the big picture, there are momentous events coming up. We need to have a serious discussion tomorrow night."

"Of course, Dad." He knew that his father was about to leave. "Looking forward to it. We'll see you and Ronnie tomorrow night, sevenish."

"Very good. We're staying at the club. Back to the Mount on Friday." Smiling quickly, the Colonel rose and left.

Ashley looked out his window and wondered what "momentous events" his father wanted to discuss. *Why couldn't he discuss them here? Unless my office isn't as secure as I thought.* In addition, the Colonel's visit had been uncharacteristically short, especially given the occasion. Had something changed since he left for Russia this last time? No. His jet lag had returned and now was playing tricks with his mind. He needed some air and to be away from the office. He called Lana and left a message that he would see her at her loft after four.

He grabbed his hat and walking stick and said, "Roberta, please cancel all my appointments for today and the rest of the week."

"Of course. Rest assured, no one will ever know you're not here."

"Pinky said I could take leave—"

"And now it's Pinky is it? My, we're coming up in the world." She laughed. "I suppose you'd like me to oversee the transition to your new offices?"

"Since you're coming with me, that would be an excellent idea. You know I'd be lost without you."

"You're the original silver-tongued devil himself."

"Could be. Thanks a lot. See you Monday."

Out in the hallway, he smiled about Pinky. *Ever since I was a kid, I've wanted to call the old bastard that to his face. Today, I did... the best part of senior partnership.*

8.

Once out on Water Street, Ashley removed his tie. *Free men don't wear ties, and I'll be just that until Monday.* He put on his dark glasses and pulled his fedora down to cover more of his face. Then, with his walking stick, he began his trek to TriBeCa and Lana's studio. His oak stick had a stainless-steel core and a sharp point. Things in New York were not as bad now as in the early eighties. Then, one of Ashley's friends was mugged in daylight on the Upper East Side in one of Manhattan's supposedly safest neighborhoods. Ashley had the stick made after that. He had actually used it once and inflicted significant damage on the would-be mugger.

Feeling anonymous on lower Broadway, he thought about what he could do before joining Dole. When Sasha called again, he would catch the next flight to Moscow, Charles's ban on foreign travel be damned. He would not enforce such a ban on a senior partner, especially when he brought back a valuable signed document. That would also show Dole's ivory tower boys what a Gules' senior partner could do. It would be a win all the way around.

He felt the mysterious tingling in his chest and checked his surroundings. He turned to see George's bodyguard approaching him. "Mister Cooper, I'm Anghelina DelaVega."

"Yes. I know. Now, why're you following me?"

"I'm not. I'm warning you."

"OK. About what?"

"We need to keep walking." She put her arm in his. She was almost as tall as him. "There's a Cuban DI agent named Jorge across the street. The young man about a block back is Bleu."

"Why're they following me?"

"You're important. Mister Drew certainly doesn't want to lose his most valuable colleague. George has a big investment in you as his son-in-law and principal heir."

"You're going to have to do better than that."

"George said you were stubborn. The guy from Bleu has been protecting you and your daughter for about four years now."

"Why's Annie involved in whatever this is? She's just a girl."

"She's almost seventeen, hardly a 'girl' anymore and very bright as well. Bleu has kept a discrete eye on you for over thirty years."

"Why?"

"As I've said, you're important to a lot of people. Now, since you're wearing your shades, your hat's pulled down and you look guilty, I assume you're on your way to see Svetlana. That is, Lana. I know her. Very clever. Be careful."

"How do you know about her?"

"My job, perhaps even my life, depends on knowing all about the people who matter in this town. And their enemies."

"All right."

"Now again, be careful. She's subtly playing you and wants you to underestimate her as just a dumb, buxom blonde. Today, she wants your baby."

"What about tomorrow?"

"I don't think she'll impact whatever's going to happen, at least directly. Stay with her and let it play out naturally. Otherwise, she might get violent."

Ashley nodded. "OK. Now, why're the Cubans interested in me?"

"Today, they're merely shadowing you."

"And later?"

"Things change."

"Has Nick Stevens been following me?"

"Oh, I doubt it. He's way beyond that. Deep cover at one of the agencies."

"So, what's really going on? You obviously know a great deal more than you're telling me."

"Not really. At this point, nobody knows anything for certain. What's coming may be big, or it could be nothing. So, be more aware of your surroundings."

"OK. But it involves not only me, but Annie as well?"

"Probably. Look, when and if it happens, you'll know it. Until then, enjoy your life. These guys won't bother you. When anything significant happens, I'll be in touch." She paused. "I saw the way you looked at me at the Firm. I'm not your adversary."

Ashley nodded before shaking his head and watched her go back downtown. It appeared that all this cloak-and-dagger stuff had something to do with the Colonel's momentous events. And that was why Bleu had resurfaced after all these years. *But why the Cubans? Enough of this. Nobody knows jack. Angelina said I should enjoy my life. I can't think of a better way to spend some of my time than with Lana, despite her warnings. Besides, my intuition will protect me.*

THREE

Wednesday and Thursday, 19 & 20 May 1993
New York, NY

1.

Ashley lay naked on Lana's gently fluctuating waterbed, eyes shut, remembering the reception at the Colonel's Quaker Mount house after Penelope's funeral. Lana had said, after giving birth to the ambassador's son, she was free, and they could begin their affair immediately. Although interested, Ashley declined. But after a "decent interval," they began. He could now feel Lana's soft breathing on his chest with her lush breasts pressed against him as he smelled the lavender in her hair and body lotion.

"You are happy, *Kitzi*. So rarely do I see your feelings, that makes your smile all brighter."

When Ashley opened his eyes, Lana's greens looked back. "Thanks. You're not the first person who's complained about me not smiling enough."

"Oh no, *Kitzi*, not complaining, I—"

"I know. Love your studio. Reminds me of my youth."

"No doubt truly defiant." She laughed and ran her hand softly across his chest. "Were you Beatles fan with long hairs?"

"No, Lana, while I like their music and all, they came after my time. I was a Beat with a beard, loved reading Ginsberg, Kerouac, Ferlinghetti, Cassady and Boroughs. In music, Monk, 'Trane, Diz, Bird, Miles, Mose and O'Day and people like that."

"Beatnik Ashley." She laughed and kissed him. "Certainly fooled me." She shrugged. "However, sexy men are always ageless. I have great excitement about tonight."

"It's going to be hell. So close to you, yet—"

"Not so. Everyone knows we are friends. Besides, it would not be unusual for me to flirt with attractive man, especially my escort. Ambassador, should he hear anything, would not mind. He likes you and knows I am free spirit."

Ashley wondered what she was planning. "However, he has very good sources. We still need to be discreet."

She bit him playfully on his shoulder. "Of course. I can be very discreet when I need to. I will make us tea, yes?"

"Sure."

When she rose, he noticed a light brown circular blemish on the underside of her left breast. He smiled. Lana's beauty was imperfect, which made her more human. He sat up and looked around the large room, which seemed to take up about half the space of a usual TriBeCa loft. He had never seen what lay beyond. While she had set up an easel in a corner, her canvases remained blank, her paints unopened. She certainly was an artist—of sex. Although they had been together for some time, their liaisons never seemed old or tired, especially true today. Most importantly, the sex provided a simulation of the intimacy he needed.

She returned with two mugs. "This old family recipe that my mother refined. Although certain you need no help, drink it all and you will fuck me into eternity."

He laughed. "Your English is good, and you seem to have mastered all our profanities."

"Truthfully, American profanity is boring and play of children compared to rich profanity of Russian."

"Yes, I know." He nodded. "With a drug this strong, there would have to be unwanted side effects."

"First time you use it, none."

"And?"

"Yes, you want to use it again. That is where side effects happen, if you use it too often."

"Let me guess, the second time's not as wonderful as the first and you keep trying, in the face of these side effects, to get back to the original high. And that's where the harm is."

"Yes. I use it only occasionally and suffer no bad effects."

"Ok. Fair enough. Now how far is it to eternity?"

"Oh, you will know, *Kitzi.*"

"OK. But what's in it for you beyond the pleasure?"

"You will be man of steel, and I must make myself strong. Drink. You made senior partner at Firm today. Congratulations."

Ashley shook his head slightly. "How'd you know?"

"Received call from friend. You seem upset I know."

"No, not upset, just surprised. I haven't told many people, and yet everyone seems to know." His tea tasted bitter but stimulating.

"Oh, *Kitzi,* when significant event occurs to important person, everyone hears. Everyone at Firm knows, and they tell their friends, who tell their friends. You are much admired and loved by many people and me."

Ashley nodded and saw a large poster on the bathroom door… the headlamp of a streamlined locomotive slicing through the blackness and over it, a large red star shining powerfully. At the bottom, in Cyrillic was "Vanguard of the Revolution." He stared at it. "I don't recall seeing your locomotive poster before."

"It has always been here."

"OK, then tell me more."

"You are asking if I am Communist." She shrugged. "Very well, my mother, Svetlana Feliksovna, was. The poster was hers. I believe Stalin made great country out of backward Russia. But it was most expensive. I keep this as reminder of mother and also of massive human folly caused by Stalin's impatience."

"OK, why did you include your mother's patronym?"

"Include patronymic as form of respect. My mother was, among other things, scientist and researcher."

"What did she research?"

"People. She was Chief Researcher at Soviet Genetic Research Institute."

"She still alive?"

"No. In mid-seventies, comrades turned on her, and she died in psychiatric hospital. But was very good mother, and I miss. Her picture is on bureau."

"Understandably. Sorry for your loss." He rose to see the picture, a beautiful young woman proudly wearing a Soviet uniform.

"Picture taken when she graduated from NKVD school, at top of class in 1937. Joining *apparat* was, probably, best way of surviving Stalin's purges. At their height then."

"No doubt." Ashley waited for Lana to say more, but knowing it would not be coming, returned to the bed. "Why don't you want anyone to know you're Russian?"

"Really?" She seemed momentarily irritated.

"Well, in that case, Ukrainian."

"Very good, *Kitz*." She playfully kissed him again.

"So, why this woman of mystery act of yours?"

She brought her left hand to her neck, her elbow resting on her breasts. Ashley knew she always did this while thinking, and her body language implied she was hiding something.

"Even in our most sophisticated circles, most people do not know difference between Ukrainian and Russian. And many are still suspicious of both. When someone presses, I mention pharmacy in Vilnius. They either stare blankly or assume Lithuanian, or some other Baltic country, which like being Swedish is all right." She smiled. "Amusing to play woman of mystery. Keeps everyone guessing. My act helps me maintain low profile."

"Thanks for your candor. I didn't mean to pry. I can see all this isn't easy for you to talk about."

"It is all right. Enough about such things for now." She moved on top of him, while softly biting his earlobe. She whispered, "I can feel you are ready for me again."

As the tea took effect, Ashley felt more aroused than he could ever remember.

2.

That evening, after Ashley picked up Lana at the ambassador's brownstone in Carnegie Hill, they went down to SoHo for the black-tie, Gay Rights benefit at Gallerie Giorgi. He knew he should have been exhausted by his afternoon with her, but he still felt aroused, partially because Lana looked absolutely stunning in a sleeveless and extraordinarily low-cut red dress. The benefit, "Artifacts of Alexander the Great from Russian Federation-On Display for the First Time in the West," was already the hottest ticket in town and would open to the public tomorrow. The large main room hummed with conversation, while a combo played Broadway show tunes.

Ashley had been fascinated with Alexander since grade school at Buckley. So, in 1982, a bust of Alexander from Pella, the ancient Macedonian capital, at the Metropolitan Museum's "The Search for Alexander" exhibit had greatly intrigued him. Eleven years later, he could still remember the details of the head—the broken-off nose and the marble pockmarked by weather. Nonetheless, it still conveyed the charisma of Alexander. He wanted to see if this exhibit contained any similar treasures.

He only saw part of it before dinner. As they arrived at their table, a discussion of Alexander's sexuality raged—heterosexual, homosexual or bisexual? Tempers among the partisans flared. Ashley thought it all rather adolescent and, trying to bring peace, said that classical Greeks did not classify men by their sexual preferences. A sex partner was simply a choice and nothing more. When this earned him the scorn of his male tablemates, Lana quickly asked him to dance. "*Trakhat' ikn!* Or, as we also say in Russian, the ringleader's 'someone who appears out of farting.'"

He laughed. "*Da*. Thanks for your support."

When she kissed his cheek, it felt a lot more erotic than it should have.

Later, with Lana busy, Ashley was alone in a room no more than ten by ten. In the middle, on a five-foot Corinthian column, under glass and a spotlight, he saw what appeared to be Alexander's painted death mask. He had never heard of such a thing, so it might not be authentic. But standing next to it, he thought it must be authentic because of all the wires surrounding it and the heavy lock securing the case.

"It was made by someone we know today as Armenian after Alexander was poisoned in Babylon. Resembles rock star, does he not?" Ashley could not quite place the accent and turned to see a tall, slim man with gray, close-cropped hair, black eyes and a thin nose, a white silk scarf draped casually over his tuxedo. His posture suggested career military. "I've heard about your comments during dinner. Are you student of Alexander?"

Ashley shook his head. "I've done some research on him. Studied Greek and Latin in school, and we had some interesting discussions about his sexuality."

"Doubtless. But, given your hosts, do you think your comments were appropriate?"

"The truth's always appropriate. I don't have time for people with narrow, partisan agendas."

The man laughed. "Good for you. I'm Giorgi Boutaris, curator of the exhibit."

"And the owner of the gallery. I'm Ash Cooper." He extended his hand.

Giorgi smiled and took his hand, placing his free hand on top of Ashley's. "I'm honored."

"This is an outstanding gallery. Quite a coup to get this exhibit."

"Indeed. Thank you. I'm agent for very prominent Cartvelian family in Sakartvelo in Caucasus, country you call Georgia. Entire exhibition's from family."

"Then, shouldn't its title be 'from Georgia,' not Russian Federation?"

"Good question. Family also maintain large residence in Federation and decided on name in interest of Russian-American relations. The family, who wishes privacy, is most interested in Alexander and have one of finest private collections in world. They hid it, for safekeeping, during Soviet interlude."

"So, what can you tell me about this death mask?"

"Well, it isn't, strictly speaking, death mask. Such things came later. Armenian was multi-lingual translator at Babylon court. When Alexander died, he bribed guards before making mask. He returned home with it and painted it several years later. It became family heirloom and treasure. In about 1453, his noble family then in Constantinople, impoverished after losing lands to the Turks, were forced to trade mask to Cartvelian family in exchange for substantial cash payment and passage to safety on family-owned Genoan galley."

"Must be priceless. I'm surprised the Cartvelians would even consider letting it out of their possession."

"It's beyond priceless. When family found this, they were ecstatic and felt they had reclaimed it for its rightful owners. They had heard rumors about it for many years and had sent out agents to find and purchase it without success. Finally, what they paid was pittance compared to what they would've paid. However, Byzantine family made many efforts to steal it back once they recovered financially. All attempts failed."

"OK. But why did the Cartvelian family care so much about it?"

"Family has reasons, which I'm not fully privy to. As I mentioned, family see this exhibition as worthwhile cause."

Ashley nodded and examined the mask again, aware that Giorgi was studying him intently.

"You're husband of Penelope Farwell. My condolences on her death. Also, attorney of some renown, as I recall."

"Thank you about Pen." Ashley shrugged. "As for the latter, there are many who would dispute that."

"I doubt that. I do try to remember those people who matter."
Giorgi nodded slowly. "If you would kindly indulge me, I'm
curious about your interest in Alexander. Why him?"

"Of course, as a history major in college, I was, obviously,
impressed by what he accomplished in conquering all the way
to the gates of India and wrote my thesis on his impact on the
modern world. But, beyond that, I don't really know. There was
something undefinable that attracted me to him at a young age.
Perhaps his charisma and determination."

"Yes, I know feeling. Alexander can still serve as example
to us."

"Indeed, but now, I'd like to know more about this family.
Are they the Iskandarovs?"

"How much do you know about them?"

"Virtually nothing, I'm afraid."

"I think you know more about family than you're aware. For
start, on your Russian trips, you have been dealing with various
members of family for many years. Even here in city."

"I thought that might be the case."

"Good." Giorgi nodded. "And now, back to Alexander. You
know, Alexander penetrated into home of Colchi people, now,
Sakartvelo. However, he had to return south soon. Some of his
lieutenants were feuding, perhaps plotting against him. After all,
powerful man never lacks for enemies."

"Indeed."

"And remember. Some of his closest friends poisoned him,
even those he trusted completely."

"I thought the circumstances of Alexander's death were
unclear. Many different theories." *He's trying to warn me. This is
getting very weird.*

"I would not speak to man such as yourself out of ignorance.
I'm merely messenger."

Before he could follow up, Ashley noticed Lana leaning
against the door frame in her vibrant red dress. She began
leaning forward, teasingly, as though, at some point, her bare

breasts would have to fall out. Having caught his eye, she smiled seductively.

Giorgi smiled seeing Ashley's reaction. "Ah, I see our Alexander has to now take backseat to your beautiful and charming lady. I understand completely. What pleasure it was to speak to you tonight. We still have much to discuss. Here's my card with my direct line. It rolls over to my assistant, Una, if I'm not in."

"I didn't bring any cards. I'll call you tomorrow. You've already given me a great deal to consider. Thank you."

"Giorgi, if you don't mind, I'd like to borrow my escort."

"But of course, Madame van Rouene."

Ashley noticed Giorgi had not smiled when he spoke to Lana, and his tone was overly formal. Lana appeared quite cool to him as well. She took Ashley by the hand to the main room, where they danced among diverse couples. With her arms around his neck, he could smell her perfume and, again, the lavender in her hair. She whispered. "I'm done here. We need to go back to my studio for nightcap. I can feel you're again ready for me."

"What time does the ambassador expect you home?"

"Around two."

"Great. We won't have to rush."

3.

After Ashley dropped Lana off, he found a note from Annie on his hallway table. "Dad, this looks important. It came from Russia. A." Under the note, he found Iskandarov's official-looking envelope. He took it, but first wanted to make sure Annie had returned home after spending the evening with her friend and classmate, Deborah Speers, and her family.

Her door was closed, and he opened it just enough to see that she was not there. Turning on the light, her room was a total mess. Dirty clothes piled high on her guest bed and CDs, books, papers and magazines littered the floor. He did not check what she had been reading because that was none of his business. But he would certainly read her the riot act when he found her. He looked at his watch—2:50 a.m.—she had probably planned all along to spend the night with Deborah. When Annie had been younger, he sometimes went into her room to make sure her covers had not fallen off or to put another blanket on her and just watch his miracle sleep. That ended when she reached puberty and demanded privacy. He sighed. She often left him notes in the kitchen but found nothing there.

Going back to his study, he poured two fingers of single malt before noticing the red message light flashing. He found three messages. The first two were annoying sales calls that should not have been on his private unlisted number, then, "Dad, we were watching a movie, and it ran long. Deborah's parents were asleep, so I decided the safest thing was to sleep over here. I'll be home early to get ready for school." He had always taught her it was best to seek forgiveness than to ask permission. Well, at least one lesson had sunk in.

He went to his bedroom and very happily shed his formal attire. Once naked, he could still smell Lana seemingly all over him. That made sense… he had kept up with her until they did reach eternity. He did not believe Lana's innocent explanation about her mother and wondered what nefarious purpose Svetlana used the tea for while in the NKVD and KGB. But he remained very warm from the tea, even with only his silk robe on. He shook his head and opened the letter.

> Monsieur Avocat Cooper. I am dreadfully sorry
> that I was unable to meet with you about the
> L'Enfant Bosnian Initiative when you were
> last in Moscow, I am afraid my aides led you
> astray. At the time, I was not even in Moscow,
> but, rather in Sakartvelo on urgent family
> business. I shall be there for the foreseeable
> future. However, I look forward to meeting you
> when I return to Moscow. I shall be delighted

to discuss L'Enfant with you at that time. In addition, I have some informations that should be of the highest interest to you. When I return, I shall contact you, for security reasons, through Sasha. At that time, I shall establish the time and place for our meeting. Most Sincerely, Aleks Iskandarov

P.S. Sasha tells me you have been elevated to the position of senior partner at you most august legal firm. My heartiest congratulation on such an honour.

Ashley had expected the usual formal first name and patronym at the end, not a nickname and last name and was surprised by the cordial tone of the letter. Curiously, he was Aleks, an unusual choice. Ashley also noted that Iskandarov had spelled *honor* with the British spelling and had used the French term for *Mister* and *lawyer*. Before the Bolshevik coup of 1917, the Russian aristocracy had used French exclusively amongst themselves. So, this provided a very interesting clue about him. However, most of all, he wondered about the "informations" he had for Ashley and why he could not reveal them in this secure letter. Georgi had been trying to tell him something important, and it made sense that he, being an agent of the Iskandarovs, had the same information Iskandarov was withholding. He also noted the letter had no date, which also seemed important. Finally, Giorgi talking about the poisoning of Alexander was definitely a warning, but was it meant for him or someone he knew? He would call the Colonel in the morning with a heads up before speaking to Giorgi.

He rose, scotch in hand, and went on to his large, tiled terrace to cool down. New York seemed about as quiet as it ever gets until a car banged over a steel construction plate on Fifth Avenue below. A few stars shone dimly in the hazy sky. Standing by the four-foot wall before him, the lights of Central Park stretched out like a magic kingdom. Soon, a police siren reminded him about the lethal nature of the kingdom's nocturnal residents.

Too tired to sleep, he remembered that he had never been able to get Randell to admit there had been someone in his hospital room when he had called him in Paris. And his intuition told him that ever since, Randell had been hiding something. Even though they remained best friends, he had never again fully trusted him. Ashley knew he should have gone to Paris then. In the meantime, he had stopped over in Paris often, en route to Moscow, and had unsuccessfully tried to contact Nadia. And he had not been able to find Olga's tomb in the Andreyev mausoleum. As Randell had recently reminded him, Nadia had said that Ashley would find it when the time was right. People had been telling him most of his life that such and such would happen "when the time was right." Surely, such a time, by now, was one of life's subway stops that he had missed. Olga had, by her own admission, withheld information from him while she prepared him for his quest—whatever the hell that might be. Ronnie had also withheld information, although with much more subtlety. To an extent, so had the Colonel. And even Lana had withheld information from him. He felt like the guy in the group who never gets that everyone else is playing a trick on him.

Ashley felt an *Andronyi* coming on and sat in one of the deck chairs, staring straight up to the illuminated cloud cover. Again, this time, he only saw a single image. He thought it was the same tall, skinny girl, because, even though she was now facing him, it was the same woman restraining her. And he did now notice a commissar's gold-trimmed red star on her uniform's sleeves. This girl, probably no more than ten, bleeding and crying, had clearly been raped and had a small handwritten sign in Russian around her neck… " am wicked girl." Ashley felt even more horrified by this than the last one and said a prayer for her. The handwriting on the sign looked like that of a young person, so she had written it. He remained clueless about why he was receiving these. And, especially, why now? He thought the woman might be Lana's mother, Svetlana Feliksovna, but she could easily just be another sadistic Soviet commissar. But, he sensed from his intuition that the woman must be important to him, but he didn't know why. And obviously, the girl was as well.

Feeling thoroughly frustrated, he forced himself out of his trance to move to another topic, far removed from the horror—senior partnership, especially after achieving his life-long goal at the Firm. He now belonged in the inner circle of his chosen profession—prestige and power for the best of the best. So why could he not find any happiness in it? Would it take some time for it all to sink in? Perhaps after he had settled into the position he would feel better. Could it not feel right because, as Randell said, he "was not where he was supposed to be"? Since all his earlier *Andronyi* images held clues, these last two must as well. It had to be the location of where he needed to be. Of course, he really did not know specifically where they were.

He shook his head, again frustrated, sipped his malt and focused on Olga. Thirty-one years and counting since her death, she had remained a presence in his life. Penelope, jealous of her, always threw something about Olga in Ashley's face, even as newlyweds. Although she knew her name, Penelope never used it. Always "your Russian witch," or "your Russian whore," or if really angry, she could, doubtless, make a hooker blush.

No longer feeling warm, he moved back to his study, went to his wall safe, removed a manila envelope and returned to his easy chair. This was the first time he had opened his safe for anything more than cash since Pen had died.

He took Olga's yearbook picture out first. Raven hair, parted in the middle, cascaded over her shoulders, complementing her smooth olive skin. Her black and intense eyes, under long eyelashes, showed great intelligence. Her high cheekbones caught the light. She seldom smiled, feeling such a display to be hopelessly bourgeois and completely absurd in such a terrible world. She always reminded Ashley that "we wander the world lost in the darkness of our own ignorance." The top of her black turtleneck covered her long neck. Unfortunately, the photo could not capture her strong aura.

He took another deep drink of the scotch and reached again into the envelope. He found the black-and-white eight-by-ten he had taken of her standing in front of her light-blue bureau, completely naked. For such intimacy, she smiled serenely. Her black mane flew everywhere. Her wine-dark nipples stood erect seductively. Ashley followed the firm curve of her hips, where one of her hands rested, down the muscled grace of her long legs. The other toned arm bent behind her head, revealing typically French armpit hair that matched her pubic triangle. While not precisely beautiful, she existed in her own niche, more than the sum of her parts—exotic, erotic and eternal. She would have aged well. He began to feel aroused, but this time, it was painful, and he quickly put the picture back.

Ashley still kept all her books, and occasionally he took them down to glance through them. Most of her ideas now seemed very naïve and dated, especially the anarchy. However, the sixties would always exist as a special time and place, with its own rules, when everything seemed possible. Sometimes however, when he read her writings, he again heard the distant trumpet call of the Struggle and the lure of the Kennedyesque crusade beckoned.

He pulled out Olga's last letter, still in its light-blue envelope. It had taken him ten years after her death to summon the courage to reread it. Even now, he felt its intense pain so completely he could not get through it without tears—not just for the pain but for all that might have been. But he remembered the letter's contents as though he had just read it yesterday.

Putting it back unread, he walked over to his desk where his Sainte Elizabeta icon was placed prominently. He kept the icon's wings closed when he did not consult her. Penelope had tried to throw the icon away during one of his frequent Russian trips. Annie, then a little girl, had seen it and told him that when her mother opened the icon, the light had almost blinded her, and she quickly dropped it, her fingers singed, and she never went near it again. A few days later, Annie had opened the icon and told him she saw the Sainte's big eyes. He found this very interesting. It might be the way to begin to reconnect with her.

Sainte Elizabeta had certainly done her part in protecting him when he had carried her around, especially in Southeast Asia back in the late sixties. Now, with Giorgi's warning, Ashley felt he needed all the protection he could get in this run-up to the momentous events. After returning the envelope, he finished his scotch, dimmed the lights and returned to his bedroom.

4.

Ashley sees a red flashing light and is drawn to it before he falls and becomes aware of lying on his back on a damp surface, unable to move. He smells copper in the humid air. A steam whistle blows, lights come on, and he is at the bottom of a large round wooden tank. Looking up, he sees a huge wooden pipe from which blood begins to pour out and rises quickly over his head.

A crash abruptly woke Ashley, and he rose, putting on his robe, hoping Annie had not been hurt. He found her in the kitchen, her green eyes staring, an empty silver tray by her feet. My God, Annie must be having a vision, just like Olga. He went over and shook her lightly, as Olga had taught him, and she came around.

"Oh, hi, Dad. I was just trying a new yoga pose." She busily put her bright red hair into a ponytail. "I made some coffee. Gotta run, bye." She grabbed her backpack and headed for the door.

"Hey, don't forget, we're having dinner at the club tonight with Granddad and Aunt Ronnie at seven."

She nodded slightly. "Yeah, I know. I'll be ready. Bye."

As Ashley poured coffee, he thought that perhaps he had made some slight progress with Annie. She had actually given several word answers instead of just "OK." At this rate, they might even be on full speaking terms by the turn of the century. Nevertheless, he did not want to get his hopes up. As he searched the nearly empty refrigerator looking for something to go with his coffee, he found a Gristedes bag with some very stale bagels. Since they were not moldy, he cut one in two and toasted it. Finding an almost empty jar of strawberry jam, he made a small but sufficient breakfast. As he ate and drank, he thought about Annie. He had seen Olga having visions, and she had some special name for them, which he could not remember. Olga could always tell before they happened and prepared herself. So, presumably, Annie could learn this skill as well. But if Ronnie could teach her that, why had she not?

Back in his study, he began thinking again about Giorgi's trusted friend remark. If Giorgi's warning proved correct, this was clearly those damn Russian émigré politics again. Ronnie had been associated with Bleu in the past but had not mentioned it for many years. His Russian contacts' reports had not mentioned it for at least ten years. Now, with the demise of the Soviet Union, it no longer even had a purpose. And yet, he was being followed by one of their agents. His recent interrupted blood dream, without Olga, was a warning of some sort. He just wanted some peace, answers and certainty, which he hoped to find soon. He smiled and knew he would know a great deal more once he had spoken to the Colonel this evening and could stop thinking about these almost overwhelming mysteries.

When he went into his study to call and warn the Colonel about poisoning, he saw the flashing red light of his answering machine. He heard Ronnie's voice on the tape, hard to understand because she sobbed so hard. After several replays, he understood. She wanted him to call. The Colonel had died.

FOUR
Tuesday, 25 May 1993
New York & Quaker Mount, NY

1.

Mr. Cooper, it is Una Ivanovna again, assistant
to Major Boutaris at Gallerie Giorgi. I am
sorrowful to follow on our previous telephone
conversations of last week. Major Boutaris is
no longer missing. I have recently received
telephone call from New York City Police
Department that he was executed, and they
throw his body in East River. We are in process
of identifying and preparing body for shipment
back to Sakartvelo. I do not need to tell you to
exercise the most extremes of caution. His killers
may be coming after you now. Thank you and
may God watch over you and your family.

Later that morning, Ashley, after running in the park, sat at
his desk and replayed the message a second time to make sure
that he had not missed any key details. He shook his head when
he finished and said a prayer for the repose of Giorgi's soul.
Because Giorgi had been abducted while closing the gallery after
the benefit, Ashley never knew what information he had. But
he now knew that Giorgi's oblique comments about a powerful

man being poisoned by his closest friends was meant for the Colonel. If the Colonel had been poisoned, that opened a slew of questions—who, why and, especially, why now? How did Giorgi know, and why did he not contact the Colonel directly? Obviously, the momentous events had now begun. It would do him good to get out of the city for a while and away from the intrigue.

2.

In his will, the Colonel stipulated that Randell should officiate at the service rather than the Woodinville Episcopal priest. Randell had originally balked at this. But when the local priest told him that he was fine with it, he began the preparations with great enthusiasm. Secondly, the Colonel wanted Ashley to deliver his eulogy at the graveside. Now Ashley tried organizing his thoughts for the umpteenth time as the limousine went up the two-lane road to the colonial cemetery on Quaker Mount.

Seated opposite Ashley, Ronnie, now in her mid-sixties, remained elegantly slender. Her silvering hair, cut in a shag, highlighted a face softened, not ravaged, by age. She wore a black ensemble with a single strand of pearls. Her long, toned legs seemed nearly as enticing as the first time Ashley had seen them the summer after Olga's death.

Ashley knew he should not be thinking about Ronnie's legs. He closed his eyes and thought back to when she had driven him home in the Colonel's Ford station wagon after leaving Olga's flat. He had sat silently in the car thinking, until she told him her name was Veronique Landfear. The Colonel had helped her become a citizen, and that was one reason she had married him. She was also a professor at Vassar College in Poughkeepsie, not far from Quaker Mount. She taught psychology, with a specialization in the female. Simply, it meant that she took freshman girls, and over four years turned them into confident and independent women. Then, she told him that at thirty-one she was not old enough to be his stepmother, and he should think of her as his big sister. Her role was to protect and mentor him. She put her hand on his. "You were mentored by Professor Andreyeva. That means you are very important." The rest of the conversation had faded from memory. But for the past thirty-one years, Ronnie had successfully protected and mentored him.

Ashley saw in the valley pockets of fog lingering on the large, neatly plowed fields, with stacked stone walls marking the property lines. On the ridge lay widely separated farmhouses among the greening trees. Seeing this, he focused on the local history. The indigenous peoples retained control over the Quaker Mount area well into the eighteenth century, owing to a boundary dispute between New York and Connecticut. The Quakers were the only Europeans allowed to settle there. Quakers built the Colonel's house in the 1740s as the original Quaker Mount Post Office and General Store. The last Quaker on the Mount died during Ashley's senior year at Harvard.

All week, the Colonel's death had seemed unreal. Not until Ashley saw him today lying in the casket at the Woodinville funeral parlor did it become real, and he broke down in public. The hills reminded him that his father's cheeks were puffed out with something; probably cotton, so they appeared fuller than they had been in life, and he had not liked that. He looked at Annie, seated next to Ronnie, trying, not successfully, to maintain her world-weary attitude despite the massive hurt he knew she felt. Her grief raised his pain.

Randell, sitting quietly on Ashley's left wearing his clerical robes, was looking at his blue *Book of Common Prayer*. Ashley wanted to thank him for being such a great friend but could not speak without totally losing his composure.

3.

Once out of the limousine, Ashley smiled. Unlike the already humid, oppressive air of the city, on Quaker Mount the air had a clean, vernal smell. Ashley saw Randell hugging his wife, Monica, as she emerged from the second car with their eldest daughter, Deborah. The three of them walked, holding hands, a perfect family. Brown-haired Deborah was thin and almost as tall as her father. Monica, the mother of three, was now voluptuously plump. Penelope had often snubbed her because of this, saying, '*Tout le Monde* is thin.' Ashley shook his head. Monica possessed a centeredness missing in Penelope and her chic crowd, probably remaining unaware they lacked anything.

A large black Cadillac limousine stopped, and the chauffeur opened the door for Ambassador van Rouene, who went directly to Ashley. He offered condolences and told Ashley that the Colonel had been a mentor to him when he was at the Firm. He then said he would like to meet Ashley at the Racquet Club tomorrow at two o'clock in one of the Aldrich Rooms. After Ashley accepted, van Rouene made his way over to the other mourners without a word about Lana. Ashley had neither heard from nor seen her since the benefit. Their arrangement provided that only she could call him.

The aroma of freshly dug earth brought Ashley's thoughts back to the Colonel. The polished mahogany casket, suspended on the chrome lowering device above the pit, reflected the sun. Splatters of brown earth already soiled the red felt around the grave.

Randell conducted the burial service with appropriate dignity and solemnity. Upon hearing Randell call his name, Ashley stepped forward. If he lost his composure now, no one would say a word. However, weakness would never be acceptable to him. He slowly folded his hands, relishing the silence of the moment, broken only by a cardinal's cry.

Looking out at the crowd, he paused for a moment at Charles Drew, standing next to his always dignified, somber wife Delores, who stood next to her older brother, the ambassador. To Charles's right was a delegation from the Firm, including two former secretaries of state and the two remaining senior partners emeritus. Beside them, he saw Roberta Cromwell, his assistant. To van Rouene's left stood many distinguished representatives from other law firms. Ashley recognized members of the Colonel's many clubs plus his golfing and poker cronies. A few steps away, Ronnie and Annie, both weeping, hugged each other. George Farwell stood conspicuously in the front row, with Anghelina on his left. George's narcissism so annoyed Ashley that it demolished his grief.

He began with a brief description of his father's childhood in the red-clay country of South Georgia. He lingered over his service in France and Russia in World War I. Describing his father's arrival in New York and start at Gules, Argent and Orr, Ashley found his cadence. He told how David Cooper had won Gwenneth Drew, the daughter of Horatio Drew, the Firm's managing partner, with his gallant Southern charm. Their marriage ended with Gwen's death in childbirth. Ashley's half-brother, Corey, survived a few hours past his mother. Ashley looked over at Charles, blinking back a tear at the memory of his older sister. Charles nodded, a brave smile appearing under his moustache.

Ashley continued with the "Dark Period" of working late, weekends and holidays in a nearly empty office. David's protégé, Spencer Talbott, finally pulled David out of his grief and back to normal life.

Ashley chose one of the Colonel's poker cronies to look at when he told about World War II. "David, then a major in the army air force, was charged with seeking volunteers for the first air raid on the Ploesti oil works in Romania. First Lieutenant Spencer Talbott, a bombardier, volunteered. David never truly recovered from Spencer's death in the raid. He was posthumously promoted to captain." Ashley noticed some of the older men, perhaps, lost in thought about buddies who had not made it back.

He looked directly at Annie as he related how Lady Patricia Sternwood, an RAF nurse helped heal David's grief over Ploesti when they married. Patricia bore Ashley at RAF Roughton's Hospital. Patricia had begun calling David "the Colonel." David never cared for it, but Patricia, used to titles, insisted. This brought some murmurs in the crowd.

Ashley smiled as he recounted David's rapid rise to prominence after the war, a golden period for him, which ended abruptly when Patricia died of a heart attack in 1958 at age fifty.

David, now twice a widower with a teenage son, resolved that he would not marry again. But that did not stop his friends. After a series of dinners with ladies arranged by mutual friends that came to naught, a French lady walked into his office. Ashley looked at Ronnie as he spoke. Veronique Landfear was having some legal difficulties with the Russian government. When David straightened them out, he thought that would be the last he would see of her. Surprisingly, she asked him to dinner. Before long, they were dating. Veronique, then in her early thirties, caused much tongue wagging when they married in late 1961.

"However, for the last thirty-one years, Veronique, who we all know and love as 'Ronnie,' has been the light in my father's eye. He hung in there for the last innings, and I think they were the happiest of his life. He told me, not long ago, that he had had a very good run for a Georgia Cracker." Ashley smiled. "That's how he referred to himself."

After a pause, Ashley's tone changed, his speech slowing. "I've known David Cooper not just as my father, but because I also had the privilege of working with him. I've also come to know him as a man and as a person. If anyone had a right to bitterness, he did. But he never allowed himself to be seduced by that easy way. He always remained boundlessly optimistic, believing tomorrow would be better than today. And people would be as well." Ashley paused. "Born into a society of carriages and candles, he lived to see all we have now." Ashley gestured with his right arm. "On his ninetieth birthday, I asked him about the most significant event of his lifetime. He surprised me with his answer… Lindberg's flight across the Atlantic, which shrank the world and has continued to shrink it ever since." Ashley shook his head. "While I don't think trans-Atlantic jet travel has shrunk enough, I think the world has shrunk a bit more today by David's passing. I remember his optimism, his grace and dignity. They all made him that currently unfashionable type of man, the gentleman. If we remember all this, he will live on in each of us. Thank you all for honoring my father by your presence."

As Ashley said his final words, his voice cracked. He quickly walked over to Ronnie and Annie and felt them hugging him.

With the casket lowered into the rocky earth, Ashley picked up a handful of moist dirt from the pile and threw it on the casket. As he did so, he offered another prayer for the repose of the Colonel's soul. The other mourners followed, each pausing to offer a final thought or prayer.

During this time, Ashley went over to where Penelope lay buried. It seemed as though he had just been to her funeral. He stared at her tombstone before moving on. It still bothered him that he could still not feel anything for her, especially here. Ashley then led his family and guests up to the Colonel's house for the receiving line and reception.

4.

After the receiving line, Ashley went to the bar for his drink. He relished the aroma of the lime and the throat burn of his first sip of straight vodka—a pleasure that Olga had introduced him to. He closed his eyes, saying a prayer for the repose of her soul. As he finished, he felt the tingling in his chest.

Charles and George greeted him warmly. After offering their condolences and praising Ashley's eulogy, Charles said, "I've let the Republicans know that you won't be joining them for a while."

"Pinky, I want to get back to work as soon as possible."

"Ash, if you were listening to your own words, you should know burying yourself in work does nothing for grief. As you well know, we have a policy for that."

"Yes, well I suppose two weeks wouldn't hurt."

"A month, Mr. Senior Partner."

"Very good, I'll take the time off. I've a number of things to get caught up on."

"All right, but no legal work. Have some fun." He smiled. "Oh, by the by, again, no foreign travel without the permission of our executive committee." Charles sipped his drink. "You haven't seen Fischer, have you?"

"No, of course not. Oh, you mean here?"

"Yes, I told him he was in the delegation. It's going to take your expertise and his contacts to get L'Enfant done."

"Pinky, I'm game. Fischer's always difficult, but I can work with him." *Yes*, thought Ashley, *that little bastard's not going to steal my initiative any time soon. I get the call from Sasha, and I'm on the next plane to Moscow and both Fischer and Pinky can kiss my ass.*

"Good man. I've given him both your numbers."

"Very good, Pinky."

As Charles and George left, Anghelina came over. "In case you missed it, it's begun. There've been about a half-dozen connected murders since the Colonel's, including Jorge, the Cuban who was shadowing you. Bleu's actively protecting you and Annie. I'll be in touch soon." Before he could ask her anything, she was gone as Randell came by.

"Who's your friend? She's quite the looker."

Ashley smiled. "I thought you were a happily married priest."

"Indeed, I am. But I'm still allowed to look, aren't I?"

"Take it easy. She's George's Cuban bodyguard, Anghelina DelaVega."

"Interesting name." He paused. "Great job on the eulogy. Remember that time we got into the Colonel's liquor cabinet?"

"God, do I. I don't think I was ever sicker."

"Me too, but my stepfather made me come over the next morning to apologize. I thought I was toast. The Colonel just laughed and said I'd suffered enough." Randell shook his head. "But he did add he'd appreciate it if we wouldn't guzzle his best Kentucky bourbon in the future. It was meant to be sipped. I offered to pay him for it, but he wouldn't take my money."

"And then we did the afternoon of yard chores for him."

"Yeah. I felt great afterward. Got rid of the hangover. After that, I had a great deal of respect for the Colonel and bourbon."

Ashley nodded his agreement. "We were, I recall, younger than Annie. And I'll kill you if you tell her about that."

"Oh, cut it, Ash. It might make you seem more human to her. Deborah knows most of my dumb adolescent moves. So, I'm sure Annie already knows yours."

Ashley shook his head, sighed and sipped his vodka. Out of the corner of his eye, he saw Annie and Deborah having one of the deep conversations, totally shutting out the rest of the world—just like he and Randell used to do.

Randell asked, "I don't suppose you're up for tennis tomorrow?"

He nodded. "Why not? I'll be back in town tonight."

"Great. I do have an ulterior motive. I want to hear all about you making senior partner."

"Sure thing… tomorrow then."

"Cool. I've got to buzz. Presiding at another funeral in the city."

"Thanks for coming. I know this was out of your way."

"Hey, don't mention it. I'm just glad the Colonel lived to see you make senior partner."

They hugged briefly.

Monica Speers came up, and they hugged. "I think you really nailed your father's essence, a gentleman. God knows, the world needs more of them." Ashley nodded his thanks. She kissed him softly. "Anyway, I'd love to take Annie down to the lake with us. Give you some time to yourself. Unfortunately, we've got to dash back to the city."

"Well, thanks for the thought. I owe you one."

She smiled. "You owe me a whole bunch, but that's another story."

"Never should have let you slip through my fingers." He smiled.

"I don't see where you had much choice in the matter. I was so angry at you then and thought you were a complete bastard."

She paused. "It's better I married Rand." She shook her head. "You know, I never figured out why you married such a harridan like Pen. You could've done so much better."

"Well, that makes two of us."

They both laughed, and she kissed him on the cheek.

After she left, Roberta Cromwell came over. "I've news. Let's find a quiet place to talk." Ashley led her out to the deserted back porch. "Fischer's disappeared. I checked with Rebekka, his assistant. She confirmed it. Doesn't know much more."

"Well, I can think of about a dozen people who would want to get rid of him."

"No doubt. She thinks this has something to do with L'Enfant."

"Interesting. Anything else?"

"Of course. Lana has disappeared. The office rumor mill says the ambassador found out about the affair. It seems the two of you were being most indiscreet at the benefit."

"Amazing. I didn't think he cared about it after the birth of his son."

"Hot rumor there as well. His son's not actually his. There's an office pool about this. You're the number one suspect."

"While I'm honored, it's not me. We began the affair only after the boy was born. I assume you're also telling me pretty much everyone at the Firm knows about the affair."

"Of course. No secrets at the Firm."

"Look, I'd like you to take two weeks leave starting Friday. Some down time. Once I come back, we're going to be very busy. And then that will give you two weeks to supervise our office transition… and find out what has happened in your absence."

"Sounds great. Count on me. There's an island off the Maine coast I've been dying to get to. I hear it's a fun place for single ladies."

"Then, by all means, go find out. Good luck. Check in when you get back."

5.

Later, at the bar, Ronnie asked, in her lovely Parisian accent, "Ash, a moment of your time." She led him into her study, just off the living room, closed the door and motioned him to the loveseat.

"Thank you for your very kind sentiments about me in your eulogy, which was magnificent. Now, I'd like you to come for lunch at L'Auberge Friday."

"You're welcome, and I'd love to."

"Marvelous." She sat beside him. You and I have had many happy times in this house, have we not?" She put her hand over Ashley's.

Ashley nodded. "Yes, many."

"I know this house's very important to you. And David and I decided it should be yours."

"Thank you. But where will you live?"

"Most of my personal belongings are now in my cottage at Rhineheuvel. I'm content to live over there, for a time."

"You certain? It doesn't look very big."

"Absolutely. I adore the view of the Hudson River. My needs are simple, and this house is too big for only me." She smiled. "You should know me well enough by now to know if I truly desired to remain here nothing could dislodge me."

"Oh, yes, I know and can tell you've something on your mind."

"Yes. The night David died, we had a great dinner and the show was fabulous. When we went to bed, he said he felt 'peculiar, but in a good way.' The next morning, he didn't wake up, and I knew he'd been poisoned, but not by whom."

"Do you know anything further? Like why?"

"I've an idea, but I want to do more research first. I should be able to tell you on Friday."

Ashley nodded. Ronnie, as usual, knows more than she's telling. She sipped her vodka before rising to retrieve her purse. "This is the key for my desk. Inside, there's a legal-sized envelope with all the documents for David's estate." She handed it to him. "Take the folder with you. Have a look at them before Friday in case there's a problem."

Ashley nodded. "Of course, but I'm sure everything's in order."

"But yes, please check anyway."

"All right. But if you ever need anything, and I mean anything, please don't hesitate."

"Thank you. Similarly, if there's anything I might do for you, let me know." She kissed both of his cheeks. "I was watching you in the limousine. There's something, despite my best efforts, you've never learned." She put her hand on his shoulder. "Ash, truly, it would be all right for you to show your emotions some time. No one would think you weak."

He shook his head while taking her hand. "I don't want to give anyone the opportunity. I learned a long time ago, at Lawrenceville, a simple proposition. 'If you're vulnerable, you're attacked.'"

"Ash Cooper, surely, you're a long way from boarding school at the Firm." She shook her head sadly.

"The Firm, being mostly a bunch of preppies, is simply a continuation of boarding school. Only this time we're playing for much higher stakes."

She shook her head. "You, sir, are incorrigible. *Alors*, we both have guests to attend to."

Ashley watched her leave. Still the free spirit, living life by her own rules. She had left Vassar when she turned sixty, saying her credibility was shot, being too old to teach young girls any more. Then, surprisingly, right after Vassar, she had opened her Provençal restaurant over on the Hudson. Amazing woman for that and so much more.

6.

The last guests left slightly after three. After supervising the cleanup, Ashley went upstairs and down the hall, hearing the oaken boards creak underfoot. He stopped at his father's office and cautiously entered. The rugged, brown-shingled Quaker meetinghouse next door dominated the view. Also built in the 1740s, it had served as a hospital for Washington's troops during the revolution. The adjoining cemetery ultimately became a burial site for non-Quakers as well. Today the Colonel had joined Patricia, near the neat stone fence around the perimeter. Even though he detested Patricia, he said a prayer for the repose of both their souls.

After idly looking over the Colonel's immaculately clean desk, Ashley inspected his photo wall. The Colonel had met many famous men—Generals Pershing, Eisenhower and Arnold. Presidents Roosevelt, Truman, Nixon, Kennedy, Carter, Reagan and De Gaulle. As well as Walter Cronkite, Ed Murrow and Governor Tom Dewey. He had met most of the Soviet leaders starting with Stalin. But he kept their pictures in a drawer. Next to the leaders were pictures of Ronnie, Patricia, Ashley, Penelope and Annie. The picture of First Lieutenant Spencer Talbott, still draped in fresh black, hung apart.

Back in the hall, he stood outside his father's bedroom and peered in. He supposed this would now become his bedroom. But that would be a difficult adjustment. He would be more comfortable in his old room but knew he should move into this one. He would, someday. He then moved down to Ronnie's bedroom. She had added a sundeck and French doors to the former guest room with her own funds and had turned it into her sanctuary. Thus, when the door was closed, she was not to be disturbed. She was either doing yoga or sunbathing, both *au naturelle*. He had only violated this once, using a mirror, during that first summer. He heard Annie calling because she needed to get back to the city for several hours of homework. Downstairs, Ashley unlocked Ronnie's desk, picked up the folder and left the key.

7.

Driving down to the city in his Volvo station wagon, Annie appeared miffed that he had not taken his Porsche 911 and seemed utterly fascinated by the trees along the Hutchison River Parkway. He wanted to talk to her to get his mind off the many times he and the Colonel had driven this together. All his efforts met with monosyllabic answers. He felt surprised when she asked, "Dad, do you believe in visions?"

"Visions? Yes. Before I joined the air force, I had one that I wasn't coming back alive. Why?"

"Just wondering."

Ashley waited for her to say more as she continued looking at the trees.

At the time, the vision seemed so real that he told Monica about it. He did not want to leave her a young widow. She thought him overdramatic. Unable to compromise, they broke up. Had he ignored the vision, he would be married to Monica, and Annie, in her present form, would not exist.

"How'd you make out with your paper about the wisewomen I helped you with?"

"Oh, got an 'A.'"

"So, why this sudden interest in wisewomen?"

"It's for Eurohistory. I just find it horrible these very independent healing women were denounced as 'witches' and were raped, tortured and killed."

"Unfortunately, in many cultures today, those who don't fit in are still killed and mistreated."

She nodded.

"Now tell me about your visions."

"Me? I don't—"

"You forget I saw you last week when you dropped the tray. And I know something about this because Olga at Harvard had them as well."

"Dad, I know about your relationship with her. We read about her in my feminist studies class. Do you have any idea how embarrassed I felt when I found out about you two?"

"Annie, I'm sorry. I was just waiting for the right time to tell you."

"And when would that be? When I'm in a nunnery because all the boys my own age think I'm a freak?"

"No, Annie, you're not." He hit the steering wheel hard and looked straight ahead. "God, I prayed you'd be spared what I went through growing up."

"Dad, do you have even a clue how geeky it is to zone out in front of your buds, like I'm epileptic or something. I don't want the visions."

"Of course I do, I've experienced it myself. I felt the same way about my intuition. In time, though, I realized two things. First, I had gifts, even though they might not be the ones I wanted. Second, they can be a powerful tool to make a better world. OK, now tell me about your visions."

She folded her arms across her chest, revealing her black nail polish. "No way. This is very personal."

"All right. Whatever you tell me stays in the car."

Annie rubbed her shoulder. Ashley knew she did this while thinking about something difficult. "They started shortly after I got my period." She looked at him to see if he was shocked by her frankness.

Ashley nodded. "OK. Continue."

"As I said, I go into a trance and see things."

"What do you see?"

"Well, there's a common one. An old lady. I've never seen clothes like she wears. And she's in this fortress-like building. I don't know if she's a prisoner or maybe a nun or both."

"Is this something happening in the present, past or the future?"

"No clue."

"How often have you had this vision?"

"Several times."

"When was the last time?"

"Yesterday. At school."

Ashley nodded. "How long did it last?"

"Just long enough to be completely embarrassing. Only Deborah stood up for me."

"Look, it sounds like you have what Olga had, but she had learned how to control them."

"Really? They can be controlled?"

"Yes. I don't know how to do it though. Ask Aunt Ronnie."

"She's been helping with this, but she doesn't have them."

"Well, in that case, we need to find someone who does."

"Thanks, Dad." Annie put on her Discman headphones from her knapsack.

Later, when Ashley passed Yankee Stadium, his emotions again rose. The Colonel used to take him to games there. They always had great seats very close to the field. Ashley, starting varsity pitcher on his Buckley team, sought inspiration from the great Yankee dynasty of the forties and fifties. He would never forget October 8, 1956, game five of the World Series, Yankees and Brooklyn. Yankee Don Larsen pitched the first perfect game in World Series history. Although it had been historic, Ashley still puzzled over its sheer improbability. Don Larsen, then with his third team, had spent his career as a journeyman and after that day had never had an outing nearly as good. In game three of the Series, he had left in the second inning. So how did it happen, on this one day, that he was able to achieve absolute perfection? The Dodgers were the defending World Champions, and four of their lineup were future hall of famers, and two more should have been. And yet, it had happened for no apparent or reasonable explanation. In any given year, the Series, obviously, featured the best pitchers. If any pitcher could suddenly get hot one day in the World Series, then there should be many perfect games and, yet, there is only the one.

What Ashley most remembered from the game was watching Larsen in the dugout sitting alone with his thoughts and demons. His teammates honored the ancient superstition that when a pitcher gets hot, he is to be left alone, lest someone break the spell. Ashley had pitched one perfect game for Buckley last spring and had a game the next week that was a disaster. Each in their own way, had learned the loneliness and temporary nature of perfection. And perhaps more importantly, they also knew very well the only direction from the top of the mountain was down. The question is whether you fall or climb down slowly.

8.

Later that evening, Ashley entered his study, put Prokofiev's sixth on the CD player and poured two fingers of scotch. Quickly disposing of the accumulated mail on his desk, he opened Ronnie's envelope. It held the will, life insurance policies, trust documents, copies of letters of instruction to various parties, all in order. At the bottom, he found a white envelope, neatly addressed to "Ashley. Eyes Only." He quickly opened it.

> 1 October 1988
> Ashley,
>
> Today I turned ninety. I was once told by a tarot
> card-reader in Russia that I would have a long
> life. You may find it curious that I put stock in
> what she said. However, everything she predicted
> back in 1919 has, indeed, come true. I want to
> get this down on paper while the Good Lord
> permits, and I still have my marbles. Although I
> have loved you as a son, I am not your father and
> Patricia was not your mother. We raised you after
> your parents were killed. Your mother, Charlotte,
> was Patricia's younger sister. Your father was my
> protégé, Spencer Talbott.

I won't reveal Spencer's real name at this point, in the event you don't wish to pursue this. I will simply say he was the young man I rescued, along with his mother, from Odessa during the Russian Civil War.

Now, you have a choice to make. If you are content with your life, destroy this letter. If you are curious, and I suspect you will be, Ronnie will provide the next steps.

You are reading this now, after my death, because nothing, according to the tarot, will happen until I die. Be aware that if you choose to delve into your real family's history, you will find some very unsettling things. Also, it could be dangerous. That is one reason I have not told you about this before. Whatever you decide, I know this will be the right choice for you.

Ashley, I have always been extraordinarily proud of you. You have been a wonderful son and I have been blessed to have had the privilege of raising and knowing you.

Your Stepfather, David.

The pain, fear and anger he had contained for the past week burst forth. He became angry that neither Ronnie nor the Colonel had told him this much sooner. Ashley wished he could have had a longer and more pleasant final conversation with the Colonel. He refilled his glass and went out on the terrace to clear his head and, perhaps, bay at the moon. It seemed long past time to do that.

FIVE

Wednesday, 26 May 1993
New York, NY

1.

Randell squeezed Ashley's shoulder entering the Racquet Club's Taproom. "Ash, you played an incredible game out there, totally focused. And, I might add, angry."

"I was." Ashley looked over the bar at the venerable barkeep. "Good day, Francis. The usual, please, this time on Dr. Speer's tab." He was spinning his racquet as he spoke. "Oh, but two iced teas instead. And I don't need your magic elixir today. I'm feeling great. Old Dr. Speers could probably use it though."

Randell shook his head. "No thanks, Francis, I'm just fine."

Francis slowly shook his head. "I must say this is highly unusual. It appears the two of you are conspiring together to confuse Uncle Francis for some, no doubt, nefarious purpose. Your usual table awaits you, unless, in addition to everything else, you've decided to change that as well." He paused. "Mr. Cooper, the ambassador has asked me to remind you of your meeting with him at two in room four of the Aldrich Rooms."

"Thanks, Francis."

"Pleasure, as always. It seems someone's being called on the carpet. Ah well, here's my magic elixir anyway, just in case. You can always count on Uncle Francis." Ashley nodded again and put the elixir in his pocket for future use.

"Good news. We'll be at our usual table."

"Oh, praise the Lord for tradition. Your lunches will be up shortly."

Once at their table, after emptying the ice water pitcher, Randell said, "Tell me more about your game today. And your anger."

Before Ashley could speak, Francis came over with their teas and sandwiches. "Ah, silent now, are we? Not good to keep secrets from Uncle Francis."

Ashley replied, "Actually, we were discussing you and how up the creek we'd be when you retired, only to be replaced by some 'whatever' kid."

"Fear not, gentlemen. Uncle Francis has no plans to retire for many years yet."

"That's great. Thanks for the update."

"Of course."

Randell laughed. "I just looked around. I think we can get in at least five minutes of uninterrupted conversation. So, again, how're you doing?"

Ashley leaned in, and Randell mirrored him. "When I got here this morning, I was angry. I took my anger out on the ball and am feeling a lot better now." Ashley looked around to see if anyone was eavesdropping. "I don't want this getting around. Not yet anyway." He paused to sip his tea and lowered his voice. "I'm adopted."

Randell nodded. "How'd you find out?"

"After the funeral, Ronnie gave me a letter from the Colonel, written on his ninetieth birthday. I recognized his handwriting as I read it last night. Patricia wasn't my mother but my aunt. My mother was Patricia's younger sister, Charlotte. Spencer Talbott, the Colonel's protégé, was my father. He said they were both killed, but my intuition's ambiguous. I must be very careful not to confuse what I want to be true with the actual truth. So, until such time as I can prove they're alive, they remain dead."

"And how do you intend to prove this one way or another?"

"I'm meeting with Ronnie tomorrow, and she has more information. I hope, if all goes well, I'll have this all cleared up by next Wednesday so I can beat you again." He smiled.

"Dream on, Clyde. Keep me in the loop though. Harvey Jacobs, my real father, was the pilot of the B-24 'Jezebel' on the '43 Ploesti raid. Talbott was the navigator and bombardier."

"You've never mentioned this before." He sipped his tea to relieve his dry throat.

Randell shrugged. "Until now, I never had any reason. My mother kept a picture on her bureau of my father, Talbott and herself in army air force uniforms. I asked her about the three of them a couple of times. They were pretty close."

"My God, we really are attached at the hip then." He laughed. "Until I started doing research for the Colonel's eulogy, Talbott was merely a face on his photo wall, draped in funereal black. And the Colonel only mentioned him once, at your mother's summer birthday party, the only time I ever saw him drunk. We were sitting on your porch swing as he kept repeating, 'I can never forgive myself for what happened to Spencer. It was all my fault.' I asked him who Spencer was. He replied, 'A very brave man I knew in the war.' This was about a year after Olga died."

"So, it would've been August the first, 1963, the twentieth anniversary of our fathers being shot down."

"Damn. Why didn't the Colonel only select single men for that mission? My father was killed five days before I was born. He never even saw me."

"My real father was given special leave in May of '43 to be at the RAF hospital for my birth. He saw me for all of one day." Randell crossed himself.

Ashley looked out the window as the East River's surface color changed when the wind skimmed over it.

"All right, what do you want to do about all this?"

"Obviously, it depends very much on Ronnie's information. As for being an orphan, I was initially angry, but as I worked it out, I felt a great sense of relief. Good to finally know the truth."

"What do mean 'know the truth'?"

Ashley's anger returned, and he fought to keep his voice low, but the anger and hurt came through. "Everyone I know seems to be playing 'Mushrooms' with me. You know, keeping me in the dark and feeding me bullshit. Ever since my intuition started, at around thirteen, I've known two things. First, my intuition said I was adopted. And this wasn't like most teenagers who decide they must've been adopted because their parents are so lame. No, this was real, but I suppressed it because, in the overall scheme of things, it really didn't matter. And also, it was a relief to know Patricia wasn't my mother. Nonetheless, when I can't sleep, this has usually bubbled up. That's why I sometimes felt I belonged elsewhere, like you said last Wednesday. Second, I've known the people around me were keeping something important from me. I can't tell you how many times I've tried to get the truth. For instance, when I called you in Paris back in '62, I sensed you had someone in your room coaching your replies."

"Hey, I'm a priest. I'm not supposed to be a good liar. However, I've known for a long time you knew. After all, just trying to protect you."

"Damnation. That's the response I get from everyone."

"Well then, perhaps it's because it's the truth. I've been your guardian for the past thirty odd years. I've just been an extra set of eyes to keep you out of harm's way. So, let me clear the air."

Francis came over. "Gentlemen, I hope I can still use that term with you, we disapprove of altercations in the Tap. If you cannot maintain decorum, I must ask you to leave the Tap until such time as you can converse without disrupting the meals of other members."

"Francis, we were not arguing in the slightest. Dr. Speers and I were simply having an intense discussion, which is now over."

"Uncle Francis is very concerned about the two of you today. You're both in a most peculiar mood."

Randell smiled. "OK. We'll behave ourselves for the rest of the meal. Promise. Beyond lunch, I can't say what will happen."

Francis shook his head and walked away, muttering.

"Good. I see our little Franciscan episode has calmed you down. So, in Paris, Cosette, a very attractive middle-aged lady was with me. I don't recall her full French name. Her Russian was Ilsa. Anyway, she was, among other things, Nadia's assistant. They both felt, in the wake of Corinne's murder, Paris was really too dangerous for you. And, at that time, they couldn't provide adequate security. Bleu has been protecting you and Annie for the past four years with a very good young man, who's nom-de-guerre is 'Sabreur Bleu.'"

"Thank you for finally coming clean. And I know about Sabreur Bleu, and I assume Annie's involved because of her visions."

"Yes, and there are people who want her for those. Don't worry, she's well protected." He paused. "Corinne recruited me into Bleu. I'm an associate agent. And please, never mention Bleu to any outsiders. We've survived for a long time because very few outsiders even know we exist. I only have one person I'm responsible for. You."

Ashley nodded. "Now, that I know. And I understand why you couldn't tell me before. My father, that is, the Colonel had to die before all this could begin. Had something to do with tarot cards."

"I know more. Sophia, the Russian countess who co-founded Bleu made a prophecy back in 1919, based on the cards. Cosette told me this and referred to her, in French as 'sorcière.' This can mean either sorceress or witch."

"You sure about the translation?"

"Yes. Why?"

"Annie had a paper for school Eurohistory about wisewomen. Or, as they used to be called, witches."

"Deborah hasn't had a paper for that class in two months. I keep a close watch on her homework."

"Interesting." Ashley took a bite of sandwich. "You know, the pieces are beginning to fall into place. Olga said she was preparing me for my quest. That's what this is all about. The Colonel, however, mentioned pursuing who I really am could be very disturbing and even dangerous."

"But why? Your father was shot down with my father. Your mother's likely dead. No doubt, very tragic. But dangerous?"

Ashley nodded. "Now, I know that's why I've recently been followed by various persons. But after reading the letter, I went out on the terrace and yelled and screamed and cursed until I felt better. I sat in one of the deckchairs and thought about Patricia. I sensed Patricia hated me for two reasons. First, I wasn't her real son. And second, I'd taken her away from being the leader of a corps of RAF nurses. So, instead of being someone important, she was changing my diapers and other domestic chores. In fact, if it hadn't been for my nursemaid, Rose, I'd probably be in an asylum now."

"I don't think Patricia liked anyone very much. With the possible exception of the Colonel."

"Right, and the Colonel was gone on Russian trips a lot when I was young. While I said in my eulogy this was a golden period for the Colonel, it certainly wasn't for me."

"Now, I had the exact opposite problem. My mother was very nice, and my Irish nursemaid was a terror. Remember, I was the only one in our third-grade class at Buckley still in short pants, even in the winter." He took a big swallow of tea. "Back to my original question. What do you want to do?"

"Look, my life now's pretty good. Not perfect. But certainly better than most."

"Right. You probably have everything you need, want or desire and then some." Randell shook his head. "But emotionally, you're a basket case. Your unlamented wife is dead, and you're estranged from your daughter. Plus, you're having an affair with a woman who's young enough to be your daughter. That's a cry for help, for sure."

"What are you talking about?"

Randell sighed. "Lana van Rouene. Counseling people's my bread and butter. Reading the signs and asking people if they need help before they ask me is how I've progressed up the food chain in the diocese."

"Damn it." Ashley frowned. "Who do you suppose knows besides you, the ambassador and everyone at the Firm?"

"Don't know. These things have a way of getting around. Annie and Ronnie may find out."

"God, I may have totally blown everything with this—thing with Lana." Ashley sighed. "I resolved yesterday, I'm going to break it off. Just haven't seen her yet." He drank his tea. "Anyway, it's not like I'm attracted to her on the same level as Pen."

"Well, of course not. You'd been with Pen for so long—"

"No, that's not it. As I've confessed before, I was like a junkie and Pen was heroin."

"All right, I know what it means, but what does it mean to you?"

"Well, we had an incredibly passionate relationship. We really hated each other, but I was so drawn to her aura and she to mine that sexually we were like wild beasts. And then once sex was over, we went back to our corners until the next time. An endless cycle until fairly recently, when her aura disappeared, and I lost interest."

"Ash, I believe you believe that you and Pen have auras. But if you do have them, they're well hidden from everyone else."

"Surely, you've seen Ronnie's. It's very bright."

Randell shook his head. "Look, I know you well enough to know you're not crazy, a little weird sometimes, but not crazy. You all may have auras. I'm just saying I can't see them."

"OK. But Olga had one as well. And it was stronger than Pen's."

"So, you're saying Pen was jealous of Olga for her aura?"

"Yes. Now, I know Pen had visions, especially when she was younger. She told me that the day Olga was killed, and I didn't believe her. She also said, 'When that old witch's dead, you'll come back to me.'"

"Hold on. Are you thinking Pen had Olga killed?"

"Look, I've no proof. But had Olga lived, we'd be living in Paris, far from Pen. Secondly, if she asked George for help, I'm sure he knows people who could do it."

"OK. But what if George refused?"

"Pen indicated several times she had something really big she could blackmail him with. And, no, she never told me what."

"Look, this is all very interesting, and thank you for your candor. But really, there's nothing to be done here, even if Pen arranged Olga's death." He paused. "No, I'm concerned about your judgement getting involved with a dangerous woman like Lana. You're about to turn fifty, a very perilous time for a man. You're no longer young and you're not really old, but you want to do something to recapture your youth before it's finally gone. Hence, the affair with a younger woman, a woman you have no intention of marrying because you know such marriages are, ultimately, doomed by the age gap. As I've said before, you need to get married again to someone closer to your own age. There are a number of lovely widows in the parish. You could still have the son you've always wanted."

"Sounds good. But, I don't think I'm ready yet. There's too much uncertainty…"

"OK, fair enough. You'll know when you are. Now let's look at the possibilities right now. You've a new position at work, a new identity as a widower and time to explore and decide what you want."

"You're back to what I should do about the Colonel's letter. In truth, I'm very ambivalent. I've no plans to change my name or anything else. I mean 'Ashley F. Cooper Esquire' is a brand. It would be professional suicide to change it. The people I deal with don't like change. But I've time now so, as I've said before, I'll see what's up before going back to work in a month. Maybe sooner."

Randell sat up. "Look, I never knew my dead father, so I see things differently. If I heard he was, somehow, alive and I had a chance to go in search of him, I'd be out of here so fast. I can't tell you how many times I've gone to bed wondering about my father, wishing I could have a chat." Randell finished the last of his tea. "I still see myself as the kid without a father. My stepfather was fine. It wasn't the same though. I don't think you understand that yet. You haven't begun to internalize you're adopted and an orphan. But one day, it'll hit you. Hard. When it does, you'll know what I'm talking about. And you may wish you'd followed up when you had the chance. Regardless of cost."

Ashley nodded cautiously. "All right. But tell me. What if you went in search of your father and found out something really upsetting?"

"He wasn't perfect. He was human. If he needs it, I'd like to forgive him."

"What if you had to go against Monica to find out?"

"I'd still do it. I like to think she'd support me. If she didn't, well, some things are simply critical and non-negotiable. This is right at the core of my being."

Ashley nodded. "You make an impressive case." He shrugged. "Look, thanks for listening to me ramble and carry on. I appreciate your input and empathy."

Randell nodded. "I know it's a tough call. I'll pray for you. And, if you happen to find anything out about my father—"

"Of course, you'll be the first. Let me give you a quick summary of my making senior partner."

After he had finished, Ashley looked at the clock over the bar. "I've got to run, time for the ambassador."

"OK, one final thing, quickly. I know you've puzzled over the deaths of Olga and Corinne, even Pen. And about why Ovals threatened and tried to kill you. Seems it's beginning to make some sense now these other facts are coming out."

"That's the problem. If I go looking for answers, I'm sure I'll soon be neck deep in those damn Russian émigré politics, a place I don't want to be."

"Very understandable. However, consider that could be the place you're supposed to be. Good luck with the ambassador. If you want to talk afterward, I'll be in my office at church."

2.

After showering and dressing, Ashley was still pondering Randell's last words about where he should be as he went down to the second floor. Ambassador Linus van Rouene stood erect in his dark-blue pinstripes, his ancient briefcase in his left hand. Even though he looked every one of his ninety-two years, his handshake remained firm. Ashley, who seldom wore his Phi Beta Kappa key, noticed the ambassador's shiny one, dangling from the watch chain across his vest.

"Thank you for escorting Lana the other night and congratulations, Mr. Cooper, on your recent promotion. Well deserved, I've no doubt. On a sadder note, again my most heartfelt condolences on the loss of your father. And wife." He brought his hand up to cover a cough. "I've reserved Aldrich Room four for us. Please follow me." They went into a sunny room with two plush leather chairs, each with a table on the side. Closing the door, he motioned for Ashley to sit. "I know you're wondering why I've asked you to join me." He placed his briefcase on the table with leather flakes falling.

Ashley smiled. "Indeed I am. But first, with respect, I sense you have a recording device in your case. And, if it's running, I request you turn it off. Or our meeting is done."

The ambassador nodded. "I see you're very careful, and your intuition is everything people say it is." He reached into his case and brought out a small black device, which he turned off. "Now, what questions do you have for me?"

Ashley could not tell if there was a second device, so he would proceed cautiously. "I'm curious. I haven't seen Lana out and about since the benefit."

"I'm sure you are. She had to go up to Montreal for something or other. She's due home tonight." A slight smile crossed the ambassador's thin lips as he sat. "As I mentioned at the funeral, I was an associate at Gules. Once I moved from the theory of international law at college into the actual practice at Gules, I decided I didn't wish to make a career of it. I spoke with your father about my interest in foreign relations. He had a friend who was in foreign service. Gave me a superb referral." He nodded. "We kept in touch over the years."

"When were you at the Firm?"

"Before the war... 1937 to '38."

"So, you knew Spencer Talbott?"

The ambassador nodded slightly. "Yes. Truly, a lady's man. Charming as all get out. Brilliant too. Seemed as though the law just came easily to him. Why do you ask?"

Ashley heard the anger in the ambassador's response. "He was my father's protégé. Just curious."

The ambassador smiled and reached into his briefcase. "This envelope has a key to a safe-deposit box. Your father gave it to me several months ago. He said I should give it to you after he died." He shook his head. "No. I've no idea about the box's contents. Only that it's located at the First National City Bank branch at Madison and Ninetieth."

Ashley took the envelope, recognizing his father's handwriting. "Ambassador, did my father say why he was conveying the key to me in this manner?"

"No. Only that it was very important you receive it. Oh yes, you should speak with your stepmother, Veronique, before going to the bank." He coughed again and looked out the window. "I've debated as to whether I should speak to you about this next matter. I decided, in the final analysis, it's far better to know than not. Therefore, I wish to raise a few matters of a personal and confidential nature. I married Lana in hopes she would produce the male heir my late wife couldn't. I'd no illusions about Lana when we married. Nor, I'm certain, she about me. She was to receive a very generous life estate if she produced, by me, a male heir. She has fulfilled that responsibility admirably. Ours is strictly a business relationship. At my advanced age, I could expect nothing more."

"Ambassador, surely there were hundreds, if not thousands of young women who would've jumped at such an opportunity."

He nodded slightly. "Especially since it involved artificial insemination. I was merely seeking a womb. Anything else would be a bonus."

"Yes, but why Lana over all the others?"

"This was what they call a 'blind pool' at the 'gentleman's sperm bank,' the Reinheiser Institute. Each applicant submitted a résumé and a DNA sample anonymously." The ambassador paused, thinking. "May I assume you have an account there as well?"

"Yes, the Colonel set it up many years ago. In case of serious injury. Why?"

"Oh, idle curiosity. I assume most of our gentlemen have such an insurance policy as a matter of course."

"And?"

"Lana's DNA appears to be extraordinary. I wanted to give my son every possible advantage since I knew I wouldn't be around—"

"Of course. Do you know why her DNA's so extraordinary?"

"No, sadly not. I should add again, in strictest confidence, her résumé was largely fabricated. She remains a woman of mystery to us all."

Ashley nodded. "That's the part I don't understand—"

"I know. Why did I choose a woman with a totally fabricated CV? Who, in all likelihood, wouldn't remain here to raise my son."

"Well, yes. Exactly."

"If Lana turns out to be unreliable as a mother, I've a backup plan with a young couple I know very well. It's contained in my will. However, thus far, she's been a most attentive mother."

Ashley felt concerned about the ambassador's dubious explanation of selecting Lana and sensed that the whole process had been anything but blind.

"Moving on. I know you've been having an affair with Lana. Since my arrangement with her is strictly business, I'm not bothered. And frankly, I'm pleased it's you and not some ne'er-do-well. In fact, had I been in your shoes, I would've probably taken advantage of the situation myself. However, that's not why I've mentioned this. As I noted earlier, Lana's résumé is largely fakery. In my experience, such women can be, and usually are, dangerous. So, *caveat emptor*."

"Of course. Nevertheless, do you know absolutely that her DNA sample was authentic?"

"On that score, I've no suspicions. She's an extraordinary woman in so many ways, as you doubtless know."

"Indeed, I do. Just to be clear, may I assume this whole procedure was carried out at Reinheiser from DNA sample to insemination?"

"Yes." The ambassador studied Ashley. "Do you know something I don't?"

Ashley shook his head. "I'm uncertain. When it comes to her, I've learned to be suspicious of almost anything she says… or does. I know virtually nothing about her, and for the record, I emphatically deny having an affair with your wife."

"But I know absolutely you are."

"Nonetheless, I again deny any involvement with Lana beyond being her part-time escort, occasional lunch and doubles partner."

The ambassador smiled. "I see. All right. Point taken, as you wish. Now, I can assure you the blind test was done properly. After all, I had a great deal riding on it. Nonetheless, if you discover anything definite—"

"Of course. Now, how did you learn of my alleged involvement?"

"It was Lana. I had her shadowed by a trusted and discreet associate of mine. Sadly, she captured Lana's infidelity with a young man, Joe Stevens." The ambassador paused to cough.

"Where was this?"

"They met at the Oak Bar at the Plaza and soon went upstairs."

Faithless wife's even unfaithful in her affairs, Ashley thought.

"Joe's the son of Nick Stevens, a fellow Crimson alumnus. Not one of your favorite people, as I recall. In any event, Nick disappeared into the Maze years ago."

"You mean Nick Stevens is in Intelligence?"

The ambassador nodded.

"Do you happen to know where Nick is now?"

"I believe he's on an assignment here in the city."

Contrary to what Anghelina said, Ashley sensed Nick was the person following him.

"My associate seems to feel Joe's in the Maze as well. That makes sense to me."

"How good's your associate?"

"All my associates are impeccable. That's why they're my associates."

"Ambassador, with respect, Joe's the president of Windermere and Associates, Pen's firm. If this were some operation, why would he be there?"

"Not the foggiest. Simply, in the course of doing research on Lana, my associate discovered some information that led her to believe some sort of operation was going on. That's all I know on that score." The ambassador paused. "Sadly, she also followed Joe to your wife, Penelope."

Ashley nodded without expression.

"My condolences, Mr. Cooper. Of course, I don't expect you to accept my accusation without proof." He again opened his briefcase and handed Ashley another envelope. "In this is a floppy disk. There are photographs on the disk, the proof of your wife's infidelity. There are instructions in the envelope on how to view them, in case you are, like me, totally ignorant of such matters. Also, there is the card of my associate, if you choose to contact her."

"Thank you, Ambassador, but was it necessary for this woman to spy on my wife?"

"While young, she came very highly recommended by an old colleague as one of the best operatives in the business. I permit her a great deal of latitude. She did this on her own initiative. I understand completely if you choose not to view the pictures." He paused again, coughing. The ambassador rose, signaling the end of the meeting. "Good day, Mr. Cooper."

They shook hands, and Ashley returned to his chair. He now sensed van Rouene's son was not actually his, and the ambassador knew it. Also, van Rouene knew a great deal more than he was saying. For instance, he knew why Lana had gone up to Montreal, and what operation Joe Stevens was running. Could Joe be keeping an eye on Lana? Or, were they allies? Ashley rose; he had enough on his plate without worrying about this. He opened the floppy disk envelope and took out the business card. Ashley was not surprised when he read, "Anghelina DelaVega Delgado, Suite 901, 276 Fifth Avenue, New York, N.Y. 10001" and an old Murray Hill exchange phone number. He called the number and only heard the answering machine.

3.

Before leaving the Racquet, Ashley had debated whether to go down to Anghelina's office or not. The Empire State Building was at 350 Fifth Avenue, and her office was in one of the seedy, old, office buildings south of there on the west side of the avenue. He would not waste time going there, but he put her card in his wallet. It might come in handy later on.

Later that afternoon, Ashley sat with the two envelopes on his study's desk. He put the safe-deposit box key envelope aside and debated whether he should put the floppy into his desktop computer. Presumably, van Rouene wanted him to see it. He inserted it and began looking intently at the pictures for something besides the obvious and found nothing. Except it amazed Ashley how much Joe Stevens resembled his father. If he half-closed his eyes, it could have been Penelope and Nick walking together in Cambridge.

Before she met Nick, Ashley and Penelope had carried on as intense a love affair as their respective boarding schools would allow with many passionate letters and phone calls and the occasional tea dance, where hours of loving kissing led nowhere. Penelope said she wanted to make love to him. However, she always heard her mother's voice telling her no. She told Ashley that it would be different in college and promised she would make his wait worthwhile. But, at college, before that could happen, they argued at a freshman dance over a seemingly trivial matter. Unfortunately, it fell on the female-male fault line, so it quickly escalated into a major event. Penelope, in tears, ran out of the room, refusing to take Ashley's calls or speak to him for a week. After one final attempt at reconciliation failed, he saw her the next day with Nick.

Returning to the screen for a second look, he followed Joe and Penelope all the way to *in flagrante delicto*. Ashley tried to feel something about her with a younger man, especially one who resembled a young Nick Stevens. But he simply could not. This was as involving as watching a pair of porn stars. What troubled him was how Anghelina had been able to get such intimate shots in a Plaza Hotel bedroom. She must have had extraordinary help and sophisticated photographic equipment. But, had Lana been secretly filming their sex? He feared he had been very careless, letting himself be set up for blackmail.

"Oh my God, I can't believe you're looking at such degrading, sexist porno."

Turning around, he saw Annie, still in her turquoise school jumper, standing motionless.

Ashley held her gaze. "This is definitely not what you rushed to assume. Have a closer look."

"Oh no. Jesus, that's Mom, isn't it? I knew I should've told you."

"Told me what?"

Ashley rose to hold her, and she buried her face in his chest, crying and shaking.

4.

About twenty minutes later, Annie sat opposite Ashley, speaking with unambiguous anger. "About a year ago, I came home from school shortly after getting there. I was sick. This was while you were in Russia. When I went by Mom's bedroom, she and that guy, Joe, were asleep on her bed, naked. I knew who he was." She shook her head, as though trying to shake out the image. "I didn't know what to do, so I very carefully tiptoed to my room and quietly closed my door. Later, when I came out after resting, Mom was gone, probably shopping at Bloomingdales." She shook her head sadly. "You know, she had these piercings in her nipples."

Ashley nodded. "Yes, I saw them."

Her face contorted disgustedly. "It's just so totally vile. A woman, a mother her age." She shook her head. "You know, we never spoke of anything important after that."

"Yes, it hurt your mother very badly."

"Well, not as much as she did me." She smiled. "Dad, I'm so glad you don't try to be choice like her."

Ashley smiled at her left-handed compliment. "I want you to think very carefully. Had you ever seen Mom with anyone else but Joe?"

She shook her head.

Ashley knew her denial could not be considered definitive. Pen always wanted to be the life of the party. She might have spontaneously had some one-night stands. However, he knew that Annie with her visions, had to be his daughter.

"Dad, I want to know the real reason why you didn't marry Monica."

"OK, fair question. I was going to be in the air force, and I told Monica my intuition indicated I'd be killed in Vietnam. I didn't want her to be a young widow. We talked about this late into the night. She cried, convinced I'd die." Ashley looked out over Annie at the park. "I was ordered to Monterey, California for the accelerated Russian language program. After that, and additional training, my orders were for Southeast Asia. Before I shipped out, I received a letter from Monica saying she and Rand were going to be married. They wanted me to be their best man."

Annie shook her head. "That's so weird."

"Not really. We all grew up together. We three were very close as teenagers. I came home on leave and stood with Randell."

Annie shrugged. "But you didn't die. What did Monica say when you got back?"

"That was the really strange part. I was in Bangkok one night, and a guy shot me. No words or anything. Just comes up and bang, I'm on the ground, and he's about to put a second bullet in me when I hear shots. He crumbles, next to me, dead. I look up. Here's this Brit saying something about a 'bloody blighter' before I lost consciousness. Now, that's like some bad spy movie. No real Englishman speaks like that anymore. Anyway, next thing I know, I'm in a military hospital with the doctor telling me I'm very lucky to be alive."

"No way, Dad. That's too creepy." Annie shook her head violently.

"Absolutely. But it's the truth. You've seen the scar on my chest, just above my heart."

"Who were these guys?"

"I don't know. The Brit just disappeared. The Russian, I later found out, was an assassin."

"Why did he want to kill you?"

"Don't know. Perhaps he knew I interrogated captured Russian advisors at NKP."

"What's this NKP?"

"I've told you about it before. It was a huge Royal Thai naval and air base in Northern Thailand on the Mekong River. On the other side of the river is Laos. Recon, counter-insurgency, black ops, B-52s, the whole nine yards were run out of there."

"Cool. I remember now. It stands for Na Kon Phanom, right?"

Ashley nodded.

"Did you ever, you know, kill anyone you were interrogating?"

"Truthfully, I shot a Russian captain, but I guess it was self-defense."

"Why didn't you ever tell me about that or getting shot before?"

Ashley shrugged. "I don't know. I guess I wanted to wait until you were older."

"Is there anything else you've been waiting to tell me?"

"Actually, yes. Let's give it a few days until I know more."

"What is it?"

"At this point, I'm not completely sure. When I find out for certain, you'll be the first."

Annie nodded.

Ashley asked, "Is there anything you'd like to tell me?"

She smiled. "No, I'll wait until you're older."

"Nice try."

"Oh, I've got a new recipe from my gourmet course I'd like to try tonight."

"Before you go, Rand told me today Deborah didn't have any papers in Euro History for the last two months. Care to explain about yours?"

"OK. Just doing some independent research for extra credit."

"Why?"

"Well, as I've said, wisewomen intrigue me."

"I sense it's tied in with your visions."

"I can't really talk about that."

"Why not?"

"All I can say is Aunt Ronnie is helping me." She went over to his desk and picked up Sainte Elizabeta.

"Why can I pick this up when mom couldn't?"

"Again, I think it's related to your visions."

"Cool."

"I had the icon with me when I was at NKP to keep me safe, and I had it in Bangkok. So, along with the Brit, it may have saved my life."

"Dad, that is just too freaky. Whatever it was, I'm glad you survived." She quickly added, "Otherwise, I'd be an orphan now. I'm going to start dinner. Hope you're hungry."

"I am. I just hope it's better than that Chinese-Mexican concoction you made last time."

"Yeah, that was kinda a disaster. Trust me, this will be much better. It's French."

"*Bonne chance* then." Ashley smiled.

"*Merci, Papa.*" She left the room humming.

He took the floppy out of the computer and opened the other envelope. The bank key had a twenty-four-hour phone number. He put it all in his wall safe before going out on the terrace to gather his thoughts.

Sitting in a deck chair, he felt an *Andronyi* coming on. Again, a single image of the skinny girl. She is wearing a blue smock and is up on her toes, smiling, doing a ballet pose. The woman is not in the picture. She had sent this to show the other side of her life and that she remained alive. He vowed he would find her.

SIX
Friday, 28 May 1993
Dutchess County, NY

1.

Last evening, after Annie's excellent meal, Ashley had been watching the lights of Central Park come on when he heard a rifle bullet hit his terrace's wall about a foot left and down from where he stood. He retreated to his study, closed the curtains and downed a glass of scotch. *Damn*, he thought, *getting shot at in NKP is one thing. Totally different in my home, my sanctuary.* Annie, after hearing three additional shots, ran in, scared and crying, and Ashley hugged her. She asked if Sabreur Bleu had saved them. Ashley did not know. She then asked if she could have some scotch. Ashley nodded and gave her a finger with an ice cube. She downed it, coughed, made a face and asked how he could stand the taste. She spent the evening close to him until she fell asleep on the living room couch. He put a blanket over her, kissed her forehead and turned off the lights.

2.

Today, Ashley, wearing dark glasses, with his blazer neatly folded on the passenger seat, piloted his Porsche 911 north along the Taconic Parkway toward the old Dutch settlement of Rhineheuvel for lunch with Ronnie. The parkway's curves made it a great drive through forests, particularly today when traffic was light before the weekend. He focused on the beautiful purr of the tuned engine, the smooth shifting of the five gears and the car's responsiveness. Nonetheless, the bullet sound remained, but each time he shifted, it receded a bit further. With the top down, his nose felt a bit stuffed. As the sun shone on his face, while enjoying Weather Report's "Birdland," he downshifted when his radar detector started flashing, just in time to see a state trooper, hidden behind a bush. He smiled at his little victory and noted that his mobile sanctuary and music always improved his mood and made his problems and dilemmas eventually disappear, except for his concern about Annie, which he would probably never lose.

Later, he felt an *Andronyi* coming on and remembered a scenic overlook a short distance ahead. Once there, he kept the car running, planned out his escape route and scanned his surroundings for trouble. Satisfied he was alone, he looked out over the parkway to the Hudson River Valley in the distance and beyond to the Catskill Mountains, where Rip Van Winkle slept off a twenty-year hangover after drinking with Henry Hudson's ghostly crew. Although north of Sleepy Hollow, this area retained its mystical beauty. After deep breaths and relaxing, the images began moving, and he could feel them as they, surprisingly, brought back strong memories of the summer of 1962.

* * *

Ashley sees himself getting up early to drive the Colonel to Idlewild Airport for his Soviet Union trip. On his way home, he stops at the Woodinville "five and ten" to buy the Kingston Trio's latest release, "Goin' Places." Knowing how much Ronnie enjoys the Trio, he rushes into her bedroom without knocking. She stands, arms folded, still damp from the shower. Stunned at seeing her naked for the first time, he stops. It is not just her physical beauty, but her aura, which shines brighter than he has ever seen, like a homing beacon drawing him closer. He desperately wants to go to her, but something holds him back, beyond her being his father's wife. He is startled by her expression, having seen it with Olga on several occasions. The elegant lady he knows has disappeared and now Olga's sister appears to be a predatory she-wolf. As she approaches him, she makes no attempt to cover herself, casually takes the record from him and tosses it. She presses herself against him, and Ashley's penis struggles to get free of his boxers before it explodes. He backs away and quickly strips.

Ronnie smiles, "*Trés bien.* Now, turn slowly around." After he does, she takes him in her arms, and as he kisses her, she tongue-kisses him. Ashley shoots all over her hard stomach. Abruptly, as the lady returns, she pulls away. "We have now seen each other *au naturelle.* Enough for now. We were about to take a most *formidable* step. And once we began, no turning back, and our lives shall radically change. Your father is absent this week. We have time to calmly discuss this. So, please be patient." She pats his cheek, "I truly love David. *Alors*, we have a separate relationship."

"I don't care. I'm still totally ready. You're the one I want. Damn the consequences."

"*Non.* Right now, you are still far too excited to think clearly. I know what you think you want, but I know what you need." She pauses. "Now, time for tennis." As she leaves, he hears her say, "Sister was truly right."

* * *

He is playing tennis at the Quaker Mount Country Club with Ronnie in a hard-contested match, which he ultimately loses. Over lunch on the club's patio, he sulks, doubly humiliated today. "Ashley Cooper, grow up *et fais attention!* You hate to lose. Today, I shall teach you how to lose gallantly. So, in the future when you fail, you shall not, ah, fall apart, but move forward with great élan." After she tells him how, Mac, the golf pro, tells Ronnie she has a call in his office. When she returns,

Ashley cannot read her expression. "My plan has been canceled. We must never speak of this morning, until, when the time is right, I shall explain everything. Until then, today we are going to Quaker Lake, and I feel certainty Monica Martin shall be there."

"So?"

"Have you not seen the way she looks at you?"

Later, for the first time, Ashley sees Monica as more than just a girl he grew up with.

That night, when Ashley returns from their first date, Ronnie asks, "How was your rendezvous?"

Ashley smiles broadly, and Ronnie hugs him.

* * *

After the images stopped, Ashley did not care who had sent them, because he grasped their significance. The time must now be right for these answers as well. He had not fully trusted Ronnie for a long time after that day. And that Kingston Trio record remained the only one in his large collection he never opened. Looking around, he saw he was still alone, although he sensed something had changed.

3.

As Ashley drove through Rhineheuvel, a town of some three thousand people, he saw many white fences, manicured lawns and a number of Dutch colonial houses. From a few blocks away, the breeze carried the aroma of Ronnie's Provençal dishes. This helped relieve his feelings of uncertainty about their meeting. A block away, he saw *L'Auberge Provençal*e, a white, authentically colonial two-story building with gray shutters and a covered veranda. When he pulled into the parking lot, Ronnie was standing under the veranda, chatting with some of the diners at the six front outdoor tables. She came down to greet him, wearing a knee-length denim skirt, a white blouse with the top three buttons open and sandals showing her brightly painted red toenails.

Putting on his blazer, he noticed her salt and pepper hair had been replaced by bright and shiny raven black, and her makeup seemed light. He began to feel aroused and thought her she-wolf's right below the surface today. After hugging and kissing him a bit longer than normally, Ronnie asked, "What's your *tvarsch* telling you?"

"My what?"

"Your famous intuition."

"Well, whatever it's called, it's not working, although I'm not surprised. It never worked with you."

"Of course not. Later, I'll explain why. Come, I've prepared a meal with all your favorite Provençal dishes and a very fine bottle of a 1982 Mourvedre blend."

"Ah yes, love it."

"I know." She smiled as she took him by the hand past the end of the restaurant parking lot and led him to her ornately decorated cottage, which he had never been in. From the outside, all the gingerbread decoration and pinnacles reminded him, a bit ominously, of Hansel and Gretel. Inside, not surprisingly, her décor seemed more Russian than French. Like Olga, she had an icon corner in her parlor, which they passed on the way to her small dining room.

"Who's on your icon shelf?"

"Sainte Xenia, an Iskandarova."

Ashley nodded politely, expecting more. Instead, Ronnie said, "I heard from Sabreur Bleu you were shot at yesterday."

"Yeah. Whoever it was missed me."

"According to Sabreur, he shot and killed the shooter after knocking the rifle away. He took his Cuban DI identity card and sniper rifle for his collection. All before the sirens."

"Damn Cubans again. Why do they want to kill me now? Sabreur's very impressive. But it scared Annie, and I spent a while calming her down."

"The Cubans usually act for the Russians on sensitive missions. You all right now?"

"I'm still a bit shaken, even though I've been shot at several times, and all but one missed. Besides, after NKP, I became fatalistic. When your number's up, it's up. When Annie and I walked over to the garage to pick up the car this morning before I dropped her off at Chaplin, we felt pretty safe, sensing Sabreur watching over us."

"*Bon*, now we'll have a pleasant meal."

During the meal, they laughed, flirted a bit and made clever, humorous conversation. When they finished, Ronnie said that now they must be serious about matters at hand. They carried their wineglasses with them as Ronnie led him to her deck, which she had added to the back of the cottage. He stood at the rail, enjoying the sun on his face, the clean air and the spectacular view of the Hudson River below and the Catskills as he sipped his wine.

"How are you doing after the funeral, the revelations and everything else?"

He sighed. "I can't say I'm thrilled to be an orphan and all. But, on the bright side, Annie and I had two actual conversations over dinner the last two nights."

"*Bon*. But now, you've a choice to make."

"I know." He took a larger sip of wine than he had planned and coughed.

Ronnie smiled. "You may ignore David's letter and go on with your life. Or, you may come with me and begin your identity search. I appreciate it's a very difficult choice, and I know you've already given it a great deal of thought."

"Yes, I have. First, though, I want to hear what you have to say."

4.

Ashley followed Ronnie upstairs to the back of the house, past her bedroom on the left and into her office opposite. The picture windows on three sides gave the room a sunny, open feel, enhanced by blond Swedish modern furniture. Ashley thought,

How typical. Ronnie always modifies her accommodations to precisely meet her needs. After he removed his blazer, they sat opposite each other a few feet apart, with a small file cabinet next to her. She demurely crossed her legs. "I'll begin with your intuition, your *tvarsch*. That's what the Iskandarov call it. Originally, a Cartvelian word transcribed into Russian. That's the case with virtually all our special words. It's not working for you now because, like you, I'm of the Iskandarov. Among us, there's no need for it because, we've the Iskandarov Trust. In order to survive, we learned long ago to speak truth to each other, regardless how painful or unpleasant that might be. Agreed?"

"Yes. I like that very much."

"OK. First, you can't proceed until the past's been accounted for, and that's Olga." Ronnie crossed herself in the three-fingered manner of Russian Orthodoxy.

"I've never seen you cross yourself in all the time I've known you. But I'm not surprised either."

She nodded as she unlocked her cabinet, took out a file and began flipping through the contents. "Ah, yes. This is a letter to me in Russian from November 1961. Even though I know your Russian's quite good, I'll translate, so there's no misunderstandings.

Dear Rushka.

Ronnie looked up, smiling. "That's what Sister called me." She looked back down at the letter.

> I have now seduced Ashley Cooper. He
> is extraordinary in so many ways. And so
> remarkable I would have done so even had he
> not been Iskandarov. He knows nothing about
> who he is. He thinks he is Scotch but is as Scotch
> as samovar. No matter, he is bright, inquisitive
> and brave. Just like Sergei Dmitrovich. Also,
> he is over six feet tall with lean athletic body
> and blonde curly hair. One only need look into

his blue eyes and there can be no doubt who his
father is. Pure Iskandarov. He has the Iskandarov
magic, although so far it has been largely wasted
on scared bourgeois American girls. In the
spring, with classes done, we will go away. I will
carry his child by then.

Ronnie looked up. "Sister was always headstrong. No
patience. Remember, you can't rush God's time, or disaster
results."

"Wait, now, hold on. Why do you have a file of Olga's letters
you've never shown me?"

She sighed. "It's complicated. Now, examine her letter to
satisfy your skepticism." She handed it to him, and he carefully
read it, recognizing Olga's particular handwriting and largely
agreeing with Ronnie's translation.

"I wanted to show you Olga's plans for the two of you and
how your life would've changed, had she not been murdered."

"Yeah, I get that. Could've been great."

"I must say you don't seem at all surprised you're Iskandarov."

"No, my intuition, my *tvarsch* has known this, on some
level, since my adolescence. But now I need to know if Ovals
actually murdered her."

"Of course. But, there's so much I need to tell you first for it to
make sense. Now, what're you prepared to do about your future?"

"I'll allocate at least a week to find out who I am. If necessary,
I can extend to the whole remainder of the month leave I have
from the Firm."

"Sorry, Ash. Once you begin, it'll take you at least a month
to even know enough to begin asking the right questions."

"But I need to get back to the Firm."

"I won't ask you why you feel that need right now. Instead,
I'd like you to make a clear and concise case why you want to
continue your life as it has been. Then I'll offer a rebuttal." Her
long fingernail tapped lightly on her wineglass.

He smiled. "A rebuttal, is it?"

"Of course. I've been surrounded by lawyers for well over thirty-five years."

"OK. First, I've achieved my goal of reaching the inner sanctum of one of the most prestigious law firms in the world. I'm now in a position to influence policy. That gives me real power, which I can use for positive change. However, you, among others, have always said I should never rest on my laurels. My next goal's to become undersecretary of state in the next Republican administration. And then, secretary of state. That would give me a certain amount of immortality. And as I approach fifty, that's not inconsequential. Besides, the Firm's executive committee has sanctioned my ambitions. Now, let's say those goals aren't met. I'm still in an excellent position to become the Firm's next managing partner, a feat my fathers, both of them, never achieved. Further, I've made a very good life for Annie and myself. In all likelihood, it'll now get better. Surely, I've fulfilled the promise you saw in me years ago."

Ronnie smiled before sipping her wine. "Very well put. But you, a life-long Democrat, want to work in a Republican administration?" She incredulously shook her head. "Now, I've some questions. While you do have a great life, you left out a key point. Are you happy? Don't answer yet because now I've some true and false questions."

"Ronnie, really?"

"Humor me. First, your birth father's real name was Spencer Talbott?"

"False. But I don't know his real one."

"Correct. His real name was Sergei Dmitrovich Iskandarov from our ancient Cartvelian noble family, who Russified their name. You're half-Russian half-Cartvelian, with Scottish-English from your mother's side. Sergei Dmitrovich was also my father. My real name's Verushka Sergevna Andreyeva. This cottage is my sanctuary, a bit of old Russia and the one place I can truly be me. Next. Patricia Sternwood Cooper was your mother?"

"Absolutely false. My mother, Charlotte, was her younger sister."

"Yes, indeed."

"I know. However, I must've killed Charlotte when she gave me birth."

"No. That's not the case. As of the mid-fifties, both your parents were still alive, although in Russia."

"How do you know? Why there? How can I find out for certain?"

"Patience, Ash. Next question."

"Wait, couldn't you have told me about my real mother before now?"

"As with Olga's letters, I wanted to tell you the truth several times. There was no way to do so without raising even more questions that I couldn't answer at the time." She patted his knee before running her long fingernails along his trouser leg up his thigh. She smiled. "Focus, Ash, on the topic at hand. Next question. Are you a shoe-in to reach your ultimate goals, with the help of George Farwell?"

"Very likely."

Ronnie nodded. "You may be right. However, consider you're a Russian expert. But, now with the collapse of the Soviet Union, Russia has already shrunk in importance. We both know right now it's too weak to be a world player. And some other region or country will come into prominence."

"As long as Russia has a large supply of nukes and oil, it'll continue to be important. Also, I expect within ten years, they'll be back to strength."

"Perhaps. Moving on, what happens to you if George suddenly dies? He's no spring chicken. But even if he lives, what's his pound of flesh? If he gets you there, you'd be his puppet, working for Western Petroleum's interests. I know your goal when you set out for the Firm was to become senior partner, an honor you certainly earned, but it doesn't seem to be what you expected. Despite my best efforts to prepare you, the idealistic, romantic young man I knew had no idea of the traps, snares and pitfalls involved. And how much of himself he'd have to sell to succeed."

Ashley nodded. "Yes, I hadn't seen it from that perspective."

"Now, back to my original questions. Are you happy? And think deeply before you answer."

"I'm content."

"Not even close to the same thing. Remember, we speak truth here."

"In that case, no, I'm not."

"Then what do you need to achieve happiness?"

He thought a few minutes. "Honestly, I don't know. I've pretty much been a lone wolf most of my life. I'm comfortable being by myself. But I know true happiness will involve someone unique." He shrugged. "Beyond that, I can't say."

"Isn't Lana unique enough for you?"

Ashley shook his head. "No. While our sex is outstanding, her late mother was NKVD and KGB. So, I don't trust her. When she gets back from Montreal, I'm breaking it off."

"You don't need to. She's probably already done so herself. Now, I understand your reluctance and your resistance to searching for your identity. Prosperity makes cowards of us all. We reach a point where we have too much to lose. However, if money were truly the measure of a man…" She shook her head.

"You're saying I should risk everything I've achieved simply to find out who I am?"

"Ash, listen to yourself. If you don't know who you are, what else matters? Think about Rand still searching for his father after all these years so he can know who he really is."

"Yes, he is. Do you know anything definite about Rand's father?"

"No, only rumors."

"Damn, I sense his father's still alive, but I've no idea where. Obviously, I've never told him this. Look, getting back to cases, the Colonel wrote my journey could be dangerous and upsetting. That's why I don't want to do it. All I see is downside."

"Ash Cooper, I don't believe that for a minute. You've always been courageous and optimistic. You really can't see any advantage to finding out who you truly are?"

"I know who I am. Ashley F. Cooper, Esquire is a brand. I love what I'm doing. So why should I change one damn thing?"

"Don't you dare lie to me, Ash Cooper. You're being a selfish bastard. I see all the time I've spent with you has been wasted. We're done here."

Ashley stood up. "No, we're most certainly not. I must know more. You owe me the truth, whether I go or not."

"You're shouting. Calm down and sit."

Ashley remained standing, seething, until Ronnie said, "Ash, good for you. That's the first time you've ever really challenged me. *Bon*. I see our relationship has changed. All right, here we go. We, I, have intentionally kept you ignorant of your heritage."

"Who's this 'we'? And why did you feel the need to keep me in the dark?"

"I'm a long-time Bleu agent. We had to keep you ignorant of your heritage to protect you. All that's now changed with David's death."

"OK. I get that about the Colonel with the tarot, but more importantly, why am I important enough to need protection?"

"I'll get to that shortly."

"OK. But first, I need to know more about Olga's murder. Ovals's *nom de guerre* was Anton Stashinski. I don't even know who he was working for."

"He was working for the Stasi and ultimately, the Soviets. The KGB developed a very strong poison. It mimicked cerebral hemorrhage, which, in turn, caused her miscarriage."

"Sadistic bastards. But why would Ovals and the KGB want Olga to not just die but to suffer such agony?"

"They meant to send a very strong warning because you two would've posed a serious threat to the Soviet regime.

The Soviets lasted as long as they did because they never ignored a threat, regardless of how small it appeared. After we executed Stashinski, they left you alone for a while until that false alarm. Recently, you were followed in Moscow on your last trip. They fully intended to kill you just prior to David's death."

"OK. What about Bangkok and the Brit who saved me? Was he Bleu? And why was the KGB trying to kill me, anyway?"

"*Non*. Not the KGB. Bleu rescued you all those times from our ancient dynastic enemies, the Polinkov. They're very involved in the organs of state power, the *apparat* KGB, now FSB."

"OK. But why are these Polinkovs trying to kill me? I've nothing to do with them. And my protectors only have to fail once, and I'm dead. The end. So, again, no. I'm not proceeding. And I certainly don't want Annie being killed, held for ransom or worse. She's not involved in this."

"Ash, but she is. She is Iskandarova, one of us. Her visions, her *pyordarsch*, are very strong and becoming stronger. So, just because you might opt out, she may decide she must find out her heritage and proceed now or, perhaps, in the future. And think about your *tvarsch*. That is the collective wisdom and experience of the Iskandarov. Their gift to you. Your new journey's what your whole life's been building toward. All your substantial talents derive from your Iskandarov blood. You're most fortunate… it could have been a very different story."

"How do you mean?"

"The Iskandarov curse. Sometimes, our offspring are retarded or worse. You'll discover more on your journey." She paused. "Now, take me. I was once married before David, to Major François Landfear, a French Army commando. Between his missions, we wanted to have a child together, but it was a disaster. After a long labor, my baby was horribly deformed and mercifully died soon after. Subsequently, François was called to serve in Indo-China and was captured in Laos in 1952. François was legally dead when I remarried."

"I'm truly sorry for your loss. You were young and must have loved him very much."

"Yes, I did. He was a wonderful man, and I learned so much from him. I had a very hard time after he was reported missing and called in every Bleu chit I had to find out more. I only learned he was condemned to the gulag and subsequently killed by person or persons unknown." She again crossed herself as tears formed, which she dabbed away. "Very well then, consider if you'd been born average or worse. You'd certainly not be where you are today."

"Probably not, but you've no idea how many times I wished I could just be normal and fit in. And not always be pushed to stand out and be hated by my peers."

"Poor little Ashley F. Cooper, Esquire. Well, have no fears about being pushed any longer. I've sold my restaurant to my employees and am leaving for Paris soon."

"But why? You have your sanctuary and restaurant just the way you want them. You have your friends. Annie needs your help."

"With David dead and the Countess Prophecy now unfolding as foreseen, I'm needed elsewhere. And not just in Paris. I've a friend staying at 1192 Park, and I'll close my cottage. As far as you and Annie are concerned, I've done my best. You're now both on your own. The Iskandarov will suffer without you, but they'll probably survive, just as they have for several millennia. *Bonne chance!*"

"Did you say millennia? How far back do they go?"

"Why do you care? You've rejected your heritage. And now, they will reject you, as well."

"What do you mean?"

"Well, you wouldn't expect much protection from the people you've rejected, would you? I mean, had Sabreur not pushed the rifle away last evening, we wouldn't even be having this conversation."

"Ronnie, that's despicable blackmail."

"It is nothing of the sort. We've kept you alive all your life because we need you. But since you refuse to go on your journey, well, what's your value now?"

"But surely these Polinkovs will find out I'm not really Iskandarov and leave me alone."

"Possibly, after the word gets out. But that takes time. Your task today's getting safely back home. Annie too. A few quick calls from me and everything changes."

"Damn it. I won't be blackmailed. I'll take my chances." He paused and then said, "Look, here's the truth about why I won't go." He stared at her and said. "I don't trust you!"

"After all I've done to protect and mentor you? You don't trust me? Why ever not?"

"On the way over here, I had to stop at an overlook because I had an *Andronyi* about that day—"

"You saw me *au naturelle*." She shook her head. "Why didn't you tell me this sooner? You could've saved us a lot of time and anguish. Have you ever wondered about the particulars of that day?"

"No. I don't follow you."

"That was the only day you ever entered my boudoir without knocking, clearly excited. But, really about a record? And you just happened to catch me just out of the shower, with my arms folded, as though I were waiting for you?"

"Your aura mesmerized me. I'd never seen anything so powerful and enticing. But how?"

"All Iskandarova have our strongest aura when we're *au naturelle* and, usually, most fertile, and it signals this to our men. The result of genetic mutation long ago. I wasn't teasing you. *Non!* I wanted to have your baby like Sister did, because I knew ours would be extraordinary. I'd received a Bleu advisory I should evacuate you to Paris because it was no longer safe for you on the Mount. Two Stasi agents were spotted in Poughkeepsie renting a car. They were kidnap specialists, and Bleu knew they were coming for you. I was waiting for the confirmation call."

"So, why didn't we stay at home then?"

"That was the first place they'd look. And given your anger, staying in the house would've been very difficult. Besides, I had an Uzi in my tennis bag and knew how to use it."

"OK. Makes sense. So, that was the call after our tennis match?"

"Yes, Bleu rescinded the advisory after capturing them on North Quaker Mount Road. Ash, I know you weren't thinking clearly that day, which was completely my fault. But had I then evacuated you to Paris, which I had the power to do, the Polinkov would have kept coming after us until they killed us. And like Sister, be assured, most unpleasantly. I confess I was very stupid to let my desires get ahead of me. And that has haunted me ever since. I don't know how to express the depth of my regret about hurting you. But now we're both again free. But it's too late for us, making a baby anyway."

"Thanks, Ronnie, but —"

"No. Thank you. Truly, though, there's someone who needs you as much as you need her. However, first, before you get too excited, there's much you need to learn."

"All right." As he drank his wine, an unfamiliar pleasure began to stir in him, unrecognizable at first, until it became absolute clarity. When the last of his wine went down, it tasted heavenly.

"Ah, I see your aura shining more brightly than it has in a long time. Now, you're truly ready… for your journey."

"Yes, tell me though, does this feud with the Polinkov trace back to a painted death mask?"

"Yes, that was its genesis, but it quickly escalated into a true dynastic struggle. But now I feel you have a much more important question."

"Absolutely. I need to know how you were able to control me so well on that day?"

She shook her head. "Sorry, Ash. I can't tell you beyond it being a part of my Iskandarova gifts. You have your *tvarsch* and

Andronyi and Annie her *pyordarsch*. So, whether in your heart of heart you truly wish to be of the Iskandarov or not, you can no longer deny you are."

"All right then, what's next?"

She smiled. "When you return to your Quaker Mount house, go to the attic. You'll see three footlockers in the northwest corner. David bought the house as a family retreat after he returned from the war in 1945 and also as a safe place for the footlockers."

"Whose are they?"

"The first belonged to Colonel Dmitri Sergeyovich Iskandarov, your grandfather, the second to your father, Captain Spencer Talbott, and the third was David's footlocker from the army air force. In it, you'll find his diary from World War I. He didn't keep one in the second war. Start with him. You'll discover much you didn't know, and that'll give you a vital framework for the other two. Next, Sergei and, finally, your grandfather. By then, they'll have answered many of your questions. And raised new ones."

"OK. Got it."

"Excellent. Here are the keys."

Ashley looked at them—two were ordinary and one elaborate.

"Another thing you'll discover in the footlockers is more about your birth mother. And also, our father was in Cuba in the late sixties, and that's a new item, his journal, now in a safe place. I'll get it to you before I leave."

"If he was alive then, why didn't he come back to this country?"

"Our father's life was very complicated."

"How did you get this journal? Could it be a fake?"

"*Non.* In February, I was tanning myself around the pool at a little place on the Yucatan when I saw Maria Civilli, an attractive Cuban lady. I hadn't seen her in a long time, and we had once been quite close. I also knew her mother very well, Angelina DelaVega Delgado, who changed it to Civilli when she left Madrid. Does this ring any bells?"

"DelaVega's Anghelina's last name, so I assume that's why she's involved in this?"

Ronnie nodded. "Yes. Our father had twins with Maria, Angelina and Rosalita, who's Annie's athletic coach at Chaplin. Angelina, named after her grandmother, decided to stand out and added the 'h' to her name. Although our father was also involved with Angelina before the war, he isn't Maria's father. Anyway, Maria knows a great deal about you and David. She said she was giving me our father's journal, which she had already copied, from the first year, or so, of his stay in Cuba. By the time you get to it, all will've become clearer."

"OK. Our father certainly got around. But I don't know what to call him, Spencer or Sergei."

"As you read the diaries, you'll discover the reasons."

"Do you know anything about the key to a safe-deposit box up on 90th and Madison? It's from the Colonel, and Ambassador van Rouene gave it to me. Now, it's in my wall safe."

"Good place. I may know. But I could be well off the mark. But, if there's a journal in the box, you should read it before the Cuban one. Now, be careful of van Rouene. He's not to be trusted."

"Thanks for the confirmation. I had my suspicions after our meeting at the Racquet last Wednesday. Lana's some sort of agent working with him, right?"

"She's in deep cover. Next time you decide to get involved with a woman, ask me first. OK?" She smiled. "She's Polinkova, and all she wants from you are babies. Lots of them. I wouldn't be surprised if she's again pregnant with your baby."

"But if she wants lots of babies, then why's she breaking up with me?"

"She's Polinkova. I doubt you've seen the last of her. Further, I know for certain the ambassador and she conspired to get your semen for her artificial insemination."

Ashley nodded. "I sensed that was her game. Tell me. What was the Colonel's role in all this?"

"David was never a Bleu agent. However, he did cooperate with us on an 'as needed basis.' He was what we call 'an agent of fortune.' In Odessa, Sophia Sergevna Iskandarova, Countess Kolchaka, saw back in 1919 David would be the catalyst of her prophecy. Fate had brought him to the right place at the appropriate time. Had David not rescued Sophia and our father then, they both would've been killed. And today, you and I wouldn't exist in our current form. So, in a sense, David was your grandfather. Without David, the Iskandarov would be greatly reduced and, perhaps would have been exterminated by the Polinkov." She paused, sipping her wine and thinking. "Now, when Rand was in Paris, a kidnapping team tried to capture him that last night. That's why Corinne began shooting and took a fatal bullet for him, just hours after she'd been designated as Nadia's successor in Bleu. She knew how important Rand would be to us. By sacrificing herself, she bought enough time for our agents to kill the attackers and save Rand. However, you must never tell him this. Such a revelation would negate his role."

Ashley smiled. "OK. My pleasure. I swear to keep his status secret. After all, he kept his Bleu membership a secret from me all these years."

"Ash, you're a devil."

"Probably. I'm still curious about two things. First, did the Colonel know you were a Bleu agent?"

"Yes, he also knew I'm next in line to succeed Nadia when she passes."

"Wow. OK. Second, why did you marry a man over twice your age?"

"As you mentioned in your eulogy, there was a lot of tongue wagging, and the terms 'gold digger' and 'tramp' were loosely tossed around. But I persevered over those early years because I had married David for three reasons. Like you, I never really knew my true father, and I suppose I was looking for a father figure. Also, David was kind, a gentleman and a rather good lover. Thirdly, it gave me access to you."

"OK, very interesting. Did he know when he would die?"

"I don't know. I could never ask him such a question. But I suspect he did."

"Yes, I agree. Have you looked into whether he was poisoned?"

"Honestly, it makes no difference. Events have gone according to Sophia's prophecy. However, were I to investigate, I'd seek out friend and foe. Someone on our side may've grown impatient."

"Yes, my *tvarsch* senses that as well. Now, how're you coming with helping Annie with her vision problems?"

"You learned to control you *tvarsch* to stand out, not fit in. And I have every faith Annie will come around. She's undergone so much rapid change in the last few years she feels overwhelmed. That's a problem I can't fix. She will either outgrow it or find someone to fix it. So, our female knowledge has been our focus."

"What's that?"

"Nothing sinister. What every Iskandarova must know as they become women, especially if they have *pyordarsch*. And not knowing's very harmful psychologically. Tell me, how's your *Andronyi* coming along? Rand told me you've recently had images of a young, skinny girl."

"I think I'm getting better at controlling their timing. The overlook was farther than I remembered and yet I held the images off until I could relax and get ready. But I don't really understand their significance."

"Bravo for the first. But no, you wouldn't. This girl's now a grown lady sending these disturbing pictures to you because she wants you to know her truth. Such honesty is necessary because when the time's right, she may be able to have union with you. Natalya's your sister."

"OK. But why did she have such a horrible childhood?"

"It's fair to say she had it so you wouldn't have to."

"I'm sorry, Ronnie, but that makes no sense at all."

"You're right, it doesn't now. Later, it will."

"I can understand what she's doing. But why did she send me these images today when she's not involved in them?"

"Very good question. You should ask her first thing if you happen to meet." Ronnie smiled. "I greatly envy you as you begin to discover how astonishing the Iskandarov truly are. There's much I do know, but more I don't and, probably, never will. Now, as you delve into our history and lore, you'll be reading a lot of sex. Sex is important to both us and the Polinkov but for completely different reasons. For the Polinkov, sex is strictly about power, control and sadism, with procreation a distant fourth. For us, sex is primarily about procreation and, indeed, survival. But that doesn't mean we don't have sexual fun. The blood union brings two compatible people together in love to create the next generation in a difficult, but amazing way, where they must work together. Now, in order to restore trust between us, I'm going to share a bit of our forbidden female mysteries with you.

"What happened on that day back in July of 1962 with my very strong aura is what we call *phygynaya*. At that time, I had no more control over it than I did over my menstrual cycle. However, I later discovered I could control it with birth-control pills. I wanted to control it because it takes over your life until you find a suitable male or it passes. When I initially came after you, it didn't matter I was married or I was going against the prophecy or even what you wanted. I had to have you. I again apologize."

"OK, that makes sense, I guess, if procreation's the primary goal. But what if the woman doesn't want babies?"

"Then she's not a true Iskandarova and union is impossible. Now, I married David for another reason besides what I've told you. We wanted to have a baby. However, fate played a nasty trick on me and you. When I was driving up to Boston to pick you up, my *phygynaya* started. I knew this would complicate my relationship with you. But I also thought I could control myself. And I would've, were it not for your Iskandarov magic."

"Yes, what is that?"

"It's a naturally occurring scent you release when aroused, and all women find it irresistible. However, I'd never encountered it before. And that was why I hugged you so closely and looked longingly at Sister's mattress. That was May. In June, during *phygynaya,* I went alone to 1192 for the duration. Then, by July, David and I had been trying to get pregnant for a long time. Something was wrong, so, I decided I should have a baby with you while I had the chance. The Stasi danger perfectly coincided with my *phygynaya* raging. But when we were almost at the point of no return, I felt going forward would, long-term, destroy our relationship. I shamefully left you still aroused and, only thinking of myself, I went back to my bathroom to cry out my eyes because I knew then I'd never be a mother. The most horrible fate for an Iskandarova. I wore my darkest glasses to cover my red eyes from you because I was ashamed. In truth, the call from Bleu changed nothing."

"I now know that. But you're right. And I was being held back. I don't know by what or whom though."

"With my gift, I can see you and Olga only had a bonding. Normally, breaking a bond, unlike a union, is quite easy. But because of her horrible and premature death, she was unable to release you."

"Yes, when she sent me her memories, there was a part I didn't understand until now. She knew she was going to die soon and was desperately trying to release me. But all she could say was 'My brother, Ashley Cooper.' Looks like I'm stuck."

"Maybe not. In the future, you may find a solution to your Olga predicament. But now, a word about Monica. After my plan failed, I needed to find you a good non-Iska girl. 'Iska' is what we call ourselves in private. And even if there had been an Iska on the Mount, you would've had the same problem with her as you did with me. Nonetheless, you still could've married Monica and probably been a lot happier."

"Yes, you're right. And I intended to, if my *tvarsch* hadn't got in the way."

"Indeed. The bad news about marrying Monica was she would've had to die, so you could now search for a compatible Iska."

"I'm starting to see this whole thing's pretty brutal. Monica's death would've hit me, and, likely, our many children, very hard. I'm not sure I'd now be in a position to go on my journey."

"You're right, it's brutal. But, among other things, and there are several we haven't discussed, this is also a test to see if you're strong enough to be of the Iskandarov. Even though I'm leaving shortly, we'll meet again when you need me. Just please keep *phygynaya* and even Iska to yourself." She paused. "And you must never ever discuss Bleu with an outsider. Our existence depends on that secrecy. OK? Now, any questions?"

"OK, mum's the word. I do want to know why you dyed your hair? I rather liked your salt and pepper."

"On Wednesday, after the funeral, I decided I wanted a change. I had blonde and raven solutions. I knew I couldn't pull off blonde. But, since then, you wouldn't believe all the propositions I've had. Do you really not like it?" She paused. "That's too bad, I was prepared to give you the most incredible sexual experience you've ever had."

"Who says I don't? And how many of those did you accept?"

"Ashley, jealous? Don't be rude. That's something gentlemen should never ask, and ladies never tell." She laughed merrily. "Back to you. Well, you probably think I'm being conceited, just like you thought Sister was when she made a similar proposition. Well, compared to me, she's a blushing virgin. Because we Iska know things non-Iskas can't even imagine. I said we have a lot of fun besides just procreating. You ready?"

She took Ashley in her arms and slowly kissed him as she ran her long red fingernails down his back and arms. "I've waited for this moment seemingly forever."

SEVEN
Friday, 28 May 1993
Quaker Mount, NY

1.

In late afternoon, Ashley reluctantly left Ronnie's cottage. Back on the Taconic, he smiled. She had been fabulous, as promised. Even though she had maintained a trim, firm body, which she attributed to her superior blood, that was secondary to her aura and perfume, which completely intoxicated him. Throughout his visit, he sensed Ronnie's *phygynaya* held in check. However, he had seen her restraint slowly declining as their meeting went on and was not surprised when she kissed him. He had quickly learned her *phygynaya* had, with age, actually intensified. By the end, like with Olga, he had been changed by their lovemaking.

About an hour after leaving Ronnie, he sensed grave danger from an unidentified person. And almost twenty-five minutes later, Ashley sat in his usual booth at Earl's Restaurant, across from Woodinville's train station. While he liked its great food the jukebox music and friendly atmosphere, he especially loved Earl, the gregarious and rotund host, who always had a joke and a warm greeting for all. Since Earl knew everyone in the village, Ashley had asked him, as he led him to his booth, if he had seen any new people today. He shook his head, "Not today, Ashley, and I know just who you mean."

While Ashley felt excited to begin his search, he had stopped here with his car parked by the back entrance. Driving to the Colonel's house in daylight, he could easily be shot at as he downshifted on Quaker Mount's winding roads. He planned a leisurely meal until dark, when he would be less conspicuous and also returning later than expected, but not so late that he would arrive after Annie, who was coming up with the Speers after eight tonight. He smelled Ronnie as he hung his blazer on the booth's hook. He should have showered after their lovemaking but wanted a reminder. When Angie, his thirty-something quasi-blonde waitress, came over to take his order, she seemed very friendly. When she left, Ashley realized he was still giving off his scent.

As he bit into Earl's Famous Cheeseburger, voted "Best Cheeseburger in Dutchess County" several years running, he loved the ground sirloin, smoked Gouda, homemade BBQ sauce, rich German mustard, the onion ring on top and the fabulous homemade chips with a large dill pickle on the side, all washed down by Butler Amber draft in a twenty-three-ounce mug.

When Angie later brought his check, she sat opposite him. "Looks like somebody got lucky today. And you smell real good. Must be nice to be single when you're still young enough to enjoy it." She paused and with a knowing smile, said, "We could go out sometime. I'm off Thursdays."

Ashley looked at her dyed hair and nice figure. She was attractive, in her own way.

"Hey, no strings, just some fun. What do you say?"

He smiled. "You've almost made me an offer I can't refuse. I'm about to go on a journey and don't know where I'll be Thursday."

"No rush. Left my phone number on your receipt. Call when you're ready. Now, back to work before Earl catches me. Toodles."

He looked down at his check and smiled. Angie had added her phone number and "I'm off at 10:30." He took his time finishing his beer and, when the sun was low, left her a nice tip and grabbed his blazer, thinking, *I'm going to my country house. It's no longer the Colonel's house. And I should begin thinking of the Colonel as "David," a work colleague.*

2.

After dangerously speeding up the Mount, a half-moon was rising when he heard the gravel driveway under his tires. There were no lights on in the house, and in the moonlight he really saw, for the first time, its ruggedly austere lines. He had thought Ronnie would leave a light on for him, as she usually did when he was out late. After all, it had only been three days since the funeral. He parked and thought, *Perhaps, my antagonist's in the house and turned off all the lights.* He knew David had kept his air force service revolver, cleaned, oiled and loaded, in his bedside drawer. But that was on the second floor.

After putting on his blazer, he carried both his and Annie's suitcases inside. Coming in the back door into the kitchen, he knew he would have to replace several fuses in the cellar. In the moonlight, he picked up a box of four and a flashlight before opening the cellar door. As he went down, the stairs squeaked and groaned, and the air felt close and stale, as though no one had been here in a long time. The cellar, which had been hand-dug around rock outcroppings, seemed more like a cave, and he could hear mice and small animals running around. When he shone his flashlight in their direction, he could see their gleaming eyes and also the filmy beauty of many spider webs as he made his way through them. At the bottom of the stairs, the stone was damp and slick, and he walked carefully as he shone his light all over the room.

Satisfied he was alone, he focused his light on David's workbench, where all his tools remained neatly in place, covered in cobwebs. The fuse box was over the workbench, and as he replaced the burned out ones, he sensed something watching him, and it felt like a hostile spirit, not merely some curious animal. He finished, returned to the kitchen and turned on all the lights. After locking the cellar door with an antique key, he saw an envelope with Ronnie's handwriting on the breakfast table.

> Ash, welcome to your new house. I've made up the master bedroom for you and my room for Annie. I did a final cleaning of the entire house, including the attic. Remember, we are truly family now. And you are both safe. Have no fear. I'll see you soon.
>
> Love, Ronnie

Despite Ronnie's assurances, he still felt he was not alone, and turning on more lights did not help. After leaving Ronnie's note propped up on the table for Annie to see, he took both their bags up to David's bedroom on the second floor, holding them up as shields. Ashley found the revolver and searched the house. Impatient to get to the footlockers, he ran up to the third-floor landing. With his free hand on the attic doorknob, he paused. *My life's about to change radically. Nonetheless, I'm anxious to find out what kind of man David was before I knew him.*

He turned the knob and stepped into the large, high-ceilinged room. Moonbeams seeped in through dusty dormers, casting an eerie light. He could see he was alone before pulling the long string under the naked hundred-fifty-watt bulb.

Sitting on one of two Quaker benches, his gun beside him, he took a series of deep breaths as he looked up at the rough-hewn main beam and all the other original beams supporting the roof and the ancient brick of the chimney top. He realized he had not been there for any length of time since childhood when he had loved to play make-believe by himself. He also remembered the room seemed protected by a friendly spirit, and he felt its presence, which, at this point, just seemed to be observing him.

This room contained reminders of the people who lived, worked or prayed here and was like a time capsule. The two Quaker benches were from the meetinghouse next door, after

General Washington had commandeered it for a hospital. For about the next hundred and twenty years, the room had been divided between a meeting room and a place for the general store's storage barrels. When the post office moved to Woodinville in the 1890s, the building was sold to a Quaker for a private house. When David bought it in 1945, he was the first non-Quaker owner. Looking into the northwest corner, right next to a long-cold pot-bellied stove, he saw three footlockers. He went over to one of them and found a Post-it note: "Ash, what are you willing to give up as you begin your search? R." He thought, *The price of learning any mystery is the loss of innocence, a process I've been experiencing my whole life.*

Next to the note, stenciled in white paint on top of the footlocker was:

COL. COOPER, DAVID E.
105-693-1604
U.S. ARMY AIR FORCE

Greeted by the smell of evaporated mothballs when he unlocked and opened it, he saw David's brown tunic, replete with an 8th Air Force patch, full-bird-colonel's insignia and three rows of ribbons. He also found *Memories of the Great War and Beyond* by Dave Cooper with its bent brown cardboard covers and spent elastic around it. With nothing else of great interest, he took the diary back to the Quaker bench and opened it, smelling its musty aroma, and began quickly reading as he would a brief, pausing at the important passages.

3.

June 25, 1917

I have lived with my grandmother, Miss Caroline
McLeod, since my mother died, and my daddy
married Miss Ida. Miss Caroline gave me this
book and said I should record whatever happens
of import during my time in the Georgia National

Guard. She insisted I write proper English and not 'cracker.' I will try.

She surely did not cotton to the idea of me going off to war, having lived through Sherman's March and such. She did allow each generation needs to make its own mistakes and learn its own lessons. Besides, she knows any high school senior who volunteered for the Guard was graduated without having to sit for final examinations. That was a month ago. We had some training and were set to work guarding the bridges over the Ocmulgee River against Hun submarines. So far, this has been kind of fun.

Seems like all my kin signed up when I did. There is Bobby Petway from Wrensgate and Willy MacNamara from Four Oaks. Have we had some great, fun times since we were children! Then there is Angus and Hamish Stuckey from down Eastman way, Stevie Mitchell from Hawks Nest, Stuart McLeod from over Abbeville and several other kin I had never met from near Albany. Of course, our unit's got our fair share of woolhats too. One is a big bruiser from Americus, Lloyd something. I played football against him one time. He tackled me, and I will never forget I saw stars. He shot a 'gator in the river. (Most likely a log. No 'gators in Georgia.) Thought it was a Hun submarine. No matter, everybody now calls him 'Gator Kaiser.'

Some of Lloyd's kin showed up at our camp last Saturday. They brought some 'shine. (It is surely glorious not being temperance any more.) And some woolhat girls who 'wanted to do something nice for our fighting boys.' My girl was Molly

Sue. We took some 'shine and went off by
ourselves. I will never forget her naked creamy
white skin and flaming red hair in the moonlight.
Nor her lustful passion. In the morning, I told her
I should like to write to her. She simply smiled,
and I felt quite the fool.

August 23, 1917

We have been nationalized. We are being joined
with old boys from 'Bama and Florida to form the
31st, Dixie Division. After training, we are heading
overseas. Finally, we will get a crack at the Hun.
I am sure we will show them a good scrap. Our
insignia is a DD in red on a white background with
a red rim. I think it is very handsome.

25 September 1917

Lafayette, we are here! We arrived in France
today. I can't wait to get my crack at the Hun.
Our division has been split up and assigned to
different parts of the front.

1 October 1917

At morning formation today, Captain Stuart,
a former cavalry officer, asks if anyone in
the company can type. I had fooled around
with a typewriter a bit, so I stepped forward.
I whispered to Ham Stuckey to join me. But
he says his daddy told him 'never to volunteer
for nothin'. I was the only one. Captain Stuart
said, 'I suspect there are far more typists in our
company than Private Cooper. Perhaps, some of
your daddies fought in the war against Spain and
your granddaddies for the Confederacy. They

probably told you not to volunteer for anything. Well, men, this is the new Army and this private's now a corporal. I'm sure such a patriot will rise quickly in the new army. Dismissed.'

15 October 1917

They say I work well without supervision. My typing is getting better with practice. But as the Lord is my witness, I have never seen so many forms and pieces of paper in one place in my life. I even dream about them now. I found out the captain's great uncle was J.E.B. Stuart. Wow! No wonder he went into the cavalry.

30 October 1917

I was typing in the captain's tent the other day. Colonel McMahon comes through on inspection. Next thing I know, I am typing at HQ. Two days later, I have three stripes.

15 March 1918

I received word today Angus Stuckey took a whuff at the front near St. Quentin. I feel his loss greatly. Hopefully, he will be the last. (But I know better now.)

18 April 1918

Bobby Petway is on his way back home after being gassed. I hear Stuart McLeod is in a hospital near Paris. Colonel McMahon said my typing and 'other skills' were helping to win the war and promoted me to Sergeant Major. He is a good Joe. I now have a mess of stripes on my shimmy. I am in charge of the other typists and am truly amazed at my rapid promotions. I think it is due to four factors. First, Miss Caroline made me a 'self-starter.' I get up in the morning ready to go. Second, one of our regimental tents took a direct last week and a whole slew of high-level typists were killed. Third, I have been able to use my God-given horse-trading skills to get things we need from the Frogs and Tommies. Colonel never asks questions when I show up with more typewriters, ribbons, paper or cognac, among other things. Fourth, I've been blessed with an ear for language. I studied French and Latin at Hawksville High School. I also learned Gaelic from Miss Caroline. The 'old language', am seam chanan in Scottish Gaelic. Also, when communications are down, in my French truck I deliver dispatches and such to other units, as well as the Tommies and Frogs. This is also where I do my horse-trading. And in the process, I get shot at. Thus, I have a Colt .45 automatic.

19 April 1918

Yesterday, I delivered dispatches to a French salient. They had been attacked on three sides by the Huns. The dead bodies of too-many-to-count dead lay where they fell. Only a handful survived. Who says the French cannot or will not fight! I am also typing secret and top-secret documents in my tent with a bomb-proof safe to keep them in. The Colonel and I use our Gaelic to discuss sensitive matters.

Ashley paused as a picture of the shelled tent, the canvas shreds, the bomb crater and the horrific human remains and those of the salient dead came into focus, as had Angus Stuckey being blown apart. He put the book down and focused his breathing. He began skimming as Dave began listing all his friends killed, including Lloyd 'Gator Kaiser,' until he felt all alone.

11 November 1918

I'm totally whacked. The armistice was signed today and went into effect at 11 a.m. Guys were whuffed to the last minute. And now, there's an eerie quiet like before a great storm. But what was all this for? The whole cursed world is not worth the life of a Willy MacNamara, Stevie Mitchell or a Bobby Petway. Hell, it is not even worth a Lloyd 'Gator Kaiser'! Hun submarines on the Ocmulgee River. What an execrable joke!!!!

12 November 1918

My big questions remain. Why was I spared? What am I going to do now? It's for damned sure I'm not going back to South Georgia. At least, not for long. I owe it to all my kin and those I didn't even know to make certain they did not die in vain. My sons, if I'm so blessed, must never go through anything like this. This has to have been, as President Wilson said, 'the war to end all wars.'

15 November 1918

The Hun's beat, thus, no new fighting in 1919. The goddamned Frog government's ships they brought us over on are being converted back to civilian use. We do not have enough ships, thus, it is the usual hurry-up and wait. We're shipping

out for Marseilles shortly to await our ship home.
The whole Expeditionary Force's going to hell.
Most of the men signed up 'for the duration.'
Thus, they're now technically civilians. It's
getting harder to keep order. Men coming off the
line ignore orders. They only care about getting
home and we can use that to keep order.

20 November 1918

We've been in Marseilles for a while, waiting.
Today, Colonel Mac called me into his secure
tent and we spoke in Gaelic. He said he couldn't
order me to do what he would propose. But it
was very important, and he knows I'm the right
man for the job. Because I've been bored since
the Armistice and this may be an adventure,
thus, I agree. I must be ready to meet a ship
here tomorrow. I'll be in charge of the overall
mission, even over officers. He wishes me good
luck and from his expression, I'll need it.

22 November 1918

I'm quartermaster on the PG Gunboat Katahdin,
which came from Atlantic Station, Gibraltar.
(It's an old ship, commissioned in 1892 and this
may be its last mission.) Officially, it remains
at Atlantic Station. After Marseilles, we put
in at Nice and picked up a platoon of thirty
combat U.S. Marines, just off the line. They're
commanded by a gunnery sergeant. I don't need
to know details of their mission. My mission's
to evacuate a Russian countess and her agents
from Odessa. She's the co-leader of a very secret
White group. They've been gathering very

important and accurate information on the Reds.
There are certain people in both the State and War
Departments who see the Reds as a future threat
to our country and they value the group's efforts.
Colonel Mac gave me a book to learn Russian
on the voyage, although the countess supposedly
speaks both French and English very well. I'll
need the Russian for the others. (I can call on
'Gunny' if I need the assistance of the Marines.)

On board, I brief Skipper Jack O'Brian from
Boston, about the mission. He already knows
the mission outlines. He says he has done a
number of these missions. I ask him whether it's
unusual to have a naval lieutenant in command
of a gunboat. He says the Spanish influenza
has been decimating Atlantic Station. He's an
acting commander because the former skipper's
dead. I try my Gaelic on him and he responds
by offering a glass of Irish whiskey. It's not
bourbon, but it's most welcome. By end of our
first meeting, we're on good terms.

Damn, thought Ashley, *the odds of how David got to Odessa
are miniscule. And yet he did.* After skipping the extensive
description of the gunboat, Ashley resumed.

30 November 1918, Morning

Upon arrival in Odessa, half the Marines take
off. They'll be gone for four days. (When they
return, the other half will go out and the first will
sleep most of the time until they go out again.)
I've been warned to expect a good number of
casualties. They're very good men and I wish
them well. I also discovered our wireless to HQ
is, at best, spotty. We're on our own.

After checking a map, I make my way to
Zimyava Street and find a large shuttered
mansion and use the massive gold knocker. A
maid answers the door, studies me and tells me
to enter. I wait in a small room until an older,
well-dressed woman comes in and greets me
warmly. She tells me she's Countess X. (I won't
share her identity for security.) As she brings
me into her salon, I notice her dress has a very
low neckline. She said she would like to do a
reading and sat me at a large table and began
shuffling cards she calls 'tarot.' Thus far, I've
not said a word and I was beginning to wonder
if I'd stumbled into a carnival sideshow or some
such. The first card she drew was 'The Fool.'
She explains to me this is me, the one foretold.
'A young man with unlimited potential and an
innocent about to begin his journey.' I tell her
I'm no innocent, having survived the War. She
smiles and draws 'The Lovers.' She now, at least,
has my attention and I listen politely to her. She
appears to be a well-educated and intelligent lady
who places great stock in her cards. And yet, she
wears a strange ornate cross around her lovely
long neck. I take no stock in her ridiculous
predictions. But, for the record, she foresaw I'd
be married three times, have no children of my
own, but rather, raise one as a debt of honor. I
would also be very successful in my chosen field.
She said she knew what that would be, but did
not tell me, so as not to influence my decisions.
Finally, after a long life, my death would be the
start of momentous events. And the boy I raised
would play a central role. Pure carnival hokum!

There it was. How could this countess so accurately predict such a thing? In David's shoes, I would've been skeptical as well.

When we finished, I told her of my mission. She smiled and told me the Red commander, Grigoriev, was in no shape to attack Odessa for several months. She would be fine until then. I then told her of the important people in my government who were concerned about her. That got her attention. But she couldn't yet leave without all her agents who had infiltrated the Red partisans and wouldn't be easy to extract. My orders didn't specify a time period for the mission and Gunny had told me the Marines mission was open-ended. I told her about Katahdin, its armaments, the Marines and it could accommodate a good number of people. She asked me if we needed supplies since we'd have to wait for a time. I nodded. She said she could offer us what we needed at a rate well below the prevailing black-market rate. I shook my head as I stood up. 'We came a great distance to evacuate you, and you're making us wait and now, you want to charge us for supplies? We're done here, and I'll order my ship to return at the earliest date and tell my superiors I simply couldn't locate you nor your group. Good day, Madam.'

She rose and hugged me. Perhaps, I wasn't so innocent as she had thought. Of course, she would provision our ship without charge. She asked me to return to my ship and come back with a complete list of our needs. I would then stay for dinner. She hasn't had male company in her house for a long time.

30 November 1918, Afternoon

I returned to ship and told the skipper the
situation. He fears getting stuck in the ice if we
wait much longer. In fact, he says it's a miracle
we're not iced in already. I tell him how the
Countess will provision the ship for free. She'd
taken me down to her cellar and she has tons of
all sorts of things. (She told me there's a whole
maze of caves and passageways under the city.
I had asked her if that would be a better way of
going back and forth to the ship. She seemed
horrified at the thought. They're even more
dangerous than the streets. Various criminal
gangs have carved up the corridors and caves. I
saw the countess had armed guards protecting
her supplies from the gangs' raids and there have
been gun fights down there. Truthfully, I can't
believe it could possibly be worse than the cold,
hard streets above ground. But I take her at her
word.) I tell him I need a list of what we need.
He calls in the shavetail ensign to gather our
needs. While we wait, we again share his Irish
whiskey and talk freely about any number of
things. I found out from Cookie his granddaddy
was with Sherman. I've not told him yet mine
was with John Bell Hood. They may have shot at
each other. Of course, such things do not seem to
carry much weight at this time or place.

Ashley heard the kitchen door open and called down,
"Annie?"

"Yes, Dad, it's me. Glad you gave me a key. Where are you?"

"I'm on the attic landing, right in the middle of something
very important. I'll be down before you go to bed. Be sure to see
Ronnie's note on the kitchen table."

"Already got it."

"OK." Ashley still sensed the danger, but the house seemed secure. So, he said nothing about it. "Thanks Rand. We'll see you and Deborah tomorrow."

"Great see you then."

Ashley returned to the bench.

> And she told me her cross was Orthodox
> Christian. I never heard of such a sect. Arriving
> again at Zimyava Street, I knock. A peephole
> opens before Svetlana, the maid, admits me.
> After being announced, I see the countess. She's
> such a handsome figure of a woman. I still can't
> believe she's in her mid-thirties. She's not plain
> and pious like women her age in Georgia. She
> elegantly makes her way down the circular
> grand marble stairs and her musical voice greets
> me warmly. She leads me into her dining room
> where I find a lavish meal. I'm unfamiliar with
> many of the foods but find them all good. We
> speak of world affairs and many other interesting
> topics. With the dinner complete, she hands my
> list to Svetlana and tells her to have it all packed
> by the morning. She takes me by the hand and,
> with our wineglasses, she admits me to her
> 'boudoir.'

Ashley saw the countess as she removed her clothing, and she is a classic voluptuous beauty of the period. Why had David never mentioned anything about this? It certainly had altered many lives.

> In the morning, Svetlana drives a Ford truck with
> our provisions to the dock and the gunboat's
> crew happily unloads them. I tried to speak
> with her in the truck's cab, but her English and
> French are very limited. She really only speaks

Russian and mine is not good enough beyond a few basics. She's a very hard woman, severe in appearance and has obviously had a very difficult life. However, she seems content with her current position.

15 December 1918

We had a blizzard last night and we're officially frozen in. It's going to be a long cold winter.

25 January 1919

I'm amazed. I had no idea two people could do such things romantically. She also tells me more about her background and life and I share mine. She helps with my French and Russian and I'm learning many things about Russia and their war. She also tells me about a man named Freud and his theories. Most interesting. The waiting has become a time of great learning. I think I could be at her side for a hundred years and not exhaust all she knows. My visits have become daily. I'm entranced.

Ashley skimed, but slowed down as David rails against the famous Boulevard Steps of Odessa, "…longer than a football field and covered in snow and ice. It's dangerous and our only way into the city." He is also running out of American tobacco and calls the Russian makhorka tobacco "a black mess."

28 March 1919, Morning

I'm standing on the frozen deck of Katahdin. Icicles hang from everything, even my moustache. I see nothing save frozen hard ice in the gray, dismal light. I inhale deeply on my last cigaret and study the forward mast, its sails

furled with chunks of ice frozen on the canvas.
I hear the haunting noise of the ice scraping
against the ship. I carefully extinguish the tip
of my cigaret on an icy pole and place it in
my tobacco pouch. I place it in my greatcoat
pocket and go on in to the skipper. He tells me
he received an urgent wireless request from the
countess for me to come as soon as I can. I ask
him to reply I'll be there within the hour. He
nods, and I tell him the Marines have almost
wrapped up their mission and we should be
leaving within the next ten to fourteen days. I
almost left then, but I asked him how long he
thought we'd be stuck in the ice. He said we
have a good supply of dynamite and munitions
to blow up or weaken the ice. He also said if
we tried to slip away after the ice breaks up, the
Whites will probably try to blow us out of the
water. But we will return fire. He added he was
at the Tommie's HQ last night. They believe
Grigoriev, the Red commander, and his troops
will be here in a few weeks, at the best. The
French are planning on withdrawing as soon as
the ice breaks.

That would be my best estimate as well because
the French and their allies are shooting at the
Whites right here in the streets. I doubt the
Whites can do much to stop Grigoriev's troops
because Deniken, the White commander, is still
fighting north of here in Kiev and so can't mount
a relief effort. I ask him what his orders are if the
Whites detain us before we evacuate. He assures
me they will not. However, he confidentially tells
me he has been ordered to scuttle the ship if we

can't escape the Reds. We'll make our way to
friendly force in Romania about 100 miles due
west. But we would have to negotiate both the
Red and White lines. If captured by the Reds,
officially, we cease to exist. Our government
will not negotiate with them. I've heard the
Bolshevik's camps are pretty barren if you
survive long enough to see one. It seems we have
nothing to lose by making a run for it.

28 March 1919, Afternoon

I walk through Odessa's snowy and icy streets,
which are patrolled by troops, either French,
Polish, Greek or one of the White factions.
Dressed in my American Expeditionary Forces
greatcoat with the Sergeant Major stripes, I'm
able to get through most of the roadblocks with
little difficulty. Occasionally, I hear gunfire or
shouting. The beggar children are everywhere.
They surely are God's most pathetic creatures,
dressed in rags, caring nothing for modesty,
nothing more than skin and bones. Their eyes are
deep and sunken. And dull, as though their souls
had already departed. Their only possessions
seem to be shoes. I give them chocolate and they
scurry away. But there are more of them than
there's chocolate and I run out. Then, I must
avert my eyes to make them invisible. Women
offer me jewelry or their bodies in return for
something. I've no idea what. I never stopped
long enough to ask. Such women are often
used as bait by ruthless gangs to rob and kill.
Therefore, I keep the safety off my Colt .45
automatic and always have one hand on it at the

ready. There are few men on the streets not in
uniform. I saw one yesterday, frozen to death, his
knees to his chest and head bowed in defeat.

Countess warmly greets me and hands me an
ounce bag of American issue tobacco. It's fresh
but I notice a brown stain on the bag, most likely
blood. I don't ask her where she got it. That's
part of our bargain. I kiss her hand and thank her
before she tells me there's someone she would
like me to meet before we conduct our affairs.
She leads me lightly by the hand into her ornate
sitting room, where a man dressed in a Cossack
officer's uniform rises. Before I could salute
him, the countess begins her introductions. He's
Colonel Dmitri Sergeyovich Iskandarov of the
former Imperial Cavalry Guards.

This is Ashley's grandfather, and he paid close attention,
looking for clues.

I salute and after the Colonel returns it, he
extends his hand. We exchange pleasantries. He
allows he was expecting someone considerably
older. And I must be an extraordinary soldier to
have advanced so far, so fast. 'In His Imperial
Majesty's Army, it should take a good soldier at
least thirty years to achieve your rank.'

I nod, smile and let him think what he will. He
then asks me if it's unusual for an Army Sergeant
to be assigned to a naval gunboat. I nod and
say, 'Yes, sir.' He smiles and says I should call
him Dmitri. He likes American informality. I
ask him to call me Dave. He asks me where I'm
from. I tell him Georgia. He laughs and says he's
from Georgia as well. I smile and nod as though

I understand. (It was only later I consulted a
map and found a country called Georgia on the
other side of the Black Sea.) I finish my tale.
The Colonel nods sympathetically, commenting
these are difficult times. He then tells me he
was recently at the front with General Deniken
at Kiev. Grigoriev had seized large caches of
weapons and ammunition from the Whites at
Tiaspol and Nikolaev, in preparation for a full
assault on Odessa. He comments our boat would
probably be gone by the time the Bolsheviki
broke through. But he quickly said while his
place was at the front, he'd like to arrange
passage for his son, Sergei, who's nine. Dmitri's
wife's in Paris and he needs someone to deliver
the boy safely. Countess had told him I'm a man
of honor. He asks how much I would charge.

Ashley stops reading. This Sergei was his father, and he
began reading very carefully.

All I can think of is if I don't do this, he's liable
to wind up like those other poor wretched orphan
children on the street. Here's a chance to save
one. I tell Dmitri I wouldn't take any money
beyond some transportation costs if I decide
to take him. He asks me what it would take
to convince me. I'll do it if the boy seems all
right. (If he's some snotty-nose little aristocrat,
there's no way in Heaven I'll do this.) And I
would like to meet the boy. Dmitri smiles and
tells me again what an extraordinary person I
am. I say, 'It's OK.' At this, Dmitri lights up. He
loves that idiom he's seen in the moving pictures
and repeats it, enjoying its sound. But quickly
whispers if it's appropriate to use it in front of

ladies. I nod. He smiles and turns to countess. 'It
is OK.' They both revel in this for a while. He
says, 'If it is agreeable to countess, he should
like to bring him here tomorrow.' Countess nods.
We shake hands and salute before he leaves with
a kiss of the Countess's hand. She sits on the red
velvet love seat and tells me Sergei's a bright and
well-mannered boy. There should be no problem.
She adds this is very important to her. Dmitri's
an old friend of her late husband, the count.
So, as far as I'm concerned, it's now all settled.
Countess leads me up the stairs to her boudoir.

14 April 1919

The ice unexpectedly melted enough, and
we put to sea last week, amid someone firing
artillery at us. We lost six Marines on their
mission and added about twenty of countess's
agents. The household servants remain in the
house. She told me most of her domestic staff
were Red sympathizers, especially Svetlana,
who was a spy. Countess let her find almost true
information. On a happier note, Sergei's a fine
young man with deep blue eyes and a handsome,
intelligent face. When he grows up, the girls will
flock to him. I never took much stock in children,
but we've had some interesting conversations.
I have a gift for knowing about people. After
being in the room with Countess X and Colonel
Iskandarov for no more than a few minutes,
it became obvious they were romantically
involved. And had been for some time. The
Colonel is Sergei's father, but I suspected his
sister, the countess is Sergei's mother. When I

interviewed Sergei, he confirmed my suspicions.
Since there appear to be no bad results from
this union, I'll leave it at that. It's none of my
business, However, I wonder who his supposed
mother, Tanya, really is.

25 April 1919

We arrived in Marseilles today. I reported to
Colonel Mac with the Countess and Sergei. He
seemed very pleased to see me and confided
in Gaelic the mission had taken longer than
expected and the Reds now controlled Odessa
and he thought I was dead or captured. Most of
our regiment's now gone home. He continued
in English asking me my plans. I told him I was
honor-bound to deliver Sergei to his mother
in Paris. He nodded and said he would like to
debrief both of us separately before we left,
along with her agents. He told me we would
again be debriefed by two Secret Servicemen in
Paris. After that, I would receive my back pay for
Russia and a priority passage home. He also said
I was in line for a suitable medal. We saluted,
and the Colonel invited us to join him for lunch,
which was quite an affair.

Ashley skimmed over the meeting with Tanya, who is
described as "shy and retiring." Her English iss not terribly good,
so they really cannot communicate.

P.S. I've wondered for some time about 'Tanya.'
She's in hiding from someone, probably being
Russian, the Reds. But she's also someone
important. I'll leave it at that.

15 May 1919

The debrief in Paris was led by two Secret
Servicemen, the senior one's named George.
Whether that's his Christian or surname, he
didn't say. He's a tall man in very good condition
in a three-piece black suit with matching
Homberg. He's no nonsense as countess and I are
separately debriefed in about a half day. As we
were leaving, he told me because of some papers
I'd signed at some point, as a senior NCO I'll
not be discharged but, instead, be in the inactive
reserves for the next twenty years and can be
recalled in case of emergency. But my primary
task in the near future is to teach Military
Science to the Reserve Officer's Training. I
tell him I plan to attend Emory College in
Oxford, Georgia. He says he will make all the
arrangements for the fall semester. I don't like
George springing this on me at the last moment.
After leaving, the countess approves of his plan
and tells me I'll be a great teacher. I allow I can
certainly use the salary. She kisses me and says
she has some shopping and other errands to
attend to.

I'm content as I've not been in so long. I've
come to realize in saving Sergei's life, I've
redeemed my own. (While I've saved the
countess as well, I'm convinced she, like the
cat, has, at least, nine lives.) I've been redeemed
because there was nothing I could've done
to save either Willy or Bobby. But given the
opportunity, I saved many lives, including her
agents. I feel as though I've somewhat moved
out from the shadow of the War. Besides, I'm in

Paris. I've survived the War and Russia. From now on, there will be a more perfect world under President Wilson's League of Nations. All men will become brothers in the new world. There's a world to be built, a world of laws, not men. I decide my future course. At Emory, I will perfect my languages and read the law. My father always wanted me to be a doctor. But that seems now very quaint. The law's the way of the future. As a lawyer, I'll help create that better new world.

And yet, as I sit here, writing this down, at this cafe on the banks of the Seine, I believe my time with countess is coming to a close. She now belongs in Paris. There's no other place she could now possibly be happy, except Russia. But the news from there isn't good for the Whites. And where do I belong? Precisely nowhere! I'm not sophisticated enough for fashionable Paris and too much so for the red clay of South Georgia. Besides, my home's gone. Our plantation, New Caledonia, was sold to Ohio carpetbaggers for unpaid taxes while I was in France, a result of the cotton price crash of '14. Miss Caroline died peacefully before she could see this. Thank the Lord! My father and Miss Ida moved into her house in Pine View. What do I have to come home to? My father, the former cotton planter and still country doctor, has a thriving practice. Despite his still skeptical attitude germs actually exist. It's not now, nor ever has been lucrative, as most of his patients can't afford to pay him. He once told me he does this because 'if I do not, then who shall attend these people?' I've learned a new term for such actions. Countess

calls it 'Noblesse Oblige.' Doctor Cooper's
patients have always made certain their doctor
and his family have food. I'm certain nothing has
changed. They're fine and will be as long as they
live.

Ashley skimmed over David's return to the countess's suite
at the Ritz but stopped.

And then she says something that truly affected
me. I will try to recall it verbatim. (It is at least
a close approximation.) 'The war against the
gangsters in the motherland is not proceeding
well. They can promise the ignorant peasants
a utopian future, while we can only offer the
historic and imperfect past. And yet, one day,
because our cause is just, I swear this upon the
memory of my beloved parents. One day, my
children or grand-children shall dance in the
streets of a free Odessa or even dance at a ball
at the Winter Palace on the banks of the Neva in
St. Petersburg. And to make this so, I must now
take the first painful steps. While I should love to
stay here forever with you, my wonderful lover,
I may not. Just as the cards tell me my future, so
they have forecast yours. You may scoff at the
cards, but I knew the first moment I laid eyes on
you, you were exceptional. And you have more
than fulfilled my every expectation. Both Tanya
and I are in your debt far more than you may
ever know. I do not know how we shall ever be
able to repay you. But life often moves in strange
and unsuspected ways not even the cards may
foretell. So, sadly, these few hours we have left
to us are all the last grains in the hourglass.'

16 May 1919

After bidding the Countess farewell, I went to
the embassy and received all my back pay for
Russia. As I was counting it out, a doughboy
comes up very nice and says he knows of a
friendly little poker game, not too far away.
As I've mentioned before, I know how to read
people and that makes me a good card player.

David was much more than a good card player, and he
has taken the doughboys from the Liberty Division for a lot of
money. The group's leader is Rupert Drew from New York City.
He's a captain and seems to be the brains of the bunch. He is
also Charles's father and was the very dignified managing partner
of the Firm when Ashley had been an associate. Rupert is very
impressed with David's card skills.

But even when I beat him badly, Rupert takes
it in good stride because he has recognized my
gift for reading people. He's a decent sort. I gave
a good portion of my winnings to Charisse, my
pretty oo-la-la girl. She's a Belgian and her home
was destroyed by the War. She needs the money
far more than I. It'll give her a stake. She need
not earn her living 'praying with her knees up,'
as we politely say. That's no way for anyone to
live. She burst into tears when I gave her the
notes. I think it's more than she had ever seen.
I've perhaps redeemed another life from the War.

When I left, Rupert gave me his address. I had
told him my interest in reading the law. He said
his old man has a legal firm in New York City.
Rupert's going back to the Harvard University
this fall and the law school after that. He said a
poker player who can read people like me would

be a crackerjack asset for the firm. And we
should correspond and keep in touch. I will.

15 June 1919

I've been in New York City for about a week
now. Rupert told me to look up an old girlfriend
of his. Corliss lives in Greenwich Village and is a
poet. Like the Countess, she too is very liberated.
She took me right in without a question and has
shown me the city. I like New York City. It has
energy, vitality and everything moves very fast.
I think this may be the place I belong. It will
become, if it's not already, the capital of the
heroic new world.

With Corliss, my sexual education may well
be complete. I still shudder when I think of my
naivety with Molly Sue that night a thousand
years ago in the Georgia woods. That boy will
not be coming back to Georgia for he no longer
exists.

6 October 1919

I'm now a freshman and instructor at Emory,
which is now in Atlanta and a university. After
leaving New York, I was briefly in Pine View.
It was very awkward. College is my refuge.
I get together with the other veterans and we
talk late into the night about the War and the
future. To me, the students who aren't veterans
seem like children. And the girls. Well, after the
women on my adventure, they seem innocent
and childlike. Without comprehension of the
world or how it works. But perhaps that's a good
thing. That may be the ultimate contribution of

all those Americans who laid down their lives, the prolonged innocence of those who remained behind. I think of Charisse and all she had to endure simply to survive. I'm certain such innocence should be a great treasure to her.

15 March 1920

I used part of my service pay to buy a Model T Ford and go up, with my friends, to Savannah on the weekends since it is still 'wet.' (They pay for the gas.) The sheriff there doesn't hold with the current foolishness. (I swear this Volstead Amendment will be the death of us all.) Bootleggers are all over Atlanta with their swill, but in Savannah, I can buy a genuine drink and the women up there know how to treat a fellow right.

5 April 1920

I suppose I'm drinking too much. But it surely helps. I received a letter from the countess today. (I wonder how she learned of my address, but I can't say I'm surprised). She said she missed me. But her ongoing war of liberation consumes all her time and effort. I'm certain she has a new lover by now. (Countess without a lover would be like grits without eggs and ham.) I suppose I'm now over her. But I'll never forget all she taught me. What an excellent teacher! How I wish I had one like her here.

She enclosed a bank draft for fifty thousand American dollars. She said it was a small token for saving her and Sergei. This was to help me finish my education and become established, so

I may fulfill the rest of my destiny as the cards
had revealed. I'm embarrassed to receive it. I
was just following orders. And I should return it
except she left no return address.

Ashley whistled. That was a considerable sum at a time
when a loaf of bread was five cents.

9 April 1920

I've stared at the draft now for some days.
And have finally decided to deposit it to my
savings account. I now have a stake. Next year,
I will go up to Boston and attend the Harvard
University along with Rupert. My father was
opposed to such a move, saying there were many
fine colleges in the South. And, indeed, there
are. However, I'm now twenty-one and it's my
money. I'm my own man.

20 May 1920

With the gift from Countess, I've regained my
focus, which I had lost in the past year. While I
will not totally forgo the pleasures of Savannah,
they will no longer be my reason for being. I
will focus on my studies because there's still
that new world to construct. The old world has
made a down payment on the future. I now
know I, and indeed the new world, will succeed.
On a sadder note, my old benefactor, Colonel
'Mac' McMahon has died of the Spanish. And
Captain Stuart, now Major, was captured leading
a cavalry change against the Reds in far north
Russia. He's assumed dead. And Katahdin, the
venerable old ship I came to love, has been
decommissioned and sold for scrap. A fine old

gal like her deserves a better ending. The Great
War, for me, is now finally over.

Ashley closed the book and his eyes. He had just read the
genesis of his life, long before being born. And he wanted to
learn more about Sophia and her role in subsequent events. That
would be in the other diaries. *Clever Ronnie—one book in, and
I'm already hooked.*

He rose, gun in hand, and as he went down to his room he
saw the light under Ronnie's door. Hearing no noise, he opened
the door and found Annie asleep. He tucked her in and turned off
the light. He would tell her about his new adventure tomorrow.

EIGHT
Saturday 28 May 1993
Quaker Mount, NY

1.

Around four a.m., Ashley heard a noise, and after putting on his robe and grabbing his revolver, he ran downstairs where the kitchen lights were on and the cellar door was open. With the cellar light not working, he, with a flashlight in his other hand, cautiously went down the creaking cellar stairs, which seemed longer than he remembered. After the flashlight revealed nothing unusual, he felt an *Andronyi* coming on. He turned off the flashlight and sat on the stairs with his revolver next to him.

As Ashley breathes deeply, the room begins to lighten, and he sees his sister, Natalya, the tall, skinny naked girl, now older, coming out of darkness with something on her left breast. Beside her is the scowling KGB woman who looks up and, speaking Russian, demands, "Listen to me."

Ashley responds in Russian, "Certainly, but tell me, do you ever allow poor girl to get dressed? And second, why do you punish her so severely?"

"She is *zechka*, female prisoner and enemy of people. Prisoners have no names, only numbers. I call her 'Little Princess' because her parents were members of former classes. Of course she has clothes. She goes to school. I saved her life by rescuing her from camps. There, she would perish within week."

Ashley is surprised he can communicate with the woman. "I see by your rank you are colonel. And I recognize you as mother of Lana van Rouene."

"*Da.* I am Svetlana Feliksovna Polinkova. She is drugged and cannot speak, only feel pain intensely. I have recently branded her with Cyrillic 'C3' on her formerly pretty left bosom. As you know, 'C' would be 'S' in your alphabet. Today is her fifteenth birthday and that is present."

"And what date is today?"

She looks at him strangely. "It is 28 May 1970."

Ashley nods. He now knows her birth date and studies the shuddering, wet-eyed and scared young woman and her left breast. The still-red branding, just above her nipple, has a roughly three-inch diameter. "Hardly seems an appropriate present. But then I would expect nothing less from your *apparat.*"

"But it is appropriate. This is first step in her redemption. Everyone who sees it will know Comrade Stalin is her father, and I and Soviet worker councils are her mothers. It will also make it easier for you to locate her on your journey of fool."

He shakes his head. "Stalin was dead before her birth. I take my journey most seriously, and it is hardly foolish."

The woman shakes her head. "You cannot succeed without her, but if you attempt to have union, her heart will explode. And without union, you will fail. She has implanted device. You can see scar on her left side."

"You must really fear my journey if you are employing extreme measures to scare and stop me."

"Fear? I fear nothing and no one. I have been in your house since before your arrival. I burned fuses and was presence you sensed when you changed them. I thoroughly studied you and your daughter last night and now know everything about you both." She laughed. "See you in realm of the demons."

As the light faded, the two women disappeared. Ashley thought this was a level of *Andronyi* he had never experienced before. And how was Colonel Polinkova able to roam freely here? With too many questions and his mind churning, he returned to bed and placed Sainte Elizabeta on his bed. Opening her bright light, he soon fell, completely relaxed, into a deep sleep.

2.

Ashley awoke as daylight filled the bedroom. His *tvarsch* had picked up Colonel Polinkova as the unexpected person, so he knew they were safe here, for the present. He sensed his *tvarsch* had become more powerful since lovemaking with Ronnie and also his ability to receive enhanced *Andronyis*. He lay back and felt all the power of the cosmos surging into him. He could hear Annie breathing, as well as the house, and experienced a level of peace he had never known before. It passed, but his senses remained acute. He went downstairs and, after making coffee, relished the flavor and its feeling in his mouth and on his tongue. Best coffee ever!

Wearing shorts, slippers and a T-shirt, Ashley ran up the stairs into the attic, eager to open the newer army footlocker. Stenciled on the top in white was:

CAPT. TALBOTT, SPENCER D.
12-267-349
U.S. ARMY AIR FORCE

He lifted the lid and breathed in his father's magic scent… aftershave, tobacco and sweat contained in pent-up microscopic particles. *Yesterday, I wasn't conscious of these particles, dormant for fifty years holding these scents and aromas. And today, it's almost like he's standing right here.* Looking up, Ashley saw, for an instant, a tanned, wiry man in shorts and an open Hawaiian shirt, smoking a cigar and smiling. Ashley smiled back and sipped his coffee as he smelled Ronnie on his hand. *Perhaps if I never shower she will always be with me.* He sensed the unknown presence, still at a distance. Could this house somehow be a magnet for spirits? He remembered occasionally seeing the spirit of a Quaker lady, a most friendly spirit, when he used to play make-believe up here.

The top layer of the trunk was a pull-out drawer that contained things used daily. He found a shaving kit, an almost empty box of Montecristo Cuban cigars and a second one, still unopened, with a note, "For my son's birth." There was also a green and red carton of Lucky Strike cigarettes with one pack remaining, as well as training and identification manuals and GI guides to England, Egypt and Libya. These revealed where Spencer had served. In the second layer, he found Spencer's dark brown dress tunic with silver captain's bars, insignia, wings and an 8th Air Force shoulder patch on the top of the left sleeve. His overseas cap remained neatly folded over the tunic. Lifting the tunic, Ashley found Spencer's diary, sat on the Quaker bench and began reading softly out loud, so as not to miss any subtleties.

15 August 1929, Evening

I am obliged to state at the outset of this journal,
I should prefer to remain in Europe and fight the
bolshevikii. My parents have said that I must
learn American ways, for the next phase of the
conflict. That is how I will best serve our cause.
This does not please me, but I have my orders.
In addition, I commit this to paper, so others may
see how I triumphed. Or, how I failed. And, in
either case, learn from my example.

Sergei wrote in a tight cursive, like Ashley, which pleased him. And used blue ink on good quality paper, both of which retained their aromas.

16 August 1929

I start my journal with our voyage to America.
Mamman and I left Paris for Le Havre today,
where we boarded the Normandie, a most
exquisite ship. We are going to visit David and
his wife, Gwenneth, in New York City. This shall

be the first time either of us has seen David since
he left Paris ten years ago.

After our visit, they will drive us up to the
Harvard University in Boston, Massachusetts
where I commence my studies. Yesterday, Papa
came home from Berlin and threw a bon voyage
fete for Mamman and me. My blonde friend,
Tamara, kissed me passionately before she left
and said she would join me next year and warned
I should be good in the meantime. She said I
owed her that much. Perhaps I do and perhaps I
do not. Our affair is over. That is certain.

"Papa," Colonel Iskandarov, had survived the civil war,
apparently without injury and lived in Berlin. "Mamman" Sophia
was in Paris because Berlin was very dangerous in those days.
So, he must be the Bleu Agency Berlin Station Chief.

17 August 1929

Last night Mamman and I attended a glittering
gala to celebrate the commencement of our
voyage. Mamman introduced me to her dearest
friend, the Countess Mariya. The countess has
the most extraordinary daughter, Nadezdha
Mytrovna. She is known as 'Nadia,' who is
Ukrainian, but dark complexioned like her
mother, with shiny black hair and mysterious
black eyes. She is going to attend the Radcliffe
College, also in Boston. Mamman has told me
I may consider Nadia as a marriage partner,
should I find her attractive, because a marriage
alliance with the Andreyev house is to be highly
valued. Much more so than an alliance with
the Riasanovsky, Tamara's house. I now know
Mamman arranged this whole situation well in

advance. I long ago learned 'co-incidence' has no place in her vocabulary.

19 August 1929

I am entranced and enchanted as never before. Nadia is the embodiment of Mother Russia, my own Sophia. However, unlike Alexandr Blok's, mine is no dullard. There is a keen intelligence under the beauty. Her décolletage entices me with her partially exposed, magnificent bosom. She fills my days and my dreams. I asked Mamman to do a tarot reading and she sees the future favorably.

21 August 1929

It is done. I am in Heaven. The captain of the ship married us. We will have a proper Orthodox service in the United States. This will suffice for the sake of propriety. She was moved into my stateroom yesterday afternoon. I found she is experienced, like me. Some fortunate fellow has taught her very well. Magnifique!

Ashley smiled at Sergei's sophistication about Nadia, who is Olga and Ronnie's mother. She was the grand duchess Randell met in Paris in 1962. Ronnie had indicated that she was still alive. Bleu was central to the Iskandarovs, so Ashley wanted to be as fully informed as possible about her and her agency. Case preparation. Ashley read closely, but only found more of Sergei's account of life on the ship with Nadia. Nonetheless, the tragic quality of the account profoundly moved him with people overeating, loving, dancing all night and enjoying leisurely first-class days at sea. They were completely unaware of the impending financial panic that would finally destroy their fragile, doomed world, so severely hobbled by The Great War.

10 September 1929

My sweet Nadia and I were truly joined two
days ago at the St. Cyril's Orthodox Church in
Manhattan. Papa came from Berlin. Today, we
set up housekeeping in a large flat in Cambridge
and begin our classes soon. Papa has ordered me
to enroll in the Reserve Officer Training Program.
(I have secretly become an American citizen and
David eased the whole process for me as Papa
had earlier requested. I also had my name legally
changed to Spencer Dryden Talbot, as Papa ordered.
I have not told Nadia. She would never, never
understand why I would do such 'a foolish thing,' as
she would doubtless say in her great hurt and anger.
Nonetheless, I do not like having secrets from her.)
Upon graduation, I will be commissioned a U.S.
Army Second Lieutenant. Papa is a chess master
who always thinks several moves ahead of his
opponents and I shall do my duty.

13 March 1930

The doctor confirmed today sweet Nadia is with
child. My joy knows no bounds. I have written
Mamman and Papa to tell them they will soon
be grandparents. Sadly, sweet Nadia will have to
withdraw from the Radcliffe College in the fall.
Nevertheless, she will miss but a single year.

3 June 1930

We have decided to remain in Cambridge for
the summer. The doctor did not think it wise for
sweet Nadia to return home. He believes she is
bearing twins. The cards were correct, as they
usually are. This is truly a great blessing.

5 July 1930

This is, truthfully, an incredible country. Even though there is great suffering from the recent financial panic, these Americans are a very optimistic people. They see the future will be bright for them, even if the present is not. The celebration of their 154 years of independence yesterday was truly remarkable. I am coming to love this country very much. I am impressed by the vitality and energy of American culture. I especially love the jazz. She finds the culture to be 'unsophisticated and vulgar, without nuance or maturity.' However, sweet Nadia reminds me that we are only student guests here. She remains the embodiment of Mother Russia for me.

29 August 1930

Nadia has become like an anchor around my neck. As I must become more American, she becomes more Russian. A place she has never even seen and that, perhaps, is why she acts that way. She has virtually lived her whole life in France. Her father sent her and her mother to Lyon just before Great War broke out in 1914, when she was four.

11 November 1930

My sweet Nadia was delivered of twin girls. It is appropriate on the twelfth anniversary of the Armistice of The Great War, we have birthed the future of the Iskandarov. They will be known as Olga and Verushka Sergevna.

Why had Dmitri ordered Sergei not to tell Nadia his plans? And Sophia had prompted his marriage to Nadia Andreyeva, for dynastic reasons. But why, when an Iskandarova would be a much more appropriate wife?

16 May 1933

This has been a mixed day. I received word of
my acceptance to Harvard Law in the fall. Sweet
Nadia announced she has discovered my secret.
(and she acted just like I had predicted.) I told
her I was merely doing my duty. She says I am
untrustworthy and I should have told her of my
deception. Did I not trust her to understand?
Now, she desires to return to France with mes
petites filles when I complete my legal studies.
Tvarsch says if she leaves, I should probably
never see them again.

He sensed Sergei had never seen them again. What cruel punishment to have two beautiful girls in your life and abruptly have them taken away. Ashley also found it curious that after chastising Sergei for obeying his orders, Nadia, subsequently, became the leader of Bleu.

I love her still and I know she loves me.
Nevertheless, my duty pulls us apart. Damn
my duty anyway. The Stalin regime in Moscow
is strong. Many of the students here look to
Moscow as the wave of the future. I believe
we, sweet Nadia and I, have become victims
of our parents' dreams. Mamman remembers
the glittering balls in Odessa and Petersburg. I
remember a much different Odessa—dangerous
armed men, starving women and children,
corpses left in the streets. David rescued me
from all that. Papa remembers the fight against
the Germans. And yet, he now works with the
Germans against the Reds. If he can change, can
I not as well?

16 November 1933

The impossible has happened. Today, the
United States of America recognized the Stalin
regime in Moscow. Yet everyone knows what
a maniacal butcher he is. In a letter received
today, Papa has again reminded me my future is
in the United States and their army. I assume he
knew about the recognition long before it was
announced to the public. He went on to say that
the new government in Germany will take care
of everything. In the next war, the Germans will
unite all of Europe against the Red Gangsters.

3 June 1936

I have graduated from Harvard Law with honors.
I may be called up by the Army fairly soon
to begin my service. Perhaps now, I will have
time to write in my journal. My brother Alexei
Dmitrovich, stopped by today for lunch. He is on
his way to Washington to take up an important
post at the French Embassy.

Ashley did not know Sergei had a brother and wondered
why he had never been mentioned.

5 June 1936

Sweet Nadia left today for Paris. We both cried,
but know it is for the best. I have lost my light,
my guide, my Sophia. As penance, I must now
stumble in the darkness. She remained constant,
but I changed. I have insisted both my daughters
return to this country for their college. Sweet
Nadia agreed. And yet I still sense something
will intervene to prevent this.

13 June 1936

I will spend some of my summer doing my
reserve training for the Army Air Corps in the
deep South. On the bright side, Papa has written
to assure me Nadia and his grand-daughters will
be well provided for. And I should seek out a
native-born girl to teach me American ways.

27 June 1936

David has sponsored me, and I begin my work at
Gules, Argent and Orr tomorrow.

22 August 1936

I have never been so busy in my life as I have
since joining the Firm. David does nothing but
work. He has not yet recovered from the loss
of Gwenneth and his child. I must find a way to
cheer him up before he kills himself. Because I
cannot show myself in Red Russia, I am working
very hard under my partner, Carlos Matarazzo,
who is Cuban. We are working, primarily, in
Cuba, Venezuela, Argentina and Chile.

10 September 1936

Nadia has written today saying she has filed for
divorce. While I will not contest it, I know her
and she either has, or soon will have, a lover,
preferably, titled and rich. She enclosed pictures
of my girls. They are so adorable, it brings tears
to my eyes. I should like nothing more than
to visit Paris and see them, but that would be
terribly awkward for all of us.

22 September 1936

One of David's clients has invited him to a soiree at her apartment on Park Avenue. He asked me to go with him 'for moral support,' as he puts it.

29 September 1936

Since the party, David has been seeing a special lady. I cannot get over the change in him. I, too, have found someone. Sally is nothing like sweet Nadia. She is very American—very pretty, very rich, very wild. She thinks I am 'adorable.' I know there is no future with her. She has no interest in marriage and frankly, neither do I. She only wishes to have a good time with me. And I am more than willing. She is a wonderful solution to Papa's order.

26 October 1936

Sally's like a tonic—she has lifted my veil of grief over Nadia. She's hosting a Halloween party at her parents' house in East Hampton for the weekend. Her parents are in Florida.

2 November 1936

Sally's idea of a Halloween party was having everyone dressed in masks and not much else in the huge shingled mansion on the Atlantic. Booze, wacky dust and anonymous sex were the order of the day. (Reminds me of Paris.) A lot of Sally's friends thought I was 'adorable' and wanted to meet me in the city. Sally doesn't mind because she found a new lover. I drove back to the city with Sally's best friend,

Virginia. No tears, no regrets. 'A clean break,' as they say.

3 July 1937

I've accepted a Gules Partnership. Carlos is sending me off today for a solo tour, starting in Havana. The more I work, the less important Russia becomes. And it seems to be a lost cause. My future now truly lies elsewhere.

25 September 1937

When I arrived at my office, my secretary, Mabel, told me that Mrs. George Farwell was waiting for me in my office. Rupert Drew's son, Charles, normally handled all of Secretary Farwell's legal matters. Entering my office, I found a very attractive and fashionable blonde lady, who said her name was 'Tammy' and smiled. (What an absurd name for an elegant lady. It seems better suited to one's cat.) While I recognized her, I didn't acknowledge her and wasn't pleased to see her. She had a made-up story about having a very complicated struggle with the Cuban government and needed my expertise. She then began in Russian, saying that I hadn't been a good boy since my bon-voyage party. Therefore, I now owed her the perfect Iskandarov baby I had deprived her of in Paris. I replied she was a married lady. She then laid out a very compelling case of exactly what would happen if I refused. At the very least, it would end my career at the Firm and anywhere else I might go. We would continue until she had confirmed her pregnancy. She said she has been

sleeping with George enough that he ought not
to be suspicious. This is still a very dangerous
game for both of us, but I really had no choice.
I agreed but added that I expected at the
confirmation of her pregnancy, she would hand-
deliver all of her evidence and all copies to me.
I also mentioned if she tried to deceive, I knew
several men professionally who would be most
pleased to kill a Russian aristocrat lady slowly
and painfully. She blanched at this before finding
her voice and said that would be unnecessary.
As a 'Russian Lady of High Rank,' she's honor-
bound to return all she had. (We'll see. I like
my solution better and it's safer.) We began that
afternoon at the Waldorf-Astoria. In for a penny,
in for a pound.

Ashley remembered Tammy, née, Tamara, had been George
Farwell's second wife. Ultimately, after she had refused to give
him a divorce, George, wanting to marry a younger woman,
had her committed to an asylum out on Staten Island. Pen had
a brother, and Ashley hoped he would not be the result of this
union. He also remembered van Rouene calling Spencer a "lady's
man" who had probably seduced many of the Firm's wives, and
from his tone that included van Rouene's. And that was what
Tammy had on Spencer.

30 November 1937

Tammy's pregnant. (Although I'm being
blackmailed, she remains a very attractive
woman, so my task was not unpleasant. In the
course of the affair, I found some incriminating
evidence of her infidelity with other men. My
defense against a repeat.) I'm, nonetheless,
delighted to be finished with her. She handed
over her evidence and I've burned it. (Honor

among thieves). Even though her 'Cuban'
problem remains, she has lost all interest in it.

Ashley wondered if Sergei had ever revealed his information
to George, setting in motion Tammy's banishment to the asylum.

16 August 1938

Tammy gave birth yesterday. Today, George
handed out cigars for the birth of his son,
Robert. So, I can now devote my full romantic
attention to Jean, a beautiful platinum blonde and
Virginia's best friend.

Ashley's fears had been realized. His half-brother, Robert
(never Bob) S. Farwell, had been profiled in a *Fortune* magazine
article as "brilliant, erratic and ruthless." Pen had called him
psychotic. Robert actively avoided any publicity. George had
to force him to do the *Fortune* piece. Although George had
gradually ceded power to him, he remained chairman, the
charismatic public face of the company. Because Robert had
been held back after first grade at St. Bernard's for "behavioral
reasons," Robert and Nick Stevens became classmates and
life-long friends. At Lawrenceville and Harvard, Robert had
been Nick's favorite football receiver. After college, Nick
enlisted in the Marines and became part of the long-range
recon teams, based out of NKP. While Robert had finagled a
medical deferment from the draft, Ashley had not seen Robert
since Harvard—not even at Pen's funeral. Ashley did not care
because Robert hated him.

1 October 1938

George brought his son, although not Tammy, to
the office today. Even though the baby doesn't
resemble him greatly, the egotistical fool parades
the baby around as though it were his. I called
Tammy on her private line and, from the sound
of her, she had a very bad cold. She told me

> George suspects nothing, hence the show. We're
> in the clear.

George certainly had not changed very much in almost fifty-five years.

2 September 1939

> The war of liberation has begun! The Germans
> invaded Poland. No doubt, they won't stop
> until they reach Moscow, despite the obviously
> meaningless Nazi-Soviet pact. The Gangster will
> hang from a streetlamp by Christmas. I again
> have purpose to my life.

18 September 1939

> The Reds remain allied with the Germans in
> dismembering Poland. There's no doubt the Nazi
> bastards can't be trusted.

When the Germans invaded France in the spring of 1940, Spencer hated them for the humiliating defeat they inflicted on his first adopted homeland (of course, hiding behind an incomplete wall was never such a good strategy). The London Blitz left him ambivalent. Ed Murrow's radio accounts of the Battle of Britain merited only a brief mention. However, in June 1941, when the Germans invaded Russia in "Barbarossa," Spencer could barely contain himself. It seemed like the hanging of Gangster Stalin in Berlin would be the finest Christmas present he, and the Russian people, had ever received. But then the Japanese struck Pearl Harbor, and Germany declared war on the United States. The Bolsheviks had been saved. Spencer learned from émigré sources in this country that the Germans routinely massacred Russians as badly as Stalin had. When David received his letter commissioning him as a captain in the army air force in 1942, he joined General Henry 'Hap' Arnold's 8th Air Force staff at Bolling Field, Washington. Spencer received his letter as a first lieutenant and a bombardier/navigator. He had learned this skill at his secret reserve training. Also assigned to the 8th Air Force, Spencer went overseas in May 1942 with the crew of the B-17 "Bounteous Beauty." His Harvard classmates, Harvey Jacobs and Mac Goodwin, were pilot and co-pilot of the Beauty. Ashley paid close attention. Harvey was Randell's father, but he had no idea who Mac was.

11 September 1942

I was certain I'd cashed in all my chips. When I
opened my eyes, at first, I thought if I hadn't, I
was flak-happy. I saw a sight so beautiful that I
thought I truly was in Heaven—an enchantingly
angelic face with bright green eyes and radiant
red hair. I was also certain she was a Kraut
and I was in Germany. Therefore, I asked her
in German if I were in Heaven. She shook her
head and replied, in flawless German, I was in
England. I again lost consciousness and when I
came around again, there was the same angelic
vision, Nurse Brown. She told me that she'd be
my primary nurse and had my flight bag with
my journal in it. I asked her if she had read it.
(Like most women.) She said she felt insulted by
my question. She 'most certainly had not.' She
said that having it in my bag was rather risky
behavior. I told her there was nothing classified
in it. She nodded and suggested, after I felt up
to it, writing about neutral topics in it would be
a good way to pass the time. I asked her about
the mission and if any of the guys survived. She
quickly changed the subject and I knew. (Just
to make it official, some desk-jockey from HQ
came out later and told me Harv, Mac and I were
the only crew who made it.) I'm totally desolate.

I loved my crew guys like the brothers they truly were. I began to remember. I didn't want to, but I had to about our last raid. Most of our raids, we had fighter escorts, Spitfires from the R.A.F., as far as they could go. On this one, we went deeper into Europe. When the Spits left, we were under almost immediate Kraut attack. (We desperately need our own fighters to protect us all the way to Berlin. So, we're losing air crews at an alarming rate. Brass keeps promising us that there's a long-range fighter in the works. Hope it arrives before we're all dead!)

I now remember Beauty badly shot up but Harv managed to get us back for a single- engine belly landing (Sadly, I've heard that great pin up of Beauty was destroyed as well. Pity!) Harv's an excellent pilot and, of course, a tough old broad like the Beauty doesn't go down easily. There was an ambulance waiting on the field because there wasn't a soul on the plane who wasn't dead or wounded in some way. After dropping my bombs, I'd gone to my other post, the nose gun, and shot at the bandits. I got two, I think, but recall taking some bullets myself. My adrenaline was pumping so hard I scarcely noticed until we were in the clear. I think I might have been still conscious when the plane finally landed but passed out in the ambulance. That was all I remembered until English Nurse Brown. Last night I dreamt of her. She's simply beautiful. There's nothing extraordinary about any of her features, but the way they're composed is a masterpiece. I especially like her smile, like the sun, filling my whole world with light.

5 November 1942

What is it about this woman, this Charlotte
Brown? She's pure and clean in her starched
uniform. I can tell by the way she carries herself
and the way she speaks she's not just a nurse.
She's an aristocrat—yet one without pretension.
To this point, I've done no more than hold her
hand. I've felt her cool skin on mine as she
bathes me or wipes the sweat from my forehead.
Sometimes, she touches me with her long,
elegant fingers. I haven't touched her at all.
Perhaps with any other woman in the world, I
would, but Charlotte's special.

Oh my God, this Charlotte's my mother.

I see her smiling face when I dream and see
her lovely breasts freely bouncing as she runs
naked and uninhibited through the woods, as
my tvarsch knows she has done in the past.
I feel better simply seeing her. And I don't
know why. She's far from the only nurse who
attends to me—the place's full of them. Many
are pretty, sexy, and friendly, but as far as I'm
concerned, they're no more than wallpaper. It's
an open secret here many of the nurses take their
recovered patients out for 'sunset therapy.' And
as I've improved, I've had my share of offers
from the other nurses. I've no interest. Perhaps
it was my brush with death, but now when I
look back on the endless parade of girls in New
York, it seems extraordinarily empty. It was fun
and very flattering, but I now realize I acted
very badly. I wish I could make atonement. And
perhaps I am. Charlotte performs her nursing
duties with great care, but I know she doesn't

give sunset therapy. And that's wonderful. I now
know I can't live without this woman. I'll ask her
to marry me. My tvarsch, since the crash, is not
always working, so I'll have the pure joy or pain
of her reply.

In the footlocker, deeper down, Ashley found a framed and
bright color picture of Charlotte in three-quarter profile. Her
green eyes make strong contact with the camera. Curly, bright
red hair, done up in a fashionable complex roll, is atop her heart-
shaped face. Her cheekbones stand out in shadowed contrast.
Her eyebrows are thin, and her opaque lipstick reflects the light
of the flash. She wears a tan uniform jacket with an unfamiliar
pin on the left lapel. Her breasts gracefully round the fabric of
her dark, high-necked blouse. Across the lower left, written in
a very beautiful hand, "Spence Darling, All My Love, Forever.
Charlotte." Ashley's heart pounded so hard he could scarcely
think as, through the years, her life-like colors reached out and
intoxicated him. While he recalled having seen her before, he
could not remember where. Nonetheless, he began to study her
as a monk would an icon. Annie certainly was her granddaughter.
Why couldn't this lovely lady have raised me after giving me
life? A mischievous glint shone in her eyes, so she would have
been fun, unlike dour Patricia.

7 November 1942

I was sitting in my chair when she came in. The
light of the late fall day caught the highlights in
her hair. She said I'd be going back to duty soon.
The flight surgeon said I was 'right as rain.'

I screwed up my courage and asked her out.
She looked at me quizzically before asking if I
meant sundowning. I shook my head. I meant
a proper date. She replied there was nowhere
to really go, besides a small Officer's Club on

the base. Shaking her head, she said it would
be best not to. I didn't buy her rejection and
quickly asked her why not. She smiled and said
we were friends and she'd like to keep it that
way. I told her I simply wished to buy her a
drink. She shook her head and said she'd seen
my ilk before. Rich, smart, handsome lads who
treat women as nothing more than a vessel for
their lust. Once they finish, they hurriedly make
excuses, leave and, should the woman find
herself in a family way, she should be a 'good
sport.' After all, it was 'just one of those things
as your Cole Porter so quaintly put it.' She'd
seen her sister nurses in such straights from
Yanks. 'Not for me, thank you very much. And
even if I was fortunate that way, my knickers or
brassiere could easily find their way into flight
rooms, as a lad's trophy.'

I told her I thought she knew me better than
that. She made a gesture with her hand I thought
indicated uncertainty. Or possibility. She said
shortly I would return to duty. She would change
the sheets and another Yank would take my
place. For her, it had been a constant cycle of
brave, handsome young men, that, had she met
anywhere else, 'well, it might be a different
story, but here we are.' She smiled. She has
listened to our stories and our lives. 'You lot are
all unaware of one small detail, you all are dead.
I have already lost one husband to the war, a
pilot back in 1940. One was quite enough, thank
you very much.'

I countered that no one can help her—the pure
and patriotic war widow, 'For King and Country

and all that.' I said I may just be another sad sack
to her, but I thought she was the most beautiful,
wonderful creature I'd ever met.

Ashley stopped, so choked up he could not even speak. He
put the diary down until he regained his composure.

She was right. I was dead, or, at least, in the land
of the dead. I knew that. The war was going to
be long. However, after my 25th mission, six
more, I was free to go home. Or, wherever I
choose. She smiled mischievously, 'I know who
you really are. I recently read your journal as I
became curious about why you were so different
than all my other Yanks. You're certainly a
ladies' man. I like a man who knows what he's
doing between the sheets. As long as he remains
faithful. Would you be faithful?' I replied, 'for
you, I'd be totally faithful to the end of time.'
She nodded. 'Was I truly Sergei Dmitrovich
Iskandarov?' I nodded. 'I am ready for our date.'

At the O club, we spoke about the War and she
asked me, among other topics, if I was fully
committed to a non-Soviet Russia? I nodded.
She said she was too. I didn't press the point at
that time. During our second drink, I realized,
regardless of how long I may have left, I simply
couldn't live without her. I asked her to marry
me. 'I should love to be your wife.' She kissed
me like no one ever has. There are still a million
questions in my mind about all this. I'm sure
they will be resolved in good time.

10 November 1942

Yesterday, we were married in the small
Anglican chapel on the hospital grounds. David

helped us get a two-week leave and we found
a hotel. The first time, as she eagerly guided
me into her, I paused, ever so briefly, enjoying
a moment of pure bliss. Being there felt so
completely right I knew she was the one for
whom I had waited my whole life. I looked
down at her and her sublime smile said she felt
the same. She's tender, loving and giving, the
fulfillment of all I ever wanted or desired in a
woman and companion and she's promised me a
houseful of children. I'd like nothing more.

25 November 1942

Even though we only left our hotel once, in order
to meet Charlotte's parents, our time together
seemed only an instant. We talked about the
future, and the past. We laughed, we cried and
achieved a level of intimate communication I've
never experienced with anyone. Not even Nadia.
We parted tearfully, and I've already written to
her. The memory of our time together will keep
me warm through my next six missions. Indeed,
the rest of my life.

Glued to the page, a small picture showed Spencer and
Charlotte in their dress uniforms, both smiling happily outside
the stone chapel where they married.

26 November 1942

I went up to London with Harv and Mac to
meet with David. He has asked us to go on a
very important mission, a low-level bombing
in a B-24. Harv replied he's a Fortress pilot
and knows nothing about the '24. I made the
same protest about my bombing experience,

which is all high altitude. David smiled and said
he needed all the experienced crews he could
get his hands on and we would be thoroughly
trained beforehand. I said OK and Harv and Mac
nodded. We're replacing a pilot, co-pilot and
bombardier killed during an especially nasty raid
on the Taranto Italian Naval Base. We're leaving
today to join the crew on their practice runs
in another location. I know I risk never seeing
Charlotte again, but a love like the one we have
is truly eternal. Besides, with my recovery, my
tvarsch has returned. I'll be OK.

Wow, his tvarsch *could be as fallible as mine, and he was
playing for much higher stakes.*

22 July 1943

I have been so busy training for the big show that
I haven't had time to write almost anything. In
the time I'm not training or sleeping, I think of
little else besides Charlotte. I should be with her
for support and for the birth of our child. At the
same time, I can't abandon my buddies. When I'm
sleeping, I still have vivid nightmares about the
final mission of the Beauty and my dead crewmates
who continue to haunt me, even when I'm awake.
It's also hot as blazes here and hard to sleep in the
first place. I wonder who came up with the twenty-
five missions? Some desk jockeys at HQ probably
did psyche stress tests and found all crews cracked
up after twenty-two missions, or something. Even
if I should make that goal, I'd like to become an
instructor, so I can be close to Charlotte.

I'm probably drinking too much at night in the
O club. The time's dragging. I don't know when

the show starts, but scuttlebutt says it'll be soon.
I want to get the damn thing over with, so I can
then be back in England with my Charlotte and
our child. My tvarsch's not good on my chances.
Nevertheless, I think that's more a reflection of
my mood right now. I remain confident our crew
will successfully return to base after bombing the
crap out of our target. The Intel guys tell us that the
target's lightly defended because the Krauts think
it's beyond our bomber's range. But now, I want to
write to Charlotte while I still have a little free time.

That was Spencer's last entry. But Ashley found two letters
pinned in the diary. The first was from Spencer to Charlotte,
dated 22 July 1943.

My Dearest,

I am in receipt of your letter of the fifteenth.
And I'm not pleased I must go on this mission.
However, since it's David asking, how can I
reasonably refuse him, after all he has done for
me, for us? After all, had he not rescued me
from Odessa, I wouldn't even be alive, in all
probability. I hope I will return before our baby
is born. However, if I'm delayed in transit, I
know you will be fine in childbirth.

Yes, we should have been more careful when we
were together, and this is a terrible time to bring
a new innocent life into the world. However, I'm,
as always, the optimist. We must build the bright
new world, which with God's help, we'll live to
see. I can't imagine any lady stronger than you.
I know you'll be as wonderful a mother to our
baby as you are in every other aspect of your life.
I count the minutes until we are reunited.

All My Love, My Most Precious, Spence.

P.S. I've been told that after this mission, I'm free.

The second letter from Charlotte to Spencer was dated 29 July 1943.

My Dearest,

I'm overjoyed about your freedom, but when I received your last letter, I cried. For you have caused me shame. I was being selfish. I desire so much to have you here with me. To hold me, to put your hand on my big belly, when our love kicks. You're right. As I'm now Mrs. Spencer Dryden Talbott and we're truly one, we may refuse David nothing after all he has done for us. I know your mission's important and you'll return safely. That's all that matters. To be the wonderful father I know you will be to our love. I was also wrong in my letter. A love like ours cannot be careful. I'm right where I have always dreamt to be. Carrying the baby of the man I adore.

Should we be blessed by a girl, I should like to call her 'Love, Amour,' or something like that. If blessed by a boy, I would suggest something. You and your father are estranged. Therefore, I think it should be a lovely gesture if we named him 'Dmitri,' or perhaps the Anglicized version of the name, although I am uncertain what that may be. As you point out, our baby's the future and the new world. Such a world begins with reconciliation between fathers and sons. Finally, have no concern for me as I bring our love into the world. I count the seconds until you are back in my arms, my most beloved. C.

Charlotte wrote with green ink in a small precise cursive that gracefully flowed. How strange and wonderful to read your parents' most intimate thoughts about you and each other. But the incredible, wonderful fact that he had grown in this magnificent lady's womb and her willing acceptance of the pain of his birth made him feel wanted as never before. After nearly fifty years, he had his real mother in the glamorous, yet mysterious, Charlotte. He knew she would have been wonderfully loving to her little Dmitri. No, he would be Spencer like his father, Spencer Talbott Junior. He reveled in the sound of it. Despite what he may have thought previously about Spencer's pre-war life, when it counted, he had stood up. He also loved the way Spencer respected and adored Charlotte. He was someone to be proud of. Someone to call "Dad." He silently asked if he would ever meet Charlotte. Then it struck him. Spencer's mission, according to Randell, had been August first. And Charlotte's letter was scented with lavender, while Spencer's had both of their scents. Spencer never saw this wonderful letter. And that made Ashley first sad and then angry. He turned the page and found a brief entry and immediately recognized Patricia's overly fussy cursive in black ink.

10 August 1943

I am Lady Patricia Sternwood, Principal Matron
of Princess Mary's Royal Air Force Nursing
Service. My younger sister, Charlotte Elizabeth,
known in these pages as 'Nurse Brown' and
'Charlotte' gave birth to a healthy male baby,
half a stoneweight, at this facility earlier this
week. Sadly, there were complications and she is
now gone. The father, Captain Spencer Talbott,
U.S.A.A.F., did not return from his mission.
(He was posthumously promoted.) I hate this
abominable war. We have already lost far too
many good men since 1940. As closest relative
to my beloved Charlotte, I am adopting the

baby and am affianced to Major David Cooper,
U.S.A.A.F. We met at an embassy reception
some time ago. The major is a widower. I am a
widow. In the event, he had promised Captain
Talbott that he would provide for his wife
and baby should he not return. These events
have necessitated a change in our plans. Our
nuptials are set for one week from today, so
we may provide the baby a proper home. As to
the question of a name for the baby, we have
decided that the baby should have an American
name. In light of the major's Southern heritage
and because the baby bears him such strong
resemblance, we have decided upon Ashley, after
the Leslie Howard character from "Gone with
the Wind", Ashley Wilkes.

Ashley felt as though he had been punched in the stomach.
To be named after an indecisive wimp like Ashley Wilkes
seemed really too much to bear. Damn Patricia had done this to
him. David would not have. As he began to wonder if he could
change his name, he closed his eyes and cursed the emotional
rollercoaster of the diaries.

Ronnie had said both his parents were alive in 1955. And he
knew Natalya was born in 1955. But what were his parents doing
in Russia? And why would a strong woman like Charlotte have
allowed her daughter to be raped, whipped, branded and generally
abused? Because she was not there? But, he now understood what
Ronnie had told him yesterday… "It's fair to say she had that life
so you wouldn't have to." Natalya could have been born first
and he second, given the randomness of multiple births with the
same couple. His sister could now be reading about her brother,
a *zek*, and the horrors inflicted on him by Colonel Polinkova. He
felt the wetness in his eyes begin to spill over onto his cheeks.
Looking up through blurred eyes, he saw Charlotte wearing

a white nightgown, her long red hair flowing and speaking in Russian, "Sergei Sergeyovich Iskandarov, I have always been with you whenever you needed me, and I held you and kissed your forehead. You must come to me and your sister, Natalya, in our houses. Your father remains the love of my life. Do not fear Colonel Polinkova, because you are smart and strong. *Adieu*."

Ashley wiped his eyes on his sleeve and heard Annie. "Dad, are you all right? Why are you crying?"

"I've just received some wonderful news. How long have you been standing there?"

"I heard a noise and just now came up. Obviously, you fell off the bench."

Wow, he thought, *I didn't realize I'd done that. But my mother actually spoke to me. And I remember when the red-haired lady came in my dreams to comfort me after a hard day at Buckley.*

Annie went over to the picture of Charlotte. She picked it up and stared. "Who's this? She's so beautiful and has the most extraordinary eyes." She laughed. "I bet she really turned you on."

"Not so much. She's your grandmother. Don't you the see the resemblance with her red hair and green eyes?"

"Dad, you've been working too hard. This is a black-and-white photo from a long time ago. Based on her hairstyle, mid-forties I'd guess. No, wait. I think I know." Annie sat on the floor, legs crossed, holding the picture against her chest as serenity and contentment swept her face. Gradually a smile came. "I'm certain this is the lady I've seen in my visions." She laughed. "I'm sorry, and my comment wasn't appropriate. She's the one, and she's alive. And yes, she has green eyes and red hair."

Ashley nodded. "Apology accepted. Now, where is she?"

"In that fortress or nunnery. Remember? That's all I know." Annie looked around at the two opened footlockers. "Dad, what's going on? What's all this stuff?"

He briefly told her about his visit with Ronnie and the two diaries. When he finished, she smiled. "Sweet. This is so cool.

I've seen that picture of Spencer. God, what an amazing couple these two must've made."

Ashley nodded and held up David's diary. "You should start with this one. It's grandpa's diary from World War I. Some of it is disturbing, but I know you can handle it. Since you're in your tennis whites, it must be time to get ready for our doubles match with Rand and Deborah."

NINE

Saturday & Sunday, 29 &30 May 1993
Quaker Mount, NY

1.

During tennis, lunch and a leisurely afternoon at Quaker Lake, Ashley was able to compartmentalize to forget about the diaries. But, upon returning home, while he remembered his mother Charlotte's dreams' loving nature, he had forgotten details. Clearly, in her most recent visit, she had called him Sergei. But what had she called him when he was a child? And, most importantly, he could not remember whether she had ever revealed being his mother before her nocturnal visits ended in the late summer of 1957, just before he left for Lawrenceville. He wanted to search his dreams for important clues about her but had never searched his *tvarsch* to recover a faint memory. Knowing this would tax his brain, he took Uncle Francis's magic elixir, went to his old room, closed the door and lay on the single bed where she had come to him and focused his *tvarsch*. Through billions of thoughts, ideas and memories, he began to sort them out until he heard "Farewell, Sergei, I have soothed you as well as I am able. You, my most beloved son, are no longer a child. Now, as a young man, going off to boarding school, my charge is done, and I must, with great reluctance, leave you. Your sister needs my full-time protection, and your father, the love of my

life, is in serious trouble. Never doubt I always have, and always
will, love you."

As Ashley tried to open his eyes, his head and eyes throbbed,
and he could dimly see by the clock that about an hour had passed.
He closed them again and slept. The wonderful aroma of Annie's
cooking interrupted his sleep, and he awoke feeling very hungry.

2.

At dinner, he answered Annie's many questions about David's
diary and quickly realized that she had a very different take on it.
While interested in his wartime experiences, she was captivated
with Countess X, "a very strong and smart woman." Annie
also knew that the countess was Sophia, her great-grandmother
and that being the fourth generation, she would have a strong
pyordarsch and the power eventually to prophesy.

Once back in the attic, Ashley went to Dmitri's large wooden
trunk, at one time elegant. But now, with most of the decoration
stripped off and its wormholes, bullet holes and many cracks and
scuffs, it seemed very stark. But, from the highly polished brass
plaque over the locks, Ashley translated the French:

> Dmitri Sergeyovich, Prince Iskandarov,
> Colonel of the 23rd Russian
> Imperial Guards Cavalry Regiment

A smaller wooden plaque below had the same information in
Russian. As Ashley opened the trunk, the wail of the hinges filled
the room. First, on top, he found a framed, face-down picture
and, in faded black ink, someone had written in French: "General
Mikhail Aleksandrovich, Count Kolchak, Sophia Sergevna
Iskandarova, Countess Kolchaka. Brother of Countess, Colonel
Dmitri Sergeyovich, Prince Iskandarov at the Helicon Estate,
The Crimea, Saint Sergius Day, May 4th 1912. The Confirmation
of the Countess's Second Time Being With Child."

Turning it over, he studies the hand-colored photograph.
Two men, with Sophia in the middle, stand before large, ornate

open doors to a ballroom, washed in late afternoon light. A young Sophia, dressed in green, smiles and displays her classic hourglass figure—full pushed-up corseted breasts, cinched waist and wide hips. She wears a gold chain with a large, gold Orthodox cross and is holding the arm of the count, a very tall man on her right and considerably older than her. He has a pointed black beard over a white, heavily bemedaled tunic with black trousers and is also smiling. On her left is Dmitri, who very much resembles Sophia. He is in a dark-green officer's dress uniform with a large, waxed handlebar moustache obscuring his mouth. All three are wearing black boots.

Under it, in Russian, in a different hand, written in faded red ink, now almost brown, is:

> Those who were born in years of stagnation,
> do not remember their way.
> We, Children of Russia's fearful years,
> can forget nothing.
> Years that burnt everything to ashes!
> Do you bode madness or bring tidings of hope?
> Aleksandr Blok

Ashley shook his head. In 1912, these people were about to go through the hell of war, followed by civil war and terror with neither comprehensible nor rational limits; years that literally burned everything to ash. Nonetheless, Ashley had found a picture of his grandfather, grandmother and the count. Sergei would be about two at that time. Sophia's second child would be Sergei's brother, Alexei, but which man was his father? No doubt, this picture was meant to impress anyone who saw it with the count's height and virility, more than a memento of a particular day.

Below the picture, Ashley found Dmitri's thick diary. He smiled at the Iskandarovs and their diaries. All strong egos. He again sat on the Quaker bench and began reading aloud.

10 July 1917

In all my previous journals, I have written in French, as would be expected. However, I shall write this one in English, so that the Hidden One shall have a clear understanding of what I am about to commit to paper.

Ashley wondered if he was the Hidden One, like Moses, but did not fully understand the term. No, Sergei was Dmitri's hidden son in America. That made more sense. His *tvarsch* remained annoyingly mute.

15 July 1917.

I shall remember this day for ever. As I mentioned in my previous journal, we had been advancing with General Kornilov against the Austrian Third Army of Tersztyansky in Galicia for the past two weeks. The Austrians are terrible soldiers. However, today we encountered Germans dug in with machine guns situated at the far end of a field. Or, at least, what had formerly been a wheat field. Stray stalks remained amongst the rotting corpses from a previous battle. The field was in a Carpathian valley with very steep walls. With no way around it, we must go through. And my will shall accept nothing less than breakthrough. The Huns, unlike the polyglot Austrians, have strong will. We must show the Krauts we are no less warriors. I have read Nietzsche in the original German, which I speak fluently.

For approximately two hours, I led my men attacking the German on foot. Although we had success at points, we were, overall, unsuccessful and retreated with great loss of life. Back at our

lines, the socialist representatives of the enlisted
soldiers said that they could no longer continue
either the attack or the offensive. Realizing
that refusal of their request was tantamount to
death, I thanked my men for their valor and we
withdrew. That was the end of my war. As we
withdrew, our formation began to disintegrate.
Ever since the Emperor was forced to abdicate,
we live in a strange twilight world, neither
government nor anarchy, where nothing is clear.
The 23rd, formerly Imperial Guards, Cavalry
Regiment no longer exists. There is no longer
anything imperial to guard. And we have not
been anywhere near full force for quite some
time, what with no replacements or supplies.
Today, most of my most valiant and dedicated
troops were killed and my will had also failed.

Ashley put the diary down. For some reason, he ached and
felt drained, as though he had gone through the attack himself.
He picked up Colonel Iskandarov's high collared, faded gray-
green tunic. The light-gray piping remained firm on the sleeves.
A thin brown leather strap ran from the thicker Sam Brown belt
to the right epaulet. He felt the unknown presence in the attic
as he breathed in the fabric. Nothing could mask the smell of a
combat officer—gunpowder, blood and sweat. Dmitri had been
wearing this as he led his men, slaughtered by machine guns, the
lethal technology of a new world. Ashley left the trunk open, the
diary on top of the picture.

3.

When Ashley came down from the attic, the house was quiet, and
he fell into bed, quickly asleep.

Later, Ashley finds himself riding a horse and is immediately
annoyed by the large moustache tickling his nose, which reeked

of nicotine and smoke. Looking down, he is not only wearing Colonel Iskandarov's uniform, but the hands are larger and younger than his.

"Thunder, Your Grace? Or artillery?" Someone asks in French.

He looks back at another man riding a few paces behind him. "Your Grace?"

Uncertain what is going on, he searches the tunic's pockets for the watch Dmitri must have and takes it out. Almost four in the afternoon and by the position of the sun, they are going east, in retreat. All around him on a vast, dry plain, he sees soldiers in dusty uniforms individually or clustered in groups, all dully trudging in the same general direction. He also sees the few remaining cavalrymen and feels the sun beating down on him and has an incredible thirst, as well as overall fatigue. Who could this other man be? Yes, his batman. What to call him? Yes. Georgi?

He asks in French, "Georgi, what is the date today?"

"It is Monday, the seventeenth of July, Your Grace."

"Thank you, Georgi. I think it is nothing more than summer thunder. The Germans could not be advancing so rapidly."

Ashley knows he is lying.

"Very good, Your Grace."

Even though Ashley finds it irritating to be called "Your Grace," he could not tell Georgi to call him Dmitri. Besides, he needs to accept what has happened and focus. This is July 17th, and the battle in the wheat field has been over for two days. These troops could easily turn on him and Georgi. Ashley is armed with a revolver of some sort, which he un-holsters to check the chambers for bullets. He also has a sabre on his left. He had done some sabre fencing in school. This one appears larger than he was used to, but the basic principles remain the same. He looks at some foot soldiers as he rides by. Their uniforms are in tatters. Pants are ripped and dirty, their feet are bare and bloody, and they reek of sweat, filth, cordite and rot. Their eyes frighten him as he feels the hatred directed toward him, only restrained by a thin tissue of tradition and order. Had he been in their situation, he would have been angry as well. These aristocratic officers did not lead their troops to Berlin and victory… only to death and defeat. Now, Mother Russia lays prone and helpless, waiting for the German gang rape.

"Hey there, I want your horse."

At first, Ashley does not realize he is being addressed in Russian. "Hey, old shit, I said I want your fuckin' horse."

Ashley looks down at a tall ragged man with a rifle and a long bayonet pointed directly at him. Ashley slows his horse and says in Russian, "Move on, soldier, I shall not report you."

"Report me? You act as though we still have fuckin' army here. Well, guess what, you dumb son-of-shit, we don't." He fires a bullet at Ashley, who feels it barely miss his ear. Scared, he refuses to give in to his fear.

"Now, move on. I know you're tired."

The man shakes his head as he reloads. "Tired? What does son of whore exploiter like you know about tired? I'm almost fuckin' empty. I want your fuckin' horse. Get off before I count to three or my next shot will blow your shit-full head off."

Ashley looks around him. The troops have stopped and stare at him. He knows, given any excuse, they would tear him to pieces.

"One."

The tissue of tradition has begun to rip. He looks briefly at Georgi. Some troops surround his horse and appear ready to kill him. He looks back at the soldier and notices his dirty red Bolshevik armband and hears the cock of his rifle.

"Two."

All right, you Red bastard, enough. Ashley quickly dismounts and stands opposite Red.

Ashley speaks loudly in Russian, so all can hear him. "If you want my horse, you can have it. However, you'll have to kill me first. And you don't have the cock to do that, do you, comrade? We still have enough army that they hang mutinous troops if you are not half-flogged to death first. Right now, someone is writing down your name." As expected, Red momentarily looks to his right. Smoothly, Ashley pushes the rifle away with his left hand while un-holstering his pistol with his right. Red accidentally pulls the trigger, discharging the rifle into the air. "You are not much without bullet, are you, comrade?" He fires directly into Red's face, and he falls at Ashley's feet.

"Your Grace, behind you."

He turns to confront a bear of a man charging him with his bayoneted rifle. No words this time. Ashley draws his sabre, deftly moves out of the way and slices Bear hard in his side before a second blow to his neck. He hears the breaking of bone and strikes his neck again before Bear falls. Mercy for a wounded man? No. This isn't Fifth Avenue. No place for the quality of mercy here. He fires final bullets into both men's heads and looks around for other attackers. Instead, a cry goes up from the troops. "Three cheers for Colonel Iskandarov."

Ashley remounts and, standing up in his stirrups, raises his bloody sabre in triumph for all ranks to see. "All right men, fall in. Look sharp there. We marched out as an army, and we'll march back same way. Mother Russia needs us now more than ever, to defend our wives, mothers, sisters and children from Hun. We have fought good a fight, only to be betrayed by our own cowardly government. We have nothing to be ashamed of, so let us return to our homes as soldiers, not a mob. Fall in and form up two neat ranks."

Again, a cheer goes up as the men form into relatively neat ranks. Marching, the lines become straighter, until finally they march as a functional unit. So much so, that as they pass by, other stragglers fall in.

Georgi says in French, "Your Grace, I fear your leg is bleeding. That second soldier cut you with his bayonet."

Ashley looks down and shakes his head. "It is nothing. A mere scratch."

"Pardon, Your Grace, but who knows where that bayonet has been?"

"Georgi, you make an excellent point. But I cannot stop right now to tend to it. The formation will break up if the troops see me wounded."

"Very good, Your Grace. I shall attend to it later and wash it out thoroughly with iodine."

Ashley nods and thinks, *Great. I wish antibiotics had been invented by now.* Nonetheless, he feels great pride in what he had done, even though he knows he is swimming against history's tide. In this small piece of the world, he has restored a sense of order, at least for a day. More importantly, he survived and gave his troops something they needed.

"If I might say so, Your Grace, you were magnificent back there with those men."

"But?"

"Your Grace?"

"I hear the hesitation in your voice. Go ahead and tell me what you truly think. I need to know."

"Very well, Your Grace. You seem slightly different this afternoon, and when you seemed to hesitate, I became concerned. In the past, you would have dispatched such a man without a moment's thought."

"True, but now we live in a republic. So, we must at least try democratic measures before we resort to the old ways."

"Very good, Your Grace. I sincerely hope I have not overstepped my—"

"Not at all, Georgi. I asked for the truth. You gave it."

"Thank you, Your Grace."

They rode in silence until another bolt of thunder woke Ashley. Shaken and drenched in sweat as he went to shower, he felt pain in his right thigh where he had been wounded. After drying off, he carefully cleaned the wound with liberally applied antibiotic cream. Sitting naked on the closed toilet, he felt nauseous because his fear was rising up as he realized Red or the Bear could have actually killed him. And what would have happened had he died in 1917? Would he wake up and be back in

1993? Or, would his whole existence be wiped out as though he
had never existed? Or, would Annie find him dead in his bed of
a gunshot or bayonet wound? And what of Colonel Iskandarov?
Would he die as well? And what would happen to young Sergei?
Where would he be? Without his father, his life would have been
very different, just enough so that Ashley, in his present form,
might not exist. He quickly rose and lifted the seat as red, green
and brown from his mouth poured into the bowl and would not
stop even when nothing remained.

Later, on his knees, still clinging to the porcelain, his
brain began to work. He did not even know what to call what
had happened with Colonel Iskandarov. For the first time in his
journey he had felt real fear. Finally, able to get up, he decided
that a slight wound, confusion and fear were no reason to stop.
The journey was a test he could not afford to fail.

4.

Early the next morning, Ashley awoke with the pain still in his
leg, put on his robe and limped up to the attic. He knew the answer
to last night would be there. He sat and eagerly began with the
next entry of 17 July 1917.

> I rode my horse east back to Sakartvelo with my
> batman, Georgi. He remains loyal. Perhaps out of
> custom, or, perhaps, he needs his salary. (I have
> been paying him out of my own pocket for some
> time. Although, I have not been paid either.)
> As I made my way home, I am very aware that
> many officers have been fatally shot either by
> their troops or by stragglers and deserters. A
> bolshevikii with his rifle and bayonet stopped
> me as I was riding. He demanded, in a most
> coarse manner, my money and horse. Knowing
> he meant to kill me as well, I dismounted
> and walked straight up to him and stared him

down. When he turned away, I drew my sabre
and shattered his spine at the neck before then
running him through. If he would not respect his
superiors, he would, in his last moments, respect
his betters. I felt great surprise at my strength.
It was as though I was actually two men. And
it was a sensation that did not endure much
beyond the encounter. Otherwise, there was no
way in Heaven I should have bested my second
assailant. Georgi warned me of another attack,
this time with a huge and angry man who came
at me with his rifled bayonet. I dispensed him as
well, although with a slight wound that Georgi
later cleaned out with iodine. I recognized him,
Zauryad-Praporshchik and thirty-year veteran,
Mikhail Brodinski, up until now, my highest
ranking, most loyal non-commissioned officer.
He was heavily involved in the wheat field battle.
I assume that was what caused him to break faith
with me. I truly regret his loss, but if he is no
longer loyal to me, I fear I have almost no one
left, aside from Georgi. I, thus, felt surprised
when my formation reformed after I made a
brief speech about how we had been betrayed
by an incompetent and corrupt government. We
had fought with honor and bravery. We need to
protect our country, our families from whatever
is coming next. We left as soldiers and so shall
we return. Despite my brave words, as we rode
on, I smelled trouble, borne on the hot summer
wind, although I do not know in what form.
Perhaps, the Huns, perhaps worse. Whatever it
is, at this point, we are impotent to stop it.

Ashley was struck by Dmitri saying that in the encounter he had the strength of two men. He had felt the exact same way with his combat and had initially thought this was his adrenaline. The metaphysics of this were way too complicated to untangle, but he sensed this had not only been important, but also would be in the future. He put the diary down and left for his morning coffee and breakfast before church in Woodinville.

As he ground the coffee, his hand fell from the grinder. He knew his *tvarsch* had become much more powerful, but it could now be powerful enough to have sent him back like that. Also, it could not be an *Andronyi*, which seemed to belong to women. The attic's unknown spirit had left, and must have been Dmitri, who, presumably, would have had the power to do such a thing. Resuming grinding, he wished he knew more about his *tvarsch*. Why wasn't there some kind of user's manual?

5.

After breakfast, Annie questioned Ashley's limp on the way to church. He asked her if he had hurt himself playing tennis or if she had noticed a wound on his leg at the lake. She studied him before shaking her head. Ashley thought she knew something but did not press it. After lunch, he returned to the attic.

6 August 1918

I have learned this day the bolshevikii gangsters
in the Urals, at, or near, Ekaterinburg, have
murdered not only the Emperor and the Empress
but also the Heir and the four Grand Duchesses.
I can find no words to express over this outrage.
These bandits have shown their true colors. I
hope the peasants shall now see this filth for
what they truly are.

27 March 1919

Today, I arrived at Odessa, where I shall be
visiting with dear Sophie. She has written me
that her lover, David Cooper, an American
Expeditionary Forces Sergeant-Major, will be
able to get her and her agents to Paris. I found
David very bright and resourceful. I did notice
that after our conversation, he went to another
room, took out his journal and pen and tried
to engage the pen on paper but could not. I
know this problem well. When you have seen
the horrors of war first-hand, it is often very
difficult to clear your mind to record quotidian
events. I gave him my advice and he was soon
writing. I have new respect for him as he is more
of a warrior than I first thought. However, I
should add that we were not completely honest
with the young man. He thinks he is delivering
Sergei to his mother, Tanya, in Paris. In reality,
he is delivering Sophie, Sergei's mother, to
Tanya, who, in reality, is Tatiana Nikolaevna,
the twenty-two-year-old former nurse, who has
only recently come out of hiding after her rescue
from the bolshevikii. She has learned how to
be inconspicuous and now moves around Paris
as a middle-aged French woman. However,
she also knows everyone of importance in the
émigré community and has been busy fund
raising and recruiting agents for our Bleu agency.
Once Sophie joins her, we shall have a most
formidable organization!

Ashley smiled. He had researched Tanya. Tatiana with her
patronym, *Nikolaevna*, meant she could well be Czar Nicholas's
second daughter, who had been a nurse during the war and

would then be twenty-two. It all seemed to fit. Perhaps her jewel-encrusted corset had saved her life, and she had been rescued prior to being tossed into an old mining pit by the Bolsheviks. Ashley wanted to learn more about this very intriguing woman. Ashley again wished David and he could have spoken about this.

2 September 1919.

I rode into the ruins of Kiev today. During the past year, the city has changed from German occupation to Ukrainian nationalist rule, which degenerated into anarchy and inflation. The bolshevikii seized the city in February and Ukrainian and Russian White forces recently deposed them. General Deniken sees Ukrainian forces as our enemy. I am not so certain. We need allies against the bolshevikii. I am to report back to the General.

As I ride my horse, Decius, I see people left hanging from lampposts along the streets and boulevards. The people scurrying out of the ruins are skeletal and hollow-eyed, as though they do not fully comprehend anything. It is like progressing through a city of the dead. I hear shots and arrive to see several chekists, badly beaten, be executed by firing squad. I feel nothing for them. Most chekists in Ukraine are Jews. Damned clever of Dzerzinskii to play on religious hatred like that. But then, that is why he is the overlord of the cheka. Clever and shrewd with no morals or conscience—a master butcher. Proceeding on further, I see our soldiers looting what little remains and raping ragged, skeletal women and girls who lie passively and silently, too starved, deranged or exhausted to care. For

all I know, they may already be dead. As I near
the railway station, a pogrom is in full swing in
the ghetto. This war and the last one, now some
five continuous years, have warped my soul.
May God have mercy on me, but I have seen so
much death, suffering, blood, cannibalism and
starvation that it now seems commonplace. I
had a dream last night that I shall spend the rest
of my life fighting an endless war. In which it is
all against all until civilization is ripped away
and once more barbarism is supreme. Until two
ragged barbarian armies meet on some field that,
once upon a time, grew wheat. They fight and
slaughter for one final wheat stalk that remains.
When we have won, we begin to fight amongst
ourselves until there is only one. I, as that lone
victor, eat the raw wheat kernels. I look around
and see vultures so gorged on human flesh they
are no longer able to fly. Rats as big as dogs, and
wild dogs running in packs, now with a taste for
human flesh. They attack me, and I am too weak
to resist. That is how it shall all end. With the
most pathetic of whimpers, the Third Rome is no
more.

Ashley remembered this Third Rome theory was controversial
when he studied it in college. After Emperor Diocletian split
the Roman Empire into east and west in the fourth century AD,
the west empire fell in 476, while the east, as the Byzantine
Empire, with its capital at Constantinople, lasted until 1453. The
Byzantine emperor had sent now St. Cyril to Christianize their
northern neighbors. Cyril succeeded and also gave the Russians
an alphabet, the Cyrillic. So, it made sense that the last Byzantine
emperor's niece, Princess Sophia Palaeologa married Prince
Ivan III of Muscovy, bringing all the pomp and ceremony of

the Byzantine court to this backwater. The prince became czar (caesar), and the Roman tradition continued in Moscow until 1917, with the abdication of Czar Nicholas II. Unfortunately, Sophia had no legal right to do what she did. Nonetheless, this was a story that never really died among Russians.

On a positive note, I met my cousin, Andrei
Ivanovich Iskandarov, a Major in the Guards. He
is preparing for a highly secret mission here in
Ukraine. Suffice to say that when he succeeds,
it shall have great bearing on this infernal war.
He is also the man who rescued Tanya from
the bolshevikii and brought her to Paris in the
summer of 1918.

Ashley began to skim as Dmitri continued his descriptions, but the slaughter, the burning of villages, the torturing of spies and partisans nauseated him. Finally, Dmitri reported favorably to General Deniken, who, nonetheless, ruthlessly suppressed Ukrainians and encouraged pogroms in the lands he controlled. As a result of lack of popular support, the Reds stopped the White drive on Moscow in September 1919 at Tula, and they began a long retreat. Dmitri knew the war, thanks to Deniken's stupidity, had now been lost. After a scorched earth fighting retreat, Dmitri and his troops evacuated Sevastopol, in the Crimea, in November 1920. He made no further comments about the success or failure of his cousin's mission. In the end, it probably made no difference.

3 June 1921

It is good to be back in Paris with ma chere
Sophie and Sergei. I treasure my time with
them, since it is so rare. It is also wonderful to
be among normal people again. I feel as though
I am beginning to regain my soul. The struggle
to recover the Motherland now intensifies with
financial backing from my principals. We shall

attack the gangsters from so many directions,
they shall truly be overwhelmed. Victory and
liberation shall be ours.

16 August 1922

With the Paris agency now fully staffed, I arrived
in Berlin yesterday with my assistant, Georgi.
We are here to build a new agency. With both
of us fluent in German, it should make our task
considerably easier. (While I somewhat admire
the Germans, I truly hate them simultaneously.)
It would be ideal to have Tanya with us, but
Berlin is full of cheka and so, far too dangerous
for her. We are all staying at the magnificent
Adlon Hotel, hard by the Brandenburg Gate. I
registered as Prince Iskandarov and the manager
insisted I have the suite our late Emperor
occupied when last here. May God have mercy
on his soul and those of the Imperial family.
Georgi has my second bedroom. We have British
pound sterling notes as well as American dollars
and Swiss francs from our salaries. So, we
will live well during the increasingly desperate
inflation, which is destroying Germany. I do
not care. The Germans have brought this on
themselves, by borrowing large sums for a short
war the Kaiser knew would end victoriously.
However, I have already discovered how
annoying it is when some group goes out on
strike and the lights disappear or the hotel no
longer has waiters.

Berlin is the new battleground with the
bolshevikii. Ever since Polish Marshal Jozef
Pilsudski defeated the red army at Warsaw, the

cheka has made Berlin its regional headquarters.
Should, God forbid, the reds triumph here, we
shall soon be fighting in streets of Paris, then
London, perhaps even New York one day.
Victory here and we contain them. Then we
attack.

18 August 1922

Yesterday I was walking in the Tiergarten, a
lovely park not far from the hotel, with my
security following at a discrete distance. I was
approached by three very pretty women I took
to be prostitutes. So, I sent them on their way.
I also observed couples freely and publicly
copulating in the park. Apparently, the prostitutes
are controlled by the government and fornication
is not against the law. But I developed an idea of
how I could humiliate German men.

Today, I put my plan into action. I spotted
an impoverished beauty and took her to the
luxurious department store Berliners call
'KaDaWe' on the 'Ku'damm,' as the main
avenue is known in the local vernacular. Having
purchased an ensemble worthy of a princess, I
brought her back to my suite. She dressed, and
we promenaded on the Unter der Linden. The
looks I receive from the humiliated German
men are worth the whole amount I have spent. It
would be a fortune for her. For me, it is merely
pocket change. My other purpose is, while
walking or promenading, studying Berliners. I
see many sullen men, presumably demobilized
veterans cheated by the government, who
'stabbed them in the back.' This is a myth that

appears to be gaining credence and does not
bode well for the future. After a while, I just
ignored them. They are not the ones who interest
me. I come from an ancient tradition that allows
me to do things that others cannot. However,
I know there are other traditions extant and I
wonder if I may detect them by some unusual
characteristic or trait. I always focus on the eyes,
but in summer on the streets, many of the most
interesting people are sporting sun-glasses. Are
they hiding something or merely shading their
eyes? Question with no answer.

15 October 1922

I have a newly issued League of Nations Nansen
passport for Russian émigrés and others who are
now officially stateless. Of course, I was able to
secure French citizenship for my entire family
some time ago. Having two different types of
passports is a very useful tool to have in my
profession. Especially, as I was able to get the
Nansens issued in several different names.

28 November 1922

I have made contact with officers of the German
Freicorps. They helped suppress the sparticists'
Rosa Luxembourg and Karl Leibnitz, who
had led a bloody and unsuccessful revolt to
create a bolshevikii 'republic' here back in
'19. The Freicorps are fighting the bolshevikii
in the Baltic States. I am also in contact with
representatives of Marshal Pilsudski of Poland,
who is still fighting and defeating, Trotsky's
red army. These two groups are our northern

bulwarks against the red plague. My backers are deeply involved in the financing of both groups. There are other anti-bolshevik groups forming in the so-called Cordon Sanitaire, those states bordering red Russia. They bear looking into and I have informed my principals about them. It is becoming clear the Germans shall be critical in the struggle because with the British and Americans substantially abandoning the anti-bolshevikii cause and the impotence of France, the Germans, by default, must.

1 May 1923

I received orders today that I should make contact with a 'Fraulein Ulrika,' My tvarsch tells me it is imperative I do this myself. She, reportedly, has some very valuable contacts and people I have not been able to reach. However, she is involved in the sex trade here, as a 'boot girl,' that is, a domina (goddess) or dominatrix. Her 'suitors,' her paying clients are all very important men, and some women, both in government and industry. Thus, it will very difficult to find her. I began investigating the Berlin prostitutes and found I had much to learn. They provide the wide range of perversions I am aware of. And some of which I cannot even conceive. Teutonic efficiency has been applied to vice. Prostitutes are organized according to specialty / perversion and are regularly checked for disease. Ironically, in a country where government seems totally impotent, it is able to regulate the joy girls. As a result, they are all catalogued, to be had for a modest fee. (Both

the directory and the girls.) It should also be
noted that the ranks of the girls are growing so
rapidly that any directory in existence is already
out of date on publishing. I bought a directory
and found twenty girls named 'Fraulein Ulrika.'
When I interviewed them, I found they ranged
in age from eight to about eighty. Most of
them were highly specialized and none of them
had even heard of the woman I was seeking.
However, one was a boot girl and I learned to
be wary of them. Their specialty is indicated by
their boot color and sub-specialty by the color
of their laces. For instance, the cruelest sport
venomous green boots, so the client has been
warned. Yellow laces indicate a piss domina, red,
a severe beating. I also learned that homosexual
men and women have a completely different
order. One prostitute suggested I should become
a regular at the hottest clubs. The police do
not make any arrests for vice because they
are primarily concerned in combatting the
armed bolshevikii and fascist gangs fighting in
the streets. I swear Sodom could never be as
degenerate as this.

5 May 1923

After becoming a regular at the Scala nightclub
on Lutherstrasse in the Schoenberg quarter,
I also frequent the bars and cabarets of the
Friedrichstrasse. While I have some leads, Ulrika
is clearly a woman who does not wish to be
found.

31 May 1923

I recently happened into a cabaret at Jagerstrasse
18 called the 'Weisse Maus' (The Little White
Mouse). There was a performer there I should
never forget. Anita Berber had a dancer's lithe
body and grace. She wore heavy dancer's
makeup on her face to the point where she
appeared to be a vampyr. Besides black heels,
she wore nothing else. Even though she appeared
androgynous, she was the most erotic creature
I have ever seen. She danced to classical music
and her dances were highly choreographed,
apparently a representation of her drug and
sexual experiences. I had never seen anything
even similar. She was absolutely captivating
as she danced by herself or with a partner in
pornographic dances. She would move between
tables in her dance and if she felt someone was
not paying sufficient attention to her, she would
urinate on their table. Imagine!

I cautiously approached her after her show
and, with her bladder presumably empty, made
inquiries about Ulrika. Already highly drugged,
she sniffed some cocaine from her wrist vial.
She began to speak very fast, almost too fast for
my German and she wandered from one topic to
another. I fought hard to keep her on task. What
I learned from her, in snippets, was that Ulrika
actually existed. But that I was looking for her
in the wrong places. I needed to search for her
in the upper-class lesbian bars, of which I was
completely ignorant. I asked if she could give me
some name of these establishments, which she
did. She then said she had to get to the studio,

where she was filming a moving picture that
would soon be released. As she was leaving in
just her sable coat, she said 'Fraulein Ulrika is
the Supreme Domina of Berlin. Be very careful!'

10 August 1923

As the street violence escalates, Berlin, in effect,
exists in a state of near anarchy. Therefore,
Germany is ripe for being conquered by the
bolshevikii. The Freicorps and their allies are
all that stands against such a takeover. Should
our cause lose Germany, all of continental
Europe will be red within a decade. I must find
this woman at the earliest date. However, I
have reached a dead end. The lesbian women in
these bars are very hostile and some have even
threatened to kill me if I persist in my search.
Ulrika has become an obsession with me. I really
need to know more about her. She surely knows
I am looking for her. I will retreat for a while. It
is now her move. My tvarsch tells me she is as
interested in meeting with me as I am with her.

10 November 1923

There has been an interesting development in
Munich. A group called the Kampbund attempted
to overthrow the government of Bavaria. It
failed, but what makes it intriguing is that
General Erich Ludendorff, second only to Paul
von Hindenburg in the German High Command,
took part in the putsch, as it being called. His
colleague in this venture was a former Austrian
corporal, Adolf Hitler. I know of him tangentially
because of his links to the Freicorps and his

National Socialist German Worker's Party
(N.S.D.A.P.). It is most curious, his party sounds
left-wing, but he is associated with right wing
groups. And he must be very impressive to be a
partner of Ludendorff. I shall be watching him
with great interest.

15 April 1924

I have finally overcome my hatred of the
Germans. My personal feelings must not
interfere with the crisis we face. Actually,
I applaud the Germans. Late last year, they
introduced a small coin, the Rentenmark with
the buying power of a trillion paper marks.
Nevertheless, the great inflation is now over. I
am not sure how this was accomplished, however
if the Germans can defeat such a great opponent,
they shall surely be able to defeat the bolshevikii
in time and with proper guidance. Nonetheless,
in yet another setback, the great inflation has
substantially wiped out the bourgeoisie, the
backbone of any society.

25 April 1924

Out on the Ku'damm, I passed a moving picture
theater and, on the marquee, "Anita Berber,
Berlin's High Priestess of Debauchery." I confess
I went in and enjoyed the show. I also learned
that she travels around the city only wearing her
sable coat with a pet monkey and cocaine vial.
Sometimes, she forgets her coat.

30 April 1924

I must discover if Ulrika truly possesses
a superior will or if it is merely theatrics.
Logically, men going to such a woman are
looking for dominance and would be most
receptive to her commands. On the other hand,
what attracted a woman to such a position?
Hatred and contempt for men or something much
more interesting? I am again making discreet
inquiries at the clubs around the city. Yesterday,
I came to Cafe Domino at Marburgerstrasse 13,
it featured jazz, dancing, luxurious cocktails
and privacy for wealthy and elegant lesbians.
After numerous inquiries and rejections there, I
found Uschi, a close friend of Ulrika. She wore
a tuxedo and had bobbed auburn hair. Uschi
told me that Ulrika would be expecting me
tomorrow evening at one of her closed sessions
at a private address in Charlottenburg, a very
fashionable address between the Ku'damm and
Hardenburgstrasse.

The next evening, I made my way to the very
quiet street, went up the front stairs and gave
the password for entrance. The gatekeeper told
me that I needed to remove all my clothes. I
told her that was not my intention. I was here
on with a business proposition for Ulrika. The
gatekeeper was a truly forbidding Amazon, taller,
stronger and larger than me. Nonetheless, my
will eventually cowed her and she permitted me
to pass.

I stopped before entering the large, smoke-
filled ballroom that had been transformed into a
classical Greek temple. As I surveyed the room, I

saw approximately two dozen women of varying
ages, sitting at cafe tables, drinking, smoking
and sniffing cocaine and who knows what else?
Their 'pets,' collared naked men, lay silently on
the floor beside them. I watched in some horror
as the women were cheering on a tall, leanly-
muscled woman, who had reduced some poor
male to a humiliated, abused and dehumanized
state, so that, wet and bleeding, he was carried
off the stage by two pets. I was shocked to
see that when they passed me, he was a rather
prominent minister in the Weimar government.
The show over, I now entered the room, which
smelled of perfume, opium, blood and sweat and
heard murmuring spread around the room. The
woman left the stage and came straight at me.
She wore a fitted gold mask and a thin white silk
robe, with gold cords crisscrossing her chest and
another gold cord around her waist. Her robe
was partially open from just above her knees to
reveal her strong thighs and calves. She called
me by name and introduced herself as 'Fraulein
Ulrika' and scolded me for defiling her temple by
not being naked, as I had been instructed. I told
her it was not my usual custom to take orders
from a woman. She shrugged, and I watched
her deep blue eyes, shining through the mask,
neatly framing her long, platinum hair. Those
eyes betrayed a deep intelligence, a strong will
and, surprisingly, a slight innocence. Had she
been merely an actress, I would have left at that
point. She told me she was neither a chonté, nor,
especially, a bienl. That is, she was an artiste, not
a prostitute. I told her that was as may be and
she was to be at the Imperial Suite at the Adlon

at 1800 the following day. She said she knew it
well. I told her I had a wager and wished to test
her to see if she truly possessed a superior will.
She asked me my terms. I told her all would be
revealed when she arrived tomorrow evening.
She nodded her acceptance and I left, without a
word further.

Ashley paused, fascinated with Ulrika and this superior will.
He had a strong will, which had led to his considerable successes.
However, *did* he have a superior will? Would a strong will and
focus plus *tvarsch* equal a superior will? In the diary, he had seen
that Dmitri never quit, and that had to be, along with the slaughter,
why the wheat field seemed so important and annoying. He had
failed, brought down by soldiers without vision or honor.

1 May 1924

When Ulrika arrived, sans mask, last evening,
she wore a silver fox fur and high-heeled green
boots. She told me she was the reincarnation
of the Valkyrie Brunhild before asking me the
wager. I told her that if she could defeat my
will, I would submit to her without reservation.
Conversely, should I overcome her will, she
would submit to me. She laughed merrily and
replied that if I required proof of her superior
will, I merely had to look into her eyes. She
knew I possessed such a will and so, it should
be easy for me to recognize hers. I replied that
her eyes had impressed me the previous evening.
It was only now that I saw the black laces in
her boots. I asked her what that meant. She
again laughed merrily and replied I would soon
discover she observed no limits in punishing her
wicked suitors because all men are either evil or
pathetic. And that I, as a warrior, a soldier was

especially evil. I had made war, killed, maimed and, perhaps, raped. Worst of all, I had not led my men to Berlin and victory, only to death, maiming and defeat. I must have great guilt over that. I replied that while I mourned the loss of my men, such is a soldier's lot and they knew that. Besides, we have not lost my war, which will be a long one, but we shall prevail. She shrugged indicating uncertainty before she told me I was a prideful and hate-filled man. She said she knew who I was when I arrived at the Adlon, Herr Blau, so long ago. Because of that I wasted a great deal of time, offended many women and, ultimately, failed to find her. I replied that I had found her. She laughed and said she had allowed me to find her. Now, when I had been walking in the Tiergarten that day, she had sent the three prostitutes to me. Since I would not deign to pay for their services, I sent them away without so much as a single Mark, even though they were all very hungry. She learned three things from this. First, I had been very prideful and not a compassionate man and, third, that I had truly hated all Germans, even the joy girls. And she knew from that she could not work with me until I changed. Therefore, she led me a merry chase, leaving real and false clues all over the city until such time as I did change my attitude about Germans. I asked her how she knew I no longer hated Germans. She smiled and said there was little in Berlin she did not know. She then said that since she had already bested me in my search, I should forego the wager and submit to her. I replied that I would never submit to any woman who called herself after a pagan goddess.

When she removed her coat, she was naked and
said for the wager to be fair, I should be naked
as well. I agreed. Soon, we were standing about
a meter apart, studying each other. I have to
confess she was one of the most beautiful women
I have ever seen with glowing skin from the sun
and completely blonde. Not to mention again her
incredible blue eyes. She stood casually, arms
lightly folded under firm, full breasts When she
spoke she said that when I could no longer resist
her, I should back up and crawl to her like the
worm I was, kiss her left boot and await further
commands. I laughed and replied when she
broke, she would assume the traditional posture
of female submission before me. I thought I
saw the slightest hint of a smile momentarily
cross her bright red lips. We resumed our silence
and I began to lose track of time. I confess that
I have never been so tempted by any woman,
except Sophie. I again studied her eyes and
realized she was trying to hypnotize me. Her
secret. I took counter measures, remembering
the mutilated Weimar minister and telling myself
that she was the wife of the German officer who
had slaughtered my troops in the wheat field.
I could not allow myself to betray my troops
by submitting to this pagan witch. We carried
on like this for some time until, on the verge
of giving in, I looked down to see her kneeling
before me. She said she was my slave and would
do anything I commanded. I told her to rise.
She would be my guest for the evening and we
would soon have dinner en suite. She kissed me
hard on the lips and then told me that had I given
in to her, she would have left me immediately.

Because I would be pathetic and not worthy to
work with her, which would begin soon now
she knew who I truly was. She kissed me again,
saying she never had sex with her suitors before
taking me down on the thick carpet.

Ashley began to search the trunk for a picture of Ulrika,
which he felt certain Dmitri must have kept.

TEN
`Sunday, 30 May 1993
Quaker Mount, NY

1.

Ashley found Ulrika's picture, an approximately eight-by-five, black-and-white photograph in the back flap of Dmitri's diary. Except for black pasties on her breasts and stiletto heels, which emphasize her powerful thighs and calves, she is naked. With legs spread, toned arms folded and platinum hair down past her shoulders, she appears sleek and graceful. Dmitri had written "her skin glowed from the sun," his way of saying she had an overall tan. She looks down at the camera, her face showing displeasure with any viewer. Across the bottom is "EINREICHEN!" (SUBMIT!) and the name, mark and address of the Berlin photographer.

Ashley could feel her power by the way she dominated the space. But he now sensed that for Ulrika this had always been a merry game, and she never had any intention of winning the wager. Despite her taunting words, she had been ordered by someone to seduce Dmitri. He reopened the diary to 1 May 1924 to find out who and why.

> I now sensed Ulrika is a lady of rank as I
> answered the door in my black silk robe for
> the waiter to serve us in the main salon. Ulrika,

naked, reappeared, smiled and called the young
waiter by name. Flustered, he could only mumble
and blush before rapidly taking his leave. She
laughed, and sat, presiding over the food-packed
table as though hosting an important diplomatic
dinner at her schloss. Nonetheless, as we spoke
of general topics, we were both studying each
other. While I was enchanted with her, my guard
remained up. Although a lady of rank, she is
a prostitute, a not uncommon situation here.
The doorbell rang again. I went to the door
and there stood a lady's maid, the well-lit and
bright corridor behind her, who said she had a
suitcase for her mistress, Baroness Ulrika. There
was something peculiar about the maid, but I
could not quite place it. I thanked her, took the
suitcase and gave it to Ulrika, calling her by
her title. She smiled mischievously, accepted
the case and responded to my puzzled face by
explaining about her maid. She had been one of
her regulars, a thin and effete man, who wished
to be a girl. Ulrika knew a Berlin surgeon who
was experimenting with gender-changing. The
only giveaway was the maid's voice, which could
not be fixed. I would have been shocked by this
anywhere else. Here, it seemed almost normal.
Ulrika retired to the bedroom and returned
wearing a Parisian negligee and I invited her
to be my guest for the foreseeable future. She
thanked me and asked me why I had not enslaved
her when I had the opportunity, rather than treat
her like a royal guest. I replied, 'The superior
will does not seek to enslave, rather, to fight
the wrongs that must be righted. Moreover, it
requires no titles, and most importantly, it must

bear the unbearable, when necessary. She nodded, as though she understood.

2 May 1924

After an unforgettable night, late this morning, Ulrika had some business to attend to and would be back in time for dinner. I knew she would report on the events of yesterday. About 1400 the door-bell rang and, not surprisingly, Ulrika's maid had come with an even larger suitcase. A lady needs to be well dressed, after all. I was marveling at the maid's surgery when she told me what time to expect her mistress.

Ulrika arrived later that evening in a green flapper dress with a matching cloche and high-heeled shoes. While there could be no doubt that she had a superior will, whether she possessed the discipline and focus to use it properly remains open. In the Adlon's dining salon, we spoke of the situation in Germany, Europe and related topics before she revealed her anti-bolshevikii organization and proposed a meeting with her brother, who commanded a secret agency. I asked her why she had led me on her merry chase. She replied that all the time, she and her brother had been checking my bona-fides and I had passed all the checks. Now, I began to have some doubts about my earlier triumph over her. She revealed that her domina persona is merely a way of gaining information by persuading her suitors—prominent men and women, in and out of the government—to speak with her brother, in order to further the agency's agenda.

She paused and confessed I was the man she
had been waiting for. She knew my situation in
Paris and did not care. She wanted babies when
the time was right which would be 'soon.' (Now,
how could I, as a gentleman, refuse this lovely
lady such a request?) After asking her several
questions about the agency, which she skillfully
parried, she said that all would be revealed on
Monday the 5th. I smiled and drew my hands up
in a gesture of surrender, 'Baroness, you have
won.' She said she did not care to be addressed
as Baroness and said, 'The superior will requires
no titles, Prince Colonel Iskandarov.' I laughed
again and asked her why the meeting was set
for Monday and not Saturday. She replied her
brother was out until Sunday night. And she
always spent the weekend with her Nacktkultur
friends on the Baltic Coast. She asked me to go
with her and show me off to her friends. Such
things are totally alien to me. But she insisted,
and I agreed. After dinner, we promenaded in
the Tiergarten along the Landwehr Canal to the
place where sparticist Rosa Luxemburg's corpse
had been dumped after her failed revolt. I gave
Ulrika a kiss, which was sincere. That night, we
truly made love for the first time. I have felt,
at times, that this was all moving way too fast.
However, given the uncertain nature of the times
when anyone could be caught up in a street
brawl and killed, or assassinated or murdered, it
makes sense. After all, most life is very cheap in
Weimar Berlin.

4 May 1924 P.M.

We returned from the Warnemünde Baltic camp
Sunday evening. Saturday morning, we left
Berlin by train and a few hours later we were on
a bus to the camp. Some people began disrobing
before we arrived there. This led me to believe
it would be merely a continuation of the Berlin
decadence, but I was wrong. Once in the camp, I
cannot remember a more tranquil, peaceful place.
I met a wide variety of very interesting people.
I was amazed how simply being naked changes
the entire social dynamic. I had also assumed a
beauty like Ulrika would have a higher status
than a plain girl. If that existed, she did not
acknowledge it and was gracious and friendly
to all, whether she knew them or not. Again, she
has opened my eyes to many things I did not
even know existed. And that is why I am coming
to love her. On Sunday, as we lay in our beach-
chairs on the sandy beach with the sun bright
above and a cooling breeze from the sea, Ulrika
began to ask me questions. Why had I become
so anti-bolshevikii? I though the answer obvious.
In an illegitimate and brutal coup d'état, a gang
of thugs had seized my homeland, destroyed all
legitimate institutions and executed many of my
friends and family. She nodded sympathetically
and said she knew Bleu was part of something
larger. I replied Bleu was the intelligence and
counter-intelligence agency of the United White
Russian Government-in-Exile, head-quartered
in Paris. She said she knew of it. She then
asked me what would happen if the bolshevikii
suddenly disappeared? I replied I would prefer

a constitutional monarchy with the last of the
Romanovas married to an Iskandarov and a
strong Duma running the government. She asked
if I had aspirations to be the Tsar? No, my place,
if anywhere, is in the Duma on a council of
elders, who would direct the Duma. Kerensky's
government was a failure because it was weak
with too many conflicting factions. Russians
want a strong central government. Because they
know that a weak one invites invasion from the
West and / or the East. She laughed and said I
was most gallant not to mention, by name, her
ancestors in the Teutonic Knights. I leaned over
and kissed her.

5 May 1924

Today, Ulrika von M. introduced me to her
brother, Reinhardt, Freiherr (Baron) von M.
He was some ten years older than Ulrika and
tall, about 183 centimeters. (6'3"). Although
wearing a suit, his close-cropped hair and large
scar on his right cheek, left me no doubt, he
had been a combat officer in the War. I said that
since he obviously knew my military history,
would he share his? He nodded. After graduating
from the University of Leipzig in 1912, he was
commissioned as a leutnant in the Imperial Army
and rapidly rose to hauptmann (captain). He was
mostly on the Eastern Front, Poland, Galicia,
Austria and Ukraine. He casually noted that our
paths had crossed in Galicia in a wheat field.
Since I do not believe in coincidence, this had to
be a test. I never saw the German commander.
I sensed he is lying, thus I revealed no anger

at this. I replied that we had been following
orders from our respective high commands.
Reinhardt then told me about his scar. In 1918,
he was transferred to the Western Front and led
a team of storm troopers who raided trenches,
mostly at night. A British bayonet had cut him
before he killed its owner. He informed me
that he is associated with a group of certain
prominent industrialists. This group, in turn,
utilizes the services of demobilized veterans
from the National Socialist German Worker
Party, popularly known as Nazis, to battle
the bolshevikii in the streets. I mentioned to
Reinhardt that, for the time being, their leader,
Herr Hitler, remains in Munich's Landsberg
Prison. He laughed. 'It is more of a house arrest.
He is writing his manifesto, presently without
a title, and once published, every German
patriot will then rally to his standard. This is the
absolute best thing that could have happened
to him.' I agreed and asked him if these people
I was to meet truly felt they could contain and
control Hitler for long. He replied they thought
so. I shall draw my own conclusions when I meet
them. Subsequently, Ulrika and I accompanied
the baron, in his Daimler, for a meeting in
Potsdam, the former capital of Prussia. We
chatted pleasantly on the way, but, by getting in
the car, I already know this is not a club from
which one resigns.

5 June 1924

Today, Georgi and I moved from the Adlon
into the house Ulrika shares with Reinhardt.

However, he travels a great deal and is only
there sporadically. The four-story house is in
Charlottenburg, near Ulrika's temple, where I
first met her. There is a sunroom on the top floor,
overlooking a well-tended garden in the back.
I am certain we shall spend a great deal of time
there. I have my own office, which Georgi shall
run for the foreseeable future. He remains my
batman, friend and confidant. Ulrika and I have
adjoining bedrooms for propriety's sake. Georgi
has a very nice room on the ground floor in the
servant's quarters. He is already charming one
of the maids, Gisela. I warned him to make sure
she is actually a she. We have been going up to
Baltic to escape Berlin and clear our heads on a
fairly regular basis.

3 September 1924

Georgi and Gisela married yesterday, and they
shall share a bedroom downstairs. There was
also a large street brawl during our wedding
celebration. What is Berlin coming to with such
goings on in Charlottenburg?

Ashley noted that Hitler had been released from jail on
Christmas Eve, 1924, after only serving nine months of his five-
year sentence. The hyperinflation of the early twenties, although
now controlled, remained a very strong memory, and most people
feared it could return. This led to widespread discontent with the
left-of-center Weimar Government. Germany was fracturing into
Fascist Right and Bolshevik Left.

16 February 1925.

At the office of Herr von J., I was initially
amused and recognized Herr Hitler from

pictures of his absurdly cut-off moustache.
He was also taller than his pictures. Gassed in
the War, I believe he still had not recovered
completely. His warm handshake and street
toughness and, especially, his eyes impressed
me, (They are dark blue, but appear brown in
the newsreels. They are hypnotic, like Ulrika's
and his will is intensely strong. Perhaps, even
stronger than mine. However, I also sense he
lacks the discipline to completely control it.
Such combination usually leads to disaster. The
industrialists are using him to achieve their goals,
but I am not convinced they shall ultimately
contain him.

11 November 1928

I noticed today in the Berliner Tageblatt, an
anti-Nazi newspaper, that Anita Berber, now
seemingly addicted to every substance on earth,
died yesterday at age 29. All that remains is her
painting in a red dress and heavily made-up face
by Otto Dix. She was truly 'the High Priestess of
Weimar Berlin,' the public face of decadence.

Dmitri commuted with Ulrika on a regular basis to Belgrade,
Munich, Warsaw, Vienna, Prague, Budapest, Bucharest and
Sophia. Ashley deduced they involved the same sort of bridge
building Dmitri had done in Berlin, bringing his principals
together with the other industrialists and intelligence agencies.
Georgi now worked for the *Abwehr*, German Military Intelligence,
but continued to live with Gisela and her son, Heinz, in the
Charlottenburg house.

15 June 1932

Thanks to our efforts, the Cordon Sanitaire
against the bolshevikii is holding well.

Increasingly, the leaders of Eastern Europe are emulating Mussolini in Italy. They are becoming progressively Fascist in their outlook and operations.

30 January 1933

We have returned to Berlin. Hitler has been proclaimed Reich Chancellor of Germany, answerable only to President von Hindenburg. His S.A. storm troopers roam the streets freely, beating up or killing any 'Enemies of the Reich,' real or perceived. On a happier note, Ulrika is pregnant with our child and shall give birth in the autumn.

23 March 1933

The Dachau concentration camp, near Munich, officially opened yesterday. The Nazis have rounded up mostly leftist politicals, enemies and undesirables. Tanya visited us today. Given her precarious position, I told her that Berlin is cheka-infested. And she remains high on their list for execution. Tanya replied since she is living on borrowed time, every day is a gift. I told her that I wanted her to take over our very key office in Prague in Czecho-Slovakia. She said she would be honored. I think she shall make an extraordinary successor for Sophie in Bleu. Sophie continues to enchant all she meets and has won us valuable friends in England, France and Italy as she continues her meetings with high officials.

5 May 1933

I have returned from Ukraine. Bolshevikii efforts
to collectivize the farming there is meeting stiff
resistance from the peasants, who are at war with
the chekists. The bolshevikii hold on Ukraine
has never been all that strong and there remain
many anti-Bolshevikii elements active there. We
are supplying those groups with weapons and
promoting disturbances, which, at a minimum,
will cause a redeployment of resources from
elsewhere, making us stronger.

16 January 1934

I learned that the situation in Ukraine has
reached crisis levels. Lenin always hated the
peasants, but this is too extreme. Chekists are
confiscating the peasant's grain and leaving them
with nothing to eat or plant. Millions of them
have already starved as the grain is being sold
abroad for hard currency. This is the proof we
need to convince the world of the monstrousness
of the regime. We shall counter the lies of the
New York Times' Moscow bureau chief, Mr.
Walter Duranty, that there is no famine.

15 June 1934

Back in Berlin, something is afoot. Rumors of
coups and counter-coups are everywhere as are
S.S. and S.A. troop movements.

2 July 1934

Several days ago, Hitler moved against his old
comrade, Captain Ernst Rohm and his S.A. storm

trooper bullyboys. In a few days, they have
ceased to exist. Only the S.S. remain.

21 August 1934

After von Hindenburg's death in early August,
Hitler moved quickly to consolidate his power
as leader (Führer) of Germany. This was ratified
by public vote on the 19th. The Army has pledged
their personal loyalty to him, not Germany, a
most disturbing development.

2.

Ashley heard footsteps, looked up and saw Annie, barefoot in
cut-offs and a red Coors T-shirt. "Dad, lunch is ready. I'm looking
forward to reading the third diary. OK?"

Ashley nodded.

"I've finished Sergei's diary. I didn't like him at first. But,
with Charlotte, it was so romantic and heartbreaking all at once.
I'm sorry he's dead. I would've loved to speak with him. What an
interesting grandfather he would've been."

"I'll explain more at lunch, but I don't believe he's dead."

"Then why hasn't he come back to see us? Or, is he still with
Charlotte who's alive somewhere?"

"Sergei's life after the war was very complicated. There's
still a lot I don't know."

Annie nodded. "OK. Let me know what you find out." She
saw the picture of Ulrika. "Wow! What a beautiful, powerful
woman." She laughed. "She is really hot, in a retro way. Who's
she?"

"She was a friend of Dmitri's."

"Friend or lover?"

"Lover, spy and high-priced prostitute."

"This is an incredible picture. Must have been airbrushed or
altered in some way. No one could possibly look this good."

"This was taken in 1920s Berlin. It hasn't been altered, based on Dmitri's description. Her name's Ulrika, and she's not a relative."

"Too bad we couldn't have gotten some of her genes. What does the word on the bottom mean?"

"Submit!"

"Ah. She's a dominatrix then. That makes perfect sense. If I looked that good, I wouldn't take any crap from anyone."

"How do you know about dominatrixes?"

"Dad, I'm not a little girl."

"No, I don't suppose you are. I'd estimate she's mid-to-late twenties in this picture. When you get to be that age, I suspect you'll be just as beautiful."

"I wish." She went over to the framed picture, briefly studied it and said, "This lady has to be my great-grandmother, Sophia. She's very pretty, and she absolutely hated her corsets. When the count left for the war, she threw all of them out and bought a new wardrobe."

"How do you know all this?"

"Aunt Ronnie told me. But I've also seen her in visions, and most of the time, she's not wearing a corset. Dmitri was a very handsome man."

"Indeed, he was. But it appears you have been withholding information from me."

"Not really. I've been doing my own studies on this. After all, you have your path, and I have mine. When they come together, we'll cooperate. OK?"

Ashley slowly nodded. Ronnie had said something like that earlier. They should begin to cooperate even more. "Now, let's eat. We've a lot to discuss."

3.

After lunch and a thorough discussion of the first two diaries and answers to why Ulrika the dominatrix was in Dmitri's diary, Ashley gave Annie a crash course in the history and politics of the period.

16 November 1934

We had to make an emergency trip to Warsaw to
see Marshal Pilsudski, arranged by dear Ulrika,
who had one of Pilsudski's chief advisors as
a suitor. (I have no doubt she knows everyone
important in this part of Europe and perhaps
beyond.). Pilsudski, the ruler of Poland, always
wears his uniform. He is not tall (1 meter, 75
centimeters or about 5'8") but is most imposing
with a very strong will and a large dark
moustache. He is also a very disciplined warrior
and patriot. He shows no emotion and is hard
to read. He sees Hitler as a threat. I cannot say
whether he is being a paranoid Pole or is seeing
something that no one else can. He wants to
launch a pre-emptive strike on Germany, while,
as he says, 'the Germans are still weak.' Poland
has a formidable army and would probably win
and oust Hitler. I share his concern about Hitler,
but there is no acceptable alternative in Germany
and his ouster would leave a power vacuum
in Germany. The bolshevikii K.P.D. party,
with Moscow's full backing, would take full
advantage. I know Pilsudski is vehemently anti-
bolshevikii and has been fighting the Russians
all his life, so he must be made to see that his
plans would be a disaster for our cause. He
reportedly has cancer and may not live all that
long. Therefore, I fear his strike shall be sooner
rather than later. I greatly admire and respect this
man—the victor of the 'Miracle of the Vistula'—
since he defeated Trotsky's red army right at
the gates of Warsaw and won the war with the
bolshevikii.

18 November 1934

We have finished our meetings with the Marshal. He understands my position but knows that both Germany and Russia desire to partition Poland when the time is right. I countered that only a strong coalition can defeat the bolshevikii and that must include a strong Poland and Germany. He thanked me for my security guarantees, but the guarantors are far distant from Poland and would never go to war with Germany if Hitler invaded. I asked him to send his foreign minister to meet with my principals. He agreed.

25 November 1934

The Marshal and his foreign minister met with my principals. The industrialists convinced him that they are still in control and would contain Hitler and reiterated their support for Polish territorial integrity. He said he would meet with all his ministers to make a final decision.

12 May 1935

That decision had been delayed for months as they endlessly debated, and the Marshal's health declined. Today, I received word that not only had the Marshal died of cancer, but the strike was now on indefinite hold. Like so many countries in Europe, no one is ready for another war, unless it is against Russia. And even then, public opinion is divided. (The British and French opposed Pilsudski because they fear the bolshevikii more than Hitler and most of Poland's neighbors favored him because they fear Hitler more than the bolshevikii, although not by much.) In the event, we have averted a catastrophe. I had proposed a German-Polish united anti-bolshevikii front. Nevertheless, both Polish historical mistrust of Germany and Hitler's racialist policies defeated that.

8 March 1936

Yesterday, the German army marched into the demilitarize Rhineland, which borders on France. The French and British offered no resistance or protest. (Similar reason as with Pilsudski.) The last allied troops of occupation left there in 1930 and it is the industrial heartland of Germany. That is why Hitler needs reunification. I know that had the French even offered token military intervention, the Germans would have fallen back, and Hitler would have been overthrown. The Versailles Treaty is now a dead letter.

17 June 1936

Nadia is far too intelligent to be a mere housewife. We have need of her in Paris as Sophie's protégé and successor, should anything happen to Tanya.

1 August 1936

Last month, Hitler intervened in the Spanish civil war on the side of rebel Francisco Franco's Fascist army. The Germans have many weapons to test out and what better place than Spain? Stalin has also sent weapons to the Republic, for the same reason. This a preview of the war that has been inevitable since the Rhineland incursion. Nadia is now firmly involved with

Bleu. I am hearing very favorable reports from
Sophie. (Perhaps now, she will forgive my
intervention in Sergei's marriage.)

11 November 1938

Two nights ago, there was a pogrom right here in
Berlin. Jews and their shops were attacked by the
Nazis. This morning there was broken glass all
over the city. It is now known as 'Kristallnacht,
the night of broken glass.' We have a Jewish
neighbor, a fine, upstanding German. When the
pogrom began, he went out, wearing his Iron
Cross First Class, to calm down the situation. We
found him yesterday morning, beaten to death, his
cross gone. This is intolerable, but the Germans
remain the only power actively opposing the
Bolshevikii. Ulrika is equally upset about this. I
shall file a protest with the industrialists.

13 November 1938

My beloved cousin, Alexei, who was killed in the
Civil War, has a daughter he never met. Although
Iskandarova, she uses her French name, Cosette.
She is eighteen and already a seasoned Bleu
agent. She arrived today from Paris to ascertain
the situation here in the wake of the pogrom.
She is staying with us for a week or so. She
has a Vestal quality and is very smart, although
her beauty pales next to Ulrika and I had no
idea how they would get on. Ulrika has already
adopted her as a younger sister and they are thick
as thieves. After Cosette leaves, she shall return,
periodically, with Sophie's messages that are too
sensitive for normal channels.

Ulrika gave birth to a girl, Marlena, in late 1933. In early 1938, Ulrika rejoined the *Abwehr*. Her brother Reinhardt's agency had been absorbed into it in 1934. She left Marlena with her family in Leipzig when her first assignment sent her to Ukraine.

15 May 1939

With war clouds on the horizon, I have been called back to Paris for a conference. Ulrika, now back in Berlin, accompanied me, as an official representative of the Abwehr. I thought about taking her brother, Reinhardt, with us. He after all, outranks her. But he is also prone to bouts of shaking and weeping as his shell-shock from the War continues to get worse. I rather like the man and have great sympathy for him.

17 May 1939

We arrived in Paris yesterday and went directly to exile government and Bleu head-quarters on Avenue Foch. I always feel a thrill seeing the six-story, impeccably clean limestone building. Going through the wrought iron and glass door, under the watchful gaze of an armed guard, we proceeded on the green marble floor to the main desk where we presented our credentials. The floor was extremely busy with people coming and going and the sound of an army of typewriters and other noisy machines filling the air. We took the lift to the fifth floor, which in America would be the sixth floor, into an enormous formal ball-room, a light and airy room offering glorious views of Paris. We were greeted by Sophie, Tanya and Cosette for our pre-meeting lunch before the conference begins tomorrow. Tonight, brings an even larger banquet in the ball-room with all the Bleu agents gathered. Security shall be extra vigilant. Sophie refers to it as 'the Repast.'

1 September 1939

The war against the Devil Stalin has begun. I remain in Berlin for the present. Despite the charade of the Ribbentrop-Molotov pact, it is only a matter of time until the invasion of Russia begins. The Germans are not yet strong enough, so Hitler has lulled the Devil into thinking he is an ally. Poland had to be sacrificed for the greater good. After the Marshal died, the Poles were never able to build a proper government and became weak, a perennial Polish problem. Nonetheless, I am pleased that the Marshal is not here to see this. I wish we could have found a better solution to the problem he posed.

14 September 1940

We have received confirmation the Devil, not satisfied with decimating the party and military leadership during the show trials, has taken to imprisoning anyone who might prove a personal threat. Leon Trotsky, his primary rival, was assassinated in Mexico City in August. When we invade, we shall be welcomed as liberators. I have been commissioned as oberst (colonel) in the Wehrmacht and am a staff officer at O.K.H., their HQ, in Zossen, about 32 km. (20 miles) south of Berlin.

22 June 1941

Barbarossa, the invasion of Russia has begun
and is being controlled from O.K.H. While I
am distressed it begins so late in the relatively
short Russian summer months, the superiority of
German arms shall again be proven.

In 1943, with the Russian campaign going badly, Dmitri
needed to fight and joined the newly formed *Waffen* SS unit, 14th
Waffen Grenadier Division, called *Galizien* (Galician) as *oberst*.
It is entirely Russian and not in the slightest "Aryan."

The racial policies of the Reich are becoming
increasingly convoluted. and the realities of the
war are taking precedence over racial theory.
Some clever bureaucrat found that Galicia,
which has been part of Ukraine from time to
time, was also a province of the Hapsburg
Empire. (They could have asked me.) Therefore,
anyone in the Division, whether or not from
Galicia, is considered an Aryan thanks to the
Hapsburg rule.

Immediately after formation, the Galizien Division was
sent to Ukraine, and for the third time Dmitri fought on familiar
territory. This time, the devastation surpassed even that of either
the Great or Civil Wars. Kiev again became a charnel house.
Encircled by the Red Army, the Galizien Division fought their way
out, but at such horrendous cost the division ceased effectively to
exist and soon disbanded. Dmitri brought something else back
with him besides his very serious wounds.

I have seen pogroms all my life and I have
participated in them. However, what the S.S.
is doing to the Jews of Ukraine is unspeakable.
We only meant to keep them in their place.
Nevertheless, the S.S. seems intent on wiping

them off the face of the earth. I am ashamed to be associated with these monsters. However, I have no choice. Therefore, I now must play the hand I have been dealt out to the last wretched card.

15 February 1943

Without a command, I am back at O.K.H. and billeted in Zossen, where I had a visitor today —Ulrika. She came dressed in a trench coat, combat boots and a fedora. She kept her coat on and I noticed her hair was very short. I immediately knew she had been captured and brutalized. She told me she had been liberated from NKVD HQ in Tsaritsyn. (She adamantly refused to call the city named after the Devil Stalin, using its pre-bolshevikii name.) She told me that she had been repeatedly raped, beaten, burned, starved, tortured in the most horrific ways and finally kept in solitary confinement. At this point, she opened her coat to reveal the chekist handiwork on her naked body. She was painfully thin and bore their scars, burns and marks. Nonetheless, she showed me these with a sense of great pride. 'I bore the unbearable, as you taught me, and was never broken.' She and the rest of the prisoners were liberated by commandos, who found her in a tiny cell, not tall enough to stand in, where she had been left to starve. After liberation, she had been in a field hospital for over a month. Nevertheless, her spirit remained unbroken. I went over and held her in my arms. She began to shake, and I realized she was crying. I kissed and held her. Later, after we made slow lovers' love,

she found all my scars, bruises and burns. In a
way, I cannot really explain, I think she is more
beautiful than before. Afterward, we had a long
discussion and I was furious when she told me
she had had a terrible miscarriage in prison and
may now be sterile. She stayed for two weeks
until she returned to her family before going
back to the Abwehr for another assignment.

Ashley now had great admiration for Ulrika, a very strong
and brave woman to be going behind enemy lines. And he now
better understood the superior will she had demonstrated in her
captivity. Dmitri became an aide to General Andrei Vlasov, a
Red Army Deputy Army Group Commander, who had grown
disgusted with Stalin before his capture by the Germans outside
Leningrad. He had been ordered to raise a new Waffen SS Division
from among Russian POWs to fight the Red Army. After initial
and mutual hostility and suspicion, Andrei and Dmitri developed
a decent working relationship.

3 September 1943

Today, Cosette made the hard trip from
Paris to Zossen. In addition to her usual high
priority messages, she told me that I am again
a grandfather. Sophie learned that Sergei and
Charlotte had a healthy boy. I am overjoyed.
Ashley shall be the 'Hidden One' until his time
comes.

Ashley had mixed emotions at definitely being the Hidden One.

2 December 1943

There is no longer any pretense here about racial
purity. The 30th Waffen Grenadier Division is
simply about getting bodies. They are all like
that bolshevikii I killed in the Great War. I need
to find suitable officers.

While touring the POW *luftstalags* in Germany for officer recruits, Dmitri noticed Spencer Talbott's name on a list of prisoners at *Luftstalag* III-B, near Furstenberg, Germany.

15 March 1944

How appropriate, today, the Ides of March, I saw my son for the first time since his marriage in America in 1929. Unfortunately, we were not able to have the conversation I would have wished for because I must assume that we were being monitored. As such, I made several anti-Semitic remarks to keep the listeners uninterested. While we have kept in touch, even during the war years, I was not prepared for the man in his mid-thirties who walked into the sparse room, unshaven but proud, in an American aviator's uniform, escorted by two guards, whom I dismissed. He showed no sign of recognition at first. I invited him to sit and I pushed my box of English Ovals toward him. He studied me carefully, wary I might trick him. I thought I saw a glimmer of recognition in his eyes but said nothing as he took the oval. I leaned over and lit it with an American Zippo, with what the Americans call a 'pin-up' on the side, a woman of fantasy proportions, 'Jezebel.' It had the desired effect. It was the name of his B-24 bomber in the Ploesti raid and I saw anger in his eyes. By my gesture with the lighter, I had indicated to him this would not be a father-son reunion. After I lit my cigarette, I introduced myself to Lieutenant Talbott. I began by saying I had interrogated many American aviators and you seem to fall into a similar pattern. You arrive in England and sweep some lovely lass

off her feet and into bed and are soon the father
of a son, with or without marriage. I asked him
if I was correct in his case. He nodded, and I
noticed a brief smile. I whispered in his ear,
'Ashley Cooper.' He grinned. Although I still
wear the insignia of the 14th Galizien Waffen
S.S. Division, I told him I was recruiting officers
for the 30th, an all-Russian division. I said I
understood he had Russian blood in him and
might be interested. He was, as expected, non-
committal. This was probably the most comfort
he has had since his capture, so I was not eager
to rush him. He asked me why he should betray
his country and fight against their 'gallant Soviet
ally.' I told him he could fight the bolshevikii
now with us or fight later against them as an
American. Also, since he has a son, that son
could fight them in the future. I advised him that
the Americans and the British were fighting the
wrong enemy. 'We shall defeat the bolshevikii
or go down to glorious defeat in the attempt.' I
paused and looked at him, the same bright boy I
once knew, and he understood what I was saying.
The Americans shall carry on the war against
the bolshevikii after the defeat of the Reich.
That shall be his task and why he has learned
American ways. I noticed the tiniest possible
crease of his lips. In that fleeting time, we had
our communion. We were one. The torch had
been passed to the next generation. I offered him
the rank of captain in the 30th and told him he
could be in uniform and strolling the Champs
Elysee within a week. As expected, he declined
my offer. He said his loyalty to his 'buddies,'
fellow prisoners, family and country was

stronger than his desire for immediate freedom.
I knew, of course, of the fate of his wife, but
remained silent so as not to upset him. I did
not want the interview to end. I wanted to tell
him how proud I am of him. However, to spend
undue time with him after we had completed
the business of this session would have attracted
unwanted attention. He saw my dilemma, stood,
snapped to attention and presented me with a
crisp, precise salute. I quickly returned it with
similar precision. The guards returned and for a
few moments after Sergei left, I stared blankly
at the gray door. As I left to rejoin General
Vlasov, I savored this bittersweet moment. I
know better than most, despite the promise of
'miracle weapons,' the Reich is in retreat in the
East and under increasing pressure from the
air in the West and armed forces in Italy. The
Americans and British would soon be landing on
the Continent. Whether they shall be successful
or not, the red army is advancing. The final
confrontation is coming. However, the fight shall
continue against the true enemy.

Ashley put the diary down and closed his eyes. He could
not help but be saddened by the tragedy of their meeting. He had
to admire both men. He also noted that Dmitri had not used the
word "death" but rather "fate" about Charlotte. Dmitri had never
minced his words about anything. Had Charlotte actually been
dead, he would have said so. Also, this entry confirmed Spencer
had not been killed at Ploesti. Ashley resumed reading and began
to scan. Bureaucracy delayed the grenadiers formation. Hitler
remained, at best, lukewarm to the idea of the 30th, which proved
to be a disaster with terrible soldiers. Many of the troops deserted
or whole units crossed into Switzerland. Dmitri stayed with the

remnants and was in Czechoslovakia when the war ended. Prior to that, Dmitri received a brief letter from Georgi. He was still living in the basement with Gisela, but Heinz has been in the Wehrmacht since he turned eighteen, and Georgi and Gisela are concerned. They have not heard anything from him in almost a year and fear the worst. The top floors of the building have been partially destroyed. Georgi went up last week and found Ulrika's brother, Reinhardt, dead in the ruins of the sunroom, a suicide. Georgi made arrangements for his funeral and hoped Reinhardt had finally found peace. They were going to try to escape to the west, if either the Russians or Germans did not kill them first.

9 May 1945

I am sitting in my tent in an American compound in Brno, two hundred kilometers south-east of Prague. This war is now officially over. Hitler is a suicide and Admiral Doenitz formally surrendered the Reich yesterday. For a few days, I was hopeful. Perhaps I might be released and make my way to America and Sergei or even find Ulrika, a foolish dream, because we have received word the victors plan to try us as war criminals. As oberst in the worst Waffen, I would be eventually tried but I never ordered any of my troops to commit war crimes. The Allies shall begin with the party leaders, at least those who survived, and work down. I wonder if they shall indict the industrialists who supported Hitler. Or shall they be absolved of any guilt? It shall be interesting to see how the victors dispense their justice, especially how they deal with the Devil Stalin. Absolutely, he has killed far more than Hitler. How does it differ if you kill someone because of their class or because of their religion? The nobility who remained

in Russia are just as dead as the Jews Hitler
obliterated. However, the Devil is cleverer
than Hitler. He twice chose the right side. It
shall also be interesting to see how long the
alliance between the West and the bolshevikii
shall stand. I wish it were not so, but I fear my
grandson, Ashley Cooper, shall fight one day
against the bolshevikii. The Americans, always
pragmatic, lack the emotional fire to attack the
Devil directly, and should be content to contain
their enemy at the periphery. Our Fascist cause
has been discredited, for at least a generation,
probably more, because of our association
with the Nazis and their ghastly extermination
policies and hence, we shall take no lead in anti-
bolshevism.

It felt very eerie for Ashley to have a grandfather he never
knew speaking about him fighting, and even more so, for Dmitri
to be correct. Ashley had fought against the 'bolshevikii' on the
periphery, Southeast Asia.

I have fought alone before. Therefore, I shall
take those first painful steps yet again, so the
day of final victory should be moved but a single
day closer. I have no illusions. I shall likely not
live to see liberation. I only know that glorious
day shall come, and my descendants shall one
day again live in an honest and powerful Russia.
However, where shall I go? The chekists moved
rapidly on the heels of the red army to liquidate
all resisters and collaborators. I know, as a
Waffen oberst, I shall be unwelcomed in the
West. Perhaps I could make my way to China
and the White Russian community in Shanghai,
assuming I am released. After the defeat of

Japan, I would organize strikes against Siberia. Perhaps we may create a free enclave in southern Siberia. The same problems that bedeviled the late Emperor in the war against Japan in 1905 shall be equally vexing to the Devil. By then, the alliance shall have broken down. I may yet find a niche for myself.

ADDENDUM. I have not written about Ulrika in a long time, although I have seen her on several occasions. After she returned from captivity, she was no longer sent back to the field. We had a conversation and she told me working with the Wehrmacht's anti-red partisans, she had seen and heard things that led her to believe that we would never conquer Russia. Hitler's policies were responsible and had alienated the population. Without that, in 1943, there could no hope of victory, regardless of how the key battle at the former Tsaritsyn on the Volga turned out. After her liberation, she returned to the Abwehr because they saw themselves as a strictly military body and hated the S.S., S.D. and Gestapo. After the bomb plot at the Wolf's Lair failed last year, Ulrika went underground, because the Abwehr had been incorporated into the S.S. Admiral Canaris had been placed under house arrest and then ultimately executed prior to the end of the war. Before this, he had kept several agents separate from the S.S. and Ulrika was one. Therefore, using the skills she learned in Ukraine, I have heard she successfully surrendered to the British and, for the moment, is safe. I still believe that had the bomb plot succeeded, the high-ranking Nazis would

have been quickly purged. The General's staff
would have taken over the conduct of the war
and perhaps, could have joined with the Allies
in warring on the bolshevikii. Reading what
Churchill and Truman and, indeed, Roosevelt
said publicly, such a scenario is not all that far-
fetched. However, in the final analysis, such is
the stuff of dreams.

9 May 1945

In my tent, I have reread what I wrote yesterday
and seems as though written it in another life.
My comrades and I have no future. An American
captain has just paid me a visit to inform me
that two days hence we shall be repatriated to
Russia. I explained to him I am a French citizen.
He nodded and said he knew. The decision was
not his. All persons of any Russian ancestry are
being repatriated. I felt sorry for him. He was
simply carrying out a cowardly decision made
on a much higher level. He was most apologetic
and gave me a Lucky Strike cigarette. We
talked for some time around the issue that such
repatriation was, at best, a death sentence. At
worst, a lingering living death in the Gulag. I
know this. He suspected it. So, what was to be
gained by spelling it out? I asked him where he
was from. He told me his name was Bill Petway
from Georgia. I told him I was from Georgia and
laughed. I remembered using the same words
with David Cooper in Odessa in another life. I
asked him if he knew David. He nodded. David
is his uncle. I knew immediately that this was no
co-incidence. Sophie has told me that David has

custody of my grandson. Someday, Ashley shall
read about me. Or, perhaps, Sergei shall. In any
case, I do not know where Sergei is. Or shall be.
I asked Captain Petway to ensure my footlocker
made its way to David. He agreed. We nodded
and drifted into silence. He left me a full packet
of cigarettes. He is an honorable warrior and I
am certain I may trust him.

10 May 1945

Today, all is ready. I have written a letter to
my beloved Sophie, Sergei and Ulrika and
put them with my footlocker. Captain Petway
said he would mail them. My small world has
now collapsed totally upon itself. If I could
only survive for a few more years, I know
professional soldiers and spies are always in
demand. My survival is now meted out in days,
or even hours, not years. And I do not know
the whereabouts of Marlena, my child with
Ulrika. I sincerely hope she is alive and well
with her mother. Tanya has disappeared. When
I last heard, she was commanding a group near
Krakow, Poland, launching raids on the red army
behind the lines.

I have just now re-read the relevant portions in
this journal. Hitler started so well, putting the
German people back to work in government
programs and the army. He made Germany
prosperous, more so than any other major
country. By the summer of 1940, he was master
of Europe. And then everything started going
wrong, slowly picking up speed until most of
the country now is in ruins. Especially, Berlin,

which has been destroyed as badly as Sodom.
Was this God's revenge for the decadence of the
Twenties?

That damned Austrian corporal had the gift of
promising exactly what everyone wanted. Myself
included. When one makes a pact with Satan,
one must be certain to read the fine print. There
was the cost, the complete obliteration of Mother
Russia in the name of Lebensraum—living room
for the Germans. I was the ultimate fool in the
ultimate bargain of fools. My tradition did not
help me one jot and it certainly did not prevent
me from failing and badly so. I know I shall not
likely have a tombstone, but if I do, I have my
epitaph selected. It is some lines from Aleksandr
Blok I have committed to memory.

In our hearts, once full of fervor,
there is fateful emptiness.
Let the croaking ravens soar above our death-bed
May those who are worthier, O God, O God,
Behold Thy Kingdom.

On the next page was a letter from Captain Petway to Colonel
David Cooper. Ashley knew Bill pretty well, but he had never
spoken about his wartime experiences. Not uncommon among
combat veterans.

12 May 1945
Dear Uncle David,

Per your instructions, I found Colonel Dmitri
Iskandarov yesterday. Unfortunately, there was
little I could do for him. When I came back
to see him today, I suspected that he might've
killed himself with cyanide rather than surrender
to the Reds. Instead, he was gone and only

left a note. THE WILL SHALL NEVER BE
VANQUISHED. That part I understand, having
read his diary. But the next part is a complete
mystery and I was hoping you might know
something. THE BLOOD IS ISKANDAR. MAY
HE SPEAK TO YOU!

Anyway, I think we'll hear again of Colonel
Iskandarov. Maybe in China. Like the true warrior
he is, he won't ever quit as long as his enemy is
still alive. I suspect the Bleu organization arranged
his escape. I also suspect Ulrika will rejoin him.
They belong together. I found her picture in his
diary's flap. My God, no woman has the right to
be that beautiful and powerful!

I can't say I'm sorry Colonel Iskandarov
escaped. When we handed the S.S. troops over
to the Reds at their lines east of here, we heard
machine gun fire. I think the Red bastards were
killing as many of them as they could, right on
the spot. They didn't even try to hide it. In fact,
they were laughing at us. I've never been more
ashamed to be an American. I think Colonel
Iskandarov was right. We'll soon be at war with
the Red bastards. Then we'll wish we had the
knowledge that was slaughtered today.

Bill

Ashley was very shocked by this slaughter, this murder of
unarmed prisoners and that the Americans could do nothing to
stop it. But Dmitri's writing about the blood also struck him. He
remembered Olga saying the same thing but had no idea what it
meant. Or even who Iskandar might be, beyond the presumed
founder of the House of Iskandarov. With the trunks done, Ashley
went down to his office to consider his next move.

ELEVEN
Monday, 31 May 1993
Quaker Mount & New York, NY

1.

"Ash, sorry to call on a holiday, but I need to see you. Most important."

"OK, Pinky. When?"

"This afternoon."

"All right, it's now 10:27. I can catch the 11:05 and be in your office about two."

"Perfect. Thanks, Ash."

Ashley went to the shower, thinking that again getting away from the Iskandarovs for a while would do him good. Before leaving, he called the bank's twenty-four-access number so he could get into the safe-deposit box on a holiday after his meeting. With any luck, he could still make the afternoon train and be back in time for dinner with any items of interest from the box. Annie said she would be busy reading Dimitri's diary. She needed to know about her great-grandfather—both the good and bad. As she had said, she was no longer a little girl.

Once on the train, Ashley reflected on the very intriguing Ulrika. Dmitri had written that she had surrendered to the British. But had they imprisoned her or sent her back to the Soviets, who, doubtless, wanted their former prisoner back? And if she had survived all that, did she ever reunite with Dmitri? Further, not being Iskandarova, how did she get her superior will? She must belong to one of the other traditions, like the Teutonic Knights, Dmitri had searched for in Berlin. Ashley now sensed she remained alive, even though she would be in her nineties, but there was no one among the living who knew or understood Dmitri better. He had to find her. And what about Georgi and Gisela and their son Heinz? Getting out of Berlin in the last days of the war would have been incredibly difficult. The Soviets would kill them, after raping her. And if they avoided the Soviets, fanatic Nazis were hanging deserters on sight. He stopped and began to clear his head for his meeting while trying to determine what Charles had that was so damn important it could not wait for Tuesday.

2.

After detraining at Grand Central, Ashley saw Fred Grieber, the firm's chauffeur, at the end of the platform. Being tall and fit, he was easy to spot above the crowd and looked much younger than his fifty-odd years. "Mr. Cooper, Mr. Drew sent me to bring you downtown. Had there been time, I would've picked you up at your country home."

Ashley smiled. "Good. Thanks, Fred. I wasn't looking forward to the subway."

"No, sir. In addition, you'll find a very nice lunch in the car's fridge. Afterward, I'm to bring you back upstate, if that's where you want to go."

"Yes, but first, I need to make two stops uptown."

Ashley thought Fred momentarily appeared confused before he nodded his assent. Perhaps Fred had been assigned to watch him, or maybe, over him. Once in the limousine, Ashley contentedly ate pheasant and wild rice off bone china and drank a nice red on a folding mahogany table as Manhattan passed by his smoked glass view. Life as a senior partner, for the moment, was good.

3.

Ashley, tea cup in hand, looked out Charles's window at the harbor. The ant remained between the windows. It had followed its basic nature to squeeze through a small gap to get to something it wanted. And now that it had it, the ant remained. But why? Was it happy there or was it trapped? So much had happened since he last saw it. At least now, Ashley no longer felt trapped.

"Ash, there's no way to sugarcoat this first piece of news. Yesterday afternoon, gunmen broke into Ambassador van Rouene's brownstone and shot and killed him and three former State Department officials who were having a meeting in the drawing room."

"Pinky, unless this was an ordinary robbery, which doesn't sound likely, why would anyone go to the trouble of shooting a man with late-stage terminal cancer?" He shook his head. "Makes no sense."

"No, it doesn't. As you probably know, the ambassador was a long-time client of Gules. He'd spent even more time in Moscow than you have. Funeral will be at St. Jerome's on Wednesday. I want you to be in the delegation."

Ashley nodded. "Of course. What about his wife and baby?"

"Ah yes, thought you might be interested in her." From the way Charles smiled, he knew about his affair. "Both mother and child are missing and presumed kidnapped by the gunmen."

"Any ransom notes?"

Charles shook his head. "NYPD is doing a thorough investigation. Just be aware they might call you. I'll keep you posted on progress."

Ashley nodded. He thought Charles had concocted a great reason why, when the time came, he could not leave the country.

"And that leads me to Larry Fischer. I received another call from NYPD Saturday morning. They fished him, naked, out of the East River. He'd been tortured and had *Juden*, German for 'Jew,' carved on his chest, and they had to identify him from dental records. On this we need containment. No scandal near the Firm. I know you two didn't get on. Have any idea who might have done this?"

"No, Pinky, I don't. Moreover, I didn't like him at all. He was a pushy and obnoxious weasel. So, did I do it? I may have motive, but frankly, he wasn't worth my trouble."

"Good. Nonetheless, Ash, no one deserves to go like that. Especially, a Gules partner."

Right, thought Ashley, *get all righteous about a guy who served as the butt of your endless anti-Semitic jokes.* "No, probably not. However, the guy didn't exactly lack for enemies. As you well know, he had a way of rubbing people the wrong way. Face it, he always had his nose out of joint about something."

"True. Nevertheless, I still don't like this one damn bit. Too many deaths recently. Your wife, then your father, van Rouene and now Fischer. I've no idea who'll replace him on L'Enfant. But I'd like you to keep your eyes open, especially at the van Rouene funeral."

"All right. Anything in particular?"

"No. Just use your sharp powers of observation."

Charles would ensure Fischer officially died in bed of a heart attack from overwork—a more fitting end for a Gules partner. Within a month, a Jewish associate would make partner, and everything would return to normal. In a year, people would not even remember Fischer. Guys like him did not get their pictures on the wall. Not right, but the Firm's way.

Ashley thought, *Surely, Charles had not called me all the way into the city for something he could have done over the phone.* He checked his watch. "So, let's get down to cases, shall we?"

Charles grunted his agreement. He would have reamed any partner who dared say that. "Yes, well, ah, thank you for coming in on a holiday. I wanted to speak to you in person about a rather delicate matter."

Ashley sipped his tea, smiling behind the cup's rim. He had flustered Charles who lit his pipe and almost disappeared in smoke before placing an old, dark-blue file on his desk. He kept his hand on it as he spoke. "This is Spencer Talbott's Firm dossier. I'm particularly concerned, as you doubtless know, with the smooth running of the Firm. And it can't run smoothly as long as one key member is unsettled."

"And why would this person be of interest to me?"

"Ash, the Colonel sat in your chair the last time he was here, and we had a long discussion about Spencer. I've known he was your father since I did the paperwork for David and Patricia to adopt you."

Ashley studied Charles's face before speaking. "I can't say I'm surprised. The Firm's always been pretty tight knit. Before Spencer, do you know what happened to my mother, Charlotte?"

"Take what I'm about to tell you with a grain of salt. It's hearsay. Very soon after your birth, someone from her past abducted her and took her to the Soviet Union. And, no, I don't know who this person was."

"Must've been very clever to get her out of the hospital and off the RAF Wroughton base."

"Precisely. That's why I'm inclined to dismiss this as hearsay." He paused. "I met your mother once, at their wedding. She was a beauty. And now, I'm going to choose my next words very carefully. She had been very wild when younger, and there was a cloud of scandal that followed her. There were probably any number of men in various countries who wanted her dead after birthing you."

Ashley nodded. Ronnie had said Charlotte was in Russia in 1955. And he briefly wondered why no one had ever rescued her and Spencer. "Right, Pinky, good point. Thanks for telling me."

Charles nodded as he pushed the dossier over. "Go ahead and open it and have a look at the document on top. The German translates as... list of prisoners at Luftstalag III-C, near Alt Drewitz, 24 April 1945."

Ashley saw 1st Lieutenant Spencer Talbott, U.S.A.A.F., G.S. about two-thirds of the way down the page, along with Captain

Harvey Jacobs, U.S.A.A.F., G.S. The sheet had German, Russian and American seals on it.

Ashley looked quizzically at Charles as he spoke. "Alt Drewitz was about fifty miles due east of Berlin, on the Oder River, the *luftstalag* where the Germans sent their most dangerous prisoners, either those who'd made multiple escapes or those whose politics set them apart. Your father was there for his several escapes."

Ashley nodded. "Good for him. However, all this proves is that my father wasn't killed at Ploesti and was still alive two weeks before the end of the war."

"Yes, but notice the G.S. next to his name, and indeed, all of them."

Ashley drank his tea before shrugging.

"That's short for *Geheime Staatspolizei,* the official name of the Gestapo. It meant he and the others were marked for execution. Secondly, there's a report in the file from the Red Army major who liberated the camp in early May 1945. No live prisoners were found in the burned camp. In the ruins of one building, they found many charred bodies, who were subsequently identified as Allied and Soviet POWs. All had been executed. David tried to get to the camp, but it was deep behind the Red Army lines, and he was unable to see the site or the bodies. The German camp commandant was hanged for war crimes after the war."

"I've been told by someone I trust that Spencer was alive in Russia as late as 1955."

"Ah yes. Iron Cage, of course. It's a myth propagated by a Fascist agency called Bleu." He shook his head. "Such an innocent name for such a lethal gang of thugs and killers."

"I've heard they were more anti-Communist than Fascist, per se."

"A distinction without a difference. Look, Ash, don't let them or anyone else manipulate you. After all, while you're very intelligent, you can also be gullible by strongly believing in something you want to be true, even if it isn't so."

Ashley could recall several times when that had been true, but it usually involved a woman. And now who had issued his challenge? Another woman, Ronnie. He would be careful. "Perhaps, but what's this Iron Cage?"

"As I say, it's a myth about the closing days of World War II. Supposedly, as the Red Army routed the Germans, they also rounded up refugees, displaced persons and some Allied POWs, and all were sent to the gulag, the Soviet slave labor camps."

"So, I'm assuming that if that were the case, the Allies would have raised holy hell to get our troops back. After all, we had the atomic bomb, and the Soviets would not get one until 1953."

"You make a very good case for its mythic status. I also know about the Iskandarovs. They were Uriah Gules's first foreign client back in the 1880s. But now, they have set up a very sophisticated scheme to lure you to Russia. Once there, both you and Annie will be held for ransom. I've done some preliminaries on this and have a report from a reputable consultant on foreign kidnappings. He estimates they will demand a million for Annie and five million for you."

"Come on, George, that's small potatoes for such an elaborate ruse."

"Very true. The high end is sixty million for you both."

"What proof do you have about the Iskandarov?"

"Only that they now need money desperately. And if they don't get it, you two will simply disappear. The gulag still exists."

"Just out of curiosity, how much would you be willing to pay for our release?"

"I can go as high as six million. However, George says he'd go as high as sixty for both of you."

"Well. That's flattering. Why's he willing to go so high?"

"Simple. You're both family. Annie's his granddaughter, and you're his son-in-law. Plus, he places great value on both your skills."

"What specifically about Annie?"

"Hmm." Charles shook his head. "He only told me she was important. But not why."

Ashley nodded and thought, *He probably wants her for her visions, and I hope that's all. I've heard rumors about him and young girls.*

"Now, I'm willing to structure a tax-free bonus of three million immediately, if you will drop your search and return to work next Monday. That, of course, is in addition to your regular quarterly senior partner's share."

"Very tempting, Pinky. And I truly appreciate the thought. However, I still have some of the Colonel's affairs to be settled. You know how probate judges and estate attorneys can be, especially up in Dutchess for outsiders. I'll give you my answer on Wednesday at the van Rouene funeral. OK?"

"Certainly. I appreciate how busy you are in the wake of your stepfather's death. He was a very fine man and a great asset to the Firm."

"Thank you." He was not surprised Charles knew so much about his search and related matters. He had spies throughout the Firm. And what he did not know, George Farwell, who literally had spies everywhere, did. "Well, if there's nothing else, I have some business to take care of before going back to the Mount."

"Then I won't keep you. And I'll see you Wednesday. I doubt you'll have time to get in your Wednesday tennis at the Racquet. Randell's presiding at the funeral."

"Interesting. I've been so busy I haven't had time to even think about that."

"Yes, well." Charles looked at his watch.

Ashley rose. Their meeting over.

3.

In the back of the limousine, Ashley thought about Charles and his opinions about Bleu, who were, and had been, his protectors. But then, perhaps he was being gullible again. He wanted to believe Bleu were the good guys. After all, anyone fighting against Stalin had to be on the side of the angels. But then, they had sided with Hitler. As Ulrika had said, "Russian émigré politics are very complicated." Perhaps they had protected him so they could cash in later. Damn, he was no better than that ant, following his romantic and fair-minded nature, and was now squeezing through the narrow gap phase of his journey to get to where he thought he wanted to be. But he also felt the Iskandarov's motives could be less than honorable. An Iskandarov ruse could have begun in 1962 with Olga and the Cuban Missile Crisis. After that, actual detente with the Soviets began, although not formalized for several years. Such a time must have been hard for Bleu as was the recent fall of the Soviets. Financially speaking, peace is the nemesis for any intelligence agency, but especially Russian-focused Bleu as contributions dried up. So, yes, they probably did need money now. Although Ashley knew there were non-Iskandarovs in Bleu, in his mind, they were one. He would be careful and skeptical as he moved forward. And Charles's telling of Charlotte's kidnapping to Russia fit with what he knew. What he, personally, needed was definite proof Spencer was alive after the war. And, also, he needed to know much more about this Iron Cage. Moving on, he thought about the death of Ambassador van Rouene, in this case, an act of mercy. But he felt that Lana, also known as Svetlana Polinkova with the KGB mother, was the most likely suspect. She certainly had motive and the expertise to do it. And his proof was Fischer because he remembered Lana had inquired about Ashley's "Fischer problem" that day of the benefit. And Lana was an agent, who after going to Montreal, came home mid-week, and Fischer showed up dead on Saturday and the ambassador was shot on Sunday. But who were the three former State Department officials meeting with van Rouene? If, on the other hand, Lana had been killed, he would mourn for her. But now he had to stop at his apartment and pick up the safe-deposit key before going to the bank.

4.

When they arrived at the bank on the corner of Madison and 90th, Ashley told Fred he would be a while. Once alone in the private safe-deposit room, he found in the box, among other things, a roll of cash, a gold bar, a portfolio of bearer bonds and real estate land deeds, jewelry, keys, bankbooks and memorabilia. Ashley smiled. David, having gone through the Depression, always hedged with hard assets that would retain their value better than currency. At least he had not stashed it all under his mattress, as many of his generation had done. Last, he found a dog-eared folder—Spencer Talbott's army air force file with "Top Secret" on the top of the cover page. The usual code word after that had been replaced with "Eyes Only-R. D." for "Restricted Distribution." He noticed a stapled note in the upper right corner.

Dave,

This settles our debt in full. We're done. Don't even ask me for so much as a paperclip!

H.A.K.

Ashley scanned the control list on the first page, noting the initials. He recognized the most prominent four. D.D.E. had to be Dwight David Eisenhower, so J.F.D. was John Foster Dulles, his secretary of state. A.W.D. would be Allen Welsh Dulles, head of Central Intelligence and G.S.F. would be George Simpson Farwell. Ashley could understand George's interest in Spencer, but why Ike and the Dulleses? The seal on the file had been broken. Ashley had worked with enough classified documents to know this was authentic. As he went through the file, nothing seemed remarkable... until he came to an addendum with typed pages, stamped again "Eyes Only-R.D." in red on every page.

My name is Spencer Dryden Talbott. No, actually, now as I sit here, I realize Spence Talbott's dead now some ten years. He died in a cattle car, moving north into a Russian Hell. It has been some time since I actually had a name, rather than a number. Therefore, now some twenty-five, or so, years since I abandoned

it, I'm again proud to say my name's Sergei
Dmitrovich Iskandarov. I think some six weeks
has passed since my mission ended. I'm not
really sure, but as best as I can tell, it's now
November of 1955.

My God, Ashley thought. *I recognize my father's handwriting. This is just what I need right now. In 1955, ten years after Luftstalag III-C, my father remained alive, verifying what Ronnie told me and debunking Charles.* The "Russian Hell" was the gulag, where his father had spent those ten years. Incredible to have survived there that long. Ashley sensed that this new journal would be painful, but it would also shed light on Iron Cage. He would read it in the privacy of the limousine.

Going down the hill on 96th Street toward the FDR Drive and the East River, Ashley recalled that, in November, 1955, then twelve, he went daily to seventh grade, not far from here, completely oblivious that his father even existed. He wanted to start the journal, but he just needed more time.

Once on the Drive, Ashley looked out the tinted window at Randall's Island, the scene of so many of his youthful athletic triumphs. They now seemed distant, trivial and far removed from anything that mattered. The time had come. "Fred, don't take it personally when I raise the privacy window. I've something I really need to focus on."

"No problem, Mr. Cooper. I've had assignments when I had no idea who was back there. Let me know if you need anything."

Ashley smiled and raised the window and after rereading the first paragraph, continued.

The trees outside my one small window are bare
but still free of snow. There was a time when I
might now be rhapsodizing about the change of
seasons, but such things belong in another life,
another world.

I have no idea where I am. I haven't seen another
human for several days. Before that I was
subjected to a constant round of interrogations
and how shall I put it? 'Inducements to
cooperate' is their favored term. Last week, I
wrote down and signed a confession, just as I
was ordered. I also told them about Iron Cage
and that may be the only reason I'm still alive.
Since I'm not going to be shot, I now want
to record the true events. I know how soon
memories fade. I've had to keep the truth straight
in my mind, so as not to interfere with my cover
story. Before every interrogation, I've relived
the events in minute detail. But this is a story
that must be told. Thank God, the journals of
my imprisonment in the Soviet network of slave
labor camps—the Gulag—are safe.

There it was. Sergei had definitely been in the gulag as a result
of Iron Cage and in typical Iskandarov fashion had kept a journal.

I made a deal with Chichikov. The release of
Binkie in exchange for my 'volunteering' for
this assignment and its successful completion.
He doesn't know about my journals. I know I
can't trust Chichikov or Svetlana Feliksovna, for
that matter, but what choice did I have? Neither
one of them would have hesitated to pour acid
on Binkie's face—or worse, to get what they
wanted. The chances Chichikov has, by now,
kept his word are so infinitesimal that an ant
would tower over them. Yet slender as that thread
of hope may be, it was the only one Binkie had.
Besides, I suspect without me present, their
sadistic games have lost their edge. Still I pray
that Binkie has been released and is safe.

As Ashley looked out at the South Bronx, it sounded like Svetlana Feliksovna had not only tortured Natalya but this Binkie as well. He pondered Spencer's naming subterfuge for a while. Binkie sounded English or American, although he had never heard it. Spencer loved Charlotte and Binkie and probably they were the same person. That meant Charlotte and Spencer had been reunited in Svetlana Feliksovna's hell house. Had Chichikov been the one who abducted her? Sergei had been in the gulag and, for some reason, Svetlana FelikOvna had brought him back to her "institute." It almost fit together beautifully with gossamer wings. He just needed proof. Come on, Dad, give me a hint. Receiving nothing, he turned to Iron Cage. Clearly, the men responsible for it had destroyed any proof of their actions. And with his initials on the document, George Farwell was deeply involved and, even, the group's leader. This was the reason he did not want Ashley going back to Russia to search for the diary. Thus, George believed it still existed.

> I entered this country under a forged American
> passport, my handler sitting beside me on the
> Lufthansa flight. I briefly felt great joy and
> pride when I saw the Statue of Liberty from
> the aircraft. I had not seen it since '42 when I
> shipped out for Europe with the Eighth. I thought
> of all the people I knew and had known in that
> other life. How today was just another day for
> them, no different from any other. Perhaps there
> was an important meeting or a birthday, but
> nothing more. How unlike my day. After we
> landed at the new Idlewild Airport in Queens,
> we took a taxi to Penn Station in Manhattan.
> There were some new buildings I saw on the
> way in but surprisingly, the city hadn't changed
> all that much. At Penn Station, it was so strange
> to be walking through the familiar giant rotunda

amidst all these people, perhaps even some I
might know, and realize I was the only person
in the huge room who wasn't free. I could've
easily overpowered my handler and escaped,
but then Binkie would've been killed. Horribly,
I'm certain. Besides, where would I go? I don't
belong among normal people any longer. It has
been far too long. I've no homeland and both my
adopted countries have made it very clear they
don't want me. All I care about in the world's
back in Russia and I know, regardless of the
outcome of the mission, I'll never see her again.
There's another person, for whom I care deeply,
although I have never met him. I've, out of
necessity, forgotten that person exists. As best I
can.

Ashley wanted to shout back at the pages, *It's all right, Dad.
I have your journal. I understand now. I'll make it right.* But
make what right?

The train stopped in Washington, D.C. and we
went to a house out in the Maryland countryside.
I was blindfolded there to condition my eyes to
darkness. I lay down and drifted between sleep
and waking until it was time to go. It was funny;
I was completely calm there, as though I had
nothing to lose. And in fact, I don't. All I have
left is my life. That and a nickel will get me on
the NYC subway, unless they have raised the
token price in my absence.

As my handler led me to a car, I could smell
his patchouli. It must have been a large car
because I was placed between two people. I can
still smell the man's sweat, mixed with cheap
Russian makhorka tobacco on my left. And the

sour, vinegary smell of an older woman on my right. Chichikov was not there. I'd know his scent anywhere. Of course, he would send his subordinates to oversee the mission.

When the car briefly stopped, I was pushed out and my blindfold removed. The car drove off quickly with lights out, so I couldn't see any of them. It was a moonless night in September. Dressed in black, I applied the black grease to my face as I'd been instructed. I looked at my watch. It was 0255 and the patrol was due by in four minutes. I should've been concerned about concealment, but I was struck, for the first time, in God knows how long, I was free. I knew I was not but enjoyed the fantasy and breathed in deeply of the free air. Someone had been burning leaves and the wonderful smoky aroma still carried on the air, mixed with something I did not recognize at first—apples. Having briefly smelled the marvel of free air, I began my fall into the sulphurous depths of Hell once more. I knew, regardless of the outcome, I'd never smell such sweetness again. And to make matters even worse, my tvarsch has abandoned me and I don't know when it would return.

I moved into the bushes, still savoring the scents. A small naval patrol passed by my location at 0259. At least the information I had was accurate.

Going into the forest, I navigated using only my back-lit compass and luminous dial watch. I've done this drill so often, I can do it in my sleep. Feeling the change of terrain underfoot at about twenty minutes into my mission, I knew I was

on the Nature Trail. I waited for another patrol
to pass before moving toward my goal. This was
the tricky part. Once I left the trees, I'd be in
the open, completely exposed. I didn't know the
patrol schedule there. Such information wasn't
available. Moving as quickly as I could, I stopped
short when I heard voices to my left. Flattening
myself on the cut grass, I felt as inconspicuous
as an elephant on a billiards table. My adrenaline
raced while my training and focus remained
strong. Slowly, something began to invade my
consciousness—the great aroma of Luckies. I
instantly remembered their red on green packet.
The smell was reassuring, and my heartbeat
slowly came down, so I could hear what they
were talking about. Not surprisingly, they were
both bragging about their girlfriends. I remained
motionless as the voices got up and faded away.
I waited two minutes before I cautiously rose
and ran in a semi-crouch toward where I'd been
told the main building, Aspen, was. However, as
I moved closer, I realized the building was too
small to be Aspen. I was lost. My first though was
Chichikov had done this. I well knew his sadistic
ways. Was this a test? Or did he wish me to fail?
After all, there aren't exactly shortages of men
like me. I squatted down and breathed deeply
until I regained my composure. I wasn't going to
fail. I couldn't. I also think that I began to calm
down then and had even smiled. I went over to
another small building. From there, I could see
a larger building, the correct size for Aspen. I
ran again in my semi-crouch for about fifty feet.
There was a light on in the structure.

I could see the Upper Terrace, just as described,
the light was coming from the Sun Room. I
crawled across the Lower Terrace and carefully
stood up. Very aware I was semi-exposed by the
Sun Room light, I moved very cautiously toward
the rightmost window. There was a light on in
there as well. Perhaps he was reading in bed. I
took a deep breath and shook my head. I drew
my pistol, an eight-shot Tokarev TT-33 without
silencer. (My planners wanted the shots to be
heard.) I looked around outside one final time
and then carefully moved one of the light green
curtains. No one was there. Typical SNAFU.
Then I noticed one of the beds was recently slept
in. I hadn't noticed initially because it almost
seemed undisturbed. However, it wasn't the one
he reportedly slept in. What if it were his wife
who was here tonight? My anger again flared
against Chichikov. No doubt, the bastard had
again set me up. Nevertheless, I couldn't turn
back now. I holstered my pistol and as quietly as
I could, climbed in through the window. I sat on
the undisturbed bed and redrew my pistol. Alert
for any noise, I looked around. The oak paneling
was painted pale pink and three floral prints hung
above the twin beds. It was hard to believe I was
in the right place, but it was exactly as described.
It seemed the boudoir of an old woman, not the
bedroom of the most powerful man on the planet.

Oh my God, he's going to really shoot Eisenhower. This is
Camp David, his presidential retreat in the Maryland hills.

I pointed my Tokarev toward the door after
heard a toilet flush. I recognized my target
from countless pictures and newsreels, plus a

'meeting we had long ago in England before our eighteenth mission. I carefully aimed, hesitated momentarily and squeezed off a single shot at his shoulder as I'd been told. President Eisenhower looked at his wound and then at me. All he could do was shake his head and ask, "Why didn't you kill me?" I smiled and carefully placed the pistol on the bed. 'General, this is a souvenir from the Lost Souls of Luftstalag III-C, whom you abandoned.'

Before Eisenhower could respond, his security detail barged in. I don't remember too much after that, except being hit and kicked until I passed out.

Eisenhower had been an icon in the Cooper household, and Ashley totally suppressed his emotions as he looked out at the trees along the Hutchison River Parkway. Probably similar to the ones Annie had found so fascinating after the Colonel's funeral. He took his Sainte Elizabeta icon from his suit pocket, and her large eyes' light began to sooth him, and he began thinking. *Luftstalag* III-C was the camp Charles had talked about earlier. Here was proof of Iron Cage—the Red Army had simply kidnapped all the POWs from III-C and sent them to the gulag where they became the "Lost Souls" and joined the swept-up POWs from other *luftstalags*. Eisenhower had not demanded their return and had broken faith with his troops. And that would be the reason that Sergei was, probably, initially anxious to go on the mission, thinking then the goal was to kill Eisenhower. Thus, the threatened disfigurement of Binkie was necessary to get Sergei to only wound him. And, at some point, Sergei must have realized that Eisenhower was only following orders from higher ups. He also knew he would be shot for the killing but only imprisoned for the wounding and might have a chance of seeing Binkie again. But the Lost Souls wanted Eisenhower dead. And that had to be the reason Sergei hesitated about where the shot would go. He had written about his mission earlier, but nothing of earth-shaking consequence. *How unlike my day.* So, he must have felt that simply wounding Eisenhower, not a young man, would make him decide not to run for reelection, which would have radically changed world history, almost as much as if he had killed him. Now, while Ashley felt satisfied, he still puzzled over why his father would have been extensively trained and come so far to only wound the president.

> As the sun arose, I began my round of interrogations. They said I had messed up, I only wounded the president. They had put out a story the president had suffered a heart attack and was rushed to Walter Reade Hospital. Therefore, my assassination attempt was a complete failure. I let them think that. I have won, in every way that counts. I remain uncomfortable with the idea of having shot an unarmed man. Especially one I used to hold in such high esteem. I still do not know why I was only to wound him. However, that was hardly my decision. Binkie is, ultimately, all that matters. And what price do I pay? It's not so bad here. And while it certainly isn't the Ritz, it is, relative to the places I have been, quite tolerable. So now, all I have to do is wait for time, either theirs or mine, to run out. Message delivered.

Ashley looked thoroughly to see if there were any other entries or items. There was nothing, even in the flaps. He now became excited to read Sergei's Cuban diaries, which would clarify this further. Ronnie had said she would drop them off before she left. With her phone disconnected, that had to be soon. He also wanted to speak to the Cuban woman who gave Ronnie the diaries and would call in every favor he had coming to find her, even if he had to go to Cuba, which would be a challenge. But as long as there remained a chance Sergei still lived, he had to try to meet him.

5.

Ashley felt great relief watching Fred leave the Woodinville train station. There was just something about him that Ashley had never fully trusted, but he did not know what. As he drove home, Ashley shook his head. He still had his "I Like Ike" campaign button somewhere. While he could not fully condone what his father had done, the lives of his father and his mother had hung in the balance. And now, knowing the basics of Iron Cage, what Sergei had done made a certain sense. No, it would be George and any other surviving members of the group who abandoned all these people, military and civilian, to a living hell, who would pay, along with any surviving Russians. He made an oath to do this. He had killed a man in Southeast Asia, so he could do it again if the opportunity arose.

TWELVE

Monday Afternoon, 31 May 1993
Quaker Mount, NY

1.

Ashley arrived home about four-thirty. "Annie?"

"Yes, Dad. Up in the attic. I'm right in the middle of something very complicated. See you later. We're having a special dinner."

"OK. Was Ronnie here?"

"Yes. Just left about a half hour ago. There's a package in your office."

"Great. Sorry I missed her. I'll be in my room with the package."

"OK, see ya."

As he passed the dining room, Ashley saw two places set with their best silver and tableware. He also noticed that Annie had opened a bottle of red wine, which was breathing on the sideboard.

He dropped Sergei's file face down on his office desk and took the brown-paper package with him. After closing his bedroom door, he changed into his jeans and sat in his easy chair, hoping this diary would clarify the many questions remaining from Camp David. But first, Ronnie's note.

31.5.93

Ash,

I leave today. I'm confident if the two of you
work together, you'll be successful. Annie
definitely has what we People of the Blood call
'pyordarsh,' like her great-grandmother, Sophia.
And you have your tvarsch. Use them to guide
you as your ancestors have for the millennia.
When the time's right, I'll find you.

Bonne Chance,

R.

Clearly, Ronnie did not want to talk to him, precisely what he
would have done. And "People of the Blood" was an interesting
term for the Iskandarov, even though he did not fully understand
why. Opening the package, he found a slender black book
with thin cardboard covers. On the front, in a white rectangle
under the Cuban flag, was "Direccion General de Intelligencia-
Interrogatorio." This was an interrogation notebook used by the
Cuban DGI, now known as DI. Ashley felt impressed Sergei had
managed to get it. Opening it, he saw the first pages had been
carefully removed. Yet another question to add to the list. The
paper was cheap and smelled of mold and mildew from careless
long-term storage.

12 June 1968

Again, I offer only truth, as ugly, unvarnished,
and uncomfortable as that may be. Should this
diary be discovered, that's God's will and I'll
perish. Nevertheless, I'm confident this diary
will one day find its way to my son when he
needs to learn about these events.

I was sitting at a small table this morning on
the balcony of our sea-side villa in Vailadero
where the Cubans have me, some two hours,
by car, east of Havana. The villa had belonged

to a rich capitalist before the revolution. All the
furnishings have long since been 'liberated by
the people.' I share the top floor where the wall's
bas relief details are caked in dust, the floor is
bare, and the furniture is coarsely utilitarian. But,
after the places I've been, it's very luxurious
and the two adjoining bedrooms are large—the
nicest jail I've ever been in. I've been told Castro
has a villa here and I may meet him. It's good to
breathe tropical air again, like in the old days.
I've been confined since 1943, almost twenty-
five years. And I had the nightmare again last
night that this was a dream and I woke back in
my cell. (Since they all looked pretty similar,
I don't know which one.) Sometimes, I hear a
heavy door slamming behind me and I flinch.
I'm so used to hearing my thoughts that actually
speaking for an extended period still seems
bizarre. I share the place with my debriefer,
Maria, such a religiously inappropriate name
for a capitan in the Cuban DGI. I'd guess she's
in her mid-twenties. Most nights I'm in my
bedroom, with the door locked, but not because
she's unattractive. On the contrary, she's dark
with a lush body and wide hips, a true baby-
making machine. God, in His wisdom, gave
such women something extra so men would be
attracted. She wears that like perfume. If I close
my eyes, she's a bit of heaven until I open them
and see her eyes—cold and dull. I've seen those
eyes before, but only on people much older.
I knew her mother, Angelina, a high-priced
courtesan, known as 'compagne' or, in English,
'companion,' a woman not merely skilled in bed
but also out of it. As opposed to the lower-class

'puta.' Maria bragged on the first day that she'd
been a puta since young. (Makes no sense to
me. It must be some proletarian bona-fides she
needs because of her very elegant mother.) She's
tried to seduce me several times and when that
fails, she punishes me during debrief by arousing
me right up to the point where I almost lose my
concentration. But she's not yet pushed me over.
(We play a complicated game in which control
is always shifting back and forth in the debriefs.)
Yesterday, she left bed naked and slipped on
a thin cotton dress. During debrief, which she
conducts in her very good English, I saw the
dark areas around her nipples through the fabric.
It was eerily like being watched by a second
pair of eyes. But also, very arousing. I asked her
to put on her bra. She frowned and told me her
bra's too small. She made a face and told me all
Cuban bras are horrible in design and comfort
and the one she has was the last of her mother's
American ones. If she performs well on this
assignment, her superior has promised her a new
American Maidenform. She was undecided about
the color. Red—the color of the Revolution or
Black—the color of the black widow. She asked
me which color I prefer. I felt confused, unless
this was a gambit. Maria isn't one for wasting
time. Yet here she was, doing precisely that. She
asked me again. I said some think red's the color
of a woman's power and black's seductive. She
responded the Red Revolution is the source of
her power and the black widow is the symbol
of the ultimate seduction. She licked her lips in
a positively obscene manner and continued her
debrief, taking extensive notes. At six, she broke

out the rum and we had a modest supper before
going for a long walk on the beach until dark.
On the beach, she asked me, in Spanish, if I
liked her. I replied, 'Like has nothing to do with
it. First, I'm married. Second, I know you're a
Rose, a female assassin, who, like your black
widow spider, kill their males after sex.' (I spoke
with, and protected, a number of former Roses
in the gulag, who had fallen afoul of Stalin.)
'One day, the order will come down to kill me
and you will. That's your job. You putas make
the best Roses because you don't give a shit
about men. Also, only a Rose has a Russian-
made steel watch, with concealed garrote.' She
replied, 'You've nothing to fear. I've not used it
in years. I simply like the watch. You're a hero.
That's all that matters.' She smiled a joyless
smile, which never fails to chill my blood. That
and her eyes make her almost like a vampire
seductress. Then she totally surprised me. 'My
mother, Angelina Civilli Mendes, who thinks
greatly of you and is a highly place official in
the DGI, has told everyone involved you're
under her personal protection. Anyone who
harms you will be terminally punished. So,
again, you've nothing to fear. And you're the
hero of Camp David.' I replied, 'Your mother's
still alive and in the DGI? I'd love to see her.'
'You will once we finish our debriefings.' Later,
when she again propositioned me, I didn't say
yes, but I didn't give her a definite no either.
While I don't trust Maria, I don't fear death
as I once might have. (I've been living on
borrowed time for so long, the interest will
come due any day now.) So, I'll chance sleeping

with her because I can gain tactical advantage.
That night, I left my door unlocked and around
midnight, in she came. The next morning,
besides being alive, I feel better than I've felt
in a long time. I know Binkie would forgive me
for Maria, just as we did at the Soviet Genetic
Research Institute. When there's no freedom,
there can be no choice.

The Soviet Genetic Research Institute. Lana had spoken
about this, where Svetlana Feliksovna researched 'people.' The
Soviets always gave their most hellacious places the most benign
names.

I made some Cuban coffee and the aroma woke
her. After breakfast— fruit and Cuban toast with
guava paste, she sat at her desk and reviewed
yesterday's notes. (I don't think there's been
a day since 1943 when I haven't rehearsed
what I was going to say. It has been one of my
disciplines that kept me alive.) We resumed
where I'd left off at Camp David. I'd just shot
Eisenhower and watched him bleed as I told
him why I was there. He had the most perplexed
expression on his face as he sat on the bed,
saying he couldn't believe I would have come
all this way simply to wound him. He looked at
his wound and nodded before looking at me. He
spoke softly, saying he was sorry about not doing
anything for 'my boys, the Lost Souls.' He'd
tried but had been repeatedly blocked by his
superiors. Then, the security detail broke in and
pinned me to the floor, where I was hit on the
head and passed out.

When I came to, I see bars all around, like the
ape cages in the Central Park Zoo, only this

time, outside, the two heavily armed guards are
the apes. The door opens, and two lugs drag me
to an interrogation room with two guys in suits.
The first guy says I should call him Mr. Stevens
and asks me why I'd tried to kill President
Eisenhower. I tell him I didn't intend to kill my
president. My orders had been to simply wound
him. Of course, he doesn't buy this. (He's a lug
who totally missed me saying 'my president.'
He was going to be trouble.) He calls me a
'fuck-up' who was just trying to cover up his
incompetence. I counter that an incompetent
would never have gotten anywhere near the
president and if I'd shot a few inches over, Nixon
would be president.

I got up to get more coffee, asking Maria if she
wanted some. This gave me time to think about
the next phase of debrief, about the second guy,
Mr. Nicholas, who would say my English was
quite good for a Russian and asked where I'd
learned it. Sure, a routine question, but I was
then in a quandary how to answer. He'd given
me an opportunity to talk about Iron Cage. But, I
doubted he was senior enough to know anything
about it. On the other hand, I could tell him I'd
learned English as part of my training. If they
thought I was simply an incompetent Russian
agent, I would be traded back in the near future.
Nevertheless, if they found out about Iron Cage,
maybe they could get all the surviving POWs
out. The new regime wants to make a break
with the past. Stalin had finally been murdered
by his closest comrades on 5 March 1953. And
the Gangster suffered in torment for a long time

because his guards were too scared to enter his
rooms without being summoned. (Serves him
right! And I got this from one of the guards
who'd been sent to the gulag.) I liked Nicholas
and had volunteered a bit of unimportant
information to him. We all know rule number
one in interrogation is never, ever, volunteer
anything. But this time, I had a gambit. I told
Maria the truth I'd finally arrived at. Nicholas
asks me about my English and I reply I'd learned
it at Harvard. At first, Stevens threatens to beat
me senseless, but I tell them I've won. Nicholas
asks me what I mean. I tell him Secretary
Khrushchev has a message. Now that Stalin's
dead, there could be a new era of cooperation.
Nevertheless, if the Americans don't cooperate,
there would be a fatal message delivered to the
next president.

Ashley reread the last lines. Oh my God, this was the genesis
of the Kennedy assassination. What a cleverly diabolical plan,
the kind Khrushchev, reportedly, favored. That was why Sergei
had only wounded the president. Sergei was giving, as promised,
the truth in his diary. Ashley knew from experience that such
sensitive information like this would never be released to the
public. And he had forgotten how the government hushed this up
after Kennedy.

They confer about this for some time. Nicholas
gives me a Lucky before he leaves, and, under
Stevens's glowering, I gratefully smoke it. (I
noticed the Lucky pack is now red and white and
I ask Stevens when the pack was changed. Not
surprisingly, he doesn't reply. Probably doesn't
know.) When Nicholas comes back, he asks me
more about my life. When I told him I was a

bombardier, he thinks I was a Russian one. When
he finds out I was with the 8th and had been
downed on Ploesti, Nicholas seems interested.
He might even be excited too. (It's hard to
tell with him.) He asks me who I was with. I
told him 'the Lost Souls.' He asks me if this
had something to do with Korea. I look at him
blankly. (I'm amazed when he tells me there had
been a three-year war in Korea. I honestly didn't
know. Both in the gulag and later with Chichikov
and Svetlana Feliksovna, my supply of external
information was limited to the glorious triumphs
of Socialism. Obviously, this war wasn't a part of
that.) Recovering, I tell him if he doesn't know
about the Lost Souls, he should ask the president,
who knows all about it and is troubled. Stevens
is sitting there getting angrier and angrier. He
gets up, throws me against the wall and grabs
me, getting so close to my face, I can see veins
bulging in his forehead. He says I have one
final chance to come clean. I spit in his face.
He smashes my face, draws blood and again
throws me against the wall. (He doesn't know
I'm sort of numb to this treatment after all my
interrogations.)

Ashley now recognized that Mr. Stevens was Nick Stevens'
father. *Being stupid and violent must run in the family. And this
hatred of Sergei had to be why Nick hated me so much in school.
And the big moron had joined his father's profession.*

Nicholas gives me another Lucky, a glass of
water and gets his handkerchief all bloody
sticking it up my nose to stop the bleeding.
Meanwhile, Stevens is over in the corner
making threatening noises. I looked at him and

laughed. I mean, I've been worked over by the
S.S., Gestapo, the NKGB, MGB, MVD KGB
(All four the same agency over eight years.)
plus Chichikov and Svetlana Feliksovna. And
these guys are playing good cop-bad cop? I
tell them they're pathetic. There's absolutely
nothing they could do to scare me. I've seen it
all. I think they're beginning to realize this—for
a moment. Stevens is up again and says he's
going to bash my head in, but Nicholas holds
him back. Stevens asks me how solitary strikes
me. I couldn't help it and laugh again. I tell him
I could do that standing on my head. I'm an
alumnus of the Icebox. Not surprisingly, they ask
what that is. Either, these guys are really ignorant
or are simply acting that way. I begin with the
gulag.

Maria commented, 'Yes, I have heard of these
slave labor camps. To me, it shows the great
weakness of the Russian communists. We,
like your country, have no such camps here
in Cuba. Only real criminals are in jail, where
they belong. Here, everyone loves and respects
Mi Fidel. (She obviously believes this fairy
tale so strongly, I won't even try to tell her the
brutal truth. All absolute regimes have a gulag
in one form or another.) She looked at me
quizzically. Again, a flicker of light in her eye,
but soon gone. The Icebox is a cell they have at
Vorkuta for troublemakers—the ideologically
unredeemable and uncooperative. They toss
you in there, naked. Vorkuta's almost always
cold, only the intensity varies. The Icebox is
unheated concrete, designed to be just cold

enough to deprive you of sleep but not cold
enough to seriously damage you. Still, after the
first week, you're a basket case. Nobody comes
out the second week. (My filthy, lice-ridden
pallet in the barracks never looked so good
after that.) Stevens says he could put me into
an unheated Quonset hut where it would get
very cold at night. I just sadly shake my head.
Stevens really is truly stupid, but even he can
see his threats aren't having the desired effect.
He whips out his pistol and jams it against my
head. I remain calm and recognize his pistol as
a skeletal-grip Beretta .25 caliber automatic.
According to my training, it's a 'disposable,'
not standard issue. I tell him if he kills me, he'll
never find out the truth. Then, totally ignoring
him, I speak to Nicholas and tell him it's obvious
Eisenhower would be re-elected next year. (That
is, 1956.) I know Nixon would be the nominee
in 1960. However, I couldn't imagine whom the
Democrats would run against him. Either Nixon
or the Democrat would be killed while in office
unless the Americans change their policies.
(I can't deliver my message too many times,
especially to this crew.) I tell them when they're
interrogating the next presidential assassin, they
could've prevented it today, but didn't because
Stevens has a bigger gun than brain. Nicholas
nods and Stevens lowers the pistol. And I remind
them again Secretary Khrushchev's message
needs to be sent to the president and his cabinet.
Otherwise, a big problem for Nixon. Nicholas
nods his understanding and asks me some more
about being a bombardier. I tell him some details.
When he asks about our targets, I tell him that's

classified. He tells me I can tell him because the
War was long over, (If only he knew. My War
is never over. I don't tell him or Maria that, of
course.) I tell him about how we were shot up
so badly on our eighteenth mission. He listens
without comment. I think he might commiserate
or tell an equally stirring war story, but he
doesn't. He probably sat out the War in DC or
someplace. He wants to know the target for the
eighteenth mission. I refuse. He again tells me
intelligence is perishable. I told him bananas are
too. And I've seen many good men give their
lives for those bananas. I tell him how an S.S.
major lined up a bunch of us in the luftstalag.
Asked first guy where his base was. He didn't
answer, and the major shot him. He went to the
second guy. Same question. No answer. Boom!
Dead! Third guy shat his pants but told him. I
guess the major didn't respect weakness because
he then blew three's head off. The major laughed
and told the rest of us we were dismissed. I'm
number four, got three's brains and blood all
over my flight jacket. I ask Stevens to tell me
what those guys died for. He shakes his head. I
tell him the Germans knew our bases. The major
was just having fun, playing with our heads. I
ask him if he'd ever seen a guy so scared, he
shits his pants. I tell Stevens I knew number
three, Captain Jack Weldon, from III-C and
before. He was normally cool as ice and I guess
he just had a bad day. Everyone has a bad day.
Some of us have had more than one. (I've had a
string going for quite a while now.) I finally get
through to my interrogators. They know they're
beaten and the same lugs take me back to my

cell. I sleep through until the following morning. My cell is the Plaza Hotel compared to the places I've been. Maria looked at me and smiled a bit. She said she doesn't believe the two American interrogators could possibly be that stupid and inexperienced. Now she's going to have to run me through the whole thing again. I made some wise guy comment 'that will mess up our social life' (She can put whatever she wants to in her report.) I did confess Eisenhower said he wanted me alive, so I knew their limits. Maria was now angry and asked if I'd left out any other details. I thought for a while and shook my head. She signaled I can take a break. She needed to catch up on her report. I went out on the balcony and lit my cigar. You can never tell about these new Cuban cigars, sometimes wonderful, sometimes horrible. I lucked out on this one. If I have to go through the interrogation again, I must be completely consistent. I ran through what I'd said, as my cigar smoke drifted out over the palm trees. After a while, I watched the sea rolling in as a seagull glided above. (I would love to come back as a gull and glide over beaches and seas.) My reverie was broken by Maria's call to come back. I puffed away and watched the smoke drift up to heaven. I don't hurry for anyone now that I'm a hero. Maria came out, stood by me, interrupted my thoughts and took my cigar, letting the smoke dribble out of her mouth. As she did so, she looked at me and I again thought I saw, for an instant, a trace of light in those dead eyes. Then, gone, she told me to come inside and continue. (I bring my cigar with me and she made me go through it again.)

We resumed the next day, I'm brought into the
same interrogation room—different guy who's
very solicitous of my well-being. I can tell
he's somebody important. He has an air about
him, 'Ivy League clubby,' that my trainers said
typified senior agents of Central Intelligence.
(Not terribly different from Donovan's OSS boys
back in the War. The camps took all my Harvard
clubbiness out of me long ago.) He tells me his
name's Baker. He has my file and reads it out
loud, noting I've been promoted to Captain. I
didn't know this. He says it's posthumous. So,
how'd I get the fingerprints of a man who was
among those the Gestapo massacred at Luftstalag
III-C in the closing days of the War? I tell him
because the massacre was a phony. He carefully
takes my fingerprints for comparison to my file.
Finally, satisfied that, at least, my fingerprints
are real, he notes my family fought against
the Reds for decades. So, why was I working
for the Commies? I shake my head. It's very
complicated. He nods and says, 'It always is with
you guys.' He then tells me Mamman Sophie
died in her sleep in Paris on 27 May 1949. (This
I'd learned in the gulag from a Bleu agent.)
My father, Dmitri, was killed at Shanghai just
before the city fell to the Chinese Communists,
the day before Sophie died, I didn't know this.
I ask him if he knows how Dmitri died. Baker
says, reportedly, he was outside an abandoned
nightclub in the former International Settlement
with a German lady. A man comes up to him and
shoots him dead. The German lady then shoots
and kills the assassin. (Father died an honorable
soldier's death fighting for the liberation of the

Motherland. I'm glad he didn't meet his end at
the hands of the Gangster. That's great comfort.)

Ashley smiled. Dmitri and Ulrika did get back together. *I
love this lady!* While Ashley felt sad Dmitri had been killed, he,
at least, had a warrior's death, as Sergei had said. At the time of
his death, he seemed to have escaped the Nazis and resumed his
struggle. And now, in death, he had also avoided the war crimes
tribunals, who were looking far down the command chain.

I thank him. However, I tell him, what I can't
stomach was the way the American government
just handed over all our people to Gangster
Stalin at the end of the War. I had many cousins,
uncles and aunts and friends, amongst the 38,000
Cossacks and their families who were forcibly
repatriated to the Gangster in Austria and
Czechoslovakia in 1945. All of my immediate
family members were French citizens. I told him
I'm an American citizen. Baker says the guy I'm
pretending to be is American and asks me how I
know about this repatriation. He claims he never
heard anything about it. (I don't believe him, not
then, not now.) I reply while most were shot on
the spot, some survived to die slowly in the
gulag, where I'd spoken with them. He shakes
his head and says such persons are an unreliable
source. Maria again smiled at the gulag reference
and wrote down something in her report. Baker
seems to feel it's necessary to convince me of the
rightness of the American position. Therefore, he
gives me a song and dance about how those
Cossacks had fought for the Germans, even for
the S.S., and the American government was
simply trying to get our own POWS back from
the Russians. I ask him why the 'Soviets, our

gallant wartime allies' weren't forthcoming with
American and Allied POWs. He replied there
was great confusion in the days following the
end of the War. Also, uncertain front lines
between the Allies and the Red Army, which, if
contact were made, could easily lead to a
shooting crisis. I reminded him that had
happened at the Elbe River, near Torgau,
Germany and there was no shooting. (That was
in a Pravda I read.) However, all POWs were
eventually repatriated. I tell him, without anger,
I'm one of the POWs caught up in Iron Cage and
not repatriated. I catch some recognition of the
term. Clearly, in one day, I've gone far up the
ladder. Maria smiled contentedly at the Iron
Cage reference. She asked me how much I knew
about this. I told her quite a bit and I asked her if
she'd ever played Monopoly. She nodded. I told
her if someone knows a lot about Iron Cage, it's
like the Get Out of Jail Free Card. She nodded as
she wrote it down before asking me a lot more
questions about Iron Cage. I answered all. Baker
said the president had asked him to ask me why I
didn't kill him when I had the chance. I tell him
my orders were only to wound him. Baker asks
why. I went through the whole message thing yet
again. On a more personal level, I tell him had I
refused to go to Camp David, my captors would
have poured acid on Binkie's face. He asks me
who Binkie is. Someone I love. He asks if
Binkie's wellbeing outweighed the wellbeing of
the president. I reply the wellbeing of the
president, at the time of my orders, was no more
than an abstraction. The wellbeing of Binkie was
paramount and under immediate threat. My

captors also said if I completed my mission
successfully, they would release her. (Not that I
trusted them one iota.) I also tell him Chichikov
deliberately gave me false information, so I
would fail. (Here I go volunteering information
again. But I have a reason.) He asks me why they
would have spent all that time training me and
then sabotage the mission. Because I would be
buried in a prison somewhere far from Binkie,
she would be blind and disfigured, and I'd be
tortured by guilt. So, when I discovered my
information was false, I had to improvise, which
they didn't know I could do. Not trusting Stevens
and Nicholas to deliver my key message, I tell
Baker about Secretary Khrushchev's message of
cooperation and the consequences of not doing
so. Baker nods and assures me he would
personally tell the president and vice-president.
(I have no idea whether he kept his vow or not.)
He then asks me about the conditions of my
confinement. 'It was tolerable, but things can
always get better.' After some further routine
questions, Baker offers sympathy for my plight,
smiles briefly and leaves. I'm moved the next
day to solitary in a military prison. I speak to no
one, not even the guards. When I try, they ignore
me. It's a decent size cell so, I can do pushups
and stuff to keep fit. I also tap Morse with the
guy next to me, a Russian spy, who told me he
works for the KGB and knows Svetlana
Feliksovna. He confirmed I have a daughter,
named Natalya, known as Nata. A few days later,
he's exchanged and is never replaced, I'm the
only one at the end of the cellblock. But out of
my cell, I have silent exercise sessions, once a

day. Maria asked me how I spent the time. I told
her I mentally built a great big palace, brick by
brick, painted every brushstroke of the frescoes,
planted every bush and tree and moved in all the
furniture, piece by piece. Then, after I'd
completed it, I took it apart, piece-by-piece, and
even replanted the grass where the palace had
stood. Also, mornings, I practice Spanish
because I sense I'm going to Cuba when I get
out. In the afternoons, Russian and evenings,
French. I knew if I stop using my mind, I'm
dead. After a year or so, I'm allowed books. It
isn't until March 1964 that I again have two
visitors. They ask me what I know about the
Kennedy assassination. I tell them I ordered it
telepathically from my cell. I'm amazed these
types haven't gotten any smarter in the
intervening years. They give me a second
chance. I tell them I didn't even know Joe
Kennedy had been able to buy the presidency.
One guy informs me it was his son, John. (All
right, the old, corrupt, appeasing bastard had
bought it for his son. Too many skeletons rattling
around in his own closets.) I can't believe it.
When I'd studied the political situation in the US
for my mission in 1955, the KGB had reviewed
all the senators and governors to establish
Eisenhower's successor if Nixon lost, a list of
148 people. John Kennedy fell dead last right
behind the Governor of North Dakota. Maria
stopped me and asked why I had studied such a
thing. I replied I studied what I was told to study
and didn't ask any questions. She nodded and
wrote something down. I ask the guys about
Nixon. I can't believe it when the other guy tells

me Nixon is out of politics and finished. Dick
Nixon, number one on the KGB's list to succeed
Eisenhower, is now an attorney in New York,
beaten by this Kennedy guy. (It just proves to me
yet again the Soviets can't understand their
adversaries. Probably never will. I'm not sure I'll
ever understand the Americans either.) The first
guy says when I'd been interviewed in 1955, I'd
predicted the next president would be
assassinated. What do I know? I tell them I'd be
willing to talk if they would get me out of
solitary. I mean it isn't bad, but again, things can
always be better. They agree. I tell them what I
know. They seem genuinely interested and, as far
as I could tell, most of my story's news to them.
During our conversation, I find out Leonid
Brezhnev had ousted Secretary Khrushchev. I
break into a spontaneous dance. Brezhnev is a
bungler of the first order. Secretary Khrushchev
was a shrewd, ruthless and very clever peasant.
The Soviet state had done pretty well under him.
Old beetle-brow is a party hack. I know the
Soviet state's doomed. Maria nods in agreement.
Both guys ask me what I'm doing. I tell him the
Soviets are doomed. I might not live to see the
demise of the Soviet state, but my sons and
daughters would. The guys are confused and
thought I'd be saddened by their report since 'I
was Khrushchev's boy.' I tell them about my
parents and all. They ask me a bunch of the same
questions as last time and leave. (They never told
me their names. Security precaution?) A few
days later, I'm transferred to another part of the
prison. It's hard labor, but I don't care. I'm with
other human beings again and I did it for three

plus years. Maria smiled and commented that's
why I'm in such good shape for a man my age. (I
think there might some sincerity in her
compliment.) I thanked her and continued. One
day, I was told to get my stuff and I'm on a plane
to Cuba, part of a spy exchange. Maria knows
the rest. She asked me where I want to go. I told
her I'd like to go piss on Eisenhower's grave,
even though he's still alive. I'm not getting out
for a while. (I'll not ever reveal my true answer.)
She asked me why I hate him so much. Because
he did nothing to stop Iron Cage. I know the
politicians restrained him, but he could have
been a much stronger advocate for his troops.
After all, we all trusted him. He violated that
trust—the trust of the warrior not to leave anyone
behind, especially when they're still alive. For
that, as far as I'm concerned, there's no
forgiveness or understanding. Maria again asked
me more questions about Iron Cage. She made
some final notes, got up, stripped off her dress,
giving me a nice little show, pinned up her hair,
took a black bra from her bureau, put on her DGI
uniform and said she'll be gone all day. I didn't
know if her bra was the promised Maidenform or
just a Cuban one. This made me very uneasy, if
it's the Maidenform, then she has already
succeeded in her mission to find out what I know
about Iron Cage and will abandon me. Or, since
she's finished the debrief, she may return and,
despite what she said before, will kill me. She
may be lying about Angelina and all.

15 August 1968

Maria has been gone for almost two months,
which, at first, bothered me. But after a while,
I started to enjoy being alone again. I had some
money and access to a special commissary for
food, rum and cigars. Most days, I'd go down
to the beach and swim for about an hour or so,
then lay in the sun before taking long beach
walks, speaking with people along the way.
Maybe stopping by a favorite seaside restaurant.
Sometimes, I could almost believe it was the
old days. I used to get down here quite a bit
before the War. My travels for the firm took me
here and also to Venezuela, Argentina Chile and
Columbia. (This also gave me access to new
recruits for the Struggle.) Cuba's no longer a
paradise, but it's warm. I like being warm. I've
been cold much of my life. I'd like to stay here,
but I have promises to keep elsewhere. However,
I've no idea how to get out of here. I sense Maria
will return one day but, in the meantime, this is
Divine retribution for having gotten involved
with the Commies. Conditions were horribly
bleak at Vorkuta. If I'd stayed in the mines, I'd
be long dead and forgotten in some mass grave.
At least I'd have my integrity and not be a traitor.
I think about my son. I'd love to meet him, but I
hear David has built a good life for him. I'd just
mess it up if I suddenly appeared out of nowhere.
However, I must see Binkie again. Of course,
I've no idea if she's still alive or even well. I also
wonder what happened to Pavel Chichikov after
I left the Institute. What an appropriate name
for a dirty son of a bitch, just like his namesake.

I never asked him if he'd read Gogol's "Dead Souls," a favorite of mine, because all I would've seen was his blank expression. Sometimes, I think of David and the guys at the firm, all living lives of capitalist luxury. I guess the sad truth is while I wasn't born stateless, I've spent most of my life that way. I don't really belong anywhere, so I must go where Binkie is, Russia, even though the Commies have totally poisoned it.

17 August 1968

Today, as I lay on the beach, I thought about Angelina. (I confess, she slips in now and again.) I saw her, for the first time, in 1937 on my first trip to Havana. As I have mentioned in a previous journal, Carlos Matarazzo was my mentor at the firm. Before sending me on my first Latin American solo mission, he handed me, with a wink, a letter of introduction to Miss Colette at Chez Marianne. Once in Havana, two muscular men in full combat gear were guarding the entrance to a large Spanish-style mansion. I showed them my letter and went through to the parlor. Miss Colette greeted me warmly, wearing a black suit with a white blouse, silk stocking and black stilettos. I'd expected to see 'the girls' lounging about in the parlor. Instead, she was alone and in a very business-like manner escorted me into her office where she proceeded to ask me all manner of personal, financial and psychological questions, telling me the house rules, expenses and giving a very thorough physical exam. Although only twenty-seven at the time, I was experienced

and confidently ran up the broad staircase
naked to Miss Angelina's Salon #22, knocked
and went in. And there she stood in her scarlet
negligee—petite, rosewater scented with shiny
black hair way past her shoulders, parted in the
middle. She appeared to be about ten years older
than me. (I had told Miss Colette I liked older
women.) She spoke refined Castilian Spanish,
'You are Carlos's protégé, Spencer Talbott. She
took me by the hand to a small round table with
two chilled daiquiris. As we drank, she told me
that she and Carlos grew up together in Madrid.
But in 1923, they began a torrid romance that
scandalized both sets of parents and 'at least half
of Madrid Society.' As a result, she was exiled
to Paris by her father, who also, unbeknownst
to her mother, gave her a very substantial trust
fund. She soon moved to Berlin, attracted by
its sexual freedom and had a wonderful time
there. Carlos was exiled to Cuba, a better place
to work out his 'urges.' After graduating from
the University in Havana, he went to Harvard
Law School and joined Gules, Argent and Orr.
As she was speaking, I became drawn to her
'come hither' eyes shining brightly through black
liner. Her dark red lipstick complimented her
light coloration. She concluded her story 'Carlos
showed up and we resumed our torrid affair for
about a year. Until, Carlos started coming less
frequently and then stopped. And now I have
you.' When she stood and removed her negligee,
I noticed she had shaved pubic hair, something
I'd never seen before. She started massaging
my back and shoulders as I remained seated,
whispering, 'I just adore a handsome young man,

especially if he is a Bleu agent.' I noticed Cuban music softly playing on her radio. 'Just tell me what you like, and I will do it. Later, you can tell me your fantasies and I will do my best to make them come true. Do not be shy.' She gave a wicked wink.

The next morning, over breakfast on her private balcony overlooking the interior courtyard, she told me 'Chez Marianne is a women's collective and its existence is only known to a selective clientele. I may come and go as I please.' After breakfast, she gave me a tour of the mansion and told me 'Chez Marianne pleases every sexual orientation, desire and fantasy. And each variety had one of the four floors. I commented I'd seen a fifth floor from the outside. She smiled and replied, 'That is just storage.' And winked again. In the back of the mansion, she showed me into a medium-sized auditorium. 'This part of the mansion is open to the tourist trade and it is for the sex shows that everyone expects in Havana. The putas come from the burdel (bordello) next door. The star of the show is Antoine, The Black Stallion, a powerfully built Haitian. If you like, on another date, we could watch the show. Our Misses never preform in public.' As we returned to her salon, I asked her more about her background. She left Berlin for Paris in 1933 and left for Havana in 1936, She also used such terms as 'free spirit' and 'black sheep' to describe herself. But was vague about why she left Paris. Arriving here with a group of young ladies, she calls 'Misses' they saw a need and set up the collective. I had to be in

Caracas that afternoon, but I make a date for
my return the next weekend. She said, 'I would
also love to show you sights in Havana, both
day and night. After taking that tour, she really
seemed to know everyone and everything going
on. And, as we went around Havana, we began
having wonderful conversations about virtually
everything. After that, I returned to Chez on a
regular basis. However, I noticed after the War
broke out in 1939, their European clientele
had declined and had not been replaced by
Americans. When the Japs bombed Pearl Harbor
on December 7, 1941, I was with her and heard
the news on her radio. I left her a few hundred
dollars as a parting gift. I had no idea if I'd return
from this war. I quickly returned to New York
and joined the Army Air Force. I never saw her
again. (But along with Binkie, these two women
have kept me going through my trials and I
thought about them almost constantly during that
period.)

Later that day, Maria, wearing a floral bikini,
lay down next to me. I asked her where she'd
been. She shook her head and made a face before
telling me she'd been debriefed on her debriefing
the whole time. I asked what happened to her
mother. She said after Pearl Harbor, tourism
dried up and Chez Marianne was forced to close
because there were not enough 'quality clients.'
Some of the Misses took their share of the
proceeds and left the country for either Mexico
or South America. Angelina moved to Santiago,
Cuba, where she lived quietly with Maria until
she was about six. One day, Angelina, returning

from the market, was kidnapped by soldiers
and forced her into a military burdel. Maria, left
alone, was sent to an orphanage. On her seventh
birthday, she was sold to Madam Isabella's—
an underage burdel. She suffered there until
'Liberacion' on January 1st 1959. Angelina
escaped from her burdel in 1950 and joined the
rebels in the Sierra Madre Mountains. When
Castro's army entered Havana on Liberacion
Day, Angelina held high rank in the rebel force.
She began her search for Maria and found her in
February and made the seventeen-year-old Maria
her aide. Angelina continued as a close aide to
Castro until 1961, when she became a senior
officer in the newly formed DGI. Maria told me
she'd like to swim with me for a while. I confess,
I'm very happy to have her back. She told me
as a reward for her very successful debrief, not
only has she received seven Maidenforms, but
her mother had granted her extended leave.
She said Angelina had always regretted that I
wasn't Maria's father. (I immediately knew who
her real father was, based on my time at Chez
Marianne.) When I showed up in Cuba, Angelina
strongly suggested Maria become pregnant by
me. And now, she was. I was overjoyed. Maria,
right now, is as free as she has ever been, and I
began to rethink my priorities. What I had here
was real and known. Even if I could get back to
Russia, and that's not a certainty, I had no idea
what to expect. My tvarsch remained silent on
this. I'll remain here for the foreseeable future
through birth and at least the first year. Later,
we went quickly to bed. After our reunion
lovemaking (Not just having sex.) I remained

awake, as too many thoughts fill my mind. While I'm happy to be here, I've also come to realize America was David's country and not mine. It was a very seductive place and it lured me away from sweet Nadia all those years ago. I learned long ago, as a zek, not to look too far into the future. This moment's all I have. Beyond that, all's murky. In the gulag, I remember a Spanish zek, Francisco, a veteran of the Loyalist cause. He'd fled to Moscow when Franco won and was granted asylum. Three years later, accused of treason, he was shipped to Vorkuta. Once there, he remained indignant that Communists could do such a horrible thing to a comrade. He maintained this was all a mistake and once the mistake was realized, he'd be released. Then, one night, a trusted comrade reminded him because he was there, he was guilty. The Party couldn't be wrong. There must be something he'd overlooked. He should search his soul. The next night, as Francisco left our barracks, he yelled, 'No tango puta ni idea.' We soon heard shots. I translated his last words for Harv Jacobs, an old Spanish proverb—'I have neither a whore nor an idea.' Francisco had somehow betrayed the cause to which he had devoted his whole life. In that moment of realization, his future collapsed in on him. Such was the power of the Party among the true believers. In all likelihood, he, like most of us, hadn't done anything wrong except to somehow run afoul of Gangster Stalin.

There it was. Randell's father, Harvey Jacobs, was a Lost Soul, and it remained possible he was still alive, somewhere in Russia.

As the zeks say, 'In the Criminal State, only
the just are in jail.' Me, I have a whore and
an idea. Therefore, I dare, for the first time in
years, to have a future. I watch this new life
grow. However, it bothers me the mother of my
child's young enough to be my daughter. Yet,
I've become her father confessor. She's told me
of her life, of those she had killed and of those
who had abused her. She cried and wailed and
cursed. However, through it all, I was witnessing
a miracle. The life within Maria is acting as the
catalyst— the child is mother to the woman.

25 August 1968

We've moved to Angelina's hacienda, outside
Havana. I was very pleased to see her again. She
has aged well, except her long hair's now gray.
She wore it very short in the Sierra Madre and
had taken great pleasure growing it out again.
It was amazing, we picked up very quickly
with our great conversations. Being in the DGI,
she has had access to books from all over the
world. Once a week, Angelina takes Maria to
her clinic for check-ups. At night, I can see the
changes in Maria's body, so divinely intimate.
How wonderful it is to see her naturalness as
compared to Nadia's societal modesty, the last
time I was involved on a day-to-day basis with a
pregnant woman. Life here is very good and I'm
truly grateful to be in the company of these two
extraordinary women. And yet, I want to return
to Russia. I'd like to see Aleks and Rini again. I
don't bear them ill will because of their mother.

They're Iskandarov and this fact can't be hidden
for long.

These two must be children he had with Svetlana Feliksovna,
and the boy had to be the minister. That might make their
negotiations easier. Or not.

If I can't see Binkie, I should like to see little
Nata. (I knew Binkie was pregnant when I left
but I never told anyone in all my interrogations
about her, not even Maria. They have no need
to know, this is most personal. Had the bastards
killed or injured pregnant Binkie, Nata would
have died as well. And it was for her, as much
as her mother that I agreed to Camp David.
(Nata's role in the next generation's important.)
Little Nata? She would be about thirteen by now.
I've actually seen her in several Andronyis she
has sent me and, although she appears frail and
delicate, she's pure Iskandarova.

Ashley now had reasonable proof Binkie was Charlotte,
Natalya's mother. And he felt relief that Natalya had sent her
Andronyis to Sergei as well.

15 March 1969

On the Ides of March, Maria delivered beautiful
twin girls. Rosalita (The 'little rose.' Our joke.)
And because none of this would have been
possible without the kindness and generosity of
Angelina, we have named the slightly older girl
after her. I feel blessed as I never have before,
Binkie excepted. My tvarsch is working again
and I know now I'll get to Russia when the time
is right.

The diary ended. Nothing else had been removed. Nonetheless,

Ashley felt very impressed with Sergei's faith. This diary had found him, not the first time his father had communicated to him. Paper-clipped to the last page, he saw a note, written in a very different hand.

> Mr. Cooper, I'm Maria Civilli. I know you have questions about your father and many other subjects. I think the two of us can be mutually beneficial. I have answers, but I need a favor. I hope you will oblige me. Perhaps, you would like to meet my other daughter, Rosalita, your half-sister. Please come to El Meson on Charles Street. Call for a reservation. Do not ask for me, I shall find you.
>
> Cordially, Maria Civilli-Mendes

Ashley knew El Meson very well. He had been there many times for the *paella,* but not recently. *At last, a person who can answer my many questions.* Reading Ronnie's note and Sergei's diary had reinforced that, for good or ill, Ashley was Iskandarov, "People of the Blood." He smelled beef Stroganoff, his favorite dish that Ronnie used to make. She had probably helped Annie prepare it before leaving. So, the two of them had ample time to talk. He realized his hunger and went downstairs, wondering what Annie would ask for. She was most certainly up to something with this fine meal.

THIRTEEN
Monday 31 May & Tuesday 1 June 1993
Quaker Mount, NY

1.

Ashley walked into the kitchen and saw Annie serving Ronnie's beef Stroganoff over Polish noodles with baby peas.

"Oh, Dad, good. I was about to call you. You must've been reading Sergei's Cuban diary. Aunt Ronnie told me it was in the package I left on your chair. I checked later, and you'd taken it. Also, I've read Sergei's file about Camp David and everything."

"I didn't want you to see that."

"Why not? Sergei's my grandfather, remember?"

"But didn't it upset you?"

She shrugged. "No. Not really. I mean, he didn't kill the president. I know from my American History course this semester President Eisenhower served out both his terms. Besides, this wasn't in the history book and was kinda cool to read about. And I thought it was so incredibly romantic what Sergei went through to protect Binkie, who has to be Charlotte." She paused. "Come on, dinner." Annie carried their plates into the dining room and poured Ashley and herself glasses of wine. Ashley sat at the head of the table with Annie on his right. Her thoughts about Camp David surprised him. She knew the outcome, while knowing "Ike" only as an historical figure, not a family icon, and had focused on Sergei's valor and integrity, which he had completely missed.

"This is really excellent. Why did you choose this particular bottle for this occasion? And remember, fine wine is for sipping, so you can savor the flavors on your tongue."

"Dad, I know that. I mean, I've been drinking beer and wine at home for almost two years now. And thank you for teaching me about alcohol. Some girls in my class have gotten into tense situations because they didn't know about its power. Anyway, my gourmet teacher spoke about this vintage, and it sounded fabulous. I almost freaked when I found it in the wine cellar."

"I know you know about wine, but this bottle's very special because it belonged to Grandpa, and he was saving it for his hundredth birthday." He savored the wine's aroma before sipping. "Now, taste the cherries, black currants and bittersweet chocolate as they play in your mouth."

Annie sipped and smiled as she swallowed. "You're right. It's fantastic."

"Good. I'd like to propose a toast to the Colonel for his largesse." Afterward, he smiled and felt pleased Annie had decided to make this dinner an occasion after his grueling day. The first bite of the Stroganoff tasted just as Ashley remembered, perhaps even better. As he ate, he focused on the spectral sunlight from the chandelier's prisms playing on the white walls before giving Annie a summary of the Cuban diary, including Chez Marianne.

"I like the idea of any women's cooperative," she said. "In this case, the women were doing something they enjoyed and were making money with it."

"So, this doesn't bother you?"

"No. Anyway, I know one of Sergei and Maria's daughters, Rosalita. She owns a women's dance studio with self-defense classes over on Madison. I go there usually three times a week before school, just to get focused and stuff. And she's also a part-time phys ed teacher at school."

Ashley nodded. "Yes. Interesting. This is really excellent."

She smiled. "Thanks. It was fun. I had a bit of help from Aunt Ronnie, who brought all the ingredients and her recipe, which she said I could share with my class."

"Good, I'm very impressed."

"Impressed enough so I can read the Cuban diary myself?"

"Yes. It's pretty grim. But I know your concern about the treatment of women in this country. Seeing how they were treated in Cuba will give you a new perspective."

"Sweet. So, what're you gonna do about all this?"

"After dinner, I'm going to make us a reservation at El Meson for tomorrow night. I'm meeting Maria Civilli there, a huge step to meet someone who actually knew my father. She can help me with the questions I have about that phase of his life and perhaps more. After that, I don't honestly know if I should go to Russia directly or stop in Paris. I've ruled out Berlin and Cuba. I'm afraid I'll need to go alone, initially."

Annie stood up. "Why can't I go to Russia? You told me you needed my help and cooperation. These people are my ancestors too, you know. I've got as much right as you do—"

"That's not the issue. You didn't respond very well to the shots the other night."

"I'll do better next time because I went through that and now know what to expect. I must go." She folded her arms across her chest.

"You *must* go?"

"Yes. When I was again studying Charlotte's picture earlier in the attic, I really felt her speaking to me."

"And what did Charlotte say?"

"You won't believe me."

Ashley felt proud that she had not given up. "Try me."

Annie studied him, raised her wine glass and sipped thoughtfully. "She told me there's a lot I need to learn, which is very true. And, if I would come to her, she'd teach me much of that."

"OK. But if you don't know where she is, how are you going to find her?"

"Grandmother lives in a Russian nunnery, and she's not a prisoner. But I can't really tell about her expression. She's always wearing dark glasses."

"Oh my God."

"What's the matter, Dad?"

"You know in Spencer's file when Chichikov threatens—"

Annie raised her hand to her mouth. "That's horrible. They blinded her anyway. Oh no. Jesus, how could they be so awful?"

"Because they had complete power over her."

Annie nodded, and they were silent for a while.

"I also think it's important Sophia and Dmitri had a child together, maybe more with Alexei."

"What do you mean 'important'?"

"This is the key to who the Iskandarovs are. And their power."

"You're saying their incest is the key to their power?"

"Yes. I just don't know how."

After nodding, Ashley returned to his dinner, thinking. How did incest relate to the People of the Blood? Could it be a way of preserving their heritage? He shook his head. No sane person or group would do that for long with all the problems of inbreeding. No, it had to be something else. Nevertheless, Annie had made some good points—things he had missed. She would be an asset in Russia.

"Dad, what do you think about Dmitri's Tanya? I don't think she's Iskandarova."

"Good deduction. I can make a case Tanya was actually Czar Nicholas's daughter, Tatiana."

"That's really cool."

"Careful. There were, at the time, a number of women falsely claiming to be Nicholas's daughter, but Tanya appears to be legit."

"OK. Aunt Ronnie told me today my visions right now are more powerful than Aunt Olga's were when she died."

Ashley thought, *Aunt Olga? Yes, that's who she'd be to Annie.* "All right. What else did Aunt Ronnie tell you?"

"She told me I needed to go along with you on your journey."

"I know. I still haven't said you can go. I need to know how comfortable you are with your visions, and then I'll give this serious consideration."

"I've been working very hard to get control of my *pyordarsch.*"

"I know the term. Did you ever discuss this with your mother?"

"Absolutely. When the visions began, I told her, and she got all weirded out. We never talked about it again."

He heard the obvious contempt in Annie's voice. Pen had never spoken to him about it.

"I mean she was OK with the usual stuff. Took me to the doctor and all and gave me 'the Talk.'" Annie rolled her eyes and shook her head. "And she did everything she was supposed to. But she never got the most important piece of it at all." Annie paused. "I'm not sure you do either." She idly stabbed some noodles with her fork. "And before you ask, no, I didn't tell my shrinks either."

"Why not? We paid them good money."

"What was the point?" She ate the noodles quickly. "I mean, I didn't have any idea about what was happening to me, and I couldn't even ask the right questions, beyond the obvious."

"Good point. What's the most important piece of it all your mother and I don't get?"

"The blood is the key to who the Iskandarov are and why they have their gifts."

Ashley had already deduced this from "Blood is Iskandar" and the "People of the Blood" but nodded thoughtfully anyway. "Tell me what Ronnie's said about all this."

"She doesn't have *pyordarsch* like Aunt Olga did. Anyway, she said there would be others, besides Charlotte, to help develop our gifts to their highest levels."

"Good news. So, you'll be able to foretell the future like the countess did?"

"Absolutely. It'll take time and a lot of work, but one day, I'll master it. Again, I'm the fourth generation from Sophia, and that's why I have the potential, which I intend to fully develop. And why I must go with you. You need answers, and so do I. Besides, without me, you won't find what you're looking for."

Ashley held his wine glass up to the light, watching the color variations in the bowl as he absorbed all she had just said. A week ago, such talk would have sounded both crazy and arrogant. No more. If she could get help with her *pyordarsch*, there would be someone to help him with his *tvarsch*. "And how do you know that?"

"Aunt Ronnie stressed we needed to work together. We each have our strengths and weaknesses, but together we complement each other. That's the Iskandarov way. I also know things you don't. 'Lita told me her mother's a senior officer in the Cuban DI. I've met Maria a few times, and she's always been very nice. But you never know. Going there might be dangerous. Or even a trap."

"My *tvarsch* says it's OK. Besides, she could've just kept the Cuban diary, and I'd be stuck. I trust her. I must."

"OK. Just be careful."

"Always." He felt pleased about her concern. He'd come up a long way on the Annie-meter in a very brief time. "You've made some excellent points. But right now, I need some exercise. I've been sitting too much today. So, I'm going to go for a run while I still have some light."

2.

After making the reservations and getting ready, Ashley, in running gear plus reflective vest and Walkman, jogged on the up and down roads atop Quaker Mount. Inspired by his running tape to run faster when he heard the Rascals' "Come On Up," he felt the blood of the Iskandarovs, not the Coopers, pumping through his body and knew he was a part of something larger than himself. The mysteries of his life had begun to fall into place and his relationship with Olga had clarified. He ran up through the trees to the fire tower, the highest point on Quaker Mount, where he had not been since before Harvard. As he ran up the metal stairs, he saw the empty beer cans, cheap booze bottles and used condoms. Things had not changed much since he used to come up here with Monica. At the top, jogging in place, he put his hand to his heart and felt wetness. His bleeding hand had left a red circle on his white T-shirt. *Damn, I forgot about that nail sticking out of the handrail. It's been over thirty years since the last time it got me.* He pulled his hand down on his shirt to create a blood Iskandarov capital "I." After turning off his Walkman, he relished the silence as he first looked east to Connecticut and then watched the sun set on mountains across the Hudson River.

No question, Annie would be coming with him. Nonetheless, while all this Iskandarov lore must seem very exciting and challenging to her, she still had to keep up her grades, and she would find that out tomorrow, her last day of school. He ran down the steps watching the moon rise. He would be home after dark, a time he really enjoyed jogging. He had been on these roads most of his life and knew every bump and pothole and loved the intimacy of the darkness as though he were the only person on the Mount.

Back on Quaker Mount Road, he turned his Walkman back on to the Butterfield Blues Band's "Got My Mojo Workin'" and "Work Song." These two, almost twelve minutes, always inspired him, and he soon went back in the zone, running effortlessly as he heard and felt the ominous and evil classic of the Doors' "Riders on the Storm" in the dark.

3.

Arriving back home, he washed out the cut and bandaged it with antibiotic cream before he found Annie watching TV in the den. "What's on?"

"Oh, it's an old tape I found. *Reilly, Ace of Spies* from PBS Thirteen about the English agent who fought against the Bolsheviks." She looked over. "Dad, what happened to your shirt?"

"Nothing. Just a small accident."

"I bet you ran up the fire tower stairs. I meant to tell you there's something sharp on the first railing."

"You go up there?"

"Of course. Everyone goes. Aunt Ronnie told me you went up there with Monica when you were my age. And I hope your tetanus shot's current, and I get the 'I.'"

"Good. And yes, it is." As he sat next to Annie, he wondered what else Ronnie had told her, but that was something he did not want to get into now.

On the TV, several Russian émigrés were having an intense argument about the Trust. This was the Bolshevik plan by Feliks Dzerzhinsky, head of the Cheka, to lure Russian émigrés back to Russia to join with the "Rebels of the Trust." All those who went back, including Sydney Reilly, were executed. Stalin finally shut down the Trust and had all its members shot. They had been "contaminated" by contact with foreigners. Presumably, some Iskandarov belonged to the group executed, so, this topic had become very real and personal in a way it had not been when he first saw the series in 1983.

"OK, when we go to Russia or wherever, we go together, provided you've maintained your grades."

"Sweet." Annie leaned over and kissed him on the cheek. "So, is all this Reilly stuff true?"

"Absolutely. Even the Trust."

"Amazing."

4.

Ashley awoke around four a.m., knowing how to absolutely verify Binkie's identity. He ran up to the attic to recover Patricia's possessions box. After her death, as a teenager, he had carried it

up there. After turning on the attic light, he found the large Lord
& Taylor box, tucked in a corner, under a dust-soaked sheet. As
he was getting the box, he sneezed loudly from the dust before
putting it next to him on the Quaker bench. Going through
Patricia's effects, he thought, *Not much to show for a life*. When
he came to the bottom, he found a worn, square, burgundy leather
box. Picking it up, he could not recall ever having seen it before.
Lifting the lid brought an unexpected scent of lavender. He saw
a picture, bound in black, of a handsome young man in an RAF
flying officer's uniform. Turning it over, written in Patricia's
fussily precise hand was:

> Colin, my most beloved. When you met your
> gallant death two years ago today, my spirit died
> with you. In place of your love within me, there
> is nothing. Where once flowed my rivers of love,
> there is now only desert. They shall not soon, if
> ever, return to me. This Sixteenth Day of August
> 1942.

Ashley had seen this picture before on her dresser but had
never asked about it, because, frankly, he had not cared who this
guy was. But now, he carefully put it aside. Under the picture
and bound by an ancient ribbon, he found a packet of letters. He
also placed them aside, unread. For the first time on his journey,
he felt like an intruder. Digging deeper, he found another large
framed picture, face down, with Patricia's handwriting. "Uncle
Neville, Mummy, Binkie and me. 15.8.39."

Turning it over, he saw a picture of Neville Chamberlain
with a quite attractive middle-aged lady, a stunning Patricia and
a vivacious Charlotte at a country estate. Binkie was definitely
Charlotte. Ashley felt the most profound relief at not having
killed his mother, who remained alive in 1955, although as a
prisoner. Further, where was Charlotte's father? Chamberlain
with the quotes was a close family friend, and Charlotte's mother
was, likely, a widow.

He next found a smaller, framed black-and-white picture of Charlotte and looked at the back. "Binkie on her sixteenth birthday, 16.3.36." Except for her bobbed hair, Charlotte then looked even more like Annie. He felt proud being the link between these two women. Charlotte was twelve years younger than Patricia, who had died at fifty in 1958. At the bottom of the box, he found another framed picture of a distinguished gentleman in the uniform of a British Army colonel. On the back, in a very feminine hand was: "Sir Hugh Sterling Sternwood, beloved husband of Lady Agnes and father of Patricia and Charlotte. Born 3.3.1883. Missing, and presumed dead, in Bolshevik Russia since 17.9.1919." Ashley wondered what Sir Hugh had been doing in Russia in 1919. If he had been part of the British Expeditionary Force, he would have been withdrawn in that April. So, he could have been part of the British Secret Service Bureau in Russia, the forerunner of MI-6. Therefore, he could have been shot on site, or, the Cheka sent him to Moscow and the Lubyanka prison for interrogation, torture and death. While Charlotte never knew her father, she certainly knew the Bolsheviks had made him disappear. And that had to be the reason she had gone on their date and then married Spencer.

He kept the three pictures out, replaced the rest in the box and covered it with the sheet. He had left Patricia's letters unread, regardless of any valuable information they might contain. He would not violate the privacy of the lady who had raised him.

As he went downstairs with the pictures, Ashley felt a certain sadness about Patricia. She had been a casualty of the war as surely as her husband or any of the tens of millions of others who had perished. He had often seen a light from under her door, late at night. Ashley imagined her sitting beside another of her usual dram of scotch, going through her burgundy box, perhaps reading an old love letter or staring at Colin, Charlotte, mother or father. Just as Ashley had not been born a proper attorney, Patricia had not been born the cold, overly formal person he had known.

Back on the second floor, he heard Annie sobbing in Ronnie's former room. He decided that just as he had done, she must work out her getting-older problems herself. If she wanted to discuss something, she would.

5.

After getting up again, showering and dressing, Ashley went down to the kitchen, placing Charlotte's birthday picture in front of Annie, who was listlessly eating her cereal. Now animated, she picked it up and intently studied it. "This is totally awesome. She looks just like me, except for her cool retro hair. I'd like to get a bob too. Where'd you find this?"

"Up in the attic. It belonged to her sister, Patricia, your step-grandmother."

Annie nodded and again studied the picture. "We have to find Charlotte."

"Agreed. We need to establish a new relationship right now. I need you to be absolutely candid with me. I'll do the same for you and treat you like the adult I know you to be."

"Sweet. But what kind of things do you want to know about?"

"Ah, your private life remains as private as you wish. But I need to know about what you're thinking and feeling about on our journey."

"OK. Deal."

"However, I'll still be available for father-type things."

Annie nodded and returned to Charlotte's picture. "I think this is the key to where she is. I've gotten everything I can out of the other one. I'll let you know when I get something."

Ashley smiled. "OK."

After pouring them both coffees, Ashley began watching TV as he ate his cereal.

A blow-dried, chisel-featured talking head said, "Washington insiders have told Action News that President Clinton will pull the plug on his embattled nominee for head of the Civil Rights Division of the Justice Department, Professor Lani Guinier. The nomination is seen as an impediment to bipartisan efforts on the stagnant economy. The Commerce Department is expected to release their index of leading economic indicators today. Action News has learned that they will either be flat or only show a modest gain."

Ashley smiled wryly. News used to be reported after the fact. Now the reports came before the fact, without regard to accuracy.

"Turning to local news, in an exclusive follow-up, Action News has learned the identity of the young white male, aged twenty-nine, shot and killed yesterday on Park Avenue at 52nd Street. The man is identified as Joseph Ulton Stevens."

Ashley stared at the screen. Pen's last lover was dead?

"Mr. Stevens was president of the very hot ad firm, Windemere and Associates. His father, Nicholas Henry Stevens, is a high-placed government official. Now, turning to sports. The Mets..."

Ashley turned off the TV.

"Hey, that's the guy I saw in bed with Mom that time."

"Right."

"Dad, you were in the city yesterday. All I know is you were in Mr. Drew's office, and you read the Camp David stuff. Did you kill this guy for what he'd done?"

Ashley was innocent, but if Annie could ask such a question, so could the cops. "No. First, I don't even own a gun. Second, I wasn't anywhere near there. And I have witnesses to account for my time." He thought that if the cops were looking for him, both Charles and Fred might get "forgetful" as an ideal way to keep him from Russia. And if the cops did not find out until after he left, leaving the country with a minor would not look good. "Finally, I don't really care what he did. It's not worth my effort to hold a grudge against him. I've even forgiven your mother."

"Really?"

"Absolutely. When your mother was even younger than you are now, she was always one of 'the really cool girls,' who always traveled in a pack with their followers. As a result, in eighth grade, all the guys in my class had a crush on her and even our home room teacher knew her name. Those days probably went on until about the time we married and were the high point, she told me, of her life. And she was always trying to recapture them. So, with Joe she could pretend she was still young too. She never really grew up."

"Yes, I kinda suspect that. But, thanks for telling me. Makes a lotta sense. But, if you didn't kill him, who did?"

"Don't know. I heard a rumor Joe was doing some sort of intel work with Lana."

"Lana van Booben was a spy? I didn't think she had the brains."

"Have no doubt. I never met anyone even half as devious as she was. She's a Russian agent and is involved with the Iskandarov."

"Are we in any danger then?"

"Only in general. I don't know anything specifically. Just be aware of your surrounding and avoid strangers for a while. And now, it's almost six. We need to be in the car by six thirty to beat the traffic." He loved Annie's nickname for Lana.

"OK. I'm on it."

6.

After finishing breakfast, Ashley walked over to the cemetery, seeing fog in the valley and hearing the sound of distant tractors. He sensed he might not return here, at least not for some time and wanted to take in his surroundings. Kneeling at Patricia's grave, he removed some small branches from the top of her headstone. "Mother…" Ashley paused. *She raised and shaped me as a child because my real mother was a prisoner in the Soviet Union. Yes, it now feels right in a way it never did before.* "Mother, I'm sorry I wasn't a better son to you. I didn't know about… you. I wish you could've confided in me. But I was just a spoiled, selfish kid, so I understand why you didn't." He said a prayer for the repose of her soul before moving over to the Colonel's grave. "Dad, I guess this is it. I've learned all I can here. The Mount's a great place, and I'll miss it, but my future lies elsewhere. Thanks for all you did for me and especially saving those three trunks. I would've liked very much if you had told me about the trunks earlier, and then I could've asked you many of the questions I still have about your adventures. I've the satisfaction of knowing because of what I've learned of my heritage, I'm not now the same person who stood here so recently to deliver your eulogy. Just know whatever else happens, you'll never be far from my thoughts."

7.

Later that morning, Ashley sat in his study, checking phone messages. Outside, he heard the noise of the city—the trucks, the car horns, police sirens, ambulances and, especially, the loose steel plate covering some sort of hole directly down from his terrace. Randell had left a message that he would have a long meeting with the bishop Wednesday morning and would not be able to make their tennis match at the Racquet. He would see him at the van Rouene funeral in the afternoon. Also, parishioner Bill Engle had offered a two-million-dollar pledge to the St. Jerome's Endowment Fund. In return, Randell had to promise that he would not go to Russia this year and would also actively discourage Ashley. Randell felt furious about this blatant bribe but said that the fund could use the money. In his message back, Ashley said he should take the easy money. Second, he shared the new information about Randell's real father, Harvey Jacobs.

Later, Ashley remembered that in 1968, when Sergei arrived in Cuba, he was in his final year at Harvard Law School, which had been pretty much a long blur of studying. In 1974, after his tour in Southeast Asia, he took the New York bar exam and that summer joined the Firm as an associate. "Working hard and playing hard," as the cliché of the time went, conveyed his work ethic. And although there had been some incredible interludes with very attractive young ladies, he could not now recall most of the details, except for one, a Greek model who, while sultrier than Olga, lacked her intellect. But he could not remember her name. What he did remember very clearly from the summer of 1975 was the Firm's annual associates' picnic at Rupert Drew's estate in Pound Ridge, NY. To an outsider, this sounded like some relaxed and carefree outdoor gathering to thank the associates for their hard work, dedication and contributions to the Firm. Without so much as an ant or a hot dog anywhere in sight, it proved to be the final obstacle for the associates to overcome in order to receive an offer of partnership. Two blackballs from the executive committee and no offer.

At the time, Ashley knew that his hard work and long hours in the office might not be enough. He had to account for the X-Factors, a profile the Firm had developed that predicted future success and had not shared with the associates. Even so, Ashley had doubts about joining the Firm because he had seen some things he really did not like. Also, he only wanted an offer made on his merits and not because he was the Colonel's son. His intuition, which he now knew as his *tvarsch*, would tell him that truth. Nonetheless, if offered a partnership, he would think very hard before accepting it.

He had little memory of the morning beyond seemingly eternal conversations and highballs until David handed him a note from Penelope Farwell asking him to meet her in the library. He very reluctantly agreed. On a day when he needed sharp focus, she would do her best to break that. Penelope wore a low-cut lilac dress—the biggest trap of all. Ashley now strongly remembered his utter annoyance at seeing her. Soon, they began arguing intensely about something, which ended with her propositioning him to take her upstairs to her room right then. Ashley told her no. She replied that he would now never make partner. George, her father, would see to that. He calmly left the room, disgusted that the selection process could be so corrupt. This had been another strike against joining the Firm. Ashley now realized that when he had left Penelope in the library, he should have driven back to the city—leaving both the Firm and her in his past. He could have easily joined the Foreign Service and probably had a better life.

Hell, had he gone into poverty law, as Olga had wanted, he would have had a better life.

She began flirting for the rest of the day with virtually all the associates and partners, her attempt to make him jealous. But when the executive committee went back to town to consider offers and the gathering became more raucous, Penelope literally dragged Ashley to her room. Once there, she warned him that the staff had instructions to report all associates who acted "inappropriately," which had a very broad meaning. He would be safe from that in her room. As he calmed down, he became entranced by her aura, not as strong as Olga or Ronnie's, but it glowed. He had no memory of Penelope ever having one before. Of course, he had not seen her very much since the spring of 1962 and Olga's death. She kissed him, and the sensation spread throughout his body, just as it had with Olga. But she could not possibly be his sister. Sometime later, as they lay in bed, he remembered proposing. She accepted and popped out of bed and began her naked dance of joy around the room, bouncing her breasts and shaking her blonde hair all around. He had never seen her happier or sexier. When she returned, she reminded him of the weekend graduation party at this same mansion in the spring of 1961. She had promised that night would be "the night." They had gone off to be alone, found a bed, and were soon nearly naked. When he had tried to remove her panties, she resisted and used tears, as she dressed, to end any discussion.

She now told him they had just made love in the same bed where she had refused him. She apologized for being aloof after that and for the fight they had at a dance in the fall of 1961. She further confessed that the fight had been her strategy to conceal she was not a virgin. And on "the night," she had been so aroused that she almost did not care if Ashley knew her secret or not. Ashley laughed and said that was simply something that was not important to him, even then. And though he tried hard, she never revealed who had first seduced her. Ashley now realized that even by the evening of the picnic it was too late. When Nick Stevens and Olga had soon entered their lives, everything changed. And yet, in a triumph of hope over sense, the following Tuesday, after Ashley accepted his partnership, their wedding announcement appeared in the *New York Times*.

8.

Ashley answered the doorbell and saw Anghelina, wearing dark glasses and a black silk business suit.

"Ashley, I've some business to discuss."

"Please, come in. Would you like some coffee? Annie recently made some."

"Thanks." She removed her glasses revealing her bright blue eyes as he led her into the kitchen.

"Now, how do you take your coffee?"

"Black, please."

He picked up the tray with the carafe and led her to the terrace's table and four chairs. After pouring coffee, he leaned back, luxuriating in the warm spring sun.

"Ashley, while I like this, given the recent shooting, do you think it's wise for us to be out here?"

"Good point, but I won't change my life for fear. After the shooting, I checked the sightlines. We can't be seen from the street, and the only danger is from someone in a building across the park. The distance and the wall make such a shot almost impossible, as long as we remain seated. I'm OK with the odds. Now, having read my, that is, our father's Cuban diaries, I know a lot more about your family. So, tell me about Rosalita."

"My mother came to New York in 1983 and eventually brought us a few years later. My sister's interesting because she's the entrepreneur in the family. Since 1991 and the fall of the Soviets, money for us has been hard to come by. And although a DI agent, 'Lita also has a knack for making money. She substantially supports us as my mother and I keep *Centrale* pleased."

Ashley nodded. "And you help out by being George's bodyguard. But what about your personal life, as opposed to your professional one?"

"I grew up in and around Havana. Both my mother and grandmother were DI, and I followed them." She sipped her coffee. "When we were young and Maria had to be away on assignments, which were frequent, we lived with Angelina. I adored her as a truly free and fearless woman. She used to tell us the most wonderful stories about people she'd known and the adventures she'd had in Europe and the Caribbean. She also told us all about Sergei. They were lovers. She dropped her fee, so the whole prostitute part with him was a cover story. And she deeply regretted that Maria wasn't Sergei's daughter."

"Thanks. That's very interesting. So, Chez was an intel operation." He now realized Sergei had sometimes hedged his bets against his later diaries being discovered.

"Yes. Their alliance was very complicated, and I don't know all the details. Now, Maria told me among Sergei's instructions about how to raise us, there was Iskandarov Trust. Number one, Iskandarov must always trust other Iskandarov and Iskandarova. Without that bond, we are doomed. I hope your *tvarsch* tells you I'm worthy of your trust."

Ashley nodded. "Of course, sister, after all you've done to protect me, you have my word." Ashley steepled his fingers. Yes, here was his half-sister, but so much younger than Olga and Ronnie he felt he should be protecting her, even though she could do so very well. He also sensed her underlying sadness and had no idea how he could help. "Your aura's very strong."

"Thanks, as is yours."

"Thanks. Our aura's are how we recognize each other. Now, does George know that you're Iska?"

"Interesting. And no, neither George nor Mr. Drew know that. George would kill me if he knew. He absolutely hates us and is always talking about how much trouble we've caused him. But, I've learned how to read him very well. I'm attuned to his moods and changes. If he decides to kill me, I'll know about it first and kill him before I disappear. Also, *Centrale* has been creating impenetrable identities for a very long time." She paused, thinking. "At the Firm and elsewhere, my persona is Anghelina DelaVega, which was Angelina's name before being banished from Madrid."

"Interesting. Well, nonetheless, be very careful. If anyone can penetrate it, it's George. And he may have done so already, just waiting for the optimal time to use it."

She nodded. "Point taken."

"Good. However, I think your blue eyes might arouse some suspicion and could result in your downfall."

"Part of my cover. I simply say when I'm frequently asked, my 'father,' Commandante Arturo, married a blonde, blue-eyed American leftist. Her picture in my wallet is my supporting documentation. And Arturo's picture's dark enough to be credible. Sergei told Maria, while he fully accepted us as his daughters, he advised our Iska name should not be used in Cuba, as it would cause us too many problems and questions."

Ashley nodded. "Tell me, though, what's your Iskandarov gift?"

"I have exceptionally fast reflexes and am an excellent athlete. My mother told us tales of our father, and I know he was extraordinary. He must've been to seduce a Rose, especially one as lethal as Maria. Although I'm twenty-four, I'm a fully-trained DI agent."

"Have you ever killed anyone?"

"When necessary. But I'm definitely not a Rose."

Ashley laughed. "But how did get your job with George?"

"I've my sponsor, my patron, in the English meaning, not the Spanish. She's not my boss."

"Who is she?"

"She's a prominent older lady who's a long-time friend of my mother and grandmother. And she made the introductions to George."

"All right. And what do you do for her in return?"

"She's a widow, and I'm her companion at her apartment over on Park. I also live there, even in her absence."

"Would I know this lady?"

"I'm sorry. She told me we must be very discreet about this, so certain people don't jump to false conclusions about our relationship. We live in a very conservative building, and there's a lot of gossip going on. The old ladies see a mature Anglo widow with a young Cuban woman, and they get the wrong idea. I also protect her as well."

"Good, but I can see where some people would think that."

She nodded. "Yes. *Centrale* ordered me to get close to George, preferably as his bodyguard, because he has business relations with a number of high officials in Cuba and elsewhere. Nothing sinister about all this, just routinely keeping my superiors informed."

"So, I assume your patron has ties to DI?"

"Yes, but only informally. Now, I've something else to tell you. *Centrale* wants you kidnapped. Since they know about my relationship with you, they've sent someone else to do the assignment."

"Do you know anything about this person?"

"They've probably sent a Rose. So be careful of strange women."

Ashley laughed. "You sound like my first stepmother, Lady Patricia." He paused. "OK. I'm surprised *Centrale* didn't just order either you or your mother to do the assignment."

"In the old days, they would've. But Maria has told them she's no longer a Rose. And I'm not sure *Centrale* trusts me enough to do it. Besides, since the money from *Centrale* is sporadic, at best, that gives us some freedom of action."

"Interesting."

She smiled. "Now, on to another matter. If you get yourself killed, Annie goes to her next of kin." She held up her hand. "Before you think that would be Ronnie Cooper, George will make sure he's appointed guardian. And none of us want that."

"You don't like George?"

"Like has nothing to do with it. He pays me, end of story. Also, my patron wants you kept alive. And don't think she carries less weight in my decisions than either George or *Centrale*. It might be even more."

"All right, I assume your patron's Ronnie Cooper. She's a widow who has an apartment over on Park in a very conservative building and has a history of helping young women from when she taught at Vassar. Finally, I know she's been mentoring a young Cuban woman for some time. I'll keep this secret as well."

She laughed. "Took you long enough. But back on topic, if George ordered me to kill you, I might just kill him instead. Or not. *Centrale* might like that." She shook her head. "I've an obligation to both my superiors at *Centrale* and George to follow their orders. If they're contradictory, as they so often are, I'd have to use my best judgement."

"So, you're saying there's a chance you might kill me as well?"

"Yes, but only as a last resort if I couldn't rescue you... to prevent you from a terrible fate, such as extreme torture and extended confinement. Or both."

"Good to know. So, who are you protecting me from?"

"You mean besides *Centrale* and George? Let's see, there's the Polinkovs, the Russian FSB, successor of the KGB, The *Mafiyah* and George's group, who conspired with the Russians on Iron Cage. And those are only the ones I know about."

He shook his head, sipped his coffee and asked, "Now, my most important question. What happened to our father after he left Cuba?"

"I've looked into this extensively. My mother doesn't want to know Sergei's fate. But, for me, it has become almost an obsession. I'm trained in finding people, especially those who don't want to be found. I've been able to track him to mid-seventies Moscow, but then nothing. Not even a death certificate. I don't know who's covering this up, but that's what it looks like."

"Thanks. It's a start, but how solid's this intel?"

"Very."

"Two more questions. Why did you change your birth name?"

"Pretty simple. I loved my grandmother, and it was she who suggested I add the 'h' to set us apart, because she predicted 'I would lead a very important life.'"

"I see, but is Angelina still alive? If so, I would love to meet her."

She shook her head slowly. "No, she died of natural causes back in 1985."

"I'm sorry, she seems like a very interesting person."

"Oh yes, she was. But now I strongly advise you might want to forget the van Rouene service Wednesday. I discovered two DI Cubans will try to get you either on the way to or the way back. But now, I've something for you." She handed him a small square envelope.

He opened the envelope, and Ronnie had written on a monogrammed card, "Ash, the prophecy begins now. Andreyeva," followed by a series of numbers. He recognized the Parisian dialing code. As he went to his study to make the call, he heard Holly come in.

FOURTEEN
Tuesday, 1 June 1993
New York, NY

1.

After making an appointment to see Grand Duchess Nadia Andreyeva in Paris on Thursday, Ashley returned to the terrace and saw Annie. "Where's Anghelina?"

"Well, you were in there a pretty long time, and after about ten minutes she said she had another appointment but would see us tonight at El Meson."

Ashley nodded as he sat. "I had to answer a long series of questions and make several declarations before getting the appointment. Not exactly like calling for pizza." He topped off his lukewarm coffee. "So, did you two get a chance to talk?"

"We did, but before I tell you about that, Aunt Ronnie told me she's mentoring Anghelina because she's showing early signs of *dhestovy*. That's a form of madness from not being properly instructed in Iska lore. She said Anghelina can seem normal for a long time and then, for no reason, explode in a fit of paranoia or intense anger. But recently, she seems more stable."

Ashley nodded. While this was disturbing, that she was carrying a gun was very alarming. "Do you know if she has *pyordarsch*?"

"Since her aura's stronger than Aunt Ronnie's she must. And Aunt Ronnie said *pyordarsch* is sometimes associated with *dhestovy*."

"Does that bother you?"

"No. I've been very well prepared, and whatever I'm missing, Charlotte can fix."

"So, then what's bothering you? I've heard you crying at night."

"Well…" She paused. "While I can't yet see far enough to see my death, I've seen the death of a close friend, and it gives me nightmares."

"I'm sorry."

"Thanks."

"Now, have you ever met Anghelina before?"

"No, I've only seen her with George a few times, and we never spoke. She seemed very nice just now, but I couldn't get over her toughness, which is so obviously there."

"Right. Hard to miss. What all did you talk about?"

"Oh, mostly Iska stuff. But just before she left, she said if the cops were looking for you about Joe Stevens, she'd take care of it."

"Good to know, and I'm grateful. But, as I've said, I've got very solid alibis."

"Good, but here's something you need to know. Aunt Ronnie told me yesterday Mom was Iska. Her father was Dmitri's brother, Alexei, stationed in Washington, and they met at a diplomatic reception in 1942."

Ashley nodded. "Good to know about Alexei. But I've suspected that for a long time. When your mother was about your age, she had a bright aura, which attracted me to her. But when I saw Olga's much stronger one, I was much more powerfully attracted to her. When I saw your mother's aura in 1975, it was much stronger than it had been, and that's why we married. But over the years, hers faded until by the time she died it had virtually disappeared."

"*Dhestovy* does that. As you probably know, the strength of your aura is based on the strength of your gifts."

"I'd assumed that. Anything else you'd like to share about Iska lore?"

She laughed. "You know I've told you repeatedly, I'm not allowed to tell you any of this lore. I can only reveal it to my husband."

He smiled. "OK. Now back to Rosalita. In preparation for my meeting with Maria Civilli, I need to know first how long you've known her and been going to her studio."

"I met 'Lita and Maria probably five years ago at El Meson. I've been going to her studio for about two years."

"I didn't know you'd been to El Meson."

"Oh yeah, I've been there many times with grandpa and Aunt Ronnie."

Ashley nodded. In 1983, David told him he had contracted food poisoning there, and Ashley began going to Victor's Cafe uptown. Obviously, David did not want him talking to Maria because she might say something about Sergei. He shook his head. "And what do you do at the studio?"

"Mostly dance routines, floor exercises and self-defense. It's a real workout. But it gets me ready physically and mentally for school. In addition, I feel safer on the street with what 'Lita has taught me. I mean, I'm no black belt, but some guy gets out of line, I can take him."

"Good, just don't get overconfident. Running and yelling are still good strategies."

"I know."

"OK. How do you feel about Rosalita?"

"She's twenty-four but seems so mature and self-sufficient. And, like Anghelina, I know it's not an act."

"OK. Now, as I've said, this trip will be dangerous, so, just suppose I died, who would you want to live with?"

"Aunt Ronnie. No question."

"How about George Farwell?"

"That old letch? You serious?"

"Has he…?"

"No, but when he's around, he's always trying to be the oh-so-charming Uncle George. It's vile. 'Lita, told me once George had come on to her after Anghelina shot him down. 'Lita told him if he laid a finger on her, she'd send him to the hospital."

"Good for her. When you met Maria did she ever say anything about Sergei being 'Lita's father."

"No. But I think the only person 'Lita fears is her sister. Maybe her mother a bit."

Ashley nodded. "Interesting."

"Oh. I maintained my A-plus average at Miss Chaplin's School for Young Ladies."

"I'm very proud of you. Now, we're leaving for Paris tomorrow night. Go start preparing your clothes for two weeks. Remember, only one bag. No more. You need two dress outfits, the rest functional. Anything we need, we buy over there. And don't forget your passport."

"Dad, I know how to travel, you know. Two weeks in one bag, that's brutal."

Ashley smiled. "Doubtless. But I know you can do it."

2.

On the way to his study, Ashley paused outside Penelope's bedroom, hoping to find some closure, as he had done with David and Patricia. He went to her writing desk and finally found their large wedding album, which he had not seen in a long time. He opened to a bookmarked picture of him in his morning coat talking to Randell, who had performed the ceremony, and Monica, in her organdy bridesmaid's dress. They all had champagne and were laughing. Wondering why Penelope felt this picture was important, he again studied it before he noticed her writing on one side of the long bookmark. *"To My Beloved Prince, let us dare to live the dream forever,"* signed with her swirling "P." On the other side of the bookmark, was a tabloid gossip column,

which Monica had brought over after their honeymoon. She had
written, "Isn't this a hoot!" across the top, and they had enjoyed
a good laugh. But why did Penelope laminate and keep it?

> Girls, in case your blood isn't blue enough, you
> missed the most fabulous society wedding of
> the season last night. Your reporter managed to
> snag an invite to rub elbows with la crème de
> la crème of New York Society at the very tony
> St. Jerome's Episcopal Church on Manhattan's
> very fashionable Upper East Side. The candle-
> lit church was magic as the bride, Penelope
> Anne Farwell, was given away by her father,
> the fabulously wealthy and socially prominent
> industrialist, George Simpson Farwell. The
> groom, Major Ashley Finlayson Cooper,
> U.S.A.F., a very prominent international lawyer,
> is a partner at a very blue-blood firm. Girls, the
> Major, 31, is a dreamboat. Moreover, the bride,
> in a to-die-for white silk and lace Valentino
> gown, was absolutely breathtaking. Your reporter
> hasn't seen anything like it since Jack and Jackie.
> Don't be surprised if lightning strikes a second
> time. Major Cooper is reportedly considering a
> political career. It certainly looks like happily
> ever after for this couple. Your reporter has
> learned that sexy Jane Fonda plans to make a…

Ashley shook his head. Where did this woman get her
information? He checked the rest of the album and found a folded
white letter dated August 28, 1992.

> Ash, my time is almost done. I know this
> because I have visions and have had them since
> I was a teen. I'm not sure why I have them, but
> Ronnie's been helping with this. I'm getting
> ahead of myself. About the time I hit puberty,

father had a paternity test done and found out
he wasn't my father. I never found out who was.
You remember he had my mother committed to
the Staten Island asylum and that was the reason.
What you don't know is that after that, he told
me I was his new 'wife' and raped my virginity.
Soon, my visions started, and he told me he
needed them for his work. And, if I disobeyed
him in any way, I'd join my mother. He
continued molesting me for several years until
he lost interest when I got my boobs. Now, you
know the truth. I've seen my death approaching
in a crash with a big truck. I fight hard to
maintain my sanity, but I can feel this madness
getting stronger every day.

There could be no forgiveness, understanding or mercy
for George. Ashley had to admit he had loved Penelope since
kindergarten. Had George acted responsibly, they could have
proceeded naturally. Ronnie would have been there to coach
Penelope on being Iskandarova and now, all three of them would
be going on this journey.

Here is my confession. I've always been
attracted to your light and, in my own way,
I loved you but, sometimes, especially when
you were gone so much, I cheated on you. I
suspect you knew about this but were too much
of a gentleman to say anything. While these
interludes were only a fuck, they made me feel
young, sexy and desirable. I've always assumed
you cheated on me on your trips with those
Russian girls you seem to love. And speaking
of Russians, I dated that lug, Nick Stevens, just
to make you jealous. But you started fucking
your Russian witch. When she got knocked up,

I knew if I didn't do something drastic, I'd lose
you forever. I blackmailed George to have him
send one of his thugs to kill her, which he did.
That guy you called Ovals was merely a decoy.
Don't know who actually poisoned her. But you
see, you've always belonged to me. So, her death
is really your fault, not mine. Besides, I fought
the law and I won. Never even asked a single
question about her death. Goodbye. P.

Penelope had been killed the next day on North Quaker
Mount Road on her way to see Ronnie. Ashley could only
shake his head. While Penelope in the *Odyssey* was the symbol
of marital fidelity, her confession was classic Penelope Farwell
Cooper—never taking any responsibilities for her actions and
always blaming someone else for her sins. However, he felt
nothing because she had simply confirmed something he already
strongly suspected. However, if Ovals had not killed Olga, then
the killer, possibly, remained out there and, with the Colonel's
death, would be after him again.

3.

As their cabbie, a recent immigrant, seemed lost in the West
Village's warren of streets, Annie began giving him directions
in Spanish. Ashley felt proud that, like him, Annie was fluent
in three languages. He remembered coming to El Meson with
David and Patricia, on one of their "bohemian adventures" in
the late fifties, later going with David and Ronnie. He took Olga
there over Thanksgiving weekend 1961 where they were spotted
by Ronnie's friend. And then there was David's food poisoning
story.

El Meson, from the outside, nestled among the residential
brownstones of Charles Street, appeared the way their clientele
wanted—a sturdy wooden door with a small neon sign above it
that could have said, *No tourists!* The distinctive aroma of black

bean soup and warmth of the kitchen felt very familiar, as did the assortment of student, academic and arty types. Anghelina met them. "Ashley, this is my sister, Rosalita."

"I've heard a great deal of good things about you," he said.

"And I you."

Their shiny raven hair, parted in the middle and pulled straight back, held by two large black combs, complemented their amber skin. Their identical high-necked, sleeveless red dresses revealed their toned arms and the slight bulge of their breasts before turning inward to slender waists. They both wore thick-heeled black shoes. "We're here for Flamenco Night. After your meeting with our mother and dinner, we'll all go back to your apartment and guard you until you leave town."

"Great idea."

Anghelina said, "I'll reintroduce you to our aunt, who will take you to our mother."

Señora Delgado, the owner, stood regally by the cash register, in a red dress with a white lace shawl around her shoulders, her gray-streaked black hair pulled into a bun. "Señor Ashley, welcome back, and good evening, Señorita Annie. As always, I am most pleased to see you."

"And I you, Señora." Annie hugged the older woman, saying something in Spanish.

Señora Delgado turned to Ashley. "Maria's in her office. I'll take you to her. And I'll look after your daughter while you're gone."

"Thank you, but that won't be necessary. She's going to the meeting as well. This is her journey too, and she needs to know everything I know and more."

She nodded. Ashley took Annie by the hand, and they followed Señora Delgado through a narrow corridor and up the stairs.

4.

Maria rose from behind a wide wooden desk in the white-stucco room. She wore a dark-blue pinstriped business suit with her black hair pinned back. She had retained her younger figure, suggesting great self-discipline. Her café au lait skin was proof why she could not be Sergei's daughter. Moving closer, he saw the dark eyes his father described with deep lines around them and her mouth. "Welcome, Señorita Annie, what a pleasant surprise. I'm pleased you came with your father. He must trust me." She laughed, and Annie hugged her. She turned to Ashley. "Commandante Maria Angelina Juanita Civilli Mendes of Cuban Security, Mister—I don't know how I should call you."

"You know, I feel as though I almost know you, and you doubtless know more about me. Why don't we call each other by our first names?"

She smiled. "Please be seated, both of you." She motioned to the chairs by her desk, turned and went over to an ornate cabinet.

"Anghelina said Señora Delgado was their aunt."

Maria set a squat bottle on a gold tray with three gold-rimmed glasses. "Not truly. The señora isn't my sister, simply an old comrade of long standing. And she taught them to dance." She placed the tray on the desk. "Annie, you now look very much the way Sergei described Charlotte."

"Oh yes, I've seen her picture when she was my age. Thank you."

Ashley leaned forward. "My father discussed Charlotte with you?"

"Of course. We discussed everything. Candidly, having had access to Sergei's dossier, there wasn't much I didn't know about him from the start." She poured three glasses. "This is Havana Club *añejo* rum, not available here. I keep it for special visitors." She raised her glass. "To a mutually productive and valuable conversation." Ashley clicked his glass with hers and Annie's and paused for Maria before sipping. "Very nice, rich and mellow." He noticed Annie had put her glass on the desk after one sip.

Maria laughed. "You're a prudent man, I see. But then you have your *tvarsch.*"

He laughed. "I see you two did discuss everything."

"Yes, we did. I've asked you here to answer any questions, and then I've a request."

"Yes. Of course." Ashley sat back on the wood and leather chair and sipped his rum. "This may seem off-topic, but it's something that's been bothering me for quite a while. What do you know about Svetlana Feliksovna Polinkova?"

"A very bright and beautiful proletarian girl who rose to be an extremely powerful commissar under Marshal Stalin. He gave her extraordinary powers to find traitors during the cleansings of the 1930s. She was also rumored to be his lover for a time."

Ashley smiled at how Maria had delicately described Stalin's purges. "Do you know why she's always referred to with her patronym? She's the only non-Iskandarov so described."

"I know. Her father was Feliks Dzerzhinski, founder of the Soviet Cheka."

"Hmm. I know he was married, but he only had one son, Jan. So, Svetlana must've been illegitimate. Nonetheless, her parentage explains a lot, especially her fast rise in the NKVD."

"Yes, it would. She was, of course, also the Commissar of the Institute where Sergei and Charlotte were. It had something to do with selective breeding. That's all I know."

"Thank you. Very helpful." She seemed fairly open. A good start.

She topped off their glasses, smiling at Annie. "It's an acquired taste."

Annie smiled weakly before nodding, clearly embarrassed at her lack of sophistication.

"So, why're you helping me?"

"You're family. Had I been interested in bourgeois marriage, I'd be your stepmother. Most importantly, you're Sergei's son. Your father helped me regain my self-respect." She sipped her rum pensively. "What you read in Sergei's diary about my early life was essentially correct, but far from complete, as it was in many other areas. Sergei didn't know the big picture until much later. After Angelina's kidnapping, I was sent to an orphanage and then, at seven, I was sold to Madam Isabella's, an American Mafia underage *burdel*. I was there for almost ten years and was kept 'jazzed' so I didn't care what those perverts were doing to me. Only my next fix mattered."

Annie seemed truly horrified. "Oh my God, I'm sorry. I can't understand how anyone could do that to girls. And I don't know 'jazzing.'"

Maria nodded. "Of course not. Rico shot us up with just enough to get us high, but still function. It's called 'jazzing' because a number of jazz musicians, such as Billie Holiday, 'Yardbird' Parker and Anita O'Day were on smack for years and still seemed to perform normally. I don't tell you this for sympathy but for how it impacted my life before Sergei. First, I survived going cold turkey at *Liberacion*, 1 January 1959, when Rico and Isabella fled. We girls helped each other. Angelina found me in February. In 1962, as a DGI agent, I found Rico and Isabella outside Miami and killed them slowly and painfully. Truthfully, it didn't bring me the relief I had hoped for. And I continued to hate myself and, as a Rose, took great pleasure in killing men. Until I met your grandfather, but even that took time. But my many killings gave me status and promotions within the DGI." She paused, smiling. "Ashley, don't look so alarmed. I haven't killed anyone since the seventies. You've both nothing to fear."

Ashley nodded, gulped his rum and tried to smile. "Tell me more about El Meson."

"Certainly. The first time I saw it was during Fidel's first visit to the city in April 1959. Angelina, then one of his top aides, brought me along as her aide. I loved New York and knew I had to get back. She'd stayed on after the trip to negotiate Sergei's release. Mr. Henry Baker, the Baker in the diary, represented the US government. Veronique Landfear, your future step-mother, Ronnie, represented the Bleu agency, and the Colonel acted as legal counsel for Madame Landfear and Sergei."

"I didn't know Ronnie knew David until the early sixties."

"Absolutely. They were working together on a number of negotiations before they finally married. You were off in boarding school at that time. I confess that when Fidel spoke at the Lawrenceville School Chapel on that visit, Angelina asked me to discreetly discover what I could about you. Among other things, I searched your room in the Kennedy House."

Although shocked, Ashley made a joke of it. "Did you find anything incriminating?"

"First, I noticed how neat your room was. I was also impressed by the number of books you had and assumed you were well-read. I did notice the Playboy pin-ups inside your closet." She laughed. "Naughty boy."

"Dad! How could you?"

"Guilty." He laughed. "But why was Angelina interested in me?"

"She knew, as Sergei's son, you'd be important in the future, and I should learn as much as I could about you. Sergei felt especially grateful for that information. Now, as I was saying, after a long negotiation in 1959 a deal had been struck for Sergei's release. Bleu's payment would be released from Credit Suisse Bank in Manhattan the following day. There was also an unnamed third party in a Cuban jail as part of the deal. The following day, someone killed it."

"I don't get it. Why even hold negotiations at all then? Have you since discovered the name of the person?"

"I've discovered it was a very powerful faction, in and out of the government, who called themselves 'Prometheus,' because they had stolen the fire from the Cold War to benefit man."

Ashley nodded. The human mind can seemingly justify anything, no matter how evil.

"Over the years, there were several more attempts to free Sergei. On the second attempt, I joined Angelina. Ronnie and I became friends, despite our being sometimes adversaries, as our interests merged. We used to meet, on a regular basis, with Angelina at different Jamaican resorts to work on new strategies."

"I see."

"Finally, Henry Baker persuaded President Johnson to release Sergei. Bleu paid Angelina. No other country wanted Sergei at that time, not even the Soviet Union. That was Svetlana's doing."

"I'm not surprised. Now, was Svetlana part of Prometheus?"

"Oh yes. Their woman in Moscow. She regarded Sergei as her property and so, all of Sergei's children were her property, including my girls. She actually wrote me a letter to order me to send them to her for 'proper socialist training.' I showed it to Angelina, who wrote back that if Svetlana wanted her grandchildren, she'd have to come to Cuba, an island she would never leave alive. And that was the end of that. Madwoman, Svetlana was."

"No argument from me. Lord Acton's 'Absolute power corrupts absolutely' covers it."

"Usually. Now, here's a part of the big picture. Sergei's 1968 stay in Cuba was entirely Angelina's operation. Commandante Antonio served only as her front man. While she didn't wish to appear immediately to Sergei, she had several goals. Most important, we had to keep Sergei alive. Second, to learn specifically how much he knew about Iron Cage. Third, I was to conduct a more detailed debrief on his captivity, including the *Luftstalags*, the gulag and the institute. Four, *mi madre* then deeply regretted she never had a child with Sergei. She'd felt, in her late thirties, a child would burden her free spirit life. She urged me not to make her mistake. And in time, I saw I wanted Sergei's child, for a variety of reasons. Now, Antonio hated all Americans and felt, as my superior, the Bleu money belonged to him. And normally, he'd be right. However, he feared me. Even though I was then merely *capitan*, I had power far beyond my rank because I often spoke for Angelina. I told him Sergei was under Angelina's protection, and after Sergei had been debriefed and left Cuba safely, I would see that Antonio would get his reward. I also told him that I wouldn't be rushed or reassigned by anyone, including him. I let him rant until I abruptly turned and left, without his permission. After Sergei left, I killed Antonio for Angelina, who gave me the money, which I sent to my Credit Suisse account here in New York. And since the fall of the Soviet Union, the money has absolutely been a life saver."

"No doubt. As you know, I stopped coming here some ten years ago. About the time you arrived."

"Yes, the Colonel's food poisoning story." She laughed and poured another glass for the two of them.

Ashley nodded. He liked Maria's laugh, which he had assumed she would not have. "I'm still curious about several things…"

"Well, we both know Sergei couldn't be my father. I'm the daughter of Antoine the Haitian—"

"You mean 'the Black Stallion'? I—"

She laughed. "I'm certain you are, and since you know Angelina's story, I've a sidelight about *Les Demoiselles de Joie*, or 'the Misses of Joy.' Now, according to Angelina, they were all 'rich, naughty free-spirits with no interest in marriage.' I know how you feel about your late stepmother, Lady Patricia Sternwood, but she was part of this group for several years in Berlin."

"Really?"

"Don't be so surprised. There's an old Spanish saying… 'Women give themselves to God only after the Devil is finally finished with them.'" She turned to Annie and smiled. "That's only true for some women."

"Yes, I know."

Ashley laughed. Of course. Patricia had been a ravishing young aristocrat. Perfect for this very liberated group. "Did Angelina ever know Sergei's father, Dmitri? They seem to have been in the same places at the same time."

"While it's certainly possible, I really don't know. Here's what you don't know about *Les Demoiselles.* During the Spanish Civil War, in late 1936, an agency of the Comintern ordered Angelina to go to Havana and set up a listening post and safe house for Cuban rebels and fraternal agents passing through in both directions from the US. She persuaded the *demoiselles* to come with her, where they would re-create the fun of Berlin, only this time, they'd get paid. Once in Havana, they, in time, supplemented their numbers with another twenty-five Cuban ladies. And the result was *Chez Marianne*. The Comintern bureaucrats were horrified when they came to inspect. However, the quality of the intel gathered and the easy movement of agents stopped their complaints, and they never came back. Angelina knew her freewheeling *demoiselles* scared them. As I've said, Angelina was a free spirit, and she played by her own rules all her life, including in Cuba. She and Sergei had a great time. Sergei didn't like Nazis. Angelina hated the rigid Stalinists. So, they also shared information." She sipped her rum. "When the war in Europe started, their European clients stopped, and the *demoiselles* had more time on their hands. Angelina, always ready to try new things, started going to ladies' night in the auditorium. And I'm the result of their union."

"Interesting. But I can't say I'm surprised. But later, after Angelina escaped from her *burdel*, I'm mystified why she didn't rescue you from yours."

"Two reasons. First, as a hunted fugitive and rebel, the Sierra Madre was the only place she could be even relatively safe. Secondly, even if she'd been free, my *burdel* was one of the best-kept secrets in Cuba at the time. Anyone, Mafiosi or customer, who broke the code of *omerta*, or silence, to anyone unauthorized was killed immediately. The select customers paid very well for their perversions. Later, Angelina easily coerced the information out of a prisoner."

"Amazing story." Ashley smiled. "Now, tell me about your relationship with David."

"Of course. First, my condolences on your stepfather. He was a fine gentleman. He made a special trip down here after he had spoken to you in your office about momentous events. He spoke with me about Sergei. That, of course, was the day before he died, and he knew."

"How so?"

"I've seen many condemned people, and they seem to have an air, some resigned and some fighting. The Colonel was the former and seemed to be at peace."

"Thanks. Good to know. Was there a particular subject he wanted to discuss?"

"Yes, several. In particular, he wanted to know if I knew why Sergei had volunteered anything about Iron Cage. He told me if Sergei had stayed quiet, he would've been exchanged within a year. But once Sergei revealed he knew about Iron Cage, he became dangerous. That's why they buried him alive and why the initial negotiation failed."

"Indeed. In the diaries, Sergei referred to it as the 'Get Out of Jail Free Card.'"

"Yes, he always thought that. In fact, it was the 'Get Buried Under the Jail and Throw Away the Key Card.'"

Ashley nodded. "However, I see a certain logic in his actions. Absent Iron Cage, he couldn't explain who he was or how he had the fingerprints of a dead man as Baker had asked. Since that situation couldn't be cleared up, he couldn't be released. Besides, his actions at Camp David worked against his release. Yes, he was buried alive, but that had to be better than being buried dead. If he'd killed Eisenhower, he would've been secretly shot by a firing squad."

"Very interesting. I'd never looked at the situation that way. And you may very well be right. But..." She sighed, stood and leaned forward with her hands firmly on the desk, looking down. "Ashley, forget about Iron Cage. If you persist in trying to uncover it by finding Sergei's gulag diaries, you'll be crushed. Iron Cage stole much of his life. He told me he wanted his son to be free of it."

"This is difficult. I want to respect my father's wishes, but..." He wondered if Maria might have a vested interest in keeping Iron Cage quiet. He crossed his arms.

"Since the Soviets no longer exist, you'll only embarrass your own and allied governments." She shook her head. "Please,

I know you may not trust me. But I honestly don't wish any harm to come to you."

Ashley uncrossed him arms as Maria sat down.

"Dad. I don't want to lose you. I think you should do as Maria says."

This was something he had not expected. Annie was right. He had to take her well-being into consideration. And yet he sensed he had to do it for his father and the Iskandarov.

Maria smiled. "You're stubborn, like your father." She threw her head back, closed her eyes and said something intense in Spanish. "Sergei was so paranoid after all his imprisonments he honestly thought I was there to kill him. It was a long, slow process to get him to trust me. We spent over a month debriefing Iron Cage, of which I was very much aware." She briefly drifted off in thought before smiling. "Your father was the most incredible man I've ever met. He was a smart and well-spoken gentleman. There was even a spiritual quality about him. Not like the priests I remember before *La Revolucion*, but a true man of God. As an atheist, at first I didn't know what it was about him. But gradually, I began to. It was his absolute faith he would ultimately succeed. However, it was this same faith that, in some ways, made him naive, like a child. It was madness for him to write a journal. When I first discovered it, I really couldn't understand how he could be writing it for a son he'd never met, one who lived over a thousand miles and a whole world away. Yet, he maintained when the time was right, it would come to you. And here we are, twenty-five years later and you have it, despite my losing it once in the archives. That's why it smells the way it does. Most incredible."

Ashley noticed as Maria had spoken about Sergei, the crispness left both her demeanor and her speech, and he saw softness creep into her eyes. "Yes, isn't it. You said his faith made him like a child. My faith isn't as strong as his was. But from what I've read about the Iskandarov, their intense faith is an integral part of who they are and their successes. So, he felt he could write the diary and no matter how things turned out, he'd be OK, even if he were shot."

"Yes, again, perhaps you're right. Nonetheless, as I've said, he was already in a very dangerous position, even without the journal. The Americans, the British and the French all wanted him out of the way. But, morally, they simply couldn't kill a man who was a bombardier on nineteen missions over Europe and Ploesti and finally became an abandoned POW. Of course, the Soviets and their allies had other ideas."

"Right. After leaving you, where did he go?"

"Back to Moscow with the KGB. Beyond that..." Maria shrugged.

Ashley sighed. "When was that?"

"It was 1973. I'm sorry I couldn't be more help. I can see your pain. Perhaps this will help a bit." She opened her desk drawer and held a scratched and dented small metal box. "This was your father's cigarette case."

Ashley took it. On the outside were his father's initials, S.D.I., in Cyrillic. Opening it, a few stale flakes of tobacco fell out, probably from his beloved Luckies.

"Sergei carried this case on all his missions as a lucky charm. He said it was a gift from his father on his eighteenth birthday. He wanted you to have it."

He nodded and handed it to Annie to see if she could get anything from it. It did help as a reminder of the man whose presence he now felt in the room.

"Thanks, Dad. I'll see what I can do once we get home."

Maria leaned forward. "Oh yes, one final thing, something I learned from Henry Baker, a reliable source, but I've not actually seen any documents."

Ashley nodded. "OK, I'll take it as such."

"Sergei's interrogation records were sent to President Eisenhower, and he went through them with Vice-President Nixon. Eisenhower had no doubt Sergei could've easily killed him. While the president was recovering, he received a letter from

Secretary Khrushchev, outlining the Soviet demands now that he had 'the president's full attention.' He and Nixon discussed this at great length. Nixon, speaking as the presumed next president and target, said we couldn't possibly agree to the terms, 'a tarted-up rehash of Stalin's demands about Europe and the Far and Middle East.' Nixon said he trusted the Secret Service to protect him, especially if they knew the Soviets were making threats. Eisenhower nodded his agreement, and that was that."

"You know, no one's secrets are now, or ever have been, secure to someone who wants to discover them. I wonder if Nixon told Kennedy about this after the 1960 election. Even if he didn't, I assume it would've shown up in some official documents. But, perhaps not."

Maria nodded thoughtfully. "Very interesting point. Now that you know the story, here's my request." She opened her desk and removed three sheets of paper and an envelope. "These are the pages I removed from the journal. I made a copy, which is in the envelope. You may read them later. I'll only read my relevant part. Here Sergei is writing about arriving in Cuba, on the way to Vailadero, after meeting Commandante Antonio at Camp Matanzas, DGI headquarters."

> In the car, the men were again silent, and I
> thought about this Maria Civilli. I imagine it
> was a fairly common last name and I knew two
> women with it. One was Angelina. I haven't
> seen her since Pearl back in '41. Could she be
> this Maria's mother? Was she even still alive?
> The other was at Vorkuta, Carmella Civilli.
> For a while, she was my camp wife, who slept
> with me and, in return, I protected her from
> the guards, the criminals who actually ran the
> place and other zeks. She told me her story and
> claimed to have been from an important Spanish
> family in Madrid. Nonetheless, as a student at

the University, she'd advocated socialist causes. When the Spanish Civil War came, she became a firebrand for the Loyalists. At the end of the war in 1939, Carmella fled to the Soviet Union with her Russian lover. Carmella lived happily in Leningrad for about a year. However, these were still the years of the Purges. One night the NKVD came for her. She learned that her lover had denounced her as a fascist spy. She bore him no ill will and readily confessed. That was what the Party wanted. And here she was in the Gulag.

Maria looked up and laughed. "When I was a girl, Angelina would tell me stories about how Tia Carmella fought the Fascists in the civil war. Now, these pages are all the family history of her I have. I even asked Sergei if he knew more than this. He didn't. When you eventually go to Russia, most likely you'll go to Vorkuta. Once there, I want you to find out what happened to Tia Carmella." She held up her hand. "You don't need to tell me the almost impossibility of this task. I can't go there myself. But I'm told you're a man of your word."

"OK, I give you my word that I'll do my best. Do you have any further information?"

She reached into the desk. "Here's her picture."

Ashley studied the dog-eared and bent, black-and-white photo of a demure young woman with intense eyes and straight, black hair. "Very good. It's a start." He handed it to Annie who put it in her purse along with the cigarette case.

Maria rose and walked over to the wall. "And now I've something else for you." As she spoke, she moved a picture, unlocked her wall safe and returned with an old envelope. "I'll leave you with this. I have another appointment tonight and won't be coming back."

Ashley stood. "Thank you. But does anyone else know whether Sergei's alive?"

"I had a comrade once who probably knew."

"So, you didn't want to know?"

"Yes. I couldn't bear knowing Sergei was dead." She hugged and kissed both of them on their cheeks. About to leave, she stopped, "Ah yes. I met with two agents from *Centrale* and told them you and Annie were under my protection, so they should get back to Cuba. They'll be back, I'm sure, in a few days. But by then, you'll probably be somewhere else."

"Thank you. That takes care of one immediate threat. And also, for your hospitality, and we'll speak again."

"You're most welcome. I'm sure we will. In the meantime, good fortune on your journey." She smiled and left.

5.

Ashley sat and opened the sealed, yellowed envelope addressed to Ashley Cooper, Esq. He began reading out loud.

5 August 1973

Dear Son, my tvarsch tells me, thanks to Maria,
when the time is right, you and this letter will
find each other. That means David Cooper, one
of the finest gentlemen I ever knew, is now
dead. That greatly grieves me. For all I know, I
may be as well. Today is your thirtieth birthday.
It's hard to believe that you're that old and
I've never seen you as you now enter into your
full adulthood. (But you are much older now.)
I'm also sorry you never knew your mother,
Charlotte Sternwood, who would've been a
wonderful mother to you. 'Binkie' was the code
name I used in my journal. And I know you've
now read all my journals through Cuba, as well
as David's and Dmitri's and that my daughter,
Verushka Sergevna, told you about your task.

Your daughter, presumably, Anastasia has very
strong pyordarsh like her great grandmother,
Sophia.

"Very impressive. But how could he have known about me
and *pyordarsch?* And I don't think I ever knew Aunt Ronnie's
Russian name."

Ashley smiled. "Prophecy, and I didn't know it until
recently."

As you know, I've lived out my days here
in Cuba but today, I'll return to Russia. I've
obligations there and before I die, I plan to learn
the whereabouts or fate of my dearest Charlotte
and Natalya. I know you're probably thinking
that if I truly loved Charlotte how could I have
a baby with another woman? Have no doubt,
many men would sell their immortal souls for
but a single night with a sultry woman like
Maria. Also, there can be no doubt Maria saved
my life. Perhaps, Maria's life, through Rosalita
and young Angelina, can be saved, as well. I
ask you to help your sisters any way you can.
I won't sugarcoat the task before you. It will
be hard, dangerous and unforgiving. But this
is good. Adversity is how we grow and mature
and learn true wisdom. You, as my son and with
your blood, are part of something larger than
yourself. Remember that 'the Blood is Iskandar.
May he speak within you.' I don't expect you
to understand this concept, yet. Remember,
you, by yourself, are nothing. You benefit from
those who came before. David tells me you are
bright and gifted. That's the result of the blood
flowing in your veins. Never forget that. Even

though you have lived your life as 'the Hidden
One,' now that you know, you must take action.
The Iskandarov have protected you for many
years from our enemies who wished you dead or
worse. Now, the time has come for you to repay
your debt. The Iskandarov need you and your
daughter. I tried to avoid my responsibility and
look where it has led me. However, I haven't
failed completely. I leave, at least, eight children
scattered around the globe to continue. The
new world awaits. Use your tvarsch to direct
you where you must go. There's still my very
important Gulag journal to be found.

When you find it, you will discover what Hell the
frozen wastes and coal mines of Vorkuta were.
I survived because of the Lost Souls, my POW
buddies from Alt Drewitz. Svetlana Feliksovna.
(Yes, that Feliks!) got in to her mad head that she
wanted me as a concubine. I resisted as long as
I could, but she was playing with a stacked deck
and the Icebox. And at the Institute, I discovered
I'd traded one Hell for another. But I also knew
this was my fate and there was a reason for it.
Do not scoff at Fate. Use your tvarsch to gain
insight. Understanding this is integral to being of
the Iskandarov. As you search, know that you, as
the fruit of Charlotte's womb, are very special to
me and I love you.

While Ashley felt dubious about fate, he felt a memory trying
to escape into his consciousness. It would come, but he would
still believe in free will. Nonetheless, another diary about the
details of the gulag and Iron Cage would be invaluable. He would
have to find it, read it and then make it public. He shook his head.
Eight children, he knew, besides himself, Olga, Ronnie, Natalya,

Anghelina, Rosalita, Aleks and Rini. On the last page, he found a faded color snapshot of Maria in her floral bikini. Her black hair is down, and she is barefoot. Yes, some men would sell their souls for a woman like her. Pasted below is a much more detailed head and shoulders shot of Sergei, wearing a Hawaiian shirt. His face is thin, tanned and deeply lined, under short gray hair. His shoulders are strong, and he is smiling broadly, revealing missing and broken teeth. After carefully studying the pictures, he gave them to Annie, who put them in her purse.

6.

Arriving downstairs, they saw a nearly full restaurant as Señora Delgado led them to "the Colonel's table." She started to make a recommendation, but Ashley stopped her and said they would have the Colonel's favorite meal and sangria for both of them. She nodded, and they turned their attention to the stage where Anghelina and Rosalita had briefly stopped. Rosalita's thick-heeled black shoes began their staccato on the hollow wooden platform, sending progressively louder echoes and vibrations through the room. Anghelina then began a more complicated rhythm, which Rosalita bested. They competed for about five minutes until the guitarist started playing. They moved in unison as though each were looking into a mirror. They would sometimes twirl their dresses' white underside or teasingly pull it up to their knees, revealing hard calves under thin black hose. Their handclaps were done with grace, precision and authority and were met with a hail of applause and whistles until they left the stage.

When Ashley and Annie had finished their meal, the Civilli sisters put down their overnight bags, sat down and poured glasses of sangria. Ashley told them what their mother had said about the two *Centrale* agents. Anghelina said, "Good. But you still have others of concern. Sister and I are armed, and we'll protect you on the way uptown. Your meal's complimentary, but a nice tip would be greatly appreciated. So, after the sangria, let's go."

FIFTEEN

Tuesday Night and Wednesday, 1 & 2 June 1993
New York, N.Y. & Over the Atlantic

1.

Ashley, having finished packing and doing almost all his last-minute trip preparations, sat in his study realizing he did not know how long he and Annie would be gone. He was not only about to leave New York but also his old life. He did not know what he was getting into or even what being the Hidden One involved, but he could not stay in New York and risk their safety. He remembered that Theodore Roosevelt had taught his young children to swim by tossing them into the deep end of the pool and letting them discover how to keep their heads above water. Somehow, it had worked, and for the first time, Ashley understood how the children must have felt. He also knew, despite being guarded by the Civilli sisters, that they would be most vulnerable leaving the building for Newark Airport. His adversaries would be watching the Air France Terminal at JFK, his work airline. He and Annie would be flying on a smaller French airline, Le Coq Gaulois, meaning The Gallic Rooster, which was the unofficial symbol of France and, he had heard, an excellent airline.

He went to his wall safe, debated whether he should bring his maroon diplomatic passport and finally decided on only the blue. Five thousand dollars, his Olga notebook, and the other diaries were piled on his desk, and he carefully put them in his briefcase. He placed his passport in his blazer's inside pocket and his Sainte Elizabeta icon in his right-hand pocket.

Finished, he relaxed as he saw the Park lights coming on and felt another *Andronyi* from Natalya. This time, she was younger than when he had seen her with Svetlana on Quaker Mount, but, of course, she was still naked and vulnerable.

Natalya stands over a naked, wet man spread-eagled on a hard-packed dirt floor. His face is round and flat, like the Mongolians Ashley once met in Budapest. He bleeds from several bullet wounds but still lives. She holds a pistol and looks up to see about twenty other similar men in their Red Army uniforms watching her, outwardly, without expression. She hears a command from Svetlana Feliksovna and fires once more, crying as she does. After two more shots, Svetlana comes over to inspect the man. Then she speaks to the others, "Monkey traitor shall soon die. I have been merciful. Next time I discover traitor I shall be merciless. Dismissed!"

She turns to Natalya. "You have done well with the Game, there will be no beating this time. You may go to your room. I shall be there shortly. Leave the pistol in the usual place."

"Mother, why this guard?"

"I randomly chose him. He must have been guilty of something."

Ashley could only shake his head at this. How could this poor girl keep going in such a hellish place? He remembered his father's letter… *Adversity is how we grow and mature and learn true wisdom.* If that were true, Natalya must be as wise as Solomon. But if so, how could she call this monstrous person "mother"? Had she completely forgotten Charlotte? Svetlana had stolen Natalya, and her birthday branding was a reminder of that. He shook his head, focused and came out of his trance before hearing, "Hello, Ashley."

"Hi, Anghelina. Back from another day of babysitting George I see."

"Tell me about it. The car service will be here in about twenty minutes. I know the driver very well, and he's well trained in losing tailing cars. Sister told me you and Annie are very good at keeping safe."

"Good. Tell me about the funeral."

"Pretty routine. Dr. Speers told both George and Charles you and Annie were on the way to Berlin for a secret meeting with Minister Iskandarov about the L'Enfant business. Has the phone been ringing?"

"Been pretty quiet until recently. And we let everything go to the answering machine… even Annie's calls."

"Good. But on the way here, I saw a guy who was obviously watching the building. He's now sleeping on the park bench across the street and will be out for another hour or so. Let's have a group meeting to run through the plan, and by then the car will be here."

2.

They arrived at Newark International Terminal B just after nine and checked in with Gallic Rooster. After that, Anghelina wished Ashley great success and kissed him on the lips, while Rosalita kissed Annie the same way before they both kissed the other sister. Ashley and Annie boarded the 747 flight leaving at 9:45 for De Gaulle/Paris Airport. As they entered the first-class cabin, Ashley smiled as he breathed in the unique aroma of the plane with the addition of several perfumes and stale tobacco. The bulkheads were all white, and the red double recliner seats with a triangular desk in between were like islands on the blue carpet. He noticed that the cabin was almost full and most of the conversations he heard, going down the aisle after Annie, were French. He saw a well-dressed young man who seemed familiar, but he did not know why. Annie had given him a quick wink as she passed. Did she know him or was she being flirty again? He had received a friendly "*Bonsoir*" as he passed the young man and returned it before getting to his own seat. When he put his carry-on and briefcase in the overhead and carefully folded his blazer on top of it, he had another opportunity to study him. Ashley nodded, still not recognizing him, and took the window seat.

"Dad, how come you get the window seat?"

"Well, when you're paying for the flight, you'll get your choice." He smiled.

"You just wait for my revenge on my mean old dad. When I'm paying, if you're lucky, you'll be riding on the wing."

"Don't be absurd. By the time you have enough money for a flight like this, we'll be riding in rockets." They both laughed. About twenty minutes later, the plane began to slowly taxi, and one of the attendants went through the safety features of the plane, first in French and then English. Once on the runway, Ashley, was pushed back into his seat and smiled when the pilot rotated, and they were airborne. As they banked toward Europe, he looked out the port window at the seemingly endless lights of the tri-state area.

The flight attendant, in her elegant blue tunic, crisp white trousers and a red cap, set at a rakish angle, came through with flutes of champagne. She offered Ashley one and looked quizzically at Annie until she reached into her purse and produced a laminated card. The attendant nodded and gave her a flute. After she moved on, Ashley very casually asked, "May I see that? I used to be a connoisseur of fake IDs." Annie smiled and gave him a Vassar College student ID with her date of birth about six months past twenty-one. But it was the name that shocked him... Anastasia Sergeyvna Iskandarova.

"Very nice. I see Ronnie's hand in this."

"Absolutely. But don't forget what Sergei wrote about me. Aunt Ronnie gave it to me as an early birthday present when she came to the house the other day. She explained when she was teaching there, until 1982, there was no problem for her special girls because the drinking age was eighteen. But then, New York raised it to nineteen, and she took action. Aunt Ronnie thinks the drinking laws in this country are insane. I agree."

"So do I. But why the change of name?"

"Well, I'm not going to be Annie Cooper much longer. You'll need to change your name soon. Aunt Ronnie said when you found out Sergei was your father you wanted to be named after him. With my patronym, I'm 'daughter of Sergei.' I like the sound of that. And I'd like it even more if it were true."

"Well, when I told her that on the phone, it was simply something I was thinking about. For a variety of reasons, I'm keeping my name for the present."

"OK. Have it your way, Mr. Ashley Finlayson Cooper. But you do need to change it." She sipped her champagne.

Ever since Ashley discovered he was named after Ashley Wilkes, he had begun to hate it. And the Iskandarov would never fully accept him until he did change. However, if, as Ashley Cooper he could get the minister to sign L'Enfant, he could return to the Firm as a star. And then he could choose to rejoin the Iskandarov or not. He always liked to have options, and this was one he had thought up earlier today. He had not told anyone about this and never would. "You know, when I was home from Lawrenceville, I knew two or three underage bars on the Upper East Side where I could always get a drink. But I also had a collection of fake IDs, just in case. Now, describe the champagne."

After she did so, the attendant came through with the dinner menu, which looked fantastic. Later, as they were eating, Annie said, "This is an incredible meal what with the rooster on the china, these big thick napkins, the elegant wine glasses with the red rooster and the miniature silverware with the long, white handles and the red stripe in the middle. And the Bordeaux is wonderful."

"Indeed, it is. Randell told me about the airline and said it was terrific, and he was in coach." He laughed.

After dinner, Ashley, with a snifter of cognac in hand, asked, "I meant to ask you before, who's that guy a few seats back you winked at?"

"Oh, that's Yuri."

"You sound as though I should know him."

"OK then. How about Sabreur Bleu? The guy who saved your life when that Cuban guy took a shot at you."

"Wow. I should go back and thank him."

"Bad idea. We can't have contact with him. He'll find us in Paris."

"OK. You sound like you know him pretty well."

"Yes, we've been going out for about two years."

"And?"

"And what? Are you prying into my personal life?"

Ashley heard her anger. "No, I told you I wouldn't do that. But he looks to be in his twenties, and your defensive response has me concerned that I should."

Annie sighed. "We're just friends. We go to movies, dinners, dances and parties. We're not wild like you and Mom were before you married."

"Well, that was a different time. I'm still your dad and just want the best for you."

"OK. He's Iskandarov, and we have the most wonderful conversations. I mean, what could be better?"

"You thinking about getting married?"

"No. I think he's a great guy, but I'll not be ready for marriage for a long time. OK?"

"Yes. I—"

"I know, you're just looking out for me. And I appreciate that. But I would also like it if you trusted me more. And you can do so by not being quite so protective and leaping to conclusions."

"No, you're right. We're partners, and I'm trying to treat you like an equal. But you need to cut me some slack. It's very hard seeing your little girl become a woman so rapidly."

"Dad, I'll always be your little girl, even when I'm old and gray and have my own kids." She smiled and reached into her purse to pull out a brown, leather-bound book with a thin, black and gold pen.

"What's that?"

"It's a diary to record everything that happens on this trip for future generations, just like the Iskandarov have done for us."

"What a great idea. But I've one final thing, and then I'll drop it. I noticed you kissed both the Civillis on their lips."

"Dad, there you go again, jumping to conclusions. We're not lesbians. It's just traditional for Iskas to do that as a token of respect and affection."

"Annie, all this Iska stuff's completely alien to me. So, because you won't tell me details, I've no idea what's normal, and I have to interpret through what I know."

"OK. Apology accepted. I'm starting by writing about our meeting with Maria last night. I paid very close attention, because I knew she wouldn't like me writing everything down. That was 'Lita's idea." She paused. "I've additional information about Carmella Civilli... she's still alive. Where she is, I don't know. I'll work on that in Paris and also on Sergei's cigarette case."

"Thanks. That's going to make finding her easier."

She shook her head.

"What is it?"

"A lot of people are smoking those stinky French cigarettes. It's so vile."

"I know. They can only smoke after we leave American airspace. I've been trying to ignore it, but as they say, nothing's perfect. And because the ventilation works well, that's a small inconvenience compared to the rest of the flight."

"OK. I suppose I can ignore it as well." She nodded and began writing. Ashley rose and got his briefcase and two blankets from the overhead and gave Annie one. He opened his briefcase on his desk and was greeted by the collective aroma of all the diaries. He took out his Olga folder and stared at the notebook for a while before looking at his watch... almost eleven p.m. New York time. He changed his watch to Paris time, finished his third cognac and put the folder on top of his briefcase. A few minutes later, he turned off his reading light and reclined in the bed-like seat, peering into the darkness, and watched the lights blinking

on the wing as the almost full moon came into view. He closed
the shade on the large port and, fully reclined and wrapped in his
blanket, said, "Good Night. Time for sleep. Tomorrow's a big
day." Annie nodded and put her diary away, as he thought, *Yeah,
they're all big from here on out.*

4.

>...and every evening,
>my only friend is mirrored in my wine-glass and,
>like myself,
>is subdued and dazed
>by the tart and mysterious liquor.

Later, Ashley, eyes closed, lay between sleep and wakefulness,
remembering Alexandr Blok's "The Stranger," which he had
originally heard in Olga Andreyeva's Seminar in Russian Silver
Age Literature at Harvard, some thirty-odd years before.

>And every evening, at the appointed hour
>—or is this only a dream that I see?
>—the figure of a girl, swathed in silk,
>moves across the misted window.
>Entranced by this strange nearness,
>I look through a dark veil
>and see an enchanted shore
>and an enchanted distance.

Olga, even now in unguarded moments, still haunted him.
That was the great unfinished time in his life. And although
he wanted to be finally free of her before going to Russia, he
doubted that would happen. But, after all, Paris was the City of
Olga, where she lay buried. At the very least, he would find her
grave and speak with her. He felt the throbbing in his temples
and knew with his parched mouth this was his prize for the three
snifters of cognac, wine and champagne. When he opened his
eyes, they were blurred and sticky. The plane was quiet, except
for preparations from the galley. Annie slept contentedly with her

sleep mask. Aside from the champagne, she had only had one glass of Bordeaux with dinner. Unlike her father, she obviously knew her limits. Smart girl. He took out his folder with Olga's yearbook picture on top. After turning on his reading light, he focused on her black hair parted in the middle and especially her intense, intelligent eyes. As he stared at the picture, her eyes seemed to glow, and he could see her aura as well. When he closed his eyes, the image briefly remained. He shook his head because that had never happened before. Had it been real or were his hungover eyes playing tricks on him? Realizing he was still way too tired to go through the notebook, he put the folder back.

When he awoke, the attendants were coming through with hot towels. Annie was writing in her diary and then looked up. "Morning. While you were asleep, I had a look a look at your Olga folder. I didn't read your diary. I just wanted to see what she looked like. The picture on top showed she was pretty in a wild kind of way, and I could see what attracted you to her. But her nude shot was amazing. I mean, here she's in her thirties and looks almost like a teenager. I've heard Iskas age well, but this is too much."

He took his hot towel and laid it over his face. "Yes, she did. Anything more?"

"Absolutely. It's hard to believe she and Aunt Ronnie were sisters. I mean, they look similar and are pretty, but Aunt Ronnie's always so chic, so elegant. And Aunt Olga's so... I don't know."

"Unkempt, Bohemian. No, a Beat, because that's what she was and didn't give a damn about how she looked. To my much younger self, she was so exotic, interesting and smart, and so very hip in her musical tastes. It was almost like she came from another planet."

"True, but she was so different from Mom and even Monica. Deborah has shown me pictures of Monica when you two were dating. You must've been a lot different when you were at Harvard."

"Yes, I was. And for a time, I changed radically."

"Oh, I know. Deborah also showed me a picture of you all in black with your neatly trimmed blond beard."

"Oh yeah, I remember that." He smiled. "When I was in college, I quickly realized I had all the privileges of an adult and the responsibilities of a child. And so, I did a lot of experimenting and sought out many different experiences."

"Thanks for sharing, Dad. But I've got to get back to my diary."

"Are you going to share your diary with me?"

"Perhaps when you're older." She laughed and began writing.

Ashley again studied Olga's picture, and as much as he tried he could not make her face glow. Yes, she would have aged well, but would that be enough? Olga at thirty-one was complete. Everything about her fit seamlessly with everything else. But today, at sixty-three, she would be lost, a person existing out of time. Perhaps it's true the good and very hip die young. He tried to picture Jim Morrison, also buried in Paris, who now would be almost fifty, trying to be the lizard king and looking so ridiculous.

Ashley turned on his reading light and opened his black-and-white Olga notebook. He felt relieved to be finished with the Iskandarov diaries with their omissions, ambiguities and, perhaps, falsehoods. He could now read something he had written. He had gone through the entire notebook just before David died and had marked certain passages he thought were significant. He also now used his *tvarsch* to find important, if unexplained, parts.

He skimmed through the early days in Olga's class when he thought of her as "the Bitch" because she was so demanding, while at the same time he was becoming madly in love with her. But then they met by accident at an outdoor café.

> She asked if I knew my real mother, a very
> touchy subject with me. No one in our family
> ever speaks about her or my real father. I told her
> that I think I might be the son of some young girl

who got herself knocked up and put me up for adoption.

Could it be that I've only known about my real parents since David's death? It now seems so much longer. God, I must find them. Even though I trust Annie's *pyordarsch,* I'm not going to get my hopes up, only to have them dashed, because she was looking at Charlotte some point in the past and didn't know it.

Olga even came to his varsity soccer games and some practices to critique his performance. Doing so in class was one thing, but soccer was out of bounds. However, she did give some very good advice for the Yale game.

"Mr. Cooper, such formidable footwork. Your kick through Dragovitch's legs was a thing of true beauty and courage. Everyone's talking about how you slew the Dragon. Just like Saint Georges. But you seem so glum."

"Sadly, professor, St. George didn't have to settle for a tie. Besides, a tie is like kissing your sister."

Professor A. smiled, "I should think that would depend on who your sister is."

Oh my God. Even though he had read this notebook several times before, this was the first time he had understood the meaning of her seemingly innocent remark. He continued skimming until he was in Olga's apartment, and they were still both naked after sex and she asked him the question about perfection and excellence he still struggled with.

"No. I've no guilt, about anything. Why should I?"

"Because you know you're a fraud."

"A fraud? What do you—?"

"You're a freak. A few genes here or there, and you could've wound up as a carnival geek.

Instead, you, fortuitously, emerged in near
excellence. You're bright, athletic and beautiful.
And what, please tell me, have you done to
deserve such distinction?"

"Well, I—"

"Not one damned thing." She crossed her arms
under her breasts. "All that stops right now. If
you've sufficient courage to stay."

He did and began to learn.

You really think you're unique? Harvard and
Radcliffe are full of people like you—freaks of
nature. Society doesn't know what to do with
really bright people. It's somehow undemocratic
to be smarter than your neighbor. However, it's
equally undemocratic to discriminate against us,
so the university and society tolerate us. And hope
we graduate without blowing the whole place up.
You wouldn't believe some of the unstables here.
All they have is their churning minds. If they
don't find an outlet, they'll simply go insane. I've
seen it first-hand many times, and it's taken me
a very long time to come to terms with that. I'll
share some of my experience with you.

Later…

"As things now stand, if you don't find that better
reality soon, you must, in the future, navigate a
narrow course between the self-murder of Scylla
and the madness of Charybdis. You're trying
to play in their world. Look at you. Freshman
sensation Ashley Cooper goes up against Yale's
star fullback, Alex Dragovitch. After you get past
him, your right wing was wide open and had a
clear shot. But you didn't pass the ball to him.

Why? Are you selfish or ego driven?" She shook
her head. "No, although those may be factors,
they would be relatively easy to cure. No, this is
much more insidious. Regardless of how great
your accomplishments are, in your mind, they'll
never be enough, because others have such high
expectations for you. Therefore, it was no longer
enough to defeat the great Dragovitch, you now
had to win the game. And when you failed at
being the *ubermensch*, you were miserable." She
looked deeply into my eyes. "Ashley, you, we,
can't exist like that. We can't let others define our
accomplishments. We also must create our own
reality and then live in it. First, you must learn to
relax your body and mind through yoga and deep
breathing. And then, you're always in control and
it's slowly killing you. You need to relinquish it,
from time to time and reassert your natural balance.
Between the poles we have our mother earth, who
gives and our father the water, who is sometimes
placid and sometimes raging. And in between these
poles, there's a place of repose, peace and harmony.
And that's what you must find. But don't assume
it's equidistant between the poles. Sometimes, it
favors the earth and then, the water."

Two pages on...

"Once we begin, we won't stop until we get to
the end."

"But how will we know when we get there?"

"You'll know, Ashley. You'll know. And our time
is limited."

Ashley reread what she said about time. Like with Penelope's
pyordarsch, and her knowing the time of her death, Olga must

have known she was going to die in the spring. And with their
time coming to an end, she did not want him to leave her for the
Columbia lacrosse game. And had she then told him her reason,
he would have thought her mad or, at least, melodramatic. But
Olga never went mad. Instead, she faced this awful knowledge
reasonably calmly. Penelope went mad because she had very
little faith in an afterlife. And even if she did, she knew, on some
level, it would be very unpleasant after breaking several of the
Ten Commandments, including murder. He had never thought
of Olga as religious, but she must have been able to accept her
fate. New knowledge now brought new questions, so he put the
journal down and closed his eyes as he said a prayer for Olga's
soul. And then his mind drifted to that place of harmony between
the poles. When he resumed reading, he discovered something
that demanded a new interpretation.

> Yesterday, when we were again making love,
> I closed my eyes and saw a red-haired and
> beautiful young woman naked with her lover,
> who was very handsome. But when her lips
> moved, I couldn't hear anything. Gradually,
> other women and men replaced them, all
> speaking silently. And even though I tried to hold
> back, I soon lost control. I kissed Olga and, as I
> did so before opening my eyes, she kissed me,
> wrapping her legs around me even tighter.

Ashley had always thought that was an illusion, caused
by Olga's pot. But now he realized she had been teaching him
Iskandarov tradition way back then. And he now knew he had
seen his real parents and grandparents and on back until he "lost
control." Olga had, presumably, seen them as well and could have
told him who they were. After thinking about the implications of
knowing that then, he smiled and also remembered Olga told him
to contact Professor Learey in the Psychology department. He
was doing some interesting mind experiments.

Later, lying on the bed, I asked her about the
vision. She looked at me strangely and began
crying. She said she shed tears of happiness and
would tell me one day what it meant, when I
better understood.

That was the last entry. Olga had died before he attained
the better understanding. Olga, in hindsight, always seemed to
be on the verge of telling him about his heritage. Ashley still
remembered those days of electric excitement and felt very happy.
Like in class, she had been very demanding, but, ultimately, fair.
But he also felt sadness, about Olga of course, but even more for
the romantic young man who spouted poetry without a cynical
thought in his head. It was not that he wanted that person back,
although he would like to capture his former sense of wonder.
He also knew that when it came to lovemaking, she was the best.
And that was because they had established a true connection,
which he still did not fully understand.

Looking out, he saw the coast of Normandy, a placid seascape
he had seen many times. But today, it was chaotic… ferocious
waves overwhelming a rocky and seaweed-snared beach or
smashing emphatically against rough, dirty white cliffs. And yet
the blue sky and the large, pillowy clouds contradicted the violence
below. And the sea birds flying or coasting above the tumult seemed
oblivious to it all. Was that really happening or were his eyes again
playing tricks on him? Looking away, he now realized more fully
how important Olga had been in making him who he needed to
be to go on his journey. As he turned to Annie, he felt a single tear
high on his cheek. She surprised him by reaching up, catching it on
her long, crimson fingernail and drinking it.

"Dad, what's wrong?"

He smiled even though he felt miserable between Olga and
his hangover and did not want to discuss it with her. But he also
knew he must. "I don't know if this is a tear of joy or sadness or
both."

"Mademoiselle Iskandarova, may I serve you some coffee."

"*Mais oui*. Cream and one sugar."

"*Et vous*, Monsieur Iskandarov?" Ashley was initially taken aback by that, but he nodded. "Black, please, and do you have any aspirin?"

"Of course." She reached into her tunic for a sealed aspirin pack. Ashley thanked her and thought, *Marvelous, Uncle Francis's magic elixir.*

Fueled by coffee and elixir, he supplemented what Annie knew about his relationship with Olga and how they planned to live in Paris after his freshman year. She asked many questions, and Ashley answered them truthfully, without leaving out anything.

"I had no idea. I'm so sorry for all that happened and what didn't."

"Thanks. But you know what? You are, and always have been, my prize for the life I did have."

"Thank you. That's so sweet." She smiled. "Would you think I was crazy if I told you I feel her presence here with us?"

"Not a bit. I've felt it for a while."

"Sweet. But what else is bothering you?"

"Not surprisingly, I'm very concerned about our journey and don't feel I've been well prepared for it. Something all three of my stepparents could've done."

"Aunt Ronnie told me the other day, Grandpa and Patricia knew they couldn't do anything because you were so young. And she did her best to prepare you for this without actually telling you about it."

Ashley sighed. "Yes, thanks for your prespective. You're right. But, and I've never told anyone, and never wrote it down either, after Olga asked me about my parents, she told me Nadia had told her my mother was an English aristocrat. Olga didn't know her name or anything else. But she was not some poor girl who got pregnant and gave me up for adoption. It wasn't much, but it gave me hope that one day I'd learn the truth."

"Oh, that's wonderful."

The attendant came back with a French breakfast and more strong coffee. As he ate, Ashley thought about Sergei and what he had said about Fate and now remembered something Oswald Spengler had written in *The Decline of the West*, riffing on Seneca. *The Fates guide him who will, him who won't, they drag.* But who were the Fates? To a pagan Roman, they were three sister godesses who weaved a tapestry of life, and every human was a thread. So, could God have taken that role? Sergei certainly thought so and believed in Countess Sophia's prophecy. If free will actually existed, life would be unpredictable, chaotic. But if Fate controlled our lives and Sophia was able to tap into this, then everyone's doing what they're supposed to for her prophecy, but thinking this is what they want to do. The whole process then becomes almost mathematical and easy to predict. So, will I be guided or dragged? I know I'm not prepared enough for whatever it is I'm going to do for the Iskandarov. But if Fate's true, I can't really fail because I'm doing what I'm supposed to do. That's why Sergei said that no matter what happened, he'd be all right. Hold on. It's so hard for me to believe this could actually be true. The Iskandarov have been deceiving themselves for a very long time. This is like a fairytale, completely unrealistic. I've been so rational for so long, it will take a major change in me to believe in this. Again, I need to learn as much as possible in Paris. What Olga taught me toughened me up so I could get through Harvard undergrad and law with honors and my associate period at the Firm. And Ronnie finished the process. But, also, in some metaphysical way, was Olga ultimately killed because she tried to rush my Iskandarov education before David's death? Just one more mystery in a long series.

He looked out again and saw the French fields below with Paris in the distance. Paris, the city Olga should have shown him after they married and were raising their son. Many years ago, on his first stopover on his way to Russia, he had found the Andreyev mausoleum in a Russian Orthodox cemetery. However, there was no sign of Olga's final resting place. He vowed he would find out from Nadia Andreyeva where Olga lay before leaving for Russia.

As they prepared to land, Ashley found the envelope Maria had given him with the three pages she had cut from Sergei's Cuban diary. While curious about them, now did not seem an appropriate place or time to read them. He put them back in his briefcase, secured it and closed his eyes to plan the rest of the day.

SIXTEEN
Wednesday & Thursday 2&3 June 1993
Paris, France

1.

About noon, Ashley and Annie, on Randell's recommendation, arrived at Chez Collette, a small hotel on La Place du Petit Pont and the Quai St. Michel. Collette gave them adjoining rooms overlooking the Seine. Annie wanted sleep, but Ashley told her they had to stay awake to reduce jetlag, and they would stay active seeing Paris. They cleaned up, had lunch and walked across the Petit Pont to L'Ile de la Cite.

"OK, Annie, as you can see, we're surrounded by tourists, so, because of the crowds, we only have time for one major sight today. It's your first time in Paris, you choose."

"All right, Notre Dame. It's close, and we can climb the north tower to stay awake."

Ashley nodded. As usual, Annie had done her homework. Fortunately, the tower line moved reasonably quickly, and they climbed the three hundred and eighty-seven steps to see the gargoyles and, along the way, Emanuel, the cathedral's largest bell, weighing about eleven hundred pounds. From atop the tower, they enjoyed the sunny, unobstructed view. As Ashley pointed out all the landmarks, he felt great pride in Annie's Parisian knowledge. After exploring the cathedral from gargoyles to catacombs and lighting some candles for luck, they browsed the shops of the Left Bank before he took her to his favorite *brasserie.*

2.

About eight, after they had ordered, Annie asked, "Why do we have an appointment with the Grand Duchess Nadia Andreyeva tomorrow when she isn't Iskandarova?"

"She's Sergei's first wife, as well as Aunt Ronnie's and Olga's mother. She's also the prime director of the Bleu agency. Therefore, she has a lot of the information we'll need before leaving for Russia. The only question is whether she'll help us."

Annie nodded and appeared to be deep in thought.

"What're you thinking about?"

"She will. I had a vision recently and saw a very large room with an elderly lady, dressed in a long gown with lots of diamonds and pearls. I think she was the grand duchess, based on what Aunt Ronnie had told me about her. Anyway, it's some sort of celebration, and there were a whole bunch of people there all dressed up. You're there as well."

"And you're there too?"

"I'm not normally in my visions, but I saw my face in a mirror. I think there's more, but I want to see the room before I say anything else."

Ashley nodded. By her expression, this was something important. "We need to be very careful tomorrow. Rand thought Nadia was an extraordinary person."

"How?"

"Very clever, observant and disciplined. So, bring you're A-plus game. Any further thoughts on Sergei's Cuban diary or cigarette case?"

She nodded. "First, the diary's authentic."

"You certain?"

"That last picture of Sergei and Maria confirmed it. The first time I had *pyordarsch,* about three years ago, I saw a very similar view of them. I had no idea who they were then, and it totally weirded me out."

"Yes, I remember your telling me that. Now, what about the cigarette case?"

"There's a big dent in it from a bullet, I think. He had on a vest, a—"

"Flak jacket?"

"Yes. Anyway, it went through, and if the case hadn't been there, it would've killed him."

"Interesting. I guess it was his lucky charm." He briefly smiled. "You remember when I asked you who you'd like to live with if I were killed, and you said Aunt Ronnie and not George Farwell. Well, before we left yesterday, Anghelina told me George wants to take you away from me because of your visions. And he would kill both Aunt Ronnie and me to get you. I'll do everything I can to ensure that doesn't happen."

"Thanks. I haven't seen Yuri since we got off the plane, but I'm certain he's watching out for us, even as we speak."

"Good. I'd really like to meet him."

"I'm sure you will," she said.

"OK. Now, I sense Nadia will want you to stay in Paris with her or even return to New York."

"But why? You won't let her do that?"

"I promise no matter what happens, here or in Russia, we aren't going back to New York until we find out our truth."

"Sweet." Annie seemed energized by this.

Ashley sipped his wine. "I think I've got a fairly good handle on Anghelina. But now that I've met Rosalita, I need to know more about her. So, why do you like her?"

"She understands me."

"How so?"

"She knows, perhaps better than anyone else, what it's like to be Iskandarova."

"More than Aunt Ronnie?"

"Yes. Being Iska means being an outsider, even more so than being an Iskandarov male. 'Lita understands that, and I've come to the same conclusion."

"But why are Iskas more outsiders than Isks, if that's a word?"

"While it's tied in with *pyordarsch* and the trances that drive people away, there's something deeper, having to do with the way you see the world differently."

"Yes, I understand completely. I guess I've been doing that so long, it just seems normal now." He paused and shook his head. "I wish my father had left me detailed instructions about *tvarsch*."

"What do you want to know?"

Ashley stared at her. A short time ago he might have laughed. "OK, why does it only work part of the time? Like when I really needed it with Ronnie or Anghelina or, even, Olga."

"Oh, Dad, it doesn't work when two Iskandarov are together. There's no need because of the Iskandarov Trust. Also, when you're stressed, tired or drunk."

Anghelina was telling the truth at their meeting. "Anything else?"

She laughed lightly. "No, not really. *Tvarsch* is simple compared to *pyordarsch*."

"As I've said before, I need to know more about your *pyordarsch*."

"Well, I can't tell you any more about it." She nodded before sipping her wine and leaning over, kissed him on the cheek and asked if they could leave. As Ashley nodded and looked up for the waiter, he saw a very large man, who seemed vaguely familiar, standing at their table, holding an espresso cup.

"Hello, Ashley Cooper. Remember me? Alexandr Dragovitch."

"My God. It's been a while. This is my daughter, Annie." He turned to her. "Alex was the defenseman I had to go against in both soccer and lacrosse. Have a seat, Alex. Would you like anything?"

"No thanks. I'm fine with my coffee. Nice to meet you, Annie. I can only stay a short while."

"OK." Ashley felt relieved. "You had a great soccer career with Milan. I followed it with some interest. You certainly did better than your pal, Nick Stevens, drafted in the sixth round by the Boston Patriots and cut in his first season."

"Sadly true. But football was never that important to Nick. He joined Central Intelligence the next year. What with his father, that was his career goal. I work with him now."

"Can't say I'm surprised." *Damn*, he thought, *these guys have government sanction to go against us.*

"So, what brings you both to Paris?"

"Annie's never been here. I thought by coming early, we could avoid the tourists. No such luck." He shook his head sadly.

"Well, have a wonderful time here with the time you have left. I've spent the off-season here for a long time." He sipped his espresso. "Anyway, for your safety, I strongly suggest you return to New York at the earliest possible date."

"I was told New York was no longer a safe place to be."

"Probably, but it would be a much safer place than, say, Moscow. In fact, Paris may not be all that safe either. I wouldn't like it if something bad happened to either of you, especially Annie."

"Thanks. We'll be careful. Since you're with Central, I was just wondering if you'd come across the death of my friend, Olga Andreyeva. You may recall she was murdered on the same day as our final lacrosse match."

"Murdered, was she? My condolences. No, I've never seen anything about that. And my memories of that day are how you got by me and scored."

"No, I didn't think you knew about her. Just a shot in the dark that you might."

"No harm, no foul. Have a wonderful time here with the time you've left."

3.

Back at the hotel, Ashley requested a move to a large double room. Annie protested that she needed her own room for privacy, but Ashley overruled her, saying he would explain upstairs. Once in the room, she said, "Dad, no offense. But this is really weird sharing a room with you. I need my privacy."

"I know, and I'll do my best to let you have it. Alex was unusually polite this evening. He hates my guts and has for a long time. I'm now concerned he would try to get to me through you."

"Is that what that was all about?"

"Yes, I know Rosalita has taught you some moves, but Dragovitch and Stevens are pros. I can defend you, but not if we're separated. I couldn't bear to lose you."

She hugged him. "Thanks, Dad. Me too." She smiled. "First dibs on the bathroom."

About a half hour later, she emerged from the bathroom in a red Lawrenceville nightshirt.

"I didn't know you had one of those. I had one long—"

"I know. You've told me. This is from a secret admirer."

"And might I know him?"

"Of course, it's you. Don't you remember? You picked it up at your last reunion." She put on her Discman headphones.

Ashley nodded. Although he had no memory of that, it pleased him she wore it tonight. At home, he normally slept naked but had brought along his pajamas as a precaution. The room felt quite warm, so he opened the large window near his bed.

After the bathroom, Ashley lay in bed, unable to sleep because of the relative quiet of Paris compared to New York. He needed some street noise. Normally on his layovers, he would be in the bar somewhere until his jet lag caught up with him and he could sleep. To clear his thoughts, he pulled the missing pages of Sergei's Cuban diary from his briefcase. He found that Commandante Antonio had greeted Sergei with a daiquiri and a large medal for Camp David.

There was nothing interesting, except for one passage.

I realize now I would have been much happier
had my sister not 'died to the world.' I thought,
as did Mamman, since Nadia and I had common
grandparents our bond would be strong. But,
it couldn't hold against the pressures we then
faced. It was another outsider, Binkie, with
whom I developed the union.

Sergei had never mentioned his sister before. In addition, what did he mean by saying that she "died to the world"? Had she joined a cloistered religious order, or did she actually die?

He shook his head and rose to do a quick check on the bedroom door and Annie, who was already asleep. He noticed a sheer black negligee on the top layer of her suitcase with an elaborate red "P" just below the lace trim. Why did Annie have her mother's negligee? Was this something she needed for her *pyordarsch*, or could it be for Yuri? Whatever it was, he had promised Annie her private life would remain so. He sighed as he heard a far-off Klaxon before turning off the light and falling into a restless sleep—trying to find a comfortable position punctuated by dreams and a nightmare about Dragovitch and hearing Annie sobbing. Finally, about three a.m., he began to relax. The sun coming in the window woke him, and he could hear Annie in the bathroom getting ready.

4.

Friday morning just before ten, their taxi pulled up in front of a six-story, immaculately clean, limestone building on the Avenue Foch. Ashley thought he had seen it before, looking just as Dmitri had described it in his diary. As they entered arm-in-arm through the massive wrought iron and glass door, the doorman, dressed like an admiral with startlingly white gloves, checked them against his entry list before passing them to the lift operator, a similarly uniformed man. Ashley became aware of the clop of his wingtips and the rhythmic click of Annie's heels on the green marble floor. The operator moved almost robotically as he closed the outside door and the car's gate.

The lift ran smoothly and quietly on its muted cables. Without even looking, the operator landed the car exactly level with the floor, and he bowed as they left. The blue door in the small entrance hall opened, and a petite woman in a black-and-white maid's uniform curtsied and asked them in French to follow her.

A thin, elegant lady in an expensive black suit rose from behind a Louis XIV writing desk. "Good morning. I am Cosette, confidential secretary to Her Imperial Highness, the Grand Duchess Nadezdha." She turned to Annie. "Welcome Anastasia Sergeyvna Iskandarova." She turned to Ashley and welcomed him as "Monsieur Cooper." Cosette's English had a very pronounced accent. While she was not the person he had spoken to when he made the appointment, she had been the one coaching Randell in the hospital.

"Now, before I introduce you to Her Imperial Highness, we clearly know who you are, perhaps better than you do. However, the question remains *what* you are. That is, are you merely passing through Paris or are you in the process of becoming? That shall be answered during your stay. *Compris?* Now, please follow me."

As they followed her, Annie appeared in deep thought as Ashley pondered Cosette's very good question. She led them into an immense ballroom. Looking for a clue about Nadia, Ashley searched his surroundings, a mixture of Louis XV furniture and Russian antiques. On the mantelpiece of the large, white marble fireplace on his left, several large Fabergé eggs were placed around an antique gold clock. The light and airy room, with a large skylight, offered splendid views of the Champs Elysées. Ashley smelled the familiar aroma of English Ovals, like Stashinski smoked. Was this some bizarre joke? Nonetheless, he focused on the left wall where a petite, white-haired lady in a high-necked, long-sleeved, white silk gown sat on a large, ornate chair with a small table next to her. She possessed an animated expression with constantly moving, mysterious black eyes. In her left hand, she held a long, unfiltered cigarette, burning slowly.

Annie whispered, "Dad, this is the place, and that's her."

"Thanks. Good to know."

Music began, and Ashley recognized Shostakovich's Fifth Symphony when the opening chord's hopefulness falls to despair. It played just loud enough to cancel out a normal level conversation from monitoring. He smiled as Cosette made the formal introductions. She then prepared marmalade tea from a highly polished, sterling samovar bearing the Romanov double eagle. After serving Nadezdha, Annie and, lastly, Ashley, she left them standing.

5.

The grand duchess remained seated and, after studying Annie, moved her focus to Ashley and began, in French, "Monsieur *Avocat* Cooper, you are the young man who caused our Olga to be killed." She raised her cigarette, inhaled deeply and exhaled as she continued. "We should add, you, Monsieur, strongly resemble your father. Both in appearance and attitude."

Smiling, Ashley bowed and said, in intentionally halting French, "Madame, I take that as the greatest compliment you could have paid me."

She sighed and responded in English. "As with most Americans, your French is an abomination. Although your friend, Dr. Speers, spoke it beautifully. Further, we are confident our daughter, Veronique, saw to your lessons, so we remain certain that if you chose, you could speak it beautifully as well. No matter, we shall continue in English."

Ashley nodded.

"We remain in expectation of a response to our original query."

"I did no such thing, Madame. I discovered her. Had I not, Olga would've died sooner and alone or, perhaps, not been found for several days. The only things I don't know are who actually killed her and how she was specifically killed. I further assume you know both and have proof."

A smile crossed Nadia's finely formed lips. "Spoken like a true *avocat*. Always, it is about the proof, is it not?" She tilted her head. "This is a complicated and delicate matter." She now motioned them to be seated. "I assure you, we may speak here with absolute confidence. Our counter-listening precautions are the finest available. You are beginning to be aware of the truth. The first truth is that the union of our Olga with the son of Sergei Dmitrovich Prince Iskandarov was not capricious." The Duchess snuffed out her cigarette and sipped tea from her sterling crested glass. "Secondly, after the murder of Olga Sergevna, because she had told you more than she should have, we determined you would absolutely learn nothing more until the appropriate time. Now that time has arrived with the death of your adopted father, a very fine gentleman whose passing deeply saddens us."

"Then that would be my next question. While I know about Countess Sophia and her prophecy, is there any other reason why I had to wait until Colonel Cooper died to begin to discover my true identity?"

"Beyond Countess Kolchaka's prophecy, you had to wait for the Bolsheviki to be overthrown. Had you come searching while they retained power, you would have simply disappeared, forever. Secondly, and of equal import, Mademoiselle Ani had to gain control of her visions, which I am informed she has."

"Absolutely. And yes, Olga began teaching me some Iskandarov lore and information." He paused. Her royal "we" already grated on him, so he would throw her a curveball. "Is it possible, in some metaphysical way, that she was punished for her actions?"

"Monsieur *Avocat,* you surprise us with such an unexpected and interesting question. Personally, we do not entertain such thoughts because we deal in facts and not speculation. We have, nonetheless, learned, when dealing with the Iskandarov, there are always fanciful questions." She shook her head and after taking another Ovals from her gold case, held it expectantly in her right hand. Annie lit it with the duchess's heavy gold lighter. She nodded. "Thank you, *ma chere*."

As Ashley watched, she released all the smoke through her nostrils and, with a well-practiced motion, flicked it away. He remembered Olga doing this in front of his young and callow self when he thought it had been devastatingly sexy. But now, he felt sadness. Had no one ever told her that she was way beyond the age where such a coquettish display would be appropriate? Such vanity could be used against her, should the need arise.

Annie remained standing by the duchess, who took Annie's hand in her almost translucently alabaster one and smiled up at her as Annie smiled back. With her smile, Ashley could picture the beautiful young lady she had once been.

"Yes, you do bear your grandmother's striking resemblance, as they say."

"Thank you, Your Imperial—"

"*Non, non,* Mademoiselle Anastasia. As the daughters of royalty, we address each other as equals. I am 'Nadia' to you, as well as to your father. My initial charade testing your father is done."

"Ashley, you inquired about proof of my Olga's murder. Remember please, there exists a world beyond the standards of proof to which you are accustomed, a rather gray world in which I have spent most of my life. Therefore, I suppose I take such grayness for granted. It is a world in which you shall yet find yourself." She again puffed and exhaled grandly. "Are you aware you have been followed?"

"No. Not specifically."

"Then, you must learn to be more careful. Please go over to that window. You shall see about twenty people milling about by the tree on the curb opposite. They are all assigned to watch my apartments for their various masters. However, Cosette noticed this morning a new man had arrived. Does the tall, blond-haired man in the lightweight trench-coat appear familiar to you?"

Ashley recognized Fred the chauffeur from the Firm. What the hell was he doing here—to protect him, follow him or something more sinister? He also surveyed the others, looking, in particular, for either Dragovitch or Stevens. While absent, he sensed they would soon appear.

He returned from the window. "His name's Fred, an employee of my law firm. They use him for many different things."

Nadia smiled. "His real name is Friedrich Grieber. Did you know, when younger, he was with the East German Stasi before defecting to your Central Intelligence, subsequently retiring to his current position?"

"No, but if he wished me harm, he has had ample opportunity, especially recently when he drove me to my country house."

"*Alors*, he is here for you and Mademoiselle Ani and is not one of my regulars."

"Right now, I'm more concerned about someone else and wondering if you'd seen a very large man—"

"You doubtless mean Alexandr Dragovitch and his partner, Nicholas Stevens. I know you have history with them. They were here yesterday. I expect them back any time. Have no fear. Here you are both now safe. I understand Dragovitch approached you last night in the Brasserie St. Michel. It is no longer safe to go to your usual places."

"Thank you. A stupid jetlagged mistake. Won't happen again." Given what had happened to Randell and Corinne back in 1962, he wondered how safe they actually were and hoped security had improved in the interim.

Nadia exhaled with a demure cough. "It is amusing. This building has always been a focus of great interest. Out there, we have representatives of many governments, the former Bolsheviki clique and several dynastic contenders. I should be happy, of course, to share any information we have on them, including Mr. Grieber."

"Thank you. That would be very helpful." Ashley looked at the framed sketch of a nearly nude harem girl on a table near his chair. "Is this—?"

Nadia nodded. "Yes, *Odalisque in a Gauze Skirt*, done in 1929. It is original and possesses great sentimental value."

Ashley waited for Nadia to say more, but she sipped her tea. Noticing a picture on another nearby table, he picked it up. "And this is your wedding picture to my father?"

"Yes, I suppose it is."

He looked at his father and found it inconceivable Sergei could ever have been so young. He studied the young, radiant Nadia with her shiny raven hair and large, black eyes and again looked at the "Odalisque." She did resemble the model, but he was not foolish enough to ask.

"Let us return for a moment to *ma chere* Olga. It was her intent to marry you. After all, she was carrying your child when she was murdered."

Ashley felt an ache for both Olga and his unborn son as his eyes began to burn.

Annie rose and came to Nadia. "The baby, by chance, a boy?"

"Yes, so it appeared. Visions?"

"Yes." Annie started to say something but shook her head. "Thank you."

Ashley felt like an outsider. What link existed between these two?

"Yes, my Olga's was a most professional execution. The Chekists developed a poison almost perfectly mimicking the effects of cerebral hemorrhage. Only a skilled doctor who knew for what he was searching could uncover the difference. We held an autopsy upon her return."

"Wait, Olga bled to death. As you may recall, I was there."

"No doubt. What you witnessed, though, was her miscarriage, a result of the hemorrhage. A particularly horrible and painful death."

Ashley remained standing unable to speak before finally getting out, "So the, uh, Chekists definitely killed Olga?"

"I see your hesitation with that term. Permit me to explain. When Monster Dzerzhinski created the Cheka, he eventually launched the Red Terror with Devil Lenin's full sanction. Since then, the Bolsheviki have changed the name of their terror organization countless times. To what end, I do not know. The organization has not changed its methods, so why should it change its names? But back to what we were discussing." Nadia shook her head. "No, that is not what I said. The Chekists developed the toxin. And while they may have been the perpetrators, there were many other interested parties."

"I'm sorry, but I don't fully understand."

"Your union possessed implications far beyond Boston. The son of an Iskandarov-Andreyeva union would become a power in post-Bolsheviki Russia. So assuredly, the Bolsheviki had interest in the mother's and baby's elimination and you, as well. Then, so did the various dynastic rivals. In addition, there were some scores left to be settled from the war years. Or, perhaps it was something more prosaic."

"Such as?"

Nadia shrugged. "Perhaps it was something more… personal. My Olga's former consort, for example. Or perhaps one of your paramours." Nadia shook her head. "But I strongly doubt such civilians could acquire such a sophisticated toxin."

He would not tell her about Penelope in front of Annie. "Do you know something along these lines?"

Nadia showily flicked the ash off her cigarette. "A person with substantial assets may acquire anything. I believe your Central Intelligence had a similar toxin." She again inhaled. "Ovals, Vladimir Stashinski, was a highly trained assassin with the Stasi."

"I've a deathbed confession he was merely a decoy. For a number of reasons, I wish to keep their identity secret at this time. But my *tvarsch* confirmed its validity."

Nadia frowned. "Very well. Under our intense interrogation, he maintained he was not the assassin and refused to name his sponsor. He was captured with a Stasi agent, Richardt Frank, one of many Nazis who joined the Stasi. But he was a kidnapper, not an assassin." She shook her head. "In the event, we executed both of them."

"Again, I know from my source that George Farwell recruited the assassin, but not his name."

"Yes, I have suspected he had been involved."

"Good. But, theoretically, Olga's killer could still be out there?"

"Ah, possibly, but, truthfully, after thirty years, very unlikely."

Ashley nodded.

After a sip of tea, Nadia asked, "Now, you have a question for me, Mademoiselle Ani?"

She nodded. "We're searching for our past."

Nadia shook her head. "Be careful, dear one. The past may be a very unfriendly place."

Annie nodded and brushed an errant curl from her forehead. "Yes, we know."

"Were I in your place, I should let the dogs of the past lie in peace. That is, what is to be gained by disturbing them? You are young and very beautiful with a lovely figure and a wonderful and gay life before you. I do not think you fully appreciate the scope of what could potentially await you in your search. I should counsel caution. Even a return to New York."

"Are we to understand you won't further help us, Nadia?"

Nadia smiled broadly. "On the contrary, Ashley. I am at your disposal. Only you may not appreciate some of what I have to say."

Ashley took a deep breath before speaking slowly. "In all of my almost fifty years on earth, I've felt incomplete. It's only recently I've discovered some of my missing pieces. Had I known about this earlier, perhaps—"

"That knowledge could have destroyed you. The Colonel, I do not think, was remiss in shielding you from your family history."

"Is our family history that bad?"

"No. They are simply associated with larger matters, which have yet to be fully resolved. Matters that could prove to be dangerous. For both of you."

"I'm willing to risk it."

"Very reckless words for an *avocat*. Doubtless, it is your prerogative to be reckless. But what of your daughter?"

Annie quickly faced Nadia, standing erect. "Nadia, with all due respect, I'm Iskandarova. The blood of the generations flows in my veins and through my body. Therefore, I must know more about my heritage, whatever it is. You say I bear my grandmother a striking resemblance. I must learn more about her—"

"Dear Mademoiselle Anastasia, I am impressed by your bearing and your convictions. But what of my responsibility to protect you from harm?"

"While I appreciate your concern for my well-being, we just heard my father confess the price he's paid for not knowing his heritage. If I simply give up now, I know one day I will pay a similar price for not knowing. And that, to me, is worse than dying young, if that should be the price for knowing."

Nadia sighed. "Very well. Simply remember, if harm befalls you at some point, I did my best to dissuade you."

Annie nodded. "I'll remember." She whispered, "Am I correct in why I'm here?"

"*Mais oui, ma chere. De la patience.*"

Ashley did not understand that whole exchange and especially why Nadia felt she had to protect Annie and why Annie accepted that she did.

Nadia smiled. "So where, dearest one, shall we begin?"

"I know I speak for my father on this. As I've said, we would like to start with my grandmother, Charlotte."

Ashley wondered how objective Nadia could be.

Nadia paused and inhaled her cigarette, her words mixing with the smoke as she slowly exhaled. "Charlotte—lovely girl. Lady Agnes, her mother, never fully approved of her. I think she was jealous. Nonetheless, a very fine operative."

Sensing Nadia was about to change the subject, Ashley asked, "What can you tell us about Charlotte's father, Sir Hugh?"

"Not terribly much. He was a highly decorated officer in the Great War. In 1919, he disappeared in Russia when meeting with a highly-placed Bolsheviki commander about eighty-five kilometers south of Murmansk, an area that should have been relatively safe for him."

"Anything more?"

"Sadly, no. The Bolsheviki never leave anything behind."

Ashley nodded. He had not expected much information, but he had tried.

"Now, let me tell you of Sophia Countess Kolchaka."

Annie leaned forward attentively.

Nadia crossed herself using her first two fingers and thumb. "Sophia Sergevna was a very strong and extraordinary lady. I realize I digress, but if I might seek your indulgence, you shall soon see my purpose. Now, you know David Cooper escorted Sophia Sergevna and Sergei Dmitrovich from Odessa to Paris during our Russian civil war?"

"Yes. The countess, as we know, had the visions. Did she ever suffer any bad side effects from them?"

Nadia looked at Ashley with a most peculiar expression. "Not in the slightest." He felt great relief. With the proper guidance, Annie would be OK.

"In 1919, Countess founded Bleu here in Paris, along with Tatiana Nikolaevna. Blue is a color of both the Russian and Ukrainian flags. The Andreyev are originally Ukrainian, from the Kiev region." She indicated two ancient crossed Imperial Russian and Ukrainian flags under glass on the wall. "After my separation, I became the protégé of Sophia Sergevna and quickly learned the innermost workings of Bleu." Nadia smiled faintly. "I know that look of disapproval on your faces, which I have seen so often before. But Bleu was a Fascist organization, how could you possibly be associated with such people?"

Ashley nodded. "Yes, Nadia, this is a challenge."

"In Europe of the thirties, democratic capitalism was considered a spent ideology, due to the world-wide depression. The collective left proclaimed with the bourgeois economy dead, as Marx had predicted, now the true communist economy would emerge. However, in 1923 with Benito Mussolini's Fascist March on Rome, Italy provided a seemingly shining example of what Fascists could do and made it a most respectable ideology, at least, until *Il Duce* became deceived by that scoundrel of an Austrian corporal and his extreme racist policies. Sadly, those excesses destroyed the legitimacy of fascism in Europe and elsewhere, securing the ascendancy of the Collectivists." She shook her head and smiled. "I do notice with great amusement, though, the Brussels bureaucrats of the nascent European Union borrow heavily from Mussolini, especially his dictum "Everything in the State and nothing without," although they are very careful to shroud such policies in their comfortable socialist rhetoric." She made a circular gesture and smiled. "However, the reason for Bleu's orientation resulted not so much from ideology, but expediency. By default, we sided with the enemies of the Bolsheviki, the Fascists. As such, one of the many groups arrayed against us in those days was the GRU, Bolsheviki military intelligence, closely allied with the Chekists. *Alors,* you may have heard of Flight Captain Jerzi Pialatov, flying with the Free Polish in the RAF."

Ashley shook his head. "No. Can't say I have."

"Then surely you know Pavel Ivanovich Chichikov, who kidnapped your mother shortly after your birth. Born Igor Polinkoff in Galicia, the Polish variant on the family name. That, however, is the only difference. To be accurate, he was actually an operative for GRU. He cleverly posed as a Polish nobleman and a pilot to infiltrate Bleu. However, Countess and

I knew his true identity. Thus, we used him as a conduit for false information to the GRU. From time to time, we would feed him verifiable information, but fundamentally we kept him ignorant of any matters of true significance. You must bear in mind we were playing three-way chess. Bleu allied with German Military Intelligence, the *Abwehr*, because their leaders, especially Admiral Canaris, strongly opposed the Bolsheviki. Bleu also commanded great support amongst the British aristocracy and Sir Oswald Mosley's British Union of Fascists. In addition, here in France, we enjoyed popular support, unfortunately because of the virulent anti-Semitism. We had also lent support to Franco and his crusade in Spain. While we shared information with the *Abwehr,* we sometimes indirectly shared information with MI-5 and MI-6 and later, the American OSS, the Office of Strategic Services, our guiding principle being that whatever was bad for the Bolsheviki was good for us. After the occupation in 1940, the situation became even more complicated. The *Maquis*, the French resistance, was predominantly and strongly pro-Bolsheviki. Therefore, we began to cooperate more with the Vichy government and the non-Bolsheviki underground, who spent nearly as much time fighting the Bolsheviki underground as the Germans. We tried to avoid the Gestapo, under former chicken farmer Heinrich Himmler, and were mostly successful."

"I'm very happy to hear that."

Nadia sipped her tea. "Now, we return to Charlotte. In May 1941, Countess received a message from her *Abwehr* contacts. Deputy Führer, Rudolf Hess, would be flying to England to negotiate a peace treaty. Under the terms, the Austrian said he would evacuate Western Europe in exchange for Great Britain giving him a free hand in attacking the Soviet Union. We, of course, knew about Barbarossa, the invasion. Countess chose Chichikov to deliver this message to Charlotte."

Annie asked, "I don't understand. If Chichikov worked for the GRU, why him?"

"Because he had to succeed to ensure his cover and credibility with Bleu." Nadia smiled. "Charlotte contacted Lord Halifax, Churchill's Foreign Secretary and an old friend of Sir Hugh. When Charlotte next spoke with Mr. Churchill, he not only had no interest, but he ordered Hess's arrest when he arrived on British soil. The Allies kept Hess locked up until he died in Berlin's Spandau Prison, just in 1987." She smiled. "We also, at that point, disclosed Chichikov's existence and his cover. But he had vital information about the coming German invasion that Gangster Stalin needed to hear. He thought the Gangster would then promote him to his inner circle. But he also knew that agents who had been abroad were often routinely liquidated upon their return to Moscow, as they had been 'corrupted' in the West. But he quickly disappeared. Knowing the Gangster as we did, despite his information, Chichikov had a rendezvous with a bullet to the back of his skull in the basement of the Lubyanka. We also started the rumor Hess had no sanction from the Austrian and having gone mad, went on a fool's errand. And thus, we felt certain we had seen the last of Pavel Chichikov."

Ashley said, "Obviously, Chichikov returned."

"Unfortunately. When Major Cooper arrived in England in 1943, everyone knew he was there to recruit for a critical mission, but not the target. By that point, all the German agents in Britain had been compromised, and only Bleu remained functional. We had to discover his mission." Nadia took a puff and let the smoke again mingle with her words. "After Serg's horrible mission, we placed Charlotte, heretofore an auxiliary nurse, to be Serg's full-time nurse. Charlotte could then approach Major Cooper when he arrived. Charlotte learned of the raid and informed us. Countess passed along information to the *Abwehr* that the target was not the V-1 site at Peenemunde, as feared, but did not specify the actual target."

Ashley put down his tea glass. "Are you saying Charlotte never loved Sergei?"

"Not at all. Serg may have begun as an assignment for Charlotte, but there may be absolutely no doubt she came to truly adore him." Nadia grimaced and inhaled deeply, momentarily closing her eyes. "Countess, obviously, did not wish to place her son's life in danger. She and Dmitri had actively tried to persuade Sergei to reject Major Cooper's mission request. It was important in Dmitri's plan Serg remain with Charlotte so their grandson, you, would have two parents. The raid against the Ploesti oil refinery, code named "Operation Tidal Wave," ultimately proved to be a failure, as Countess had predicted, failing to halt Romanian oil production for long. However, it was important psychologically, as it showed the Americans had bombers with longer ranges than the Germans thought. In addition, it showed that the Americans were serious about the war and willing to sacrifice aircrews to achieve victory. In 1944, my contacts in the *Abwehr* arranged for me to visit my Serg in the *Luftstalag* III-B near Furstenberg. I suppose I hoped, even at that late date, for reconciliation. His appearance was absolutely appalling, so much older than his thirty-four years. I told him if he would join the *Waffen* SS, his father could have him transferred as an advisor to Bleu, and we could be together again. I almost had convinced him, but he said while he still had strong emotions for me, he wished to return to England and Charlotte. I told him what had happened to her. I do not think he believed me."

"What did happen to Charlotte after the kidnapping?"

"We have been able to track her at the institute until the mid-sixties. After that, she simply disappeared."

"Do you know what happened?"

"To a degree. Our agents in Russia seemingly know where she is, but she has told them she is finished with Bleu and wishes to be left alone."

"So, as far as you know, she's still alive?"

"Yes, but again she does not wish to be found."

Ashley nodded. He knew he would find her. "And what of Sergei?"

"We know about him until the mid-seventies. And then, he disappeared. I do not like to speculate on where he might be today. Although, I suspect our agents know more than they are revealing."

"Don't you as Bleu's Prime Director have some leverage over these agents?"

"Normally, yes, but the agents in question are under command of Aleks Iskandarov. And he is protecting their privacy. I could discover the truth, but at such great cost that it would not be wise."

"It seems to me that this whole mess could've been avoided in the first place if you, Bleu, Dmitri, the countess, could have arranged Sergei's release from the *luftstalags*."

"I hear your anger, Ashley. Sadly, it was simply not possible. First of all, Serg, even though he truly wanted to return to Charlotte, would not leave his 'buddies,' as he referred to them. They were a very tight-knit group who were absolutely fearless. They had planned many escapes from the camps and several of them had succeeded, for a while. Getting out of the camp was not difficult. Getting out of occupied Europe was entirely a different matter, even with the help of the underground. Also, our hands were sometimes tied because the Germans used Serg as a virtual hostage to keep us honest in our dealings. Secondly, because of their attempts, they had come to the attention of the Gestapo, who had marked them all for execution at *Luftstalag* III-C, near Alt Drewitz. Instead, the camp was overrun by the Bolsheviki in 1945, before any of the executions could be carried out. Alt Drewitz, now in Poland, is called, ah, some Polish name I do not recall. The camp is merely a ruin."

"Thank you. Just as I thought. But Alt Drewitz was tied into Iron Cage."

"But yes. That is a very dangerous thing to know—"

"Nadia, with respect, I think you're being melodramatic."

"Ashley, with equal respect, nearly fifty years has elapsed. Most of the great secrets of the war have been revealed, save this one. That is because it would profoundly embarrass several governments, your own included, were it to be declassified. In addition, powerful people have, over the years, made certain it remains secret and any proof that might have existed has long ago been destroyed. It was of this matter I spoke earlier when I warned you of the dangers of pursuing your heritage. There were, for several years, rumors of diaries kept in the gulag by those abducted in Iron Cage." She shrugged. "Personally, I remain skeptical because any such diaries would have been detected and destroyed by the camp officials."

"But?"

"You now listen very attentively, Ashley. We know Serg revealed writing such a diary under interrogation after Camp David. When he refused to surrender it, he was imprisoned. Later, after his release, Major Maria Civilli of the Cuban DGI was assigned to ascertain whether it existed and, if so, where it was. She failed. To this day, the disposition of his diary remains unknown. Assuming, naturally, it ever truly existed, at all." She shook her head. "As you may know, I, along with Colonel Cooper, my Veronique and Angelina Civilli, negotiated Serg's release with Mr. Henry Baker. I saw Serg before he boarded the plane for Cuba. I told him I would be happy to take him back to France." Nadia inhaled. "*Bon Dieu,* I should never forget this. He thanked me, and I recall love in his voice. However, he said he must go to Cuba. I asked him why. He smiled. His *tvarsch* told him so. And you obviously also place great faith in yours."

Ashley nodded. He had not known, according to Maria, that Nadia was part of the negotiations. *Was there some animosity between them?*

"Good. Please excuse me. I am most fatigued after our discussions and must rest before our luncheon, which shall be in an hour."

"Thank you for all you've told us. We would like to remain here and review what we've learned. And we'll likely have more questions. Will the music continue when you leave?"

"Of course. If you require anything further, please, do not hesitate to call on Cosette."

SEVENTEEN
Thursday, 3 June 1993
Paris, France.

1.

The breeze coming through floor-to-ceiling glass doors and the sky blue of the dining room gave Ashley the feeling of flying over the Champs Elysées and Arc De Triomphe. Then again, it could have been the strong Roussanne wine he had at lunch. Georges, the butler, and Blanche, Nadia's maid, had already cleared the luncheon dishes and only demitasse cups, wine glasses and ashtrays remained. After Nadia lit her English Ovals, signifying the end of the meal, Cosette lit a Gauloises. The breeze swept their smoke and odor away, which pleased Ashley and, especially, Annie, who smiled.

Ashley placed his Sainte Elizabeta icon on the table, and even though shut, its light seeped out.

"Thank God for His mercies. I had feared this had been stolen in the wake of Olga Sergeyvna's murder. I am overjoyed to see it again. It was a wedding present from Sophia, and I gave it to my daughter when she left for your country. Did Olga Sergeyvna teach you how to use it? And, since you are not of the Orthodox community, is your faith strong enough to utilize her to her full potential?"

"Yes, she did. About your second question, I don't know. I use it as well as Olga did. But I don't know its full potential, as I suspect Olga's faith was no stronger than mine back then."

"Have you considered you must convert to Orthodoxy and receive a new name?"

"I have. Ronnie has already selected 'Sergei' for me. As far as Orthodoxy goes, I don't think that'll be a problem. Ever since I studied Blok under Olga's tutelage, I've been fascinated by Orthodoxy's power and mysticism. Olga's class inspired me to delve deeper into all things Russian." He put the icon back in his trousers' pocket.

"Then you and Sainte Elizabeta with her large eyes shall grow together. Since you are determined to go to Russia, you shall need help getting airline tickets, visas and hotel reservations."

Ashley noticed Nadia and Cosette now seemed much more animated and alert. And, surprisingly, so did Annie. And the effects of his wine had been greatly reduced.

"And I further counsel you to depart tomorrow morning to catch your foes off guard. Now, I can procure all these things by late this evening, one of the privileges of my station. I could also procure new identities for you and your daughter."

Ashley thought for a moment. "Thank you, we will accept your first offer, but we must enter Russia under our own names. Our adversaries know what we look like. And our friends in Russia know our true identities as well."

Nadia nodded slowly. "Friends are a rare commodity in Russia. The Russians still exhibit many negative survival traits they learned in the paranoid environment of the former regime. The rulers have changed, but not the game."

"No, probably not. But—"

"Ashley, you are stubborn like your father with a head as thick as oak."

"You're not the first to tell me that. But I usually get what I aim for."

Nadia sighed and shook her head. "*Alors*, I insist you stay with us overnight. Besides, tonight is our Friday Repast, whose date we have changed in your honors. I instructed Blanche, just before you arrived, to pick up your luggage at Chez Collette. Also, you shall be much safer here."

"Oh, of course, Sabreur Bleu has been keeping a protective eye upon us since before we left New York, and that's how you knew that."

"But yes. He shall be at the Repast, and you can thank him tonight. While in New York, he was working for my Veronique with the Sisters Civilli, but even though she is Iskandarova, he does not fully trust Anghelina."

"Interesting. I do remember Anghelina warned me about him."

"Yes. He is concerned because she works for George Farwell and, at a critical moment, she may not know where her loyalties lie. Further, I believe they were once linked romantically."

Ashley noticed Annie ignored the last comment and smiled when Nadia turned to her.

"My dear, the time has come. Inside that door by the far window, you shall find a dark-blue Chanel gown tailored for you. It is from an age of great feminine elegance and once belonged to my daughter, your 'Aunt Ronnie.'"

As she hurried to the door, Nadia whispered, "The gown is rather low-cut, both front and back. However, a young lady must learn to properly wear such gowns."

"Indeed. But it also belonged to Corinne Duval. I know its significance." Ashley nodded.

"I shall explain this tonight. Please be patient."

"Oh, it's beautiful. I've never seen anything like it. Can, ah, may we stay, Dad?"

"Thank you, Nadia. Given all of your preparations, we'll happily accept your gracious hospitality."

"The Repast begins at eight, and you shall find all you need in your rooms." She smiled. "In the morning, Georges shall drive you to the airport, and Cosette shall accompany you to make certain no harm befalls you en route. I must work now. Please go with Cosette, who has a great surprise for you both."

2.

Through the lobby's window, Ashley saw a parked silver and red Rolls Royce Silver Wraith from the late forties. Seeing Georges, in his chauffeur uniform, next to it, he asked Cosette, "Is this your surprise?"

"Ah, only a *soupçon*. Now, let us go, but first, be sure to give the gentlemen across the street a smile and friendly wave. Especially, Stevens and Dragovitch."

Ashley and Annie waved with broad smiles as they entered the car before Cosette began a commentary on the architecture and history of the buildings and monuments they would pass. While Annie asked questions, Ashley relaxed in comfort while the anarchy of Parisian traffic raged outside.

When the car stopped, Ashley remarked that they were only a few blocks north of the Bois de Boulogne, in Neuilly. Georges had already opened the car door in front of a tall whitewashed wall with a wrought iron gate, which Cosette was going through. Inside, he found a quiet place of Russian Orthodox crosses, Cyrillic letters, imperial eagles, mausoleums and crests. The noise of Paris reduced to a faint hum the further Cosette led them, broken occasionally by a distant Klaxon. "Cosette, why is there a Russian Orthodox cemetery here?"

"Ashley, you will notice that many of the graves here are raised. That is so the coffins may be reburied back in Russia when the time is appropriate."

"And when might that be?"

"When it has been reliably determined the gangsters cannot retake control of the government." She paused. "Do not believe for a moment there has been a change in Russia. When the second war ended, the Fascists, some of our comrades, were tried as war criminals by the victors. However, what of the crimes of Stalin? His many crimes were never even mentioned, much less prosecuted, and he murdered tens of millions, much more than Hitler. Now that the Bolsheviki have lost, where are the war crimes trials? Nowhere to be seen. Without trials, there can be no justice for Russia. As long as the Bolsheviki clique remain unpunished and unrepentant, they shall try to return soon, this time in a different guise."

"Interesting. You're right. But I was wondering why there's an Orthodox cemetery on this particular site."

"Ah yes. The land was donated by a wealthy Russian exile in the last century, so that, in death, we would not have to concern ourselves about the Romans, the heretics or worse. This is truly a sacred and special place."

As they passed the Orthodox chapel, Ashley could smell the almost overwhelming scent of candles and incense and watched Annie slip into a trance. He was, nonetheless, surprised when she said, "Ilsa, I shall lead the way."

Cosette bowed and said, "Very good, Countess."

Annie led them to a corner mausoleum under shade trees with a marble entrance under a Cyrillic "Iskandarov." "Ilsa, open and stand watch, please."

"Very good, Countess." Cosette again bowed before unlocking the black steel door and turning on the inside light. After Annie went in, Cosette remained by the door. "You have seen Mademoiselle Ani's visions before. Countess had the same expression when she had hers. *Alors*, there are approximately fifty wall-to-ceiling plaques in the mausoleum. However, not all have coffins behind them."

"Why not?"

"The martyrs were tossed into mass graves by the Bolsheviki. The coffins are in protected vaults behind the plaques to prevent our enemies from desecrating their sacred remains. I shall watch out for us for a time. An open door attracts undesirables. Mademoiselle Olga is on your left, Countess Sophia on your right and Prince Dmitri in their midst."

"Thank you for bringing us here."

"I know of your efforts to find the tomb of Olga Sergeyvna. Again, when the time was right, here you are. I hope you find what you seek."

Ashley nodded his thanks and, on his way to Olga's plaque, saw Annie crushing herself against the countess's plaque with her arms spread wide. He smiled and, once at Olga's plaque, caressed the cool, smooth marble and the engraved Cyrillic words from Anna Akhmatova's poem *In the Evening*.

> Yet I secretly cast spells
> over the future,
> whenever the evenings
> are quite blue,
> and I have a foreboding
> of a second meeting,
> an inevitable meeting,
> with you.

Remembering Olga reciting it in class, intense well-being spread through him.

When he again became aware, he felt his face pressed against the wet marble before unsuccessfully placing his palm on the plaque, hoping to receive a vibration from Olga.

He heard the steel door close before Cosette spoke softly. "Monsieur Cooper, I do not think it appropriate for your daughter to be in such an unladylike posture."

Ashley looked over. Annie remained pressed against the marble, now with her legs spread wide. "I don't know what Mademoiselle Annie's doing, Cosette, but I know it's important."

"Mademoiselle Ani is such a beautiful girl. It should greatly grieve me should anything untoward happen to her."

"Thank you, Cosette."

She nodded. "My daughter, Hélène, was a Bleu agent, not terribly older than your daughter when, in 1957, she volunteered for her second mission, a very dangerous one to free Charlotte. Sergei had revealed Charlotte's last location during his release negotiations. However, Hélène was killed in the failed attempt."

"I'm sorry for your loss. But it has bothered me Bleu never tried to rescue my parents. So, thank you for telling me."

Cosette nodded. "In 1943, when Chichikov kidnapped your mother, he also had stolen the list of all Bleu agents operating in Russia. That was how he survived that return to Moscow. At the time, we had ninety-eight agents in country, all very well placed. And that network had been built up very gradually since 1919. Virtually overnight, ninety-six of them were rounded up, interrogated, tortured and executed. Only two others barely escaped. As a result, we were not able to rebuild our original numbers for almost twenty years."

"That explains a lot. However, my *tvarsch* is silent on you, so you are Iska."

"Very good, you are becoming of the Iskandarov. Now, having revealed myself to you, I shall invoke Iskandarov Trust. We shall speak honestly and candidly."

Ashley nodded. "Of course."

"Excellent. First, I monitored your meeting, as I do all of hers, therefore I have several things I need to communicate. My Russian name is Ilsa Andreyevna Iskandarova, and I am Bleu's Director of Operations, a position I worked up to, starting in 1935 when I was seventeen. My father was Andreii Ivanovich Baron Iskandarov. He was killed in action during the civil war, far behind enemy lines and was also first cousin to Dmitri. My mother, Ivana Mikhailovna Baroness Iskandarova, was, at that time, Nadia's superior in strategic planning." She paused. "I love Nadia dearly, but she is simply too rational, thank God for that, to fully understand a metaphysical people like us. And that certainly played a role in her unsuccessful marriage, although she still denies it. You may recall she remarried shortly after to the late grand duke with whom she had two children, who live in Russia. Now, let us focus on Dmitri's plaque."

"Yes, thank you for the insights into Nadia."

On the way, Ashley noticed the plaque next to Dmitri's for Xenia Ivanovna Princess Iskandarova. Unlike the others, her plaque had no picture and only the Russian inscription, "MOST HIGHLY FAVORED LADY."

"Cosette, who's this?"

Cosette crossed herself before speaking. "She is one of those I spoke of earlier. Now in a mass grave. Nonetheless, a highly honorable lady who lived a most admirable life before being martyred at a relatively young age. We hold her in the highest esteem, a sainte."

"Yes. I remember seeing her icon in Ronnie's cottage, so, why doesn't she have a picture here?"

"The artist who does her icon claims he is using a picture of her but has never produced it. I think he is using his imagination because after martyrdom, the Polinkov destroyed all traces of her. That included the prince and all of her children. No one here had ever seen her and thus, we had no way to re-create her image. Almost half of our plaques, sadly, have no pictures."

"That's terrible. I'd love to know what she looked like."

Cosette smiled slightly. "Perhaps one day. Now, let me tell you more about your father. Countess, concerned about her son's well-being after the separation, asked a long-time American friend, Yvonne St. Pierre, to watch over him. Although some ten years older, she soon became his friend, confidant, and part-time lover. She described him as 'a charming and handsome man, who appeared to be lost. As though uncertain of where he was or should be.' Therefore, he sought connection through intimacy. There were many ladies, but there was one in particular."

"George Farwell's wife?"

"No, his mistress. When the baby was born, he looked nothing like George. The baby did not survive, and the lady was sent to a sanitarium, where she later died."

Ashley nodded. "I'm not surprised. He did the same to Penelope's mother. I sense in the case of his mistress, George had both the baby and the mother killed."

"Agreed. Now, Yvonne reported to Countess that George swore revenge on your father. That was one reason there were no spy swaps for Sergei for such a long time, even though Chichikov told him if he carried out his mission successfully, he would be exchanged at the earliest date. When there was an exchange, it had the proviso your father could never return to the United States. As Nadia told you earlier, we lost track of Sergei in Russia sometime in the mid-seventies."

"Do you know if he's still there?"

"I am desolate that I do not." She paused. "However, were your father dead, I think it very likely he should be resting here with his parents, daughter and kin. I know Nadia would have spared no expense to retrieve his body."

Ashley thought, *Wow, makes sense. My father might actually be alive.*

"I know you have read about the incredible relationship and chemistry between Dmitri Sergeyovich and his sister, Sophia Sergevna. I wish to speak about Dmitri's death. On 26 May 1949, when we received word Dmitri had been shot and killed at Shanghai, Sophia seemed as though she already knew. Subsequently, she seemed to lose all focus and energy, and the years, which she had kept at bay, suddenly swept over her as her hair became white. On 24 May, it had been un-dyed raven black. On 27 May, Countess went to bed early and died at only sixty-four. Colonel Iskandarov was a fine gentleman and officer. He and Countess represented the finest traditions of the Iskandarov."

"I know that only too well. But frankly, because he never gave any details, I'm very uncomfortable with what Dmitri did in Barbarossa."

"Monsieur Cooper, Colonel Iskandarov took a blood oath to destroy the Bolsheviki. He joined the Nazis, the only people committed to their destruction, even though revolted by their racist policies. Of course, he knew writings about Barbarossa could come back to haunt or get him executed one day. Remember, this was a war of slaughter on both sides between two totalitarian regimes. As for war crimes, yes, he did such things, but it was truly a case of kill or be killed."

Ashley nodded. "All right. I guess I knew that to be true, but now I understand. But how did he get from Czechoslovakia to China after the war?"

"There was an organization, in German, known as 'Spider Web.' In English, you know it by its code name, 'Odessa.' In 1945, they rescued him and his staff, and they made their way through Czechoslovakia and Austria to Italy, sheltered in monasteries and abbeys along the way. And they had several times when they were almost captured. From Naples, he set sail for Argentina. In late 1946, he secured passage, along with his staff, to China to fight against the Chinese Bolsheviki."

"You seem to know a great deal and have very strong feelings about my grandfather."

"But yes. I knew him very well." She smiled.

When she said no more, he asked, "Do you know anything about *demoiselles de joie* and Angelina Civilli?"

"I know a great deal about both. She was my first assignment for Bleu. Angelina Civilli was a very intriguing person, an extraordinary lady and a most worthy opponent for Countess. While they contended professionally, they had a strong personal relationship. Angelina was plain-looking but possessed great charisma and an air of complete innocence. Countess was equally scandalous in her private life but also had that same angelic quality. And that bound the two ladies together. I was at the *lycee* at that time and lived with my mother at the apartment. She thought Angelina the devil incarnate, while I was fascinated by her. Angelina was a 'No Chains Communist.' She felt totally free because, in her life, the chains of the state had already withered away, as Marx predicted. That earned her the great animosity of the Stalin clique, and there were several attempts on her life. She said she could smell Stalin's agents before they attacked. Despite this, she played the role of the rich, bored apolitical heiress to the maximum effect and was also shameless. For instance, when she became a regular at Countess's cocktail parties, she would approach a lady and ask if she could borrow her husband for the night. Or she might ask the husband if she could borrow his wife. On occasions, she asked both of them to join her. In time, among our guests, it became a mark of status to be asked. And there were hurt feelings among those who were not. She solved this by bringing in her *demoiselles. Bon Dieu*, some of them were absolutely stunning and asked the same questions."

Ashley nodded. "I'm not shocked by this. I've encountered similar in New York."

"*Non*, I did not expect you would. As I have said, despite her behavior and eccentric form of Marxism, she primarily focused on fundraising for Spain and, later, arms shipments for the Spanish Loyalists, just as we did for Franco's Nationalists. We both did some espionage as well, mostly to sabotage each other's efforts. On the whole, a good-natured rivalry. In truth, we were sorry when she and her *demoiselles* left for Cuba. Her successor proved a rather dull and plodding French Communist, easy to best."

"So, what was her official position?"

"She headed a small, but very influential group, called, in English, No Chains LTD."

"Clever. Was she running a blackmail operation like Baroness Ulrika?"

"*Non*, since the spouses knew about it. However, she was excellent at pillow talk, which produced a great deal of information. Countess asked me to infiltrate her organization. It was easy. Angelina was greatly attracted to me, and I allowed her to seduce me. I soon moved in with her and the *demoiselles*. This went on for a year as I came to know No Chains very well and sent the information back to Bleu. The last time I saw her, Angelina kissed me on the mouth and said, "You remain loyal to Sophie, and sadly, that means you can't join us in Cuba." There was no nastiness, only a statement of fact. It had been a wonderful apprenticeship in so many ways. So, after my adventures with the *demoiselles*, I became a courier to Dmitri in Berlin. And the result of that was my daughter, Hélène."

"Yes, your courier duties are in Dmitri's diary. But wasn't this when he and Ulrika were lovers?"

"Ah yes. She shared Dmitri with me so I could get Iskandarova pregnant. Ulrika is truly a remarkable and wonderful lady." She smiled. "And now, please excuse me as I visit Hélène and my parents."

Ashley stood before Dmitri and read, "Colonel of the 2nd Russian Imperial Cavalry Guards Division," as though none of the later unpleasantness had ever happened. He also saw Dmitri had not received the Blok poem he had requested for his epitaph. Instead, there were familiar lines from William Ernest Henley's poem, *Invictus*. Back in seventh grade, Ashley was required to memorize the whole thing and had never forgotten it.

> I thank whatever gods may be
> For my unconquerable soul.
> In the fell clutch of circumstance
> I have not winced nor cried aloud.
> My head is bloody but unbowed.
> I am the master of my fate
> I am the captain of my soul.

Ashley knelt before the plaque in silent prayer. Later, when Cosette came back, he said, "Dmitri says Sophia wishes me to come to her."

"And for what purpose?"

"I don't know."

"Of course not. However, you must be careful. The demons have been known to send out false messages to lure neophytes, such as yourself, to their doom."

"That I am. But this is something I must do on my journey."

"I see. Be fully aware. You must go to the Realm of the Spirits, both the good and the evil, if you wish to make contact. That is a place only for the dead. That is why we have the plaques safely here for veneration."

"I know. Are you saying that you won't help me get there?"

"Not at all. I am saying if you go, you shall go alone."

He thought for a moment. "All right."

Nadia shook her head and led him deeper into the mausoleum to an old, thick wooden door, reinforced by three horizontal iron beams and, in front of it, a nine-foot, gold Orthodox Cross, with the mysterious squiggle about halfway up. Cosette reached into her suit pocket and held out an old-fashioned key. "This is how you shall return here. After you leave, I shall lock the door to foil the evil spirits."

"A bit melodramatic, perhaps?"

"Not an iota. I have great concern for you. Beyond this door is a portal, and your time there is limited. Now, you shall find sixty-four steps, the same as squares on a chessboard. You shall be in darkness, and it is essential you count the steps accurately. If you do not, you shall wander, lost, until you die and then face a great battle for your soul." She shook her head. "Once you are on the floor, continue straight until you come to a wall. It is most important you then turn right. Now, mark me well. Do not turn left, although you shall be profoundly tempted. If you cannot resist, *alors*, you shall not be rejoining us."

Ashley nodded and repeated her directions. "Then what?"

"Continue on. Now, to return to us, reverse the process, except now there are seventy steps."

"But that makes no sense."

"Sense? *Zut alors*. It is not a place of anything like sense." She shook her head. "*Non*, you are not ready."

"My faith and *tvarsch* will guide me. While I'm comfortable with my intuition, I consider this to be more a test of my faith. I know I will be severely tested in Russia. So, if I fail here, I wasn't ready."

"I understand. I feel your faith is stronger than you might suspect. However, your *tvarsch* is not yet strong enough."

"Perhaps, but, again, if my *tvarsch* isn't strong enough for this, then I may as well return to New York. How do you know so much? Have you been there?"

"No. But Countess once told me of her very difficult journey. I also knew several people who never came back."

"Fair enough. When did Countess make her journey?"

"During the Great War, in 1916, in Petrograd."

"So, this was before her prophecy. Interesting. But how could she have taken the journey from Russia?"

"As I said, beyond the door is a portal. The Realm of the Spirits moves. If you fail to return promptly, the next time the portal opens, you could be in Iceland, or worse."

"And, if I don't return, promise me Annie goes to live with Ronnie, that is, Veronique. Right now, Annie's busy with her task, and I don't want her distracted worrying about mine."

"Now who's being melodramatic? But yes, I shall personally accompany Mademoiselle Ani to Veronique. Good fortune." She handed him the key.

3.

Ashley hears the door lock and remains close, adjusting his eyes to the dark. He recalls at Harvard, Professor Leary had warned, when tripping, never fight it. No matter how bad it seems, go with it. How different could this be? He hears wings above him in the darkness. Are they bats, birds, angels or demons? As his eyes adjust, he sees, turning around, that after being level for about six feet the stairs continue up. He had assumed this would be the top of the stairs, but this would make his return task more difficult. Behind an elaborate Byzantine arch on the far side of the steps, it smells of stale air, as though the area is sealed. He feels a sudden urge to explore it. No, he cannot be distracted because someone is already playing with his mind. His eyes adjusted, he takes his first step on the stairs, covered in mold, slime and mildew, and, going down, starts counting.

After carefully counting ten steps, he is at another landing and stops. On his right is an open wooden door to darkness, and on his left is a Roman arch leading to a far-off fire. As he continues down, he hears random numbers in his head, but sees no one, sensing presences just out of view. He begins hearing threats on his life, his soul and being. He is told repeatedly he does not belong there.

At fifty-one steps, he smells rot and hears a great jumble of thoughts, feelings and emotions condemning him. He focuses on his silent counting, but it becomes almost impossible. At fifty-nine, he sees, suspended in front of him, a dimly-lit demon face, palsied and drooping to the left, rotted on the right with yellow teeth either decayed or missing, his eyes a blind white. And, even worse, the demon smells like a mixture of vomit, excrement and decay. Seeing and smelling such disgusting horror, Ashley finally loses track of counting. When the face disappears, he cannot remember if he has counted fifty-nine once or twice. *I'm lost, and I can't go forward or back. Stuck! And the air now is so foul, I can barely breathe, and my fears are rising unchecked. Get a grip. I must continue. Chessboard sixty-four. There should be a landing and then four steps.*

When he arrives at the landing, he feels confident. Only four more before the floor. He has faith that when he leaves the final step, the floor will be a short drop. But he drops farther than expected and upon landing, falls. Shaken, he does not get up immediately from the smooth, hard surface, trying to remember what to do next. Again, voices try to confuse him. He rises and turns around with his hands out in the total darkness, trying to determine which direction he must go. He begins limping with his arms still out and senses when to stop. The noises, smells and taunting voices grow stronger as he tries to concentrate. He also fears there are further steps or even open pits on the floor, and if his *tvarsch* fails him, he is doomed. He proceeds slowly.

Moving on, the stench of corpses overwhelms his other senses, and a few times he gags and retches. Now, do I go left or right at the wall? He heard so many voices calling for left that he decided right must be correct. After limping for what seems a long distance, he sees a light come on at the wall. Looking down the left passage, he sees a beautiful valley, with neatly planted fields, thick forests and a red cottage in a clearing at the bottom. It is very inviting, and he sees a woman coming toward him on the steps, stopping about ten feet away. She has a wild mane of curly black hair, thick black eyebrows over heavily made-up silver eyes and bright red opaque lipstick on full lips, which are parted hungrily. Her black shirt covers her magnificent breasts and is tied underneath them, revealing a flat, smooth stomach. Her jeans ride seductively on her hips, and she is barefoot. She speaks in his head.

"Ashley, I know your parents, Sergei and Charlotte. I am present at your conception and am almost your godmother. You have many questions, and I have many answers. I can sense your gnawing and oppressive loneliness. Come to me, be my love and I shall reveal all. So happy together. Your *tvarsch* wants to commune with me. Come. Do not fight inevitable. Come to me."

Her voice is vaguely familiar, and he wants desperately to go to her, but knows he must not. *Oh my God, this is that Greek model I briefly dated as an associate.* He remembers the voice— Svetlana Feliksovna in Natalya's *Andronyis*. He focuses his mind on Natalya. This works until he feels himself being pulled.

"Please, do not try to resist. I am your destiny, your fate. I offer you peace you have never really known." She is very tempting, but he knows she is lying. He focuses even harder on Natalya and begins to pull away. Just as his focus starts to weaken, he remembers Sainte Elizabeta, and a burst of energy allows him to pull away as he opens the icon and focuses her large, glowing eyes on the demoness, who disappears. The spell broken, the valley returns to darkness.

Weak and shaken as he walks down the right-hand passage, almost blind, a great sadness consumes him as his loneliness now crushes his spirit and soul. He knows he would be selling his soul to go to her. But then, at this point, his soul and a buck twenty-five are enough to get him on the New York City subway. When he hears two dogs close to him growling loudly, fear replaces all thoughts of soul-selling. As they come closer, he can smell them and their foul breath.

"Zayus, Apollon, heel."

Although the area is suddenly candle-lit and he hears a woman's voice, he cannot see her. He feels his *tvarsch* struggling and wonders if he has wandered into another demon's trap.

"Ah yes, you are the seeker who wishes to be of the Iskandarov. Focus your thoughts to communicate. Your *tvarsch* is not that strong, therefore, I credit you for your courage in having successfully navigated to this place. You must have strong faith. Remember, your time here is limited."

Ashley focuses. "Thank you. Who are you, and why can I not see you?"

"I am Princess Xenia of the Iskandarov, killed at age thirty-two by Svetlana Feliksovna Polinkova. I know you seek information about her. However, you have much more important matters to learn. Your *tvarsch* now works with us because we are spirits of, not mortal, Iskandarov."

"Then I am confused. My *tvarsch* should allow me to see you. Further, it tells me that you are really many spirits. How can that be?"

"At this point, I do not wish to be seen, and my wish is stronger than your *tvarsch*. Nonetheless, you are here to see Sophia, Countess Kolchaka. We had best make speed. It is almost her time to return. I shall guide you to her. Here, take my hand."

Ashley feels only her hand in his. "Did you recognize the face you saw on the steps? It was your old friend, Stashinski."

"Yes, well, hardly a friend. I am amazed how quickly he has deteriorated."

"Such are the wages of evil. Ah, success, Countess remains."

Ashley thanks her and sees Sophia naked, as he saw her in David's diary in 1919, but she is as regal and imposing as if attired in her finery. He quickly studies her light-gray eyes. She is not a demon.

"I see you are not only prudent but are truly brave to come here, as there are many demons abroad at this time. And I feel your great sadness. While I understand your reasons, you must never even think about surrendering your immortal soul, lest you become a captive in this place. I know both your *tvarsch* and faith are strong. After all, the blood of the Iskandarov flows in you, the grandson of Dmitri and my son, Sergei. I felt great pride in your resistance at the wall. I know it was most difficult for you. In that cottage is trapped a woman who could be the Devil herself. She tries to lure all passers-by to torture them eternally. The image projected was someone from deep in your subconscious."

"I am overjoyed Svetlana Feliksovna is finally in Hell."

"Yes. I have heard you vowing revenge on her several times. There remain many who deserve it more."

"Doubtless. The image I saw was Eleni something or other. I was attracted to her because of her resemblance to Olga Sergevna. But that was all they shared."

"That was a thought I do not think you wished to share. Although I do admit, I see why Colonel Polinkova chose this particular woman to entice you. However, please remember her silver demonic eyes. *Formidable!* She imposed herself on your memory of this Eleni. Her cottage is deep within the realm of the demons, a place to which I must soon return."

"But why do you need to return there? It must be horrible."

"But yes, it is much worse than you can possibly imagine. However, I too feel that great loneliness when alone here. So, I return to the place where my husband resides."

"The count?"

"No, Dmitri with whom I had my blood union. My true husband and partner. Although you do not know the meaning of this term, I pray you shall. Penelope was the daughter of my cousin, the Grand Duke Alexei, as you know. He did leave detailed instructions with George's wife for an Iskandarova upbringing. But she had been locked up when Penelope began adolescence. As a result, you two never had your blood union to become an Iskandarov unity. In the event, I spend half of my time with Dmitri and half here until such time as he has paid his debt."

"Debt?"

"Yes, for all the people he killed in the course of his human existence. We negotiated it down to one hundred and fifty lives in exchange for my presence half the time there. In about another hundred years, his debt shall be repaid, and he shall be free to be here with me. Have no fear, that is not as long for us as it would be for you."

"That is very noble of you."

"No. Again, existence without Dmitri is far worse than what I endure with the demons because we are a unity. I know your thoughts. How wonderful could it be to live here in this place? The light is solely for your benefit. However, I exist half the time in our paradise, sunny, warm verdant fields bordered by the beautiful Russian forest with the Creator who is boundless and timeless. As a human, you may not yet see it. The demons exist in the dark, unable to see our paradise. The cottage you saw is actually a miserable shack on a desert of burning sand and rain. Svetlana may only venture out to one hundred meters, but for her slaves, there is no way to escape it. As the Iskandarov and Polinkov were bound together in life, so we are here. The good of both clans, along with our retainers, go to paradise, while all the evil ones remain trapped in the darkness, just as they were in life. Now, I have brought you here to tell you several things you need to know on your journey. First, the male quadriga, *tvarsch*, courage, intellect and faith. When you have mastered all four, you shall truly be an Iskandarov warrior. George Farwell is the sworn enemy of the Iskandarov, and you must kill him."

"Why me, especially?"

"You swore an oath to kill him. The Iskandarov consider oath-taking very serious. And he deserves death because he has robbed you."

"And how did he do that?"

"As I have indicated, your blood union. But also, for his child molestation of your wife. That alone is grounds for justifiable Iskandarov murder."

"I have already killed one man, and he haunts me. And now that I might have to spend time with the demons—"

"Have no fear. That was self-preservation."

"I know, but—"

"Our time is limited, so, secondly, you cannot succeed by yourself. Your teamwork is lacking. As was demonstrated when you missed the football goal against Dragovitch and Yale."

"I am learning with Annie."

"Yes, true. As for my great-granddaughter, although her *pyordarsch* is very strong and she has matured greatly since the death of your stepfather, she still has her own journey and obstacles to overcome. You should start to rely on her less and less. Your paths do not necessarily coincide. Therefore, you need to find a partner with whom you may try to have the union. Someone you can trust and share with. Thirdly, most of us have been blessed with very superior attributes. So, we do not boast of our accomplishments. After all, how could it have been any other way? Be humble."

"Yes, I see. But there is one thing bothering me. Are we pawns of fate or do we have truly free will?"

"I know why you ask me that. It is complicated. However, you are the recipient of blood from the millennia of our ancestors. When you were born, everything you needed to become a successful Iskandarov was already in your blood. This includes your predilections, choices and talents. You are an *avocat* rather than a mathematician because of your predilection for the humanities, history in particular. Your choices led you in that direction. And the more successful choices you made, the closer you were to your goal. Therefore, did you become an *avocat* because that was what you wanted to do or because your blood had already made the choice for you?"

"Interesting. But what about Sergei? Surely he did not have a predilection to shoot a president."

"Very good. Unlike you, from an early age, my son made a series of bad choices. That was why Dmitri sent him to America. By 1929, he was too self-indulgent and decadent to make a good warrior. My husband found his successors in two women, Nadia and Ulrika. And that was why Sergei never received his orders from Dmitri."

"That is pretty harsh."

"Yes, it is. That is the Iskandarov way. But I confess, as his mother, after the horrors of the Great War and our civil war, I did not want my son to be a warrior, only to be chewed up in some meaningless war."

"I see."

"No. Not fully. After he met Angelina Civilli, in the late thirties, Sergei changed when his long dormant sense of honor came to the fore. He did not need to join the air force in the war or go on the Ploesti raid or remain with his POW 'buddies' or allow Charlotte to be tortured. And yet he made all the honorable decisions."

"How was Angelina able to change him?"

"She had a gift for seeing what people needed and giving it to them."

"All right, I get that, but why was his plane shot down?"

"On Ploesti, he owed the ultimate debt to Colonel Cooper and could not honorably refuse, hence he had to be on that aircraft. Here is the key point… your lifespan is ultimately determined by your blood. Any time you have a group of people, such as a bomber crew, there may be one or more whose lifetime is going to end that day. As I remember, the co-pilot was killed, while the rest survived."

"Yes, Mac's parachute failed."

She nodded. "I can see I have not convinced you."

"I am trying. Your great prophecy is strong evidence of its truth. But it is too primitive and—"

"Now, what did I say about being humble?"

"OK. I may get there. Nonetheless, I greatly appreciate all you have told me."

"Excellent. Now, my last point is one I wish you to ponder. I am not expecting an immediate reply. Why do you wish to become of the Iskandarov?"

"That's a very good question. But now, I would like to see Olga, please."

"Oh yes, I know you would. However, she is not here. I suppose it would do no harm to tell you to try again at her plaque. Now, I hear Dmitri coming for me."

* * *

When Dmitri appears, he is not the one Ashley expected—young with a muscular body and an erection. He stops in front of Ashley and smiles as he reaches for Sophia, who says, "*Adieu*, grandson, good fortune." Once their hands touch, they disappear.

Ashley has no idea what to do. *Should I remain? Go back to the stairs? Wait for Xenia? How much time do I have?*

He is startled when Xenia appears right in front of him, naked, blonde, gray-eyed and full-term pregnant with large translucent wings and a very bright aura.

"Now you know why I possess many spirits. One is my unborn son, Pyotr, who was killed with me and your unborn son with Lady Olga. I rescued and have within me all the innocent souls I have rescued from the realm of nothing, now safe and warm within my womb. After all, souls weigh virtually nothing and have no mass."

"Of course." He shook his head. *Now why did I not think of that?* "Thank you. Will I ever see my son again?"

"Ah yes, I think you have a reasonably good idea of his appearance. Here take my hands and again focus to join us." Slowly, a young boy appears out of Xenia. "He certainly resembles you most closely."

"Indeed, he does."

As the boy disappears, Ashley asks, "When will I see him again?"

Xenia smiles. "When the time is right."

Ashley nods. "Of course. But why do you save babies and all?"

"I am named after another Iska Princess, Xenia, who condemned many maiden serfs to give their pure blood until dead into her bathing tub, so she would remain young and beautiful. As she aged, she became quite mad and even as a crone thought wearing the maiden's blood made her beautiful. She became, for our enemies, a symbol of death. Thus, I became a symbol of life and an example to Iskandarovas all and birthed as many babies as I could. I was married to Prince Evahn at eighteen. We had our blood union, and over the next fourteen years I birthed six boys and four girls. I absolutely adored being with child. Evahn thought it very arousing as well. When I maintained my maternity after death, my charge became to rescue as many Iskandarov and Polinkov innocent souls as I could. When I learned you were coming to see the Countess Sophia, I knew I had to meet you and share my experiences with you."

"Absolutely. Thank you for sharing. But I still do not understand the why."

"Of course. When the Iskandarov commit a sin or a crime, they seek to make restitution to balance the scales. And it was because of all that I did to balance the scales that the Polinkov killed me. I was a great threat to them."

"OK. Very good to know. And you truly are a martyr and sainte."

"Please, you embarrass me. I was only a true and faithful Iskandarova. Come with me. Your time grows short here, and you have been successful. I may take you to the stairs, but you must make your own way back. I could fly you back to your destination in an instant, but that would be cheating on your trial, which continues. Remember, seventy steps this time. Keep your focus and wits about you. The demons shall try even harder to keep you here and steal your soul."

"But why do they want my soul?"

"It is pure energy. In your body, it is like an electric torch that powers your whole system—"

"Like what we call a flashlight?"

"Truly? You die when your soul leaves your body. And since energy cannot be destroyed, only converted to another form, it shall live forever. You lose it to a demon and you cease to exist, and the demon becomes more powerful."

"I see. Good to know."

"Excellent. Now take my hand again." He hears her wings flapping and instantly is at the bottom on the stairs. Her aura shines brightly, and Ashley is amazed the area is so small, only about twelve feet between the last step and the wall.

"Xenia, why did it take me so long to get to the wall?"

"Good question. You were moving so very slowly, I am surprised you ever made it. Seriously, there is no time or space here."

"Then how come I have a time limit?"

"Ashley, shame on you. Your world continues normally. The Earth rotates and circles the sun. That is why." She laughs.

"Again, thank you… for everything."

"You are most welcome. Godspeed." Xenia disappears.

Svetlana Feliksovna appears in her NKVD uniform he saw on Lana's bureau. "We are not finished. Your father was *zek*, my prisoner. Your mother was *zechka* and my prisoner. Therefore, you are my property as well, to do with as I please. Surrender now, and I shall be merciful. The longer you wait, the worse your punishment. You are about to climb staircase. Most risky. You may not succeed and die here. Or after fighting your way to your destination, portal may have closed, leaving you stranded for who knows how long? As human, you need nutrients. We do not and there are none to be had. You shall slowly starve to death like stupid Ukrainian serf. I so enjoyed watching those idiots turn on each other and even eat their children, foolishly trying to extend their miserable existences. They were actually better off dead."

"Now I know why you tortured my sister and the others so horribly. I defeated you once already, so you don't scare me any more than a Halloween boo. So, go back to your shack and pound some of that burning sand."

As he climbs the stairs, the demons resume chanting numbers and making vile threats, but he knows their tricks and ignores them, keeping a silent running account. However, for some reason, it seems to take twice the energy to go up rather than down. It is not until the twentieth step landing that he sees what appears to be Penelope.

"Ash, stay with me. You see me as I would have appeared in absolute naked perfection, had you come with me after the Yale lacrosse game. It is not too late. We can still have our blood union, as we were supposed to. I have lovely rooms not far from here."

"Pen, you are still delusional. You are dead. You cannot get pregnant."

"I most certainly can, with a live person."

Ashley shook his head. "I do not believe you, and even if I did, I am not going to bet my soul on it. Now, get out of my way. I do not want anything to do with you because you killed Olga, among other crimes. You may have escaped the law, but not retribution. So, again, you have made your bed. I am certain you know the rest." He paused. "And for the record, I never cheated on you with any Russian women. Now, get lost."

After the demoness disappeared, Ashley feels very weak, and going up the stairs becomes increasingly difficult, and he begins to lose count until Xenia again surprises him. "That was your last test."

"Who was that? Svetlana again."

"No, that was your former wife. As a human she went mad because she knew she was going to be expelled by the Iskandarov and thus, a demoness. Had you now gone with her, she would have betrayed you to Svetlana. Now, take my hand. I shall deliver you to where you belong." He again hears her wings. "Now, we are outside the door back to the mausoleum." She smiles before disappearing, and Ashley finds his key still in his hand.

5.

After entering the mausoleum, Ashley no longer limped, and the Orthodox cross remained shining. Exhausted, he sat on a bench against a wall and watched as a large boulder sealed the portal. *Damn,* he thought, *if Xenia hadn't rescued me, I'd now be on the wrong side of that big rock.* He tried to get up to close the wooden door, but it closed itself, and the cross began to dim. He looked down at his messy clothes and felt his unshaved face. Unable to keep his eyes open, he was soon dreaming of flying over Moscow with Xenia, and both of them are invisible. Because he is quite familiar with the city, Xenia shows him where the Iskandarov are and where he is likely to be.

"Wake up, Ashley. We need to get you to the apartment."

He looks up to see Cosette. "But, I've only been asleep for a few minutes, I—"

"Not so. I discovered you about an hour ago and left you to regain your strength."

He felt Annie kissing him. "I'm so glad you're OK. I was very worried when Countess told me you were with her. What you did was crazy."

"Probably. But it was something I had to do, and I'm glad I did. And now I must go back to Olga's plaque." They helped him up, but he went first to Xenia's plaque. After focusing as best he could, he saw her smiling face and heard in his head, "Abide, Prince Sergei Iskandarov until we meet again." He smiled and thought, *Wow!*

At Olga's plaque, he put his hand on the marble and received a shock. He would see her again, soon. As he left the mausoleum with Cosette and Annie, he thought, *I should be exhausted, but I feel great. All I need is a hot shower, and I look forward to a most interesting evening.*

EIGHTEEN
Thursday, 3 June 1993
Paris, France

1.

Following Blanche down the long corridor to his assigned bedroom, Ashley continued struggling with Sophia's Blood Doctrine. But, as he entered and saw Olga's posters, pictures and most of the furniture from her pad, his nostalgic delight overwhelmed his thoughts. Surprisingly, given Nadia's politics, even Olga's anarchist poster with the bare-breasted maiden's heroic flag was on a wall. And he saw her most precious possession on her brass bed table... Tiffany, an authentic stained glass floral lamp that Sophia had given her on her twenty-first birthday. He had always loved the sound that the balls at the end of the dual pull-cords made when they hit the brass base under the large red rose. He pulled the two balls apart and let them go and smiled at their tone. After doing it again, he went to the shower.

Washing his hair, he suddenly felt fear. *I failed in my mission to the realm of the spirits. If Xenia hadn't rescued me, I'd now be stuck behind the boulder, fighting for my life and soul. That was the toughest test I've ever faced. And I know Russia will be even harder.*

"Ash Cooper, cut this bullshit and get a grip."

He heard Olga's voice as though she were in the shower with him.

"You, as a mortal, can't navigate in the Realm of the Spirits by yourself. You needed help, which must be earned. And you had to be humble enough to accept it when Xenia offered it. Those persons Cosette spoke about who perished were arrogant and prideful, and their deaths were horrible. Now that is failure and not even close to what you accomplished. Your *tvarsch* is strong because your faith in it is strong, especially after your ordeal. Right now, your *tvarsch* and faith are in balance. Lose that balance and you may lose everything. This was something I tried to teach you, but I guess you had your mind on something else. In any event, that's why faith and *tvarsch* are two elements of the male quadriga."

"OK, but when can I see you?"

"Whenever the evenings are quite blue."

He felt the tingling and knew he would see her tonight.

Going happily back to the room, he noticed his clothes were now in the armoire, including his black tie, which he tried it on, just to ensure it fit properly, and it did.

Later, still in his pleated shirt, vest and tuxedo trousers, he heard a light knock on the doorframe, and as he turned he saw an elderly lady self-confidently entering, wearing dark glasses, a red silk turban, a white-buttoned blouse with several unbuttoned, a Bolero jacket over it and a long, black skirt mostly concealing green, high-heeled, yellow-laced boots. "Good afternoon, Baroness Ulrika."

"And to you, Herr Ashley Cooper. Please excuse my interruption. My friend, Cosette told me where you are, and I wanted to speak to you privately before the Repast."

"Thank you for coming." He smiled. "Let's sit by the window. Would you care for some tea, or something else?"

"No thank you. However, my eyes are very light sensitive. If you would please close the draperies, I may remove my glasses." As he did so, she sat regally straight on the padded chair. "I know you have read your grandfather's journal. I saw it shortly after he wrote it, and I can attest to its overall veracity, but not to its completeness."

Ashley nodded. "I'm not surprised. And I feel as though I know you."

She smiled at her hands, which were gently folded in her lap, removed her glasses and then looked directly at him with her hypnotic blue eyes. "In 1922, after completing my studies at the University of Leipzig, I joined my brother Reinhardt in his Section IV of the then secret *Abwehr*, German Military Intelligence, which was forbidden by the Versailles Treaty. And Section IV and its unorthodox methods was the most secret."

"No doubt." Ashley studied her face and the surgeries that had left her alabaster skin tightly pulled. He especially focused on a particularly long, white scar on the left of her throat, running up past her jaw.

"As you must know, the Section financed my domina role because it was, and is, well known that many powerful men wish to temporarily cede power to a woman. It is also known that many powerful men, especially Germans, have great guilt and are looking for redemption through punishment. I was the reincarnation of Brunhild, the fierce Valkyrie." She held up her hand. "Now I know that sounds ludicrous, but that was the result of my research because, at that time, the myths of our Germanic-Aryan race's past were becoming popular."

"So, did you blackmail these men?"

"Your reputation is true. You do not waste time, and you speak plainly and employ such a sordid word. At their first meeting I told my clients they could trust my discretion. And from there, we proceeded slowly, building trust as they began to reveal their most intimate desires. Now, after our sessions ended and they cleaned up, we would relax together, talking over tea, beer, schnapps or whatever they desired. And these talks became, after a while, political. Most of these men were terrified the Bolsheviks would try to seize power again, especially after the

Berlin Sparticist Uprising and a similar one in very conservative Munich, both in 1919. And this next time, backed by the Soviet Union, they would succeed. And they all wanted to do something, even my Socialists, but did not know what or how. I told them to contact my brother to volunteer their services because I assured them Reinhardt truly did not care about their desires and could be very discreet. And they knew I would never betray them. I don't expect you to understand, but my regulars were like my family." She smiled.

"I can understand that. You were on much more intimate terms with these men and had much more trust than a typical family." Ashley very much doubted her account, but she was very entertaining, and there was no point in arguing.

"Yes, you understand perfectly." She paused. "Now, when the Director of Bleu arrived in Berlin, it was important. However, Section IV was initially divided on how to handle him. Although Russian émigré politics were highly byzantine and opaque, Bleu was a major force in the anti-Bolshevik cause. Nevertheless, we also knew the Bolsheviks were very clever and not above funding an agency against themselves, such as the infamous Trust. When Reinhardt began his research, he discovered no one had ever checked the authenticity of this new, but very essential, agency. He gave me the task of researching Dmitri. About a month later, I felt I knew him very well, thus he would eventually come to me, not because he was guilty or weak, but rather because he was strong and loved a challenge. I carefully laid a trail of clues in appropriate places. He was not to find me until all of our research had been completed. Even then, if I suspected anything amiss, I would break off contact." She smiled. "I knew the best way to win his trust was to lose our wager in a most convincing way."

"I suspected that had been the case."

"However, what started as a political relationship quickly developed into something more. He taught me so much, I cannot begin to say. Especially about the superior will and enduring the unendurable. However, most of all, as a warrior, he inspired me to follow his code. However, I confess I kept a group of about twenty regulars. I simply could not abandon them. In fact, I have one who has been with me since the twenties."

"You're still a practicing domina?"

"Yes. I surprise myself. But my regulars simply would not let me retire. So, over the years, I evolved from Valkyrie deity to warrior queen to avenging crone. You would be amazed how many older men, despite my wounds and age, still find me wickedly alluring. I saved the life of a Jew. In 1932, I had this man feminized by a surgeon I knew to protect him. She is my maid to this day, replacing my previous maid, also feminized, who was one of several by-standers killed during a Nazi and Bolshevik street brawl in 1925." She paused for a moment. "Now, I never was a Nazi. Rather, a German patriot who took an oath to restore German honor. I still feel more raped by Hitler than by the Bolsheviks."

"Thank you for telling me all this. I never knew what Dmitri's role was in Bleu."

"He was Master Strategist and Sophia, Chief of Operations. I want you to know about my debt to your grandfather. From his journal, you know when I was captured along with my group we were turned over to the NKVD in Stalingrad. I shall spare you the details. My face should give you a suitable example of their handiwork. Nonetheless, they never broke me because I had learned to never give in, and do not fight the pain, embrace it. Additionally, trust in your superior will."

"Yes, I understand."

"Excellent, I also owed your grandfather a second tremendous debt for the assistance he provided when I had to go to ground in the final stages of the war. That was when *stümper* Himmler seized control of the *Abwehr*. As the Reich was collapsing around them, the Nazis executed our *Abwehr* leader, Admiral Wilhelm Canaris, the very man they needed instead of *dummkopf* Himmler. I was one of the agents the admiral protected, and I became invisible for a period before surrendering to the British. I

worked for them until another *Abwehr* officer, General Reinhard
Gehlen formed the BND, the West German Intelligence Service.
Therefore, before I take my leave, Dmitri told me one day you
would read these texts in which he wanted to emphasize your
military heritage and your superior will, two vital attributes
needed on your journey. I noticed you were studying my face. I
chose to keep the scar as a reminder of my ordeal because I won."

"Yes, but tell me about your daughter, Marlena. The diaries
had virtually nothing about her."

"Yes, of course. In 1939, when she was six, we sent her to
Switzerland for her schooling and safety with friends. In 1951,
she returned to West Germany and matriculated at Heidelberg
University. After graduating, she came to Bleu as an agent."

"And?"

"You listen well. She is incredibly beautiful and carries on in
my footsteps." She smiled. "And now, see you tonight."

* * *

After removing the rest of his black-tie clothes and getting
dressed in slacks and shirt, Annie excitedly came in. "I just met
Baroness Ulrika. We had a wonderful conversation, and she told
me she's still a practicing domina in Berlin. Incredible. She's
such a strong, confident woman."

"Yes, she is. Now what's so urgent?"

"This is not only the place I saw in my vision, it's the place
where Yuri's going to die, along with others. And it's going to
happen tonight."

"How do you know?"

"I had another vision. We're in the big room, and I can see
I'm in my blue gown. There's an explosion."

"You're certain of this? And have you told anyone?"

"Positive. And no."

"Have you seen Cosette and Nadia?"

"Cosette's supervising the Repast preparations. Nadia's still
in her office."

2.

About fifteen minutes later, one flight down in Nadia's office, Annie had explained her vision to Nadia. "I have no doubt about the quality and proof of what you say. We have bomb scares every so often. Most of the time, nothing. Do you know the time of the explosion?"

"If your mantel clock's correct, then just before ten."

"Some consolation that our ceremony shall be over by then, and many shall have left."

Cosette spoke. "Nadia, with respect. I am seeing something further." She turned to Annie. "I know you are very fond of Yuri Aleksandrovich Iskandarov, and you say he shall die tonight. However, consider what you have said about his death."

"Yes. Oh no. I'm powerless to stop this, aren't I?"

"Yes. Countess told me long ago the power of *pyordarsch* is absolute. That is, simply because you see future events, you may not change them. Thus, you shall lose a close friend, the first of many. You cannot let your grief overwhelm that which is important. You must carry on, like a true Iska."

Annie nodded. "I'll do my best."

Cosette nodded, and Ashley spoke. "I know this is all part of Iskandarov Blood Doctrine. Cosette and Annie, you'll excuse me if I remain, at best, agnostic on this and even skeptical. If we don't find the device, Yuri dies. If we find it, then maybe he dies and maybe he doesn't, but I like those odds much better."

Cosette replied, "Monsieur Cooper, I see the change in you since this afternoon, but your *avocat* brain remains. Understand, this is a test for you as well and shall be an education, as you shall discover what happens when you try to defy fate."

Nadia nodded. "I understand both sides here. However, if there is but a miniscule chance, we must do everything we can to protect Minister Iskandarov's son. Agreed?"

All nodded.

"Good. I shall call our bomb squad to sweep the entire building and keep them on high alert throughout the evening."

Ashley spoke. "I feel I must help with that. I developed some knowledge of bomb finding while I was in Thailand, where bombs were seemingly everywhere."

"Good. Begin, please."

"The device is probably on a timer, so it can be planted before the Repast. Nadia, any new employees?"

"No. They have all been with me for years."

"What about deliveries?"

"Everything is left downstairs. Two of my staff go down and sweep and manually search before bringing anything upstairs."

"Who else lives in the building?"

"I own it, and we have a hotel on three floors above the entrance. The rest are offices."

"Thank you. Most helpful. I'll begin my search."

3.

After Ashley finished his search, he returned to his room and found the promised dossiers on Stevens, Dragovitch and Fred. After finishing the first two, it was time to get ready.

About a half hour later, in the ballroom, Ashley sipped vintage champagne while observing a hundred or so people all formally and elegantly dressed, with the ladies heavily bejeweled. Servers moved discreetly through them with drinks and appetizers. All wore ceramic nametags, written in Cosette's elaborate script, with only their *noms de guerre* for security, but Ashley's nametag read "P. Ashlei," the "P" standing for "Prince." At first, thinking it silly, as the evening wore on, he felt more comfortable.

Ulrika, in dark glasses, swept into the room and went directly to Ashley, wearing her red turban over a shiny, black silk gown cinched at the waist and green opera slippers.

"Good evening, Baroness, I like your *nom*, Valkyrie. I didn't know you were a Bleu agent."

"Yes, Prince. Of long standing. Obviously, Dmitri never mentioned that in his writings. The *Abwehr* and Bleu were closely tied all through the war."

"Is Marlena going to join us tonight?"

"Sadly, no. I think the two of you might have gotten on well." She sighed. "No, she is in Russia on a mission for Nadia."

Cosette, dressed in an elaborate gown, came across the room. The ladies hugged warmly. "We again have a bomb report."

"I should stop coming. It seems every time I do, there is a bomb report. What is known?"

"We do not know the target. However, it could be you."

Ulrika shook her head. "Then it is probably Stasi related. I am too well protected in Berlin. What time?"

"Twenty-two hundred." Cosette turned to Ashley. "We still have no success. Perhaps, Mademoiselle Annie is mistaken?"

"No, my *tvarsch* has told me of the device."

"Very well, we shall continue our search."

"Good luck. I now think the device isn't in this room."

After Cosette left, Ashley said, "Assuming you're the target, you don't seem very concerned."

"No. I am not. Stasi has been after me for decades. Of course, it could also be Neo-Nazis or Soviets." She paused. "I have had a long and wonderful life, and all because the commandos rescued me at Stalingrad. Absent that, I would be dead and forgotten in a mass grave somewhere in Russia. Borrowed time, something you know about."

"Indeed, I do."

"Then you know of what I speak. Now, please excuse me. There are many people with whom I need to speak."

"Of course. Enjoy the Repast."

After she left, Ashley noticed tobacco smoke permeating the air, where it remained with no air currents from outside. A piano quartet played by the ballroom entrance. Most of the people he met had been interesting. They knew why he was there and where he and Annie were going. They offered encouragement and advice, which he gratefully accepted. He really liked these people and felt strong kinship and happiness in belonging and seeing all the various auras.

Ashley thought he saw his mystery lady from the Moscow reception. As he made his way toward her, a young man in a military dress uniform with a light-blue sash, several ribbons and a powerful aura intercepted him. He stood erect with an engaging smile and extended his hand. "Prince Ashlei, I'm Sabreur Bleu."

"Ah yes. The young man who saved my life in New York. I can't thank you enough."

He smiled. "All part of my duties. Besides, from the dead Cuban I'm now the proud owner of a Dragunov SVD semi-automatic sniper rifle for my collection."

Ashley nodded his appreciation while looking for his lady, who had again disappeared.

"Have no illusions, sir. You're going up against strong, powerful and ruthless men and women. And they want you dead in the most painful manner possible. They also plan to capture Annie for her visions. And in captivity, she will come to envy your relatively quick death."

Ashley sipped his champagne to get the moisture back in his throat. This young man certainly spoke plainly. "Yes, I've already had a very polite, but firm, warning to return to New York."

"Yes, Alex Dragovitch at the brasserie and your old nemesis Nick Stevens are in the area and may show up here tonight. However, I suspect they'll need you alive for the foreseeable future. And remember, you have friends you aren't aware exist. You and your daughter are most important to Bleu, and we'll do everything we can to ensure your safety and survival. Our people will contact you once you're in Russia. Let me add, it's most fortunate you and Annie didn't attend the van Rouene funeral and you left town when you did. One final topic I wish to clarify. I've been accused of assassinating Ambassador van Rouene, his former State Department colleagues and abducting his heir and wife, your former lover, Lana van Rouene. Or, if you prefer, Svetlana Igorovna Polinkova. I swear to you, I had no hand in it. Yes, I was in the area, but on another unrelated mission."

Ashley nodded. Absent his *tvarsch*, he felt inclined to believe him. "All right, but if not you, then who?"

"The ambassador had many enemies. There are numerous rumors floating about, but nothing definitive. However, Lana seems the most likely. You were very lucky to have survived this most dangerous woman."

"Thank you for the information. She's a true Polinkova, like her mother, deceitful and desirous of having an Iskandarov baby. She may have already succeeded. But, no doubt she did this. The ambassador had served his purpose, and she left town, just after my stepfather died, to return to Russia. I sense I'll confront her again."

"Thank you, sir, I hope you don't. Now, enjoy the Repast."

Almost immediately two ladies swept up Ashley. Both appeared to be in their mid-thirties, expensively dressed and coiffed. Princess Irina, blonde and Rubenesque, holding a glass of vodka, wore a crimson gown with a large, gold Orthodox cross. The Baroness von Heida, holding a flute of champagne, tall and lean, had strong shoulders and long, straight red hair. Dressed in a high-collared green silk gown with a slit on the right, it seemed very similar to what she wore in Moscow. But when Ashley asked her if they had met, she smiled and said, "*Charmante*."

Applause began as the duchess made her entrance with Annie, wearing the floor-length, dark-blue gown along with a triple strand of pearls and earrings to match and a diamond tiara. As the duchess had cautioned, the gown was quite low-cut, with a plunging neckline in front and scooped out to her waist in back. However, Annie seemed completely poised and wore the gown as though she had done so numerous times. Ashley assumed she had learned this at the various formal balls she went to in New York with Penelope, who would have had no objection, except as competition for her own revealing gown.

"My dears, this is Mademoiselle Ani, great-granddaughter of Sophia and Dmitri, granddaughter of Sergei and Charlotte and daughter of our other special guest, Prince Ashlei." She gestured toward him before everyone applauded.

"Ashley, your daughter is most poised for such a young lady."

Sipping his champagne, he nodded to the princess. "Yes, my almost seventeen going-on-thirty daughter. Constant source of surprise." As he spoke, he noticed the princess had a very bright aura.

Annie and the duchess came over, and Nadia smiled. "Mademoiselle Ani, truly *charmante et ravissante, n'est-ce pas?*"

"Absolutely." Ashley turned to Annie, who smiled a bit too hard. "You do look lovely. Have fun, and don't worry." He introduced Annie to the two ladies. The baroness took Annie by the hand and said, "After we pause for a champagne, I know of a charming young man Mademoiselle Ani simply must meet."

The duchess nodded. "What an excellent idea. And now, my dears, if you shall excuse me, I must attend my other guests."

Ashley smiled and glanced at his watch. Less than an hour left. He thought, *They're both scared, like me. Earlier, I searched everywhere, including the terrace around the skylight and notified the two armed guards who were in the process of rolling out its cover. I don't need to be the star here. I'll pass the ball to the pros.*

Princess Irina turned to Ashley. "Please escort me outside. I should like some air before another cigarette." They strolled out through French doors to the spacious terrace where several clusters of people spoke softly. Ashley noticed that for a large woman, Irina moved with remarkable agility. He looked out over the lighted boulevard before looking down. The men were still there, and although Fred and Nick had left, Dragovitch remained. So, where were they?

"I just wanted to make certain I was still in Paris and not in nineteenth century Russia." As he spoke, he was also looking for anything out of place.

Irina laughed genteelly and held a long crimson cigarette, which Ashley lit. "In a sense you are." She exhaled and waved her cigarette toward the room. "It's very much as things could be today in Russia, were it not for Lenin's coup d'état in 1917. However, we look very much to the future, albeit a Russian one, not European."

Ashley sipped his champagne. "So, are you opposed to Europe and the West?"

"*Non*, not at all. Aside from the Soviets, we're opposed to no one. Russia remains the bulwark against Asia and, indeed, Islam. And Russia will, one day, be the leader of Europe into a new and glorious future, as Andrey Biely predicted."

"Tell me though, the Soviet Union has ceased to exist for several years now. So why are Bleu's headquarters still in Paris and not in, say, St. Petersburg?"

"Simply, the Communist Party has been defeated, but not the organs of state security. *Apparat* KGB, or, if you prefer, the FSB, may eventually succeed in taking over the government. Russia has always wanted strong leaders and security over freedom. The organs can provide that."

"Do you support Yeltsin, then?"

"We do, but not with enthusiasm." She sipped her vodka. "I assume you're aware of the significance of the blue Chanel gown."

"Yes, Ronnie told me about it in general terms. And I remember Corinne Duval was shot wearing a similar gown."

"Unfortunately, so. However, tonight announces our fourth-generation leader. When the duchess passes, her daughter, Verushka, your stepmother, will succeed her. And now Mademoiselle Ani is heir-apparent to Verushka. She wasn't chosen capriciously. Her tenure, hopefully, won't begin for many years. Or perhaps never. And no, she's not now a Bleu agent. But she's a primary reason my sister and I are here tonight. The other is to meet you." She puffed her cigarette. "I noticed you met my son, Sabreur Bleu."

Ashley would still speak to Nadia later about Annie. He nodded and sensed, interestingly, that Irina was clearly a full Iska, despite Svetlana Feliksovna being her mother. And that was why she had aged so gracefully.

She exhaled a narrow stream of smoke. "I know you and your lovely daughter are going to Russia, and your task there will be very difficult. Therefore, you both simply must stay with us at our dacha outside Moscow. My husband, the prince, would like very much to meet you."

"Indeed, and I've been looking forward to meeting him. Thank you."

She smiled. "Good, it's all settled." She puffed her cigarette. "I, that is, we're leaving for our cottage in the Sakartvelo tomorrow. We expect to be back in Moscow in a few days and will be in contact. Now, have you made your hotel reservations? I'm sure you're familiar with the problems that can cause if you haven't."

"The duchess is taking care of all the details. Everything ready by tomorrow."

"In that event, I should sleep soundly. Duchess leaves absolutely nothing to chance. Every last iota must be accounted for. Now, we'll see you at the dacha in few days' time?"

"Yes, of course."

"Very good. Best fortune on your journey, Ashlei." She began to leave, turned and said, "Do not be concerned about what's bothering you."

"Iska *pyordarsch?*"

She smiled and left. Ashley remained on the terrace, enjoying the relatively clean air. He finished his champagne while again enjoying the lights of the boulevard, and his thoughts drifted back to Cosette, who had confirmed, after leaving the cemetery, that his meeting with Sophia and Xenia, as well as his encounter with Dmitri in the attic, had not been unusual for an Iskandarov; further proof that the rationality, Cosette's *avocat* brain, that had served him so well in New York had already proved to be an obstacle here. He was, already, a long way from New York. Tomorrow, he would be even farther. At the same time, Cosette had told him Dmitri had wanted Sergei to marry her in 1939. Sergei, who had never met her and was angry at Dmitri for ignoring him for ten years, rejected the offer. And he and Dmitri had not spoken again until their *luftstalag* meeting. And in a final irony, Cosette lost her daughter trying to rescue the woman he had married. And what a different life he would have led as Cosette's son and a Bleu agent. This led him to thinking of all the coincidences and what-ifs that had to happen for him to even be standing here in his present configuration. And that meant no matter what happened tonight, device or not, he would be OK. As would Annie.

4.

As ten o'clock approached, Nadia found Ashley on the terrace, and they went over to a quiet corner to talk undisturbed. "Nadia, what are your people saying?"

"They have swept the whole building and found nothing. And you?"

"I've come up empty as well, and I've searched all the public areas including the terrace around the skylight."

"I fear Mademoiselle Ani is incorrect. However, as a precaution everyone has been informed to evacuate the room at five minutes before the hour, just in case, and remain out for ten minutes."

"Shall we evacuate as well?"

"You may, if you wish, but at the appointed time, I shall stand in the French doors, so I can be seen by all, setting an example and to tell those remaining to depart."

"In that case, I'll join you as well."

"That is not necessary."

"It most certainly is. I need to show faith in my bomb detecting."

She laughed. "Very well."

"Good. Now, it struck me that when you speak about my daughter you are saying 'Ani,' as in Anastasia."

"But yes, is that not her name?"

"No. Her name is Anne."

"But, you have seen the identity card Veronique gave her. Anastasia is her Iskandarova woman name. She is no longer a girl at seventeen and is allowed to marry, if she so chooses. In similar fashion, Ashley is your boy name and should have been changed years ago. Sergei is your Iskandarov man name."

"Thank you. I've never especially liked Ashley, but it has become my professional name, my brand, if you will."

"That is as may be. However, I wonder how much longer you shall be an *avocat*."

"Good question. Come, I see people beginning to leave."

For the fifteen minutes they stood in the French door, they were seemingly confident. When the guests returned, Nadia told Ashley, "Thank the Lord. Now, I am fatigued. This has been a long day for the both of us. Please escort me."

As they entered the ballroom, arm-in-arm, the quartet began playing, and everyone applauded. As Nadia waved regally, she said, "This is the Ukrainian national anthem. And these people are all my agents and retainers." She stopped and turned. "A pleasant evening to you all now that we are safe, but I must retire. Let the dancing begin."

After escorting Nadia to her bedroom door at the end of the long corridor, Ashley said, "I know what the blue gown signifies. Why didn't you tell me what you were planning?"

Nadia appeared perplexed. "Ashlei, with respect, it has nothing to do with you. She shall not, God willing, be leader for many years to come, after she is married and has her children." She crossed herself. "And by then, God willing, there shall be no need for an agency such as Bleu."

"Yes, hopefully so." He paused. "Now, you arranged for Yuri to be here, did you not?"

A truly hurt expression came over Nadia. "Have I done something untoward? They have known each other for almost four years and have been keeping company for approximately two. According to my reports, Penelope approved of this arrangement."

"I can't say I'm surprised." He had started serious dating at fifteen and thought about Penelope's negligee in Annie's suitcase.

"Nonetheless, even though she'll be seventeen on the sixth and is very poised, she's not, in my world, an adult yet."

"While I understand your fatherly fears, I should not be concerned. You and Penelope have made a superb preparation for her. I am confident she shall make all of the appropriate decisions as they arise. Now, why do you not return to the Repast? I am certain there are some ladies who should enjoy a flirtation with you. Who knows, perhaps more?"

"Thank you, but I already have a rendezvous for this blue night."

Nadia smiled. "Ah, *bonne chance*."

Ashley kissed her gloved hand. "Thank you for a most interesting and enjoyable day."

Nadia smiled. "My pleasure. I see you are not the same person who arrived here this morning. We shall speak before you leave."

Ashley returned to the ballroom to say goodnight to Annie and found her having an intense conversation, in French, with Yuri while waltzing. They stopped, and Ashley said, "I'm going to retire soon. Have fun, but don't stay up too late… we've a long day tomorrow."

"OK, Dad, don't worry. I'll be in bed before midnight." She kissed his cheek, and after Yuri shook his hand, they resumed their conversation and waltzed away. Ashley wondered whose bed she would be in before midnight. It was that obvious. However, in his new relationships with her, he was treating her like an adult and, physically, despite his protests, she was already a woman.

As he watched them, Cosette joined him. "They make a lovely couple. I remember when your president, Mr. Kennedy and his wife were dancing the night away and captivating everyone in this very room back in 1962." She smiled. "It was a thank you visit for our part in a very complex agent exchange. This received no press coverage, given the importance of the people involved." She nodded. "Even though you were in the intelligence community, I wager you never heard of Bleu before your journey."

"Well, I'd met with some foreign agents when I was at NKP who belonged to a very secret agency. But I never learned its name or any particulars. But I now sense they must've been Bleu."

"Good. Please keep us secret, to the best of your ability, while in Russia."

"Of course. Thank you, Cosette, for everything. Good night."

"Good fortune tonight, Ashley."

He smiled and nodded. "Thank you."

5.

Ashley hears Tiffany's lamp balls hitting the bronze but could not get up because of a hand on his chest and looks up at Olga, naked and unchanged. The only light is coming from the city. "Please don't turn on Tiffany. But if you look through the window, you'll see the blue against the clouds."

"Olga, at last."

"Of course, Ash. But I'm soon going to have to leave you."

"I certainly don't like that, but I now understand why you must."

"Good. But now we have unfinished business. The last time we were alive together, I had a premonition you'd be in danger if you went to New York."

"Oh my God, I remember now. Some drunk driver tried to run me over on Forty-Second Street by Grand Central."

"That was Chichikov. You, we, posed a serious threat to Svetlana's empire."

"Very interesting. Maria told me Svetlana was Prometheus's woman in Moscow. And I know Pen was behind your murder and Stashinski was merely a decoy."

"Yes. What actually killed me was some hash I bought for us, after you left. Returning from Montreal, I decided it would be fun to be stoned for the Yale game."

"Olga, my love, if you'd waited until after the game, we'd both be dead, so I need to know more. Did you buy from Blue Boy?"

"No, busted and in the joint. That left Harry something."

"Yeah, I remember Slimy Harry from my sophomore year, and he would be so very happy to be highly paid for your poison. He disappeared in December of '62. Cops never found his body."

"I can't say I'm sorry." She paused and looked deeply into his eyes. "However, I don't think you ever believed I could foretell the future."

"You're wrong. You started me on the surreal path that has led me to this moment. I didn't know at the time you were going to die. But you knew, didn't you?"

"Impressive. Yes, but had I told you the truth, you wouldn't believe me."

"You're right, but back then I didn't really understand you, as I do now."

"Yes, I know."

"And I thank you for it and all your efforts to educate me. Now, why Montreal?"

"To see my mentor, Jean-Louis, a professor of history at McGill University to say goodbye."

"Yes, I remember him from your memories."

"Of course. But, all this stuff doesn't matter now because I'm very content where I am. One of the reasons I'm here is to give you a small clue for your journey. Our father's gulag diaries still exist."

"OK, that might just keep me alive. Now, I've a burning question. How can we speak together when I had to use telepathy with Countess Sophia and Princess Xenia and all the rest?"

"We're not in the Realm, but here in my room. And like Xenia, I didn't wish to reveal myself in the shower."

"OK. Makes some sense. Now, did you influence my advisor to recommend your class to me?"

"No. Fate guided you there, just like it always does. You don't like that but remember it. That first day in class, you were so easy to recognize. That's why I was so hard on you. I wanted to see if you were a true Iskandarov."

"What's that?"

"There are true Iskandarov and those who aren't. Now, remember that time we were making love and you saw all those people, but didn't hear them?"

"Of course, that means we formed a bond that was never broken. And I know from your memories you tried to break the bond but were so far gone you could only get out, *my brother, Ashley Cooper.*"

"I'm sorry. I've been desolate ever since."

"Olga, don't. You did your best, and it's OK."

"Not so. In any event, individually, Iskandarov men and women are incomplete. I'll break our bond because forming a union is vitally important for both parties. And you'll soon be free to begin that process. And I think you've been prepared as well as any Seeker ever has been, having learned how the Colonel, Sergei and Dmitri navigated their trials and traps."

"OK, and thanks. I need to know where you've been. Sophia said you weren't with her or Xenia in paradise."

"That's true. When I died, there were demons waiting to capture my life-force because I was vulnerable, being estranged from both the Iskandarov and Andreyev. Remember in the morgue when I suddenly opened my eyes and my aura lit up?"

"How could I possibly forget that?"

"Right. That's when I fled inside you, which I could do because of our bond. Now, paradise is boring. Most of the time, I drift over the Earth, alone or with others, a most pleasant experience. But because of our bond, I always know when you need me and am back in you instantly. And earlier today, I was inside you, and that's why you couldn't see me. I didn't want to reveal myself then. Me entering or leaving you is the tingling you feel. Now, you owe me twice. When you were shot in Bangkok, you briefly died. My life-force kept you alive long enough to get you to the hospital. And today, I was your extra energy when you battled Svetlana Feliksovna."

"Thanks. So, you've been my guardian angel all this time?"

"I'm a spirit, not an angel, like Princess Xenia. But yes… farewell, Ash."

Olga dissolves into a shimmering haze, floating over him. When she completely envelops him, he feels such powerful joy and peace they again are one, until he hears, "My brother, Ashley Cooper, I release you from our bond. Godspeed."

Ashley awoke, feeling a loneliness, an aching such as he had never felt before, until he sensed someone in the room and turned on Tiffany. He felt disappointed, scared and surprised to see Nick Stevens in black-tie. "Hello, Nick. To what do I owe the honor?" He hoped his voice had not betrayed him.

"Relax, Cooper. You always talk to yourself like that when you sleep? Nutso. I'm here to warn you. All hell's about to break loose. Drago and I got wind of it from one of the mopes outside who watch this palace. The guy you know as Fred is actually Friedrich Grieber, former Stasi and now freelancing for some group who want Baroness von Manteuffel killed."

"Why? She's about ninety-four. Can't they let nature take its course?"

"They found out she helped a bunch of Jews escape Germany." He shook his head. "You know how these nutjobs are. Look, he's planted a device above the ballroom skylight, and I don't know when it'll blow, but I'd assume sooner than later. You need to get dressed and rescue as many as you can."

Ashley nodded slowly. "Why're you warning me? You've always hated my guts. And I'm not crazy about yours either. Makes no sense."

"Look. It's complicated. My orders are to keep you alive, for the present. Come on, get dressed. I know you still love to play the hero. See ya."

Ashley rose and put on his tuxedo trousers, dress shirt and black loafers, and as he ran down the corridor to the ballroom, he thought, *Damn, I should've read Fred's file before the Repast.* In the ballroom, he saw Ulrika, surrounded by many men and women and heard her discussing her theory of pain. He yelled, "Baroness," as the device went off and blew him off his feet.

As he regained consciousness, the nickel odor of blood and the foul stench of burst intestines filled his nose. He did not feel pain, except in his chest. He tried to get up but could not before hearing, "Dad, you're OK. You have a shard of glass in your chest, and Cosette says she'll fix you up. You also have a lot of small shards as well. But they're not considered serious. Oh yeah, Yuri survived the blast. I don't get it. Here let me help you up."

As he rose and his eyes focused, he saw Annie's, Cosette's and Yuri's faces, their clothes all covered in blood. "Why didn't you tell me you all were bleeding?"

"Dad, it's not ours. We've been checked out by medics. We're fine. Just haven't had a chance to get cleaned up."

"You are most fortunate. It is not yet your time and shall not be for a long while, God willing." Cosette crossed herself. "Whatever possessed you to run in here dressed like that?"

Ashley told her about Nick.

She shook her head. "Insane people. My friends are dead and for what purpose? I am pleased you did not see the true horror of the explosion."

Nadia came into the room in her blue robe. "Please, your attention. If you are not directly involved in cleanup, go to your rooms. We shall convene for a debrief at ten hundred hours tomorrow. Try to get some sleep. If you require further medical attention, please see the medics in the foyer. It is vital we clear this room as quickly as possible. I need to gain control of this news story. Reminder, Bleu must always remain out of the public eye if we are to survive."

As people began to leave, Annie kissed Ashley on the cheek, and Ashley told Yuri, "Take good care of my daughter." He nodded and left, hand in hand with Annie.

As much as Ashley did not want to leave the ballroom, wanting to assist, he let Cosette help him to his room, where she expertly removed and cleaned the shard wound and lesser pieces.

She commented that one of the smaller shards appeared to come from Ulrika's dark glasses.

After, sitting on the bed, Ashley began raging and crying. He cried for his now dead friends, especially Ulrika, and he raged because he felt terrified. *Had I run into the room any sooner, I'd be dead. Damn, that was a stupid thing to do. Why do I still need to be the hero? Had the big shard hit me a few inches to the left, I'd also be dead. Given Annie's fascination of Ulrika, she could have been standing next to her. That's why I did it. Hell of a time to lose my guardian spirit. And yet, Annie and I and Yuri and Cosette and Nadia are all OK.*

He felt Cosette holding him, and the smell of her perfume relaxed him as his adrenaline receded.

"Come, Ashlei, I need to get you cleaned up before you sleep. I shall also give you a painkiller."

He heard her turning on the shower and felt her picking him up. "How are you going to clean me?"

"I am going to get in with you. Come, Ashley, I am old enough to be your mother. Think of me that way. And do not concern yourself. I have seen many naked men." Afterward, she carefully dried him off like she would an infant and put a large bandage over his shard wound. He watched her slowly dry herself.

"*Alors*, have you never seen a naked old lady before?"

"Of course. But never one as attractive as you."

"Flatterer."

Annie burst in, wearing Penelope's negligee. "Oh, I'm sorry to interrupt, but Yuri's not responding. Please come quick." They put on robes and went as fast as possible to Yuri's room, where he was sitting up in bed, naked. "Cosette, can you do anything for him?"

She went over to the bed and, after examining him, said, "While I can find no apparent reason, *ma chere*, he is in God's hands now."

Annie began crying, and Cosette held her. "Sadly, your *pyordarsch* was most accurate. I am truly desolate for your loss. I had assumed when you made your prophecy, he would be killed in the explosion. This result had never occurred to me." She turned to Ashley. "You are the one who appears in shock."

"Yes, so much going through my head I scarcely know where to begin. I'm not certain where I should be or even where I am. My daughter's crying her eyes out, and I don't know what I can do to help her."

"I understand. But now, I shall take her back to her room, try to calm her and give a sedative. Then, I shall return to your room to give you a strong painkiller. But now take some time here to regain your composure."

Ashley nodded and began his breathing and relaxation exercises.

5.

When Cosette arrived, Ashley was in bed. "Ah *bon*, you seem better, but please, take this." She gave him a large white pill and water. "I was able to help Ani calm down somewhat. After you fall asleep, I shall return to her for the night to make sure her grief does not completely overwhelm her."

"Thank you, but now I'd just like to sleep."

"Of course. I shall remain here for a while to make certain you have no complications from your wound."

"Thank you."

Despite all that had happened, his exhaustion began overwhelming him. Here in Olga's brass bed, a reminder of so many happy times, with its now crisp white sheets, he felt clean after his wounding from the exquisite shower and cleansing Cosette had given him, treating him like her own son. He had never experienced anything so womb-like and intimate. Clearly, Patricia had never done something so maternal. And yet, at the same time, his mind was spinning in all sorts of directions. He had grown up as an Episcopalian believing in free will. And although Annie's prediction had not been completely accurate, Yuri's post-blast death had shaken his faith in free will to his core. And he was starting to believe the Fates controlled everything. But what would happen tomorrow and the day after and the day after that and all the days following about his young woman he would have to put back together again? It would be like the help Ronnie had given him as he put himself back together all those years ago after Olga died. And he wondered about what would happen until the final day when she would be better.

There could no longer be any thought of going back. They had crossed their Rubicon. The painkiller began to calm and dull his mind, and as he drifted further into sleep, he felt a kiss on his forehead and heard, "Good night and good fortune, Prince Sergei Sergeyovich Iskandarov." He heard Tiffany's chimes but no Olga before the door closed, and then a final thought—*Russia tomorrow.*